W9-DDO-113

JF
SHU

Shusterman, Neal. MBJ

Gleanings. ● ● NOV 2022

$19.99

33281300020754

DATE			

MBJ
● ● NOV 2022

Guelph Public Library

GLEANINGS

Also by Neal Shusterman

Novels
Bruiser
Challenger Deep
Chasing Forgiveness
The Dark Side of Nowhere
Dissidents
Downsiders
The Eyes of Kid Midas
Full Tilt
Game Changer
The Shadow Club
The Shadow Club Rising
Speeding Bullet

(with Jarrod Shusterman)
Dry
Roxy

Arc of a Scythe Trilogy
Scythe
Thunderhead
The Toll

The Accelerati Trilogy
(with Eric Elfman)
Tesla's Attic
Edison's Alley
Hawking's Hallway

The Antsy Bonano Series
The Schwa Was Here
Antsy Does Time
Ship Out of Luck

The Unwind Dystology
Unwind
UnWholly
UnSouled
UnDivided
UnBound

The Skinjacker Trilogy
Everlost
Everwild
Everfound

The Star Shards Chronicles
Scorpion Shards
Thief of Souls
Shattered Sky

The Dark Fusion Series
Dreadlocks
Red Rider's Hood
Duckling Ugly

Story Collections
Darkness Creeping
MindQuakes
MindStorms
MindTwisters
MindBenders

ARC OF A SCYTHE

GLEANINGS

Stories from the Arc of a Scythe

NEAL SHUSTERMAN

SIMON & SCHUSTER BFYR

NEW YORK • LONDON • TORONTO • SYDNEY • NEW DELHI

For my friend and publisher,
Justin Chanda,
who believed in this series
from the beginning,
and has always believed in me
—N. S.

SIMON & SCHUSTER BFYR

An imprint of Simon & Schuster Children's Publishing Division
1230 Avenue of the Americas, New York, New York 10020

This book is a work of fiction. Any references to historical events, real people, or real places
are used fictitiously. Other names, characters, places, and events are products of the author's
imagination, and any resemblance to actual events or places or persons, living or dead, is entirely
coincidental.
Text © 2022 by Neal Shusterman
Jacket illustration © 2022 by Kevin Tong
Jacket design by Chloë Foglia © 2022 by Simon & Schuster, Inc.
All rights reserved, including the right of reproduction
in whole or in part in any form.
SIMON & SCHUSTER BOOKS FOR YOUNG READERS
and related marks are trademarks of Simon & Schuster, Inc.

For information about special discounts for bulk purchases, please contact Simon & Schuster
Special Sales at 1-866-506-1949 or business@simonandschuster.com.
The Simon & Schuster Speakers Bureau can bring authors to your live event. For more
information or to book an event, contact the Simon & Schuster Speakers Bureau at 1-866-248-
3049 or visit our website at www.simonspeakers.com.
Interior design by Hilary Zarycky
The text for this book was set in Bembo.
Manufactured in the United States of America
First Edition
2 4 6 8 10 9 7 5 3 1
Library of Congress Cataloging-in-Publication Data
Names: Shusterman, Neal, author.
Title: Gleanings / Neal Shusterman.
Description: First edition. | New York : Simon & Schuster Books for Young Readers, 2022.
Series: Arc of a Scythe | Audience: Ages 12 and up. | Summary: A collection of stories that span
the time when humans live in a world without hunger, disease, or death and Scythes act as the
living instruments of population control.
Identifiers: LCCN 2022007022 | ISBN 9781534499973 (hardcover)
ISBN 9781534499997 (ebook)
Subjects: CYAC: Death—Fiction. | Murder—Fiction. | Science fiction.
LCGFT: Short stories. | Science fiction.
Classification: LCC PZ7.S55987 Gl 2022 | DDC [Fic]—dc23
LC record available at https://lccn.loc.gov/2022007022

Contents

The First Swing

Slicing through the air with effortless aplomb,
the moment you take your first swing,
you wield your axe
like you are a master in the art of gleaning.

Those before you are in awe.
They cannot imagine what your next move will be.
You carry yourself as balanced and poised as a performer
dancing brutally among them;
the searing star of stars,
your robe cascading to the earth
in showers of gold.

But that is not the truth.

Your worth does not matter
to those who now matter to you.
You are truly nothing but a tiny sunspot
to the eyes of others like yourself.
An insignificant fleck.
And as you take that first swing,
they laugh at you.

You try to rise above their derision,
to be noticed in some small way.
To find favor from the old ones,

who are never old.
To gain respect from the young ones,
who have slain their own youth.
To justify the arrogance
that comes with the pride
of being chosen.

But that is not the truth either.

It will be years until you come to know the truth:
That those you revere are merely servants
to the collective that we prune.
It was *their* choice to let *us* choose
all those years ago.
The awed, terrified, relieved spectators;
the real ones in power,
the puppeteers of your actions.

Standing in a perfect line before them,
a cutting edge,
wielding our axes,
each one of us is the same as the last.
We are one in all,
We are all in one, and

We.
Shall.
Kill.

Our mantra, our commandment,
our duty to remind the immortal of mortality.
To teach them
that eternal repose may be distant,
but not lost.

Who are We?
We are Scythes.
And the weapons We wield
are not by any means our friends.
The devastating force
of bullet, blade, and bludgeon
tears us apart each day, every day,
piece by piece,
and leaves us with wounds that will never heal.
This is what ties us to the masses,
yet restrains us from being one with them.
And with each new gleaning,
We bleed and break anew,
yet our resolve never changes.

For We are scythes.
Nothing will ever change that fact.
And when it is your time to bleed,
you will know,
and you will learn.

—Joelle Shusterman

Formidable

"It takes time, Susan," Michael had told her. "Soon the girl who you once were will wither into memory. You will inhabit your new identity fully and completely."

Which was easy for him to say—Michael had already been a scythe for five years. She wondered how long it had taken him to "inhabit" himself. He was so fully Faraday, she couldn't imagine him being anyone else.

I am Marie. Not Susan. It was something she constantly had to tell herself—because it wasn't just about presenting herself as Scythe Marie Curie; she had to start seeing herself that way. *Feeling* the reality of it. The public persona was one thing, but getting that persona into one's own thoughts was another. It was like thinking in a different language.

"This will cease to be a role you play, and will become who you are," Faraday had assured her. "And once it does, I have a feeling you'll be formidable!"

But so far she felt anything but. Her first few months of gleaning had been unremarkable. Utilitarian. Functional. She did her job, but was still trying to find a style that defined her. Without it, she felt sloppy and undirected.

This was her state of mind when Susan—no . . . when *Marie*—arrived at Harvest Conclave, Year of the Marlin. It was her first conclave as a full-fledged scythe. She had naively thought that the grand gathering of scythes would be easier to bear now that she was no longer a mere apprentice . . . but that couldn't be further from the truth.

While most scythes arrived in driverless vehicles—publicars, or scythe limousines for the more ostentatious among them—Marie drove herself in an old mortal-age Porsche that had been gifted to her by the son of a man she had gleaned. As she stepped out, rather than letting the car be taken by a member of the scytheguard, she turned to the gathered crowd.

"Is there anyone here who can drive a nonautonomous, off-grid stick shift?"

Very few hands went up. She chose a young man, who seemed about her age. Nineteen or so. When he realized he had been selected, he stepped forward, eager as a puppy.

"Careful, it packs a punch," she warned.

"Yes, Your Honor. Thank you, Your Honor. I'll be careful, Your Honor."

She handed him the keys with one hand, then held out her other to him as well. He knelt to kiss her ring and the sight of him doing so made a little girl in the audience squeal with delight.

"Leave the keys with any member of the scytheguard, and they'll find their way back to me," she told him.

He bowed to her. He actually bowed. She recalled that bowing began as a way to show fealty—offering a royal your head for decapitation. While some scythes loved the groveling, Marie found it ridiculous and awkward. She wondered if any scythes ever actually beheaded someone who bowed to them.

"It is a scythe's prerogative to give random tasks to random people," Michael had told her. *"Just as it is a scythe's prerogative to reward them for their service."* She had come to learn it wasn't about feeling superior—it was a way to justify the granting of immunity. In this way Michael had taught her to turn what could have been entitlement into a kindness.

The young man drove off, and Marie joined the pageant—and a pageant is exactly what it was: an intentional spectacle of scythes in their colorful robes ascending the marble steps to Fulcrum City's capital building. The ascension was as important as any business that took place within the building, because it was a reminder to the public of how awe-inspiring the Scythedom was.

There were always hordes on either side of the steps behind a gauntlet of the scytheguard, all hoping to catch a glimpse of their favorite scythes. Some scythes played to the crowd; others did not. But whether they smiled and waved, or scowled in chilling judgment, it left an impression that was essential to the Scythedom's public image.

As she ascended the steps, Marie did not engage the crowd. She wanted nothing more than to be inside and be done with this part of it. In spite of the scythes making their way up with her, she suddenly felt very much alone. She hadn't anticipated how powerful that sense of isolation would be. At her previous conclaves, when she was an apprentice, she was always accompanied by Faraday. But this time not a single scythe around her felt companionable.

There had been five apprentices who took the final test at Vernal Conclave four months back. Marie was the only one to make the cut; the only one ordained. Which meant that she couldn't even find camaraderie among other first-timers, because there were none. Nor could she fraternize with up-and-coming apprentices, because that was beneath her as a scythe, and would reflect poorly on her.

As for the rest of the scythes, they were either too absorbed by the adulation of the crowd, or too self-absorbed, to notice her sense of solitude. Or maybe they did notice, and took pleasure in it. It's not that the others disliked her—but they did dislike the *idea* of her. They hated the fact that a scythe as young as Faraday, just a few years past his own ordination, had taken on an apprentice. And so Marie bore the brunt of their disapproval.

There were many who made sport of that disapproval, treating her with dismissive disdain. Even now she was getting sideways looks of scythes who clearly disapproved of her choice of robe, a vibrant, bright violet. She had chosen such a vivid color as a way to secretly spite her Tonist parents, who abhorred anything that wasn't faded earth tones. Now she was regretting it, because of the unwanted attention it drew.

She had toyed with the idea of dyeing her hair that same color—but the hairdresser had made a face, and said her single, beautiful braid would get lost against the fabric. "Silver!" he had suggested. "Oh, how striking that would be!"

And so Marie took the advice. Now her silver braid fell along the back of her robe dangling halfway to the ground. She thought this new look would help redefine her from being Faraday's protégé to being her own scythe—but now she could see that it had backfired. She saw smirks and heard snickers, and they reddened her cheeks—which only made her more embarrassed, because now they knew they had gotten to her.

In the vestibule, where the traditional breakfast feast was set out for the eye as well as the appetite, someone finally spoke to her. Scythe Vonnegut approached, in his acid-wash denim robe looking like the surface of the moon; a fabric harkening to a time that no one quite remembered.

"Well if it isn't 'Little Miss Mischief,'" Scythe Vonnegut said with a grin. He had the sort of grin that could either be false or genuine, and she could never be sure which. As for the moniker, Marie had no idea who had coined it, but it had taken hold, spreading through the MidMerican Scythedom even before she was ordained. Little Miss Mischief. It was just one more unkindness, for she was neither little nor mischievous. She was a tall girl, slim and gangly—and far from mischievous, she was dour—too serious to ever be up to mischief of any kind.

"I would prefer it if you didn't call me that, Scythe Vonnegut."

He grinned that ambiguous grin. "It's just a term of endearment," he said, then quickly changed the subject. "I love what you've done with your hair!" Again, was it derision, or sincerity? She would have to learn how to read people better. Although scythes were so skilled at remaining unread.

She spotted Faraday across the room. He hadn't seen her yet. Or maybe he was pretending not to. Well, why should she care? She was a scythe now, not some fawning schoolgirl. Matters of the heart had no place in her life.

"You must learn to be less obvious," Scythe Vonnegut whispered to her. "Your infatuation might as well be projected on the walls."

"Why does it matter? Scythe Faraday has no feelings for me."

Again that grin. "If you say so."

A gong sounded, alerting them that they had fifteen more minutes to fill their stomachs.

"Have a good conclave," Vonnegut said as he strode away. "And eat up before the gluttons leave the display in ruins."

Michael did come up to her in the vestibule just a few minutes before they were ushered into the inner chamber, but their conversation was stilted. Both were keenly aware that they were being watched, and judged, and gossiped about.

"You're looking well, Marie," he said. "I trust you had a good first season."

"I've made my quota."

"I had no doubts." She thought he might come closer for a few more personal words, but instead he moved away. "Good to see you, Marie."

She wondered if he could sense how her heart dropped.

The ritual of conclave morning ranged from dull to torturous. The Tolling of the Names. Ten for every scythe, chosen out of the dozens each had gleaned. Ten to represent all the others. Marie's favorites had been Taylor Vega, who, with his last breaths, thanked her for not gleaning him in front of his family; and Toosdai Riggle, because she liked saying the name.

Finally the morning came round to the matters at hand. This season's hot mess of a debate revolved around what to do about the troublemakers in the old capital. But really, it was less of a debate, and more just an opportunity to complain.

"The Windbags of Washington continue to stir an increasingly rancid pot," Scythe Douglass said.

"Yes, but it's not our problem," High Blade Ginsburg

pointed out. "The old capital is in EastMerica. Let them deal with it." As High Blade, she was constantly trying to remind the MidMerican scythes to stay out of business that wasn't theirs— but this time she was wrong. This was more than just an East-Merican problem.

Marie grunted at the High Blade's dismissal of the issue. She hadn't meant anyone to hear, but someone beside her—she thought it was Scythe Streisand—nudged her. "If you have an opinion, offer it," she said. "You're a scythe now. It's time you learned to be opinionated."

"No one wants to hear what I have to say."

"Ha! No one wants to hear what *anyone* has to say, but you say it anyway. That's the way it is around here."

And so Marie stood, and waited until she was recognized by High Blade Ginsburg, who studied Marie for a moment before she spoke.

"Does our newest member care to weigh in on the matter?"

"Yes, Your Excellency," Marie said. "It seems to me that the old pre-Thunderhead government is MidMerica's problem, too—because they still claim hegemony over not just EastMerica, but also MidMerica, WestMerica, and Texas."

Then another scythe shouted without waiting to be recognized. "The paltry claims of the Washingtonians have no bearing on reality! They are a nuisance, nothing more."

"But," said Marie, "as long as they stir up trouble, they weaken everything we stand for."

"It's the Thunderhead that they rail against," said the scythe who spoke out of turn, "so the Thunderhead can deal with them."

"That's short-sighted!" Marie dared to say. "We can't deny that the Scythedom and the Thunderhead are two sides of the same coin. If one is threatened, then so is the other!"

It brought forth a low grumbling from the rest of conclave. She wasn't sure if that was good or bad.

"Let the old-world politicians broadcast their bile," shouted someone else. "If the Thunderhead allows it, then so should we."

"The Thunderhead is obliged to honor their freedom—including their freedom to disrupt," Marie said. "But *we* don't have that obligation. Which means we can actually *do* something about it."

High Blade Ginsburg folded her arms. "So what does the Honorable Scythe Curie propose we do?"

And all eyes turned to her. Suddenly self-consciousness came crashing down on Marie like a harsh autumn wave.

"We . . . we do what the Thunderhead can't. We solve the problem. . . ."

Silence. Then from across the room, another scythe bellowed in the most resonant of voices. "Could it be that 'Little Miss Mischief' is finally living up to her name?"

That brought a round of laughter so hearty from the throng that it actually echoed throughout the chamber. Marie tried to endure it with dignity, but she felt her spirit imploding.

Once the laughter died down, High Blade Ginsberg, still chuckling, spoke to Marie in her most patronizing tone. "My dear fledgling rapier, the Scythedom's stability comes from consistency and slow deliberation. You would be wise, Scythe Curie, to be less . . . reactionary."

"Hear, hear!" someone seconded.

And that was that. The High Blade called for other business, and the conversation shifted to the debate on whether scythes should be banned from taking on the same last name as another living scythe, since there was currently constant confusion between Scythes Armstrong, Armstrong, and Armstrong.

Marie let out a breath though her clenched teeth, and it came out as a hiss. "Well, that was pointless."

"Agreed," said Scythe Streisand, "but it was entertaining."

Which only aggravated Marie more. "I'm not here for everyone's entertainment."

Scythe Streisand gave her a judgmental glare. "Honestly, kid, if you can't handle a little smackdown, you have no business being a scythe."

That made Marie bite back anything else she had to say. She looked over to Faraday across the chamber. He didn't as much as glance at her. Was he embarrassed by her display? Pleased that she put forth an opinion? Honestly, there was no way to tell. He certainly didn't lift a finger to support her, but was that such a surprise? As much as Marie hated to admit it, Michael was right to distance himself from her—and not just because of rumors and gossip—but because Marie needed to establish herself without him. But with this crowd, how could she ever do anything that would bring forth something other than smirks, snickers, and folded arms?

"Scythes are figures of action," Faraday had told her during her apprenticeship, then had added with an impish grin, "and not just because they make action figures of us."

He was right. A scythe needed to act decisively and without hesitation—even when it was difficult. If Marie was going to prove herself, her choices would have to be so breathtaking the Scythedom would have no wind left to laugh.

Marie lived alone. Most scythes did. There wasn't a commandment that made solitude compulsory. *"Thou shalt have neither spouse nor spawn"* didn't mean one couldn't have a lover or companion. But Marie had already found out what most scythes already knew: Anyone who would choose to live with a scythe was not the sort of companion you'd want to share a home with.

Some young scythes returned to the homes of their youth, but it never lasted. Marie could never go back to live with her parents, even if they hadn't been members of that absurd Tonist cult. She couldn't imagine coming home after a gleaning and having to face them. Yes, gleaning was a vital, almost sacred task for humanity, but death was death, and blood was blood.

Marie had chosen for herself a large home in the woods with high ceilings and huge windows, with a view of mountains and a babbling creek. She found that the sound of flowing water calmed her. Cleansed her. She had heard there was a famous residence somewhere where a river actually ran through the home. Something worth exploring someday, but for now, her rustic home sufficed. She had purchased it using Scythedom funds, rather than just taking it from the owner, as some scythes did. After four months, it was barely furnished. Another instance of her not "inhabiting" her life.

The day after returning from conclave, she took a walk in the woods, hoping the crisp, earthy air would purge her of the foul feeling that conclave had left her with, but she came across two joggers on the path. They were gossiping. Who was cheating on their spouse in virtual brothels; who was traveling to Tasmania for outrageous body modifications; turning a corner for no good reason. It reminded Marie of the petty intrigue that plagued conclave.

Marie gleaned both of them, and immediately regretted it—because wasn't it just as petty to condemn them to death for gossiping? And they weren't clean gleanings, either. Had she done it right, their hearts would have quickly ceased beating and the mess would be minimal. But not this time. She heard Michael's voice in her head chiding her, and telling her to practice her killcraft.

When she got home, her cat, Sierra, quickly came to her, weaving around her ankles. Marie had a part-time housekeeper—the only extravagance Marie allowed herself—who gasped at the sight of Marie's blood-spattered robe. She always gasped, every single time, and she always apologized for it—but Marie was grateful for her honest reaction. The aftermath of gleaning *should* be shocking. If it ever stopped being shocking, then something was wrong.

"Debora, could you please take this robe to the cleaners?" Marie asked her. "Tell them no rush, I still have two others."

"Yes, Your Honor."

The cleaners always did wonders with her robes . . . although Marie sometimes suspected they just gave her new ones.

After Debora had gone, Marie drew herself a bath to wash the day away, and made the mistake of turning on the news while she soaked.

President Hinton of the Old America was ordering the

Army Corps of Engineers—which still existed for some strange reason—to start dismantling Thunderhead cerebral nodes.

"It is our moral duty to free this great nation from the stranglehold that the dark cloud has over it," Hinton said, in his typical bloviating tone—but it was nothing more than words in a whirlpool. Public opinion was not on Hinton's side. The fact was, fewer than one in twenty even voted anymore—because most everyone knew that the very concept of government was obsolete—and even fewer than that agreed with Hinton's negative view of the Thunderhead. But of course Hinton and his cronies claimed that the Thunderhead's polls were all lies. Hinton lived in such a miasma of falsehoods, he couldn't even conceive of an entity incapable of lying.

The Thunderhead made no effort to stop the server removal. Instead it just established new nodes elsewhere—which had the added benefit of providing thousands of jobs for people who chose to work.

It was well known that the Thunderhead had publicly offered Hinton the same thing it had tried to offer presidents for years: an honorable way to step down; friendly exile anywhere in the world for him, his cabinet, and all their families. They would be handed a new future, free to pursue any activity their hearts desired, as long as it didn't involve a position of political power. Hinton was just one more in a line of presidents who flatly refused.

"I do not fault Mr. Hinton," the Thunderhead had said, always magnanimous. "No one cedes power willingly. Resistance is a natural, expected response."

After her bath, Marie sat before a crackling fire, sipping cocoa, trying to take comfort in simple pleasures, but she remained uneasy. As if sensing it, Sierra hopped onto her lap, so carefully as to not make as much as a ripple in Marie's cocoa, and settled in. This was the cat's third life. Marie had decided to allow her nine. It felt poetic. It felt just. But not all justice had such a pleasing aesthetic. . . .

There was a thought that had been lingering in the back of Marie's mind ever since conclave. An intimidating thought. Perhaps a dangerous one. She had actively suppressed it, refusing to allow it to surface, trying to fill her mind with a hundred other things. But as she pet Sierra, she knew that this moment of gentle, purring comfort would not last.

She knew it was only a matter of time until she made a trip to Washington.

The troubling state of the District of Columbia clearly showed that the Thunderhead, perfect as it was, had a passive-aggressive streak. The expansive greenbelt known as the Washington Mall had now been mostly reclaimed by nature. Odd, because the Thunderhead was meticulous when it came to horticultural maintenance—and yet the green areas of Washington were completely ignored. Not only that, but the Thunderhead chose not to put any effort into infrastructure in the area. It had stopped repairing roads and bridges, and it had long since relocated the museums of the Smithsonian, leaving their old structures as empty shells.

At some point the Thunderhead had all the city signage changed. Now it was officially known as the "Washington Ruins."

And as if all that wasn't crushing enough, the Thunderhead had established clubs, and places of refuge for unsavories, causing most everyone without unsavory status to move elsewhere.

It was all part of a plan—not so much to discredit the venerable town, but to seal it into the past, much like the ruins of other ancient empires. Washington was still a place to be respected, but only in the way that we respect crumbling antiquity.

Even so, vestiges of the old American government still remained. Politicians who saw themselves as the last bastions of a better time. Better, perhaps for them, but, just like all other pre-Thunderhead governments, not at all better for anyone else. They had no real power anymore—all they could do was bluster, trying to find weak seams in the Thunderhead's silver lining.

Through all of their verbal attacks, the Thunderhead continued its campaign of benign neglect, treating the politicians of the broken beltway like a mortal-age landlord might treat a deadbeat tenant. It didn't evict them, but made it increasingly difficult for them to stay.

Most took the hint and headed for easier pastures. Congress had officially disbanded when the Thunderhead redefined the Americas into the various Merican regions. The judiciary now only existed to rubber-stamp the Thunderhead's infallible judgments. With the concept of "nations" gone, there was no further need for defense—which, after all, was a primary purpose of nations in the first place.

Now only the executive branch remained, the president and his cabinet clinging on like stubborn leaves defying the fall. . . .

Marie arrived on a chilly November day, two months after Harvest Conclave. She told no one what she was up to. That way, if it didn't go well, there'd be no one to ridicule her.

With the roads no longer maintained, she had blown a tire in a nasty pothole on Constitution Avenue, and had to walk the last mile.

Unsavories hung out in clusters, as unsavories tend to do, drinking themselves silly and breaking whatever was left to break. Funny how they never realized that they were doing the Thunderhead's bidding. They broke down the old city like bacteria break down the remains of a corpse.

"Yo, beautiful," one of them taunted her. "I got your immunity right here." As if offending a scythe was a sign of bravery rather than unbridled stupidity.

Marie ignored him, and the catcalls, and the rude comments that came from the unsavory shadows along the way. It wasn't worth her energy to be miffed by it. Unsavories did what they did, which really wasn't much of anything, since the Thunderhead wouldn't allow anything that was truly unsavory.

The White House was the only structure still well-kept, as was its grounds. An oasis behind a high fence, guarded at all hours. It was, of course, all theater, nothing more.

There were two guards at the main gate, armed with intimidating automatic weapons. They were in camouflage, which made Marie stifle a laugh. Camouflage? Really? They should have gone for medieval armor; it would have been prettier.

"Let me pass," she ordered.

They gripped their weapons tighter. "Can't let you do that, ma'am," one of them said.

"You'll address me as 'Your Honor,' and you'll step aside."

They hardened their gazes and didn't move—but she could tell they were scared.

"What are you going to do, shoot me?" she asked. "Your weapons aren't even loaded."

"You don't know that."

"Of course I do. The Thunderhead doesn't allow anyone to have loaded weapons. Only scythes can. You're lucky the Thunderhead allows you to play with those toys at all."

"Your Honor," said the other guard, with just a little bit of desperation in her voice, "we're just doing our job."

No, they were just wasting her time. "I am going to have a conversation with your boss," she told them. "If I have to glean you to have that conversation, I will. So what will it be?"

She waited. They didn't move. So she reached into her robe for a blade—

—and the moment she did, the guard to the left lowered her weapon, and stepped aside. The other was quick to do the same.

"Wise choice," Marie said, and strode through, onto the expanse of the southern lawn, not looking back to see if the guards dropped their weapons and left, or remained at their pointless posts.

The guards at the front entrance must have been told there was a scythe on the premises, because the door was unguarded. Had they been ordered to fall back, she wondered, or had they deserted?

Inside, everything looked as she had imagined. The beige-and-white-tiled floor. Red-carpeted stairs. A stagnant place that hadn't changed an iota since mortal days. Portraits of long-dead presidents peered down wistfully from the walls, amid grand artworks extolling the virtues of democratic rule of the people and by the people. A wonderful dream that sometimes even worked—but as long as humans were fallible, it could never be perfect. Perfection required the Thunderhead. And scythes.

Marie encountered a few more guards along the way—but not as many as she thought—and they all laid down their empty weapons before her. Only as she attempted to enter the West Wing did she encounter resistance. A single soldier holding his ground at the foot of the stairs.

"Please don't make me betray him, Your Honor," the soldier said.

He seemed to steel himself for gleaning, but when Marie didn't glean him, he relaxed the slightest bit. He didn't so much let Marie pass, as he pretended the scythe wasn't there at all. The soldier stood his ground, but only as a boulder stands its ground in a river. Marie flowed around him and up the grand staircase.

The so-called president was not in his residence, the Oval Office, or any of the standard areas of the sprawling structure. *All right, so this is a game of hide-and-seek,* she thought.

Palming a security pad, which, by law, had to yield to her, she slipped into one of the various secret hallways—hidden from the public, perhaps, but there was no information a scythe did not have access to, and Scythe Curie had done her homework well. She descended several sets of stairs into a reinforced concrete bunker beneath the venerable building—a shelter designed to withstand all nature of attack.

As she approached a steel door, as secure as a vault, she found no one there stop her. The security pad read her biometrics, the massive deadbolt system disengaged, and the door labored open.

Inside, she found a cluster of men and women huddled in some sort of war room. Maps and screens. A framed flag from the days when such banners differentiated one place from another.

There were gasps and whimpers at the sight of Scythe Curie in her bright purple robe, with a knife in her hand. She recognized each face. These were the members of the president's cabinet. And in the midst of them was President Hinton himself.

Some turned away from Marie, some let their heads drop in abject defeat, and others covered their eyes, hoping to deny what those eyes told them for a few precious moments. Only Hinton himself held eye contact with her, in blazing defiance.

"I am Scythe Marie Curie," she said. "I'm sure you know why I'm here."

"You're little more than a child," Hinton scoffed. "And you're not even from this region."

"I thought you didn't recognize the Thunderhead's regions," she countered. "But it doesn't matter. Scythes aren't bound by their regions. We can glean wherever we choose."

"You have no right to come here and threaten me."

"Of course I do, Mr. President," she responded. "Humanity has given me the right to do whatever I please. That is the law under which we now live—or did you forget?"

"You will leave here now!" Hinton commanded. "And maybe I'll forget this intrusion."

Marie released a single chuckle. "We both know there's only one way I leave here," she told him.

Then the Secretary of State leaned close to Hinton and whispered, "Scythes are known to negotiate, sir. Perhaps I could broker a deal."

"I'm not that kind of scythe," Marie told them.

"No," said Hinton, dripping disgust. "You're the worst kind.

Young, idealistic, pigheaded. Thinking your cause is as pure and gleaming as your blade."

"Maybe I'm all those things," conceded Marie, "but I'm also inevitable."

That's when one of the others tried to bolt out the door. And it began.

Marie's blade was quick. Her mastery was a wonder to behold—and soon the world would indeed behold it, for there were cameras in every corner. She knew this, but she was not performing for the cameras. She was simply doing her duty with expedience and grace. They fell, one after another, until the only one who remained was Hinton himself, now cowering in a corner, all of his bravado collapsing under the weight of the moment.

Marie instinctively knew this was a turning point. Not just for her, but for the entire world. For their entire species. Could he sense that, too? Is that why his hands were shaking?

"There is no longer a place for you," she told him. "Civilization has moved on."

"All right, I'll go," he pleaded. "I'll go into exile. You'll never see me again."

But Marie shook her head. "The Thunderhead would have been happy with that—and if you had agreed to that before today, I wouldn't be here. But you didn't accept exile. And I don't work for the Thunderhead."

"You will come to regret this," he told her. "Mark my words—if there's one thing I know it's that you will rue the day you made this choice. And when you do—"

But any soliloquy he planned was pruned at the root with a single stroke.

• • •

She climbed back up to the White House proper, trying to wrap her mind around what she had just done. She had cleared the way for the Thunderhead to rule unimpeded. She had also solidified the power and sovereignty of the Scythedom in a way no one had done before. She wondered if this would violate the second scythe commandment. Would gleaning the last trouble-some figures of mortal rule be considered bias? Even if it was, what was the worst the Scythedom could do to her? Censure her? Take away her right to glean for a year or two? Surely cutting the world free from the past was worth any price.

She found a bathroom up in the presidential residence, and drew a bath for herself. This had been a messy affair—and while she could wash the blood from her hands, the spatter streaked and saturated her robe, making it a terrible thing to behold.

But it was a thick garment, so she turned it inside out to hide the blood. She thought it might look odd, but it did not. Her robe's lining was a silky lavender. It was a subtle, subdued hue. She found that she actually liked it far better than the garish purple.

Focal points in history have their own gravity, and so as she stepped outside, she found herself faced by a small but growing crowd. The gate had been thrown open, the guards were gone. And nearly everyone in the crowd had a hand up with one device or another recording, streaming, galvanizing this moment as a new anchor point for posterity.

She realized she had not prepared anything to say, but she had to say something. And so the words she now spoke—words that would soon become known the world round—were truly from the heart.

"What I have done today is my burden, and my gift," she told the crowd. *"The future is unfettered. There could not be a brighter day. Long live us all!"*

The Thunderhead might have been able to predict what came next, but Marie certainly couldn't. In the weeks after the gleaning, her actions began to be mirrored around the world. Monarchs and dictators, and heads of state for nations that by and large no longer existed were gleaned one after the other, until not a single one remained. Nations were now officially washed away. Now the only divisions were that of region. All equal. None in competition. No more "them," only "us." And at each political gleaning, the same words were spoken.

"The future is unfettered. Long live us all!"

The Thunderhead, which did not comment on the mechanics of life and death, had only this to say, in its usual understated way: "I did not ask for this, but it will make my stewardship of the planet a little bit easier."

Even so, Marie could not get out of her mind the president's last words. She would rue the day she made this choice. She wondered when that day would come.

At Winter Conclave, Marie arrived in her Porsche, and found the same young man waiting to park her car, apparently deciding that it was his permanent calling. The moment she approached the marble steps to the Fulcrum City capital, the crowd, which had been watching the processional of scythes, all turned their eyes to her and began whispering. Soon, however, the whispers fell into silence. Other scythes saw her and stepped aside, letting her have a wide berth. Letting her go before them.

"The new robe suits you, Scythe Curie," said Scythe Vonnegut, without the slightest smirk or hint at irony. She nodded her thanks to him. Then, for the first time on these steps, she turned to the crowds on either side and faintly smiled, offering them the slightest of waves—and they looked ready to swoon from her attention. She had heard that people were now calling her "Little Miss Murder." She disliked it a lot less than she thought she would. It gave her a persona she was motivated to grow out of.

Strange, but the scythes around her no longer felt intimidating. She longed to see how Michael would be around her now. Perhaps he would see her less as a student, and more his equal. An added bonus to her now infamous gleaning.

As she crossed into the outer vestibule where their sumptuous conclave breakfast awaited, she overheard a scythe she didn't even know speak to another.

"I wouldn't doubt she'll be High Blade someday," the scythe said. "The girl is formidable."

Marie smiled, for, at last, her own future was unfettered.

Never Work with Animals

Co-authored with Michael H. Payne

Scythe Fields held the hot dog beneath his nose, taking a deep whiff, and letting it out. "Ah, the scent of a good, strong mustard under a perfect cerulean sky!" He turned and beamed at the hot dog vendor. "Nothing like it in the world, Charles."

"Yes, Your Honor," Charles more sighed than said. The fellow was melancholy to a fault. Fields would've gleaned him years ago were it not for the quality of his hot dogs. A standard brand, yes—but the skill was in the preparation. Just the right amount of mustard, and kraut—crisp, not soggy—and a bun warmed to the perfect temperature. Fields practically inhaled the hot dog, then brushed crumbs from his golden-brown robe.

"I'll have a second, I believe." Fields leaned back against the cart and watched the citizens of Oxnard, WestMerica, strolling through the shoreline park, leaf shadows dancing in the ocean breeze over the grassy hillocks and winding pathways. "If all days could be like this!" he said, and glanced at Charles for a reaction.

"They mostly are," he said in his habitual sepulchral tones. "Only rains or clouds over when the Thunderhead lets it—which is only as often as people want, I suppose."

A simple nod or a smile was what Fields was fishing for—or even something more effusive. Perhaps a wholehearted declaration that the town was as wonderful as it was due to his efforts—

not the Thunderhead's—which, as a scythe, Fields had no use for. He started to glower, annoyed that Charles had dragged his thoughts toward unpleasantness. Fields found his hand twitching for the sword cane hanging from his arm—a reflex he indulged as often as not.

Annoyance held the paramount spot on his list of gleaning offenses—something that sloppy waiters, peevish teenagers, and inattentive pet owners up and down this section of the coast had learned during the three decades he had been a scythe.

But as irksome as Charles could be, Fields's heart was softened by the loving care the man gave his craft. Even now, it was there in the way he set the hot dog into its bun like a babe into a cradle. It was this that allowed Fields to overlook his many faults.

Fields reached for the hot dog before Charles had even begun extending it toward him. "Ready a third if you'd be so kind, Charles," Fields said. "I'm trying to put on a few pounds after the shining example offered by Xenocrates—the High Blade over in MidMerica." Fields patted the barely noticeable belly beneath his robes. "Alas, no matter how much I try, my own blood continues to conspire against me." He took a bite of the hot dog, letting the sweet and salt of it wash away the bitterness of his thoughts.

A slight clearing of throat from Charles. "You could have your nanites adjusted, Your Honor, to allow you to put on weight."

The mouthful tried to go down the wrong pipe; Fields coughed, bent forward, stomped his foot, got his glottal equipment under control, and swallowed with an effort. "And admit defeat?" He straightened and shook his head. "Mind over matter, Charles! *That's* the guiding principle that's gotten this world where it is today, and—"

Just then, a dog began barking, shattering the calm of the bucolic day. The sound made Fields's gut clench and shattered his every other thought.

"Godfrey Daniels!" he exclaimed. His research had never revealed what the expression actually meant, but his Patron Historic had been known to use it in moments of exasperation, so Scythe Fields had adopted its use when he'd adopted the name. Grabbing his sword cane—yet another quaint accessory he'd adopted from his beloved Mortal Era—he spun away from the cart, ready to administer a death-infused correction to whoever might dare disturb the genteel tranquility he'd fought so long and so hard for.

It wasn't that he disliked dogs—he loved dogs. But, like children, they were better seen than heard.

As a child, he'd had a beloved dog—but dogs had short natural lives, and the cost of revival and resetting their age doubled every time. Eventually when it became too cost prohibitive, many people opted to let their pets pass. He supposed it was a way to control the pet population—after all, there were no pet scythes to glean them—but as a child he'd found it a cruelty.

As a scythe, however, everything came free—including endless pet revivals. Fields was currently bereft of a canine companion, though. His most recent dog, a cocker spaniel, had been on the frail side, and the frequent trips down to the animal shelter's revival center when the thing kept rendering itself deadish had gotten to be a nuisance. The last time that he'd dropped it off for revival, he never returned to pick it up. "Gift it to someone worthy," he had told them at the revival center. "Perhaps someone who has more patience for such an accident-prone animal."

He wasn't quite sure which direction the barking had come from, but as he turned to look, he did see a leashless dog trotting toward him through the park alongside a young couple, its apparent masters. Silky, grayish white, it caused Fields to pause. It was rather a lovely animal. It held its head high, its chest puffed out, its fluffy tail most handsomely curled up and around to touch its back.

Fields was delighted to discover that this wasn't the dog barking—in fact, from the air of self-possession around it, Fields couldn't quite imagine it *ever* barking. As if such a thing was beneath it. The sound came again, and this time Fields triangulated it to a yippy little rat-sized creature farther down the path. It was scooped up by a woman in a neon-pink outfit that was somehow louder than the animal, and she spirited the little beast away.

Fields knew this pair. The yapping dog was a Pomeranian named Tea Biscuit, and its owner was Constance Something-or-Other. He had given her several stern looks over the years, but this? The blatant interruption of a perfect lunch? There was only so much his kindly nature could endure.

But he could attend to the woman later. Of more immediate interest was this newcomer couple, and their far more dignified dog.

Quickly gulping the rest of his frankfurter, Fields deployed his cane with a flourish, and started toward them.

"Good afternoon!" he called as jovially as he knew how. "I hope you'll allow me to welcome you folks to Oxnard, the shining jewel of the WestMerican coast."

The slight twitch that tugged at their faces was an effect

he caused everywhere he went. All scythes knew it. It was the tamping down of the human fight-or-flight response that surfaced whenever people saw a scythe. Since both fight and flight would bring about a gleaning, people had learned to imprison that particular instinct, although it did, on these occasions, rattle its chains.

Their reaction was irritating, but the dog didn't bark at him and that kept his demeanor pleasant. Really, it was quite an exceptional animal.

Leaning forward, Fields dangled the hand not sporting his ring before the dog's nose and beamed at the young couple. They seemed genuinely young, too, not like so many who turned the corner at the first sign of a wrinkle.

"Permit me to introduce myself." He would've tipped his hat if he'd had one, but he didn't care for the way hats flattened the hair along his temples. "Fields is the name, local scythe and greeting committee. I'm always pleased to welcome new arrivals and make certain they understand what a fine little community we have here. Are you taking up residence in Oxnard, or just visiting?"

The couple smiled, slightly nervous. "It's a pleasure to meet you, Your Honor," said the man. "We've just moved here from the Region of the Rising Sun."

Come to think of it, they did have a mild PanAsiatic leaning—not that Fields cared about such things. It was nice to know his little seaside town was attracting people from far-flung places. Although he hoped it didn't become a habit.

"I'm Khen Muragami. This is my wife, Anjali, and our Shikoku dog here is named Jian—"

"Splendid, splendid," said Fields, having already forgotten the couple's names. The dog's name, however, stuck out sorely, and Fields couldn't help pursing his lips. "Am I to understand that you've named this fine animal 'John'?" He shook his head. "I could never understand why people would give a dog a mundane human name—and unless I'm greatly mistaken, this is a female. . . ."

The young woman cleared her throat. "Excuse me, Your Honor, but her name is *Jian*." She displayed a healthy pair of dimples. "Our girl can be quite the handful sometimes, so her name is an ancient PanAsiatic word for a double-edged sword."

"Ancient?" Fields brightened. "Well, now, I'm quite an expert on the Age of Mortality. In fact, my Patron Historic was one of the Mortal Era's greatest existential philosophers, encapsulating that bygone time in two precepts that I've found applicable even to our modern day. The first, *'You can't cheat an honest man'* shows how mortal folk who lived contentedly could never be led astray. And the second, *'Never give a sucker an even break,'* instructs us to be ruthless when dealing with those who *do* depart the path of propriety."

He placed his ringed hand over his chest, in a gesture of sincerity. "Truly words to live by." He couldn't help but notice how the couple's eyes lingered on the ring.

"Indeed," the man said, his smile showing a few more teeth than were necessary. "And thank you for the welcome, Your Honor. We'll look forward to seeing you around town."

"I'm somewhat unmissable, yes. Good day to you both." Then bending a bit farther, he met the dog's dark, unblinking gaze. "And to you, John."

He made his way back to the hot dog stand where Charles had his third hot dog waiting. "What a delightful animal. It certainly deserves a more appropriate name. But such things can be remedied."

Charles went almost entirely still behind the cart, and Fields couldn't blame him at all. Fields had come to love his profession, of course. Goddard, that eloquent scythe from MidMerica, had espoused some wonderful precepts about a scythe's relationship to his work. A pity he'd been burned beyond revival in a botched Tonist gleaning a few months ago. Well, perhaps it was no great loss. After all, Goddard *had* been annoyingly loud and flashy. . . .

Fields heaved a sigh. "I shall have to pay John's family a visit this evening—but not before breaking bread with Constance and Tea Biscuit." Then he chuckled, because more would be broken than bread.

Constance Something-or-Other had not made things convenient for him. When he had arrived at her home, she was still packing her bags even though it had been hours since she'd committed her gleaning offense. If only she'd put a bit more effort into making her getaway, she could've saved him a great deal of exertion, but no.

She unleashed a tearful barrage of pre-gleaning hysterics, but at least she put Tea Biscuit into his carrier before Fields had unlimbered his sword cane upon her.

John's owners were much more courteous. They took their gleaning in stride—although they were monotonously insistent about how special John was, and how she needed the most dutiful sort of care.

The aftermath there had proven a pleasant surprise. Fields had his tranquilizer gun, loaded and ready in his robe to use on the dog, but the animal once again showed its sterling character. She'd not even growled at him as he'd removed her old collar and tags and replaced them with new ones. Quite surprising behavior, considering the trying events she had just witnessed. But, well, one didn't acquire a dog for protection in these enlightened times, did one?

"Trixie is now your name," he told her, jingling the tags that now dangled on her neck. This was always the name he gave female dogs he adopted. He had plenty of "Trixie" paraphernalia at home—it would be a waste to choose a different name. Besides, Fields decided she looked like a Trixie. And that was that. He snapped the leash into place, and she trailed after him quite meekly into his limo. Tea Biscuit's carrier, on the other hand, went into the trunk, where the demonic creature's incessant barking would be muted.

Ten minutes later, his limo pulled up to the curb with a spine-rattling jerk. Add to that the way the dratted thing seemed to take the longest possible route tonight, and it left his mood sour, if not foul. The Scythedom's driverless vehicles were not allowed to participate in the Thunderhead's electronic traffic grid—which made them a fleet of artificial unintelligence. Even so, a glitchy automated vehicle was infinitely preferable to having a human chauffeur. Fields couldn't understand how anyone could stand entrusting themselves so completely to another person.

With Tea Biscuit's carrier in one hand, and Trixie's leash in the other, he walked toward the Oxnard pet shelter and revival center's main entrance. Mere seconds after he rang the bell, the door opened to reveal a salt-and-pepper-haired woman with whom Fields had dealt before. "Good evening, Dawn," he said, again lamenting his inability to wear hats that he could tip. "Always a pleasure to see a familiar face."

"Scythe Fields." Dawn's eyes moved down and back up, her gaze taking in the scene. "These dogs are both alive," she observed, "so you're not here for another pet revival?"

"Not tonight," he told her. "I am giving the creature in the case to the shelter, where you will, no doubt, find a more disciplined owner than it previously had. And this beauty"—he gestured to Trixie sitting on the path beside him, her ears back and her nose at work on a scent—"I shall be adopting myself. I trust the paperwork's still in its usual spot?"

He stepped through the door and headed to the reception desk.

"You know that, as a scythe, you don't need to fill out any paperwork, Your Honor."

"Nor do I need to bring animals here after I've gleaned their owners, and yet I do," Fields pointed out. "And I don't need to return animals for revival after they've proven themselves unworthy companions, and yet I do that as well. Because filling out forms, and these other kindnesses set a positive example. Although I might be above the law, I am not beyond it."

"Yes, Your Honor." She took Tea Biscuit off his hands, and Fields went to the nearest computer console. Upon his approach, the friendly Thunderhead interface vanished and was replaced by the simple, utilitarian screen that faced every scythe when they approached a computer. He pulled up the requisite forms and got to work, all the while his new canine ward waited patiently by his side.

"I've a good feeling about this one," he shouted to Dawn, who was still in the back, trying to settle Tea Biscuit. He'd gone through quite a few dogs in his years, but the truth was, a person in his position needed a certain *kind* of dog, a kind he'd yet to find despite his constant searching. So many of those other dogs had an uncanny tendency toward deadishness, but he suspected this one would be very different.

With the adoption forms all in order, he bid Dawn a fond farewell and left. But when he got to the curb, his limo was gone. He fumbled through his pockets one-handed for his hand tablet. Tapping it, he discovered that the car was back home in the garage recharging its fuel cells.

"Godfrey Daniels," he muttered. If only one could glean an inanimate object. Taking a breath, he let it go. No use wasting his annoyance on a machine. Besides, it was a lovely night, and the quietude of the town's streets was widely renowned, especially after dark when only unsavory types would be out and about. He had no use for such people and had let his gleaning send that message as far as it could travel. Not that he targeted any group, of course—but a few high-profile examples, he'd found, could start rumors and convey an impression that wasn't backed up by the sort of hard data that would get him in trouble with High Blade Pickford and her statistics staff.

Fields gave a smile to the dog sitting at his feet. "Come now, Trixie," he said in his most coaxing tone. "We'll have a nice little stroll and get to know one another."

Speaking to animals, he knew, was all about tone and body

language. But that didn't mean that the conversation, one-sided though it may be, needed to be empty. Fields had to admit, the one-sidedness charmed him. Properly behaved dogs allowed him to talk without any fear of being interrupted, sidetracked, or even questioned.

"I think you'll see, Trixie, that you've nothing to fear from your uncle Bill, and I'm sure we'll be on our way to becoming great friends and bosom companions in no time."

The dog's ears twitched forward, and she was dutifully obedient . . . but the blankness about her . . . There was nothing fearful in her manner, but nothing ingratiating, either. Fields didn't know what to make of it. He had to admit, however, a muted reaction was better than howling or barking or lunging at him as some of his previous acquisitions had done during their first moments together.

"A pleasant walk through the streets of your new hometown," he said. "That should be just the thing to perk you up."

And, of course, the dog said nothing.

Fields—back when he was just little Jimmy Randell—had fond and not-so-fond memories of his childhood dog. Towser was a sturdy and willful malamute that his parents saw fit to leave almost entirely in young Jimmy's care, which would have been fine, had he been a little older and sturdier himself. Towser was adept at bolting, and pulling out of Jimmy's grasp. The poor dog's life came to a bitter intermission when a female malamute across the street caught Towser's eye. He darted into the street, and was promptly killed by a car. Jimmy's parents revived Towser, but not without complaining about the cost, and giving Jimmy a stern reprimand. "A dog's gotta know its place," his father would constantly tell him. "They *want* to know their place. Once they know who's master they're content and relieved."

And so from that moment on, he was firmer with Towser, and wrapped the leash twice around his wrist when he took Towser for a walk. It worked at first, until Towser spied a raccoon lumbering across the street one evening. He bolted again . . . this time dragging Jimmy into the street with him, where they were both rendered deadish by a truck. As for the raccoon, it made a clean getaway, as raccoons often do.

After Jimmy's revival, he got yet another reprimand, and did not get Towser back. "We revived him and sent him to live on a ranch," his father told him. "With a more responsible caretaker," he added, just for the dig.

But as Jimmy got older, he suspected it was a lie, and they had let Towser stay dead, what with the increasing expense of pet revival. The possibility that he'd been lied to about Towser was one of the many reasons Fields had found it fairly easy to plunge that sword into his father's chest at his final apprenticeship test three decades ago. His father, of course, was revived, but never forgave him. Fields suspected that was part of the reason for the test: to emotionally distance young scythes from their families. Although for Fields that emotional distance seemed to extend to most other human beings as well. But pets were different. Their love was unconditional—and he was certain that Trixie could be conditioned to love him.

On the walk home that night, Fields let Trixie sniff at the trees and flowerbeds along the way, until reaching his beachfront home. It was sizable, without being ostentatious. A grassy yard dotted with beds of dahlias and primrose and three ficus trees to provide the most picturesque sort of shade as well as being large enough for a medium-sized dog like Trixie to get a bit of exercise. The house itself was three stories tall and painted the tasteful gray and white that Fields unofficially but strictly enforced hereabouts. He pushed the front gate open with a little thrill of anticipation. "Now then, Trixie," he said, stepping through, "let's give you the grand tour."

This time, she didn't follow, the leash going taut in Fields's hand. Turning in the slightly orange light of the corner streetlamp, he couldn't detect even the slightest wag of her tail. She was sniffing, though, her head raised slightly, and her nose pointed toward the house.

"Displaying caution." Fields nodded. "An admirable trait when entering a new situation." He tugged the lead a bit more firmly. "But enough of that. Come along inside." His father had been right about one thing: Dogs had to know the alpha. Knowing where they were in the pecking order made them feel safe. Less anxious. Even if it was just a pecking order of two. He also worried that there may be raccoons lurking about again. Those creatures had plagued him ever since that unfortunate truck incident. The last thing he wanted was for Trixie to get all worked up about a critter before even getting through the door.

Fortunately, she followed him in without him having to become more insistent; up the brick walkway to the porch and into the front hall. He closed the door quickly behind them, tapped the light switch, and undid the leash from Trixie's collar.

"Give Uncle Bill a moment to put his equipment away, and we can see the house."

As he hadn't had to use the tranquilizer gun, he simply unloaded it and placed it upon its rack within his weapons cabinet just inside the door. "A place for everything, and everything in its place." He closed the cabinet and turned, expecting to see her sniffing the floor or the carpet or curtains in the front room. Instead, she was standing exactly where he'd left her, regarding him. Her gaze was now even more opaque—he would almost have called it thoughtful had she not been a dog—but she didn't cringe, didn't growl, didn't bark, didn't leap up to plant her paws against his belly or anything untoward like that.

"Very good." Bending down, Fields patted her head, and her lack of response struck him as odd, but then he'd always found overly exuberant dogs to be a bit off-putting. "Such a good girl," he said to reinforce the idea. "The kitchen first, I think."

He showed her her bowls, the name "Trixie" inscribed upon them—he had another pair labeled "Rex" along with matching collar and tags for those times when he adopted a male. She sniffed them, lapped at the water bowl, but seemed otherwise uninterested; even when he took an old box of dog biscuits he still had in the cupboard from the previous Trixie and shook it at her with a grin, she didn't react with more than a slightly cocked head.

"You've never seen dog biscuits before?" Fields rattled the box again. "Treats? Cookies? Num-nums?" He couldn't think what else people called the things, but since she didn't respond with any more recognition to one name than the others, the point became quickly moot. "Did they teach you nothing at all?" Opening the box, he shook one out and extended it toward her. "Here you go, girl. Come on."

She merely cocked her head in the other direction.

For the briefest of instants, he imagined taking a bite of it himself as a demonstration, but instead, he returned to his earlier question: What had her previous owners taught her? "Certainly they played catch with you!" And taking careful aim, he tossed the biscuit to pass just to the left of her muzzle.

Not only did she not catch it, she shied to her right, allowing the biscuit to clatter to the kitchen's tile floor.

Feeling gladder and gladder that he'd gotten her former owners out of the way, Fields put the box of biscuits back in the cupboard. "We shall begin your education first thing in the morning," he informed her, and he turned back just in time to see the biscuit was now gone from the floor.

He blew out a breath. "Well, at least you recognize food when you see it." Nodding, he crossed the kitchen and pushed open the door to the dining room. "Come, Trixie. Come." That word, at least, she seemed to know. . . .

In the dining room, he showed her the side door with the flap that she could push aside when she felt the need to relieve herself, then he opened the door to show her the side yard where said relieving would occur. She *had* to be housebroken at her age; he refused to think otherwise and led her from the dining room out to the end of the front hall and the stairway.

On the second floor, he showed her his office and her daytime cushion on the floor across from his desk. "So while I'm seeing to the great work that's been entrusted to me, you can be waiting faithfully nearby." Heading back into the hallway and up the stairs to the third floor, he used his cane to point out her nighttime cushion beside his bed as well as his collection of vintage video disks and antique big-screen TV. "You shall retire for the evening here." He gently tapped her cushion, and she seemed to get the idea, because she stepped forward and sat upon it. The cushion was the finest pet bed there was. Highest quality, and comfortable enough to ensure that she would never have any reason to venture up onto his bed. Not that there wouldn't be the occasional misstep—but time, training, and discipline would let her know what was and was not allowed.

And then Trixie barked.

It was the first sound she had made in his presence. It was soft and very short, her eyes fixed on the windows that during daylight hours would show a lovely view of the ocean. French doors opened between the windows onto an upper deck that he seldom used, and toward this door Trixie now advanced, her head low, the hair bristling along her neck.

Fields stared. "Whatever's the matter, girl?" Nothing could be out there of interest to a dog . . . .except possibly birds or cats or—"Raccoons?"

Rushing across the room to the door now, she growled, and Fields tightened his lips. Could the little devils truly be cavorting about in the trees and bushes alongside the house again?

Only one way to find out.

Quick steps brought him to her side; he wrenched the door open, rushed out onto the deck, and cried, "Ha!"

No scurrying or squeaking met his ears, but Trixie ran straight for the western railing. An energetic stretch brought her to her hind legs, her front paws coming to rest on top of the rail, and the eager way she bent her head downward made Fields sure she'd spotted some quarry.

"What is it, girl?" Fields hurried to the spot beside her, leaned halfway over in an attempt to catch the beasts in the act of whatever it was raccoons did, but then Trixie was moving, barking, trying to squeeze between him and the railing. "What on earth are you—?" he began, taking a step back. "Heel, Trixie! Heel!"

Exactly the wrong thing to say, he realized as soon as he'd said it, for the dog was suddenly positioning herself right where he was trying to put his foot. She gave a yelp, and not wanting to settle his full weight upon her, he jumped away, striking the low porch railing about mid-thigh. Inner ear spinning, his balance shifting, his shoulders continued forward, and before he knew it, he'd gone over, the flagstone of the back patio rushing toward him.

"Godfrey Daniels!" he managed to exclaim before a painful crack jolted through him, and everything went dark.

Blinking blearily, Fields rubbed his head. More blinking revealed tasteful wooden walls with velvet hangings of a muted purple color. He pushed himself up onto one elbow, and another bout of blinking revealed an entirely too perky woman in white.

"Good afternoon, Scythe Fields!" Her eyes sparkled enough to give a mortal man an aneurism. "It's such an honor serving you for what the records indicate is only your second revival!"

"Whut in tarnation?" Fields heard himself, and shut his mouth quickly. The voice coming out of him—the *words* coming out of him did not sound like him. They were familiar, yes, but not in a good way. More in a kind of way he'd much rather forget. Although his thoughts were muddy, he forced eloquence to his lips. "Could you kindly tell me what has occurred?"

"Not our business to know." The woman grew a bit less bright and sprightly, but Fields still felt like he had to squint to look at her. "All I know is that the drones brought you in, and we did our work. Scythe Conan Doyle from the High Blade's office was here yesterday, though, and he said there didn't seem to be any sign of foul play at the scene."

"Scene?" More memories bubbled up. "Trixie!" he shouted, leaping to his feet.

Spots burst across his vision, but a steadying grip seized his upper arm. "Careful, Your Honor!"

"Let go!" Vertigo washed through him, and he couldn't stop the whininess and drawl of his youth from seeping into his voice. "Me and my dog were huntin' raccoons when I tripped and fell!"

"Sir?" The pressure of her hand lessened. "Raccoons?"

The wave of grouchiness inspired by her question didn't clear his eyes, but it did make him feel more like himself—more like the version of himself that proudly bore the name Fields. He cleared his throat. "Yes, madame! Raccoons!" A deep breath helped him focus, both on the wall of the room and on the person he was supposed to be. "Ferocious little devils! Came at us in a pack like miniature wolves! Practically wolverines, the whole gang of them!"

Another breath, and he was able to turn to the nurse with a fair amount of his swagger back. "So if you'd be so kind as to tell me what's become of my faithful dog, I'll be on my way to retrieve her." He forced a chuckle he didn't quite feel. "Retrieve my dog. Quite the witty remark were she a retriever."

The nurse's expression had gone almost completely blank, something Fields found he preferred to the bubbliness she'd been displaying earlier. "Your . . . dog?" she asked, and Fields had to smile, seeing that *she* was the one off-balance now. "Well, you've been here a day and a half . . . so . . . I suppose she'd be at the animal shelter?"

"Excellent!" A table behind her caught Fields's attention, and his smile grew, his sword cane and hand tablet lying there. "Most excellent!" He stepped around the nurse, grabbed his belongings, and started for the door.

"Sir?" she called behind him. "Perhaps you should rest a bit more? We have some really good ice cream if you'd—"

"Unnecessary!" With each step, he could feel the panache of his bon vivant personality trickling back to inhabit his various extremities. "I'm sure Oxnard has been beside itself with worry, wondering about my condition, so I shall make my departure." He gave her a flourished salute with his cane, made his way down a hall to a lobby, and exited, the afternoon blue and shimmering with just the slightest touch of a breeze.

The animal shelter was on the next block, and Fields made his way around to the emergency room entrance before realizing that regular business hours were still in effect, with people waiting their turn—and although Fields didn't mind a little paperwork, waiting his turn was certainly not in his portfolio of skills. He made his way to the front, and, of course, no one dared to stop him.

The little lobby looked much the same as it did during his late-night visit, but he actually pulled up short to see Dawn seated behind the counter. He had hoped it would be someone else, and spare him the embarrassment of having to retrieve Trixie so soon after adopting her.

"Your Honor!" She sprang to her feet, the small but sincere smile on her lips striking Fields with much more force than the large, slightly plastic one the nurse had worn. "I wasn't sure when you'd be out." Coming around to the end of the counter, she touched something that clicked, and the whole section swung open. "But I've got someone here who I'll bet is happy to see you!"

Trixie lay stretched across the floor behind the counter, and Fields braced himself, partially resigned to the inevitable barking and leaping and slobbering—

Except that Trixie just raised her head and looked at him.

Fields's heart seemed to be pressing against his ribs. That the animal should know him so well, should know exactly how to react to him, after so brief an acquaintance . . . "Such an excellent dog," he managed to get out.

"She's very well behaved," Dawn was saying. "I can't even imagine how she was trained. But she showed up here the other night not long after you took her, and when I called the scythe offices, they said you'd been taken in for revival."

Having never been through the revival process in his adult life, Fields didn't know if the upwelling of emotion he was feeling might be a residual effect or not. But he couldn't deny that the thought of this near stranger caring for Trixie while he himself had been incapacitated was tightening his throat and misting his eyes. "Dawn, my dear?" He held out his ring. "I can't thank you enough."

Her eyes went wide. "Immunity, Your Honor?" She crossed toward him hesitantly.

"You've earned it."

He tried not to flinch as she went down on one knee to kiss his ring. Fortunately, she didn't make a slobbering mess of things. Fields kept his attention on Trixie during the whole nauseating procedure. She was sitting up on her haunches now, her tongue lolling out in what Fields had always thought of as a canine smile. "That's my girl," he said, clapping his hands when the telltale red flash from his ring indicated that Dawn had finally removed herself. "At least we frightened those raccoons away, eh, Trixie?"

The jolliness of her expression seemed to increase. Beaming, Fields bent down, took the end of her leash, and started toward the door. "You've my eternal thanks, Dawn," he called, "or a year's worth, at least." He looked back to give her the usual jaunty wave with his cane, but Trixie pulled a bit harder on the lead than he'd been expecting, making him stumble a few steps outside before he could recover his balance.

He took an easy breath for the first time since his revival. "To the park, I believe, Trixie." She was walking alongside him now, her ears perked but her gaze focused ahead, no doubt on the lookout for miscreants. Fields nodded in approval and went on. "I can't wait to see how you'll respond to Charles's wonderful hot dogs."

Out on the street with his faithful canine companion, Fields puffed away the last bits of the timid uncertainty that had clouded his thoughts when he'd first awoken. He'd left that weak, frightened boy behind years ago, and it made his lips tighten to think that a little thing like going deadish should allow that person to return. . . .

But it was much too pleasant a day for such morbid considerations. "Yes, indeed," he said, putting the slightest strut into his step and nodding to the people moving aside for him and Trixie on the sidewalk. "Quite lovely."

At the oceanfront promenade, they took a right, the salty scent of the sea making Fields wonder if he should commandeer a small yacht for viewing the sunset. Perhaps Trixie had some water dog in her?

At this moment, she was nosing along the lampposts and planters in just the way Fields liked: neither impeding his forward progress nor forcing him to scurry. And when they arrived at the park, he took the hot dog Charles gave him and barely had to bend over and offer it to Trixie, before she lunged upward, snatching the offering away, nearly nipping his fingers in the process.

Fields beamed at her. "Devoured it like a true connoisseur, wouldn't you say, Charles?"

"Yes, Your Honor," the man answered in his usual baritone moan, but fortunately, he was already extending a perfect, mustard-covered specimen of his culinary art, so Fields once again forgave him all else.

After a second for Trixie and third for himself, Fields took leave of the park and headed downtown. "As a rule, I don't care much for the hustle and bustle of the city," he told Trixie—and anyone else who cared to listen during the long blocks between the water and the storefronts that strived so unsuccessfully to be quaint. "But a scythe's duties are never done."

After picking up some dinner for himself, and multiple dog food choices for Trixie, he noted a few people for future gleaning, then headed home.

"Quite the eventful day, Trixie," he said as he pushed open the front door. "What say we attempt to take things easy for the rest of the week, hmmm? No more hunting for us."

She swung her face up, but the lack of tongue-lolling, perked ears, shining eyes, or any sort of expression at all wanted to send a shiver down his spine. He shook his head. Likely he was still woozy from the procedure.

In the kitchen, he plopped a spoonful from each can of dog food into her bowl. She ate them all with equal relish, but that in fact turned out to be no relish at all. Her tail barely moved as she swallowed the scoops—nothing he would've called a wag, certainly—nor did her ears perk in any appreciable way.

His first impulse was to wonder if she'd overdone the hot dogs, but his next thought brought a smile to his face. "Not a picky eater! Yet another excellent quality in a dog!" He dumped the remainder from one of the cans into the bowl and slid the other cans into the refrigerator. "For tomorrow, then."

The soft chomping sounds of her finishing followed him across the kitchen to the sink. "There are few things I find as annoying as a prima donna," he said, glad once again to have a properly nonresponsive audience to whom he could declaim his thoughts. He filled her water bowl and carried it back to Trixie's nook. "Those who constantly call attention to themselves with outrageous demands or by presenting themselves as somehow better or more important than the rest of us." He set the bowl down, straightened, and shook his head before noticing that she was looking up at him again.

For the slightest of instants, he almost thought something might be lurking in those dark eyes. But then she was turning away, lowering her head to lap at the water bowl. "Most extraordinary," he muttered. "My recovery from the deadish condition is definitely incomplete." Shifting his shoulders, he opened the refrigerator and removed a can of his favorite beverage, grape soda—a lifeline to his childhood—or more accurately, the sweet trophy of having survived it.

With a pop of the top, he raised the can in a salute to Trixie. "A man and his dog." He took a deep draught, blew out a breath, and gestured to the kitchen door. "Now, with that unfortunate accident behind us, let's settle in for our first normal evening."

She followed him upstairs so silently, he had to look behind him several times to make sure she was there. Bypassing the second floor entirely, he climbed to the bedroom, poked the light switch on the wall by the doorway, stepped inside to direct Trixie toward her cushion—

And she was already crossing the room, lowering herself onto the gold velour, resting her head upon her forepaws.

She looked so natural that Fields had to take another swig of grape soda to clear the tightness from his throat. "A boy and his dog," he said again. Did he say "boy"? "A man, that is," although he felt self-conscious correcting himself to Trixie.

Moving to the bed, he kicked off his shoes, settled against the pillows, grabbed the remote from its spot below the lamp on the nightstand—one of his Patron Historic's films after his trying day would be just the thing! He poked the power button, and promptly fell asleep during the opening credits.

A crash made him blink, and he blinked several more times before he realized that darkness surrounded him. Yes, he often found himself nodding off as soon as he positioned himself in front of any sort of screen, but why had it shut off? Why weren't the room's lights still on? And why, he added to his list of inner questions, wasn't he holding the remote any longer?

Still only woozily awake, he swung his bare feet onto the carpet with an unpleasant *squish*, stood, and took the several steps to the light switch by the door. Each step was, oddly enough, colder and wetter than the step before.

What had happened here? Had a pipe burst in the bathroom? He looked in that direction, but of course he couldn't see anything. Annoyance tightened his lips. He and Trixie might need to collect his cane from the locker downstairs and pay the plumbers a visit.

It was then that he realized what the crashing sound that had woken him up must have been. In the shadows by his bed, he saw that his night table lamp had fallen onto the floor. He reached out and touched the light switch.

The instant the ceiling light came on, intense pain buzzed and snapped through him—and in that first instant of searing illumination, he saw bare electrical wires from the broken lamp lying against the soaked carpet.

"Godfrey—" he managed to hiss between his clenched teeth, before the electrical surge shut down all his thoughts.

• • •

This time, he didn't come awake all at once. He just seemed to notice that his gaze was fixed on a lovely wood-inlaid ceiling: the same lovely wood-inlaid ceiling he'd woken to previously at the revival parlor.

"Sumpthin' ain't right," he heard himself say. Then choked back the words, coughing, swallowing, clearing his throat, and swallowing some more to make even the memory of those words go away. Fields then rolled onto his side to see the same nurse standing beside the bed, her uniform just as white but her smile more labored, less shimmering. "Scythe Fields? How are you feeling, Your Honor?"

He sat up with a grimace. "I seem to have fallen victim to a minor domestic mishap," he said, forcing his speech to stay properly elevated. His most recent memories rushed back more readily than they had the last time—perhaps being rendered deadish got easier with practice—and after another bout of throat clearing, he asked, "Trixie wasn't injured, was she?"

The nurse's smile shifted as if she were trying to disguise the discovery of a tack in her shoe. "Trixie? That's your dog? Because the emergency crew found her sitting out front."

"Emergency crew?" Not quite ready to stand, he blinked up at her.

"Because of the water." The nurse's smile became even more strained. "And the fire. The crew said the electrical surge would've taken your whole neighborhood off-line if the Thunderhead didn't keep a firewall around your house because of, you know, the whole scythe thing."

The lights suddenly seemed much too bright, her voice

much too grating. Fields squinted at the table beside the bed, but this time, his sword cane wasn't there, of course; he hadn't had it on his person at the time of the accident.

"And I suppose that Trixie will be at the animal shelter again?"

"I . . . guess?"

It irked him that she was uncertain, for surely part of her job was to attend to such things. Incompetence was just cause for gleaning, but Fields had more important matters to attend to.

Climbing to his feet, he slipped on his shoes that some-one had seen fit to retrieve from his waterlogged house, soggy though they were. He said, "Thank you," winced at how meekly the words had emerged, turned back to show the nurse the sneer that went with his current actual feelings—

But she was already saying, "Oh, you're so welcome, Scythe Fields! We're all just honored to be of service to you!"

He gave her a tight smile, then made his way as quickly as he could to the exit.

It was a beautiful afternoon again; he just didn't know how many afternoons he'd been away this time. Two, it had been before, hadn't it? And to have gone deadish so soon after his previous bout, well, it struck him as almost unseemly, almost as if someone had—

He stopped that thought, refused to let it advance, pounded his shoes—which made squishy noises along the sidewalk toward the animal shelter's emergency room entrance.

Pushing through, he once again found Dawn at the counter staring at her tablet, but this time her hands were gripping the thing like she'd just caught it running around the room.

"Quite the eventful week it's been, hasn't it?" he said, a little too loudly.

Dawn started like she'd been bitten by something behind the counter and leaped from her chair. "Scythe Fields!" She glanced at the tablet still in her hand, and her gaze darted up toward him like some sort of small bird flitting past. "I've been keeping Trixie again while they repaired your place, and I . . . I have to ask, sir, I mean, with these two accidents happening so soon after you adopted Trixie, do you, well, do you honestly think that the two of you are a good match?"

"*What?*" Fields reached for his sword cane, remembered that he didn't have it, then remembered that he'd given her immunity yesterday—or two days ago or three days or however long his lazy, worthless, filthy hide had been lolling around—

The sudden shards of self-hatred digging into his thoughts, so familiar from his youth but carefully subsumed since receiving his robe and ring and new identity, shocked him even more than Dawn's insinuation. He had to draw a deep breath before he could recall himself well enough to say with extra enunciation, "If you're attempting to imply that I'm unfit to be a dog owner, then I shall inform you that, in the long and largely ignoble history of the human race, there has never before been a man and a dog so meant for each other as myself and Trixie. That you would even consider us to be incompatible makes me wonder if you might be pursuing the wrong profession."

Dawn's smile completely vanished. "With all due respect, Your Honor, I've devoted over eighty years to caring for and reviving animals, and considering Trixie's unusual background, it might be a good idea to—"

"Background?" Fields felt the hair at the back of his neck rise. "What could possibly be unusual about Trixie's background?"

The woman licked her lips nervously. "The Thunderhead won't talk about Trixie specifically since you adopted her, but it did direct me to some very interesting footage." Raising her tablet, she tapped it and turned it toward him.

Not wanting to, Fields glanced down, saw images of puppies quite reminiscent of Trixie wrestling and running across a well-tended and sunny lawn. "These videos," Dawn was saying, "come from the Nepal charter region in PanAsia, and these dogs, well, they call them 'enhanced pets.'"

About to repeat the word "enhanced" but add an incredulous question mark to it, Fields instead froze when a voice from the screen said, "All right, now! Let's have all the girls on this side, all the boys on that side!"

Tongues lolling, the puppies quickly separated themselves into two groups.

"And now," the voice went on, "let's have both groups line up in size order!"

Another scramble, the camera pulling back, and the puppies sorted themselves in exactly the specified fashion.

Fields had to swallow. "Well-trained animals," he murmured, but he couldn't quite get the little waver out of his voice.

"No, Your Honor," Dawn said softly, and Fields still nearly flinched; he'd managed to forget the woman was there. "The reports say that a group of scientists has been working for almost a century in Nepal, trying to give a select set of dogs human levels of intelligence. These here are just puppies, but later on, they show some fully grown dogs who—"

"No!" Fields shouted, dashing the pad from the woman's hand. "That video is nothing but some unsavory's idea of a joke. It's false, and if I even for a moment thought that it might be true, I would be on the first flight across the Pacific to personally glean everyone involved!"

He chose to dismiss it out of hand. Except that a part of his brain wasn't willing to let it go. Because if Trixie was not just sentient, but also *sapient* . . . then maybe these so-called accidents . . .

"No!" he shouted again, barely stopping himself from stomping his foot. "No more of this. I'll take my dog now!"

Her lips tight, Dawn opened the end of the counter, and Trixie was once again waiting there with silent patience. Squatting, Fields reached to grab the end of her leash and nearly flinched when she rose before he could even take the lead . . .

. . . Because her standing and him crouching put her deep, dark eyes right at the same level as his. And while he found himself staring—almost shivering, in fact—she looked back with absolute calm.

He snatched the leash, lurched to his feet, and aimed for the door, Trixie sliding silently into place beside him. "You've made a number of grave errors today, madame!" he called without turning back. "Quite a *large* number!"

"Please, Your Honor!" Something close to panic seemed to edge Dawn's words. "We've got a lot of very nice dogs at the shelter, you know that! Maybe you'll want to reconsider adopting *this* particular dog. . . ."

In the doorway Fields stopped to fix her with what he hoped was a steely glare. "And you, madame, might want to consider how short a year of immunity can be!" He wanted to rattle his sword cane at her, but of course he didn't have it, and Trixie again had kept going; he had to move quickly to avoid being pulled over sideways as they went out the door.

The farther away from the animal shelter he got, the more ridiculous that video felt. "Unconscionable!" he fumed, trying to stomp each step his uncomfortably moist shoes took along the sidewalk. "Why would anyone believe such an outrageous falsehood?"

Trixie's ears pulled back, and the look she turned over her shoulder at him had so much raw reproach in it, it froze every other sound on Fields's tongue.

Because she couldn't be reproachful, could she? She was an animal—a splendid animal, certainly, possibly the finest canine he'd ever come across, but from there, it was a long stretch to think she did not just see, hear, and smell the world, but understood everything that went on around her. Enough to develop a murderous sense of revenge . . .

"It would've been in the news!" he forced himself to say aloud, his own voice as always the most soothing sound he could imagine. "If people were bringing creatures of that sort out of a charter region, why, the nets and webs would be full of—!"

"Your Honor?" asked Charles, and Fields blinked at the hot dog stand there in front of him. Lost in horrible thought, he'd had no particular destination in mind—maybe to wend his way homeward and see if the repair crews had done anything irksome enough to have earned them a gleaning visit.

But Trixie had led him straight here; she was in fact rearing back on her hind legs with her front paws against the side of the cart and her attention fully fixed on the hot dog Charles was holding out to Fields.

She obviously detected their aroma on the breeze, he told himself. Not that there was the slightest whisper of a wind stirring the afternoon's warmth, but a dog's sense of smell was more sensitive than any person's. That Trixie had headed for the hot dog stand didn't prove a single thing: not a single, solitary thing!

"Your Honor?" Charles asked again, waving the hot dog in Fields's direction.

Fields found that he wasn't hungry—he hadn't been hungry before, and he certainly wasn't hungry *now*. Without a word of explanation, he turned to go.

The leash, however, drew taut in his hand, Trixie not following. He spun to confront her, but froze again at the calm determination in her dark eyes, now focused on him instead of the hot dog wavering in Charles's grip. She gave a slow blink, and then, still looking directly at him, she made a gruff little not-quite-a-bark that put Fields in mind of the way his mother had always cleared her throat when she'd wanted to call his attention to one of his perceived shortcomings.

The jolt that shot up his spine made his arm twitch, and the involuntary movement of his hand was apparently enough of a signal for Charles. Nodding, the man stooped, held out the hot dog to Trixie, and said, "Good dog," his voice as deep and deliberate as always.

Trixie broke eye contact, took the hot dog, but didn't wolf it down the way every other animal he'd ever owned would've—

or even the way Trixie herself had eaten her food yesterday, or the day before, or whenever he'd last been alive.

No, she held the end of the bun almost gently in her teeth, swiveled her neck till she was looking straight at Fields again, and only then did she begin. A flex of her neck sent the hot dog flipping several inches into the air, then she stretched upward, and in a movement too fast for him to make out, stripped the bun away without upsetting the trajectory of the hot dog itself. Dropping back to sit, she opened her mouth and caught the meat while the bun fell to the concrete beside her with a soft little plop.

"Wow!" Charles said, and Fields would've stared in wonder at him for this unaccustomed outburst had Trixie not been commanding all his attention.

Because slowly, one dainty bite at a time, she proceeded to pull the hot dog in with her teeth, chewing and swallowing each bite while she somehow managed to hold the rest of the item as steadily as a cigar, her gaze not wavering from his in the slightest during the entire performance. And at this point, Fields felt almost entirely convinced that it was indeed a performance.

Which meant he knew what he had to do.

Except that he had no idea how to do it.

He talked the whole way home. For him it was entirely unnatural not to, and the current situation was already more unnatural than Fields wanted to consider. So he kept up a steady stream of observations about the weather and the landscaping and the odd way people were dressing; the more inane the blather, the better. He had to convince Trixie that he still believed her to be an ordinary dog, and to do that, he had to convince her that he was an idiot.

Well, more of an idiot than the creature already mistook him to be.

Unless he was the one who was mistaken.

No. He knew better—although there were secret, silent times that he wished he *didn't* know better. Times when he wanted to drop his whole Scythe Fields act and crawl under his bed the way he had whenever Mother or Father had raised one of their carefully sculpted eyebrows too archly in his direction, saying the perfect thing to skewer his self-respect.

But this could not be one of those moments. He needed to be in control. He was the master of . . . of whatever this thing was. But before he could take any action, he needed to be sure. He had to give the dog a test, to lure her into a trap—yes, that was a more vital way of putting it. He needed to trick her into revealing the truth of her intentions toward him.

So he chattered and tried to think, following her up the walkway, entering the front gate, dishing her out half a can of food from the refrigerator—

Which was when the plan came to him, and he straightened. "Godfrey Daniels!" he proclaimed as if he'd had a sudden realization. "If I've spent so much of the last week incommunicado, I'm in danger of falling behind on my gleaning quota!" Not that he truly was; the last few months had held quite enough annoyances to have kept him truly busy—but the dog didn't know that. "I'll trust you to entertain yourself this evening, as I must be about my official duties."

Leaving the kitchen, he fought down the urge to look back

and see if she was following. "It's always a dilemma," he muttered, enunciating each word without, he hoped, making it too obvious that he was enunciating, "picking the proper method." He stopped at the weapons cabinet in the front hall, undid the lock, and pulled the doors open to reveal his arsenal. Handguns, knives, rifles, axes, shotguns, several racks of assorted poisons. Yes, he usually went with the sword hidden in his cane, but knowing that he had other options open to him always made him feel more professional.

"When I get back," he muttered, striving for the manner of a person making a mental note, "I must clean these shotguns, take them out onto the beach, and discharge them harmlessly above the sea, to make sure they're in good working order." Unable at last to stop himself, he glanced over his shoulder, ready for whatever he might see.

Trixie sat in the middle of the front room, her head cocked cutely but her eyes brimming with a not-so-cute intensity.

A part of him wanted to deny that she had any motives whatsoever—she was just a dog listening to the incomprehensible garble of her master's voice. But the rest of him wasn't so sure.

"Delicate instruments, shotguns," he told her in the same breezy, offhanded fashion he'd employed during the walk home; nothing more than a man talking to his dog. "If not maintained and discharged regularly, the entire thing might just explode upon firing." He took the smallest shotgun from the rack, weighed it in one hand—

Then pretended to be distracted. "And my muzzleloaders!" Leaning the shotgun against the wall beside the cabinet, he took the black powder flask from the next shelf, made a show of undoing the cap and sniffing it. Moving it about enough to fill the area with its sulfuric stink. "Yes, I'd best see to my firearms when I return this evening."

With a nod, he replaced the flask, pushed the cabinet closed, and stepped to the front door, the air still heavy with black powder aroma. To any observer it would appear he had simply forgotten he had left a shotgun leaning against the side of the cabinet. But there were no observers. Or at least no *human* observer.

"I'll be back soon, Trixie," he said with a jauntiness he didn't at all feel, turned the knob, and walked out into the evening's twilight.

A few minutes later, Fields slunk back toward the house, trusting that the sulfurous scent of gunpowder he'd left behind would mask his own. The windows beside the front door would give him an unobstructed view of both the entryway and weapons locker, and as much as he didn't want to know, he crept up, peered through—

—and saw the hallway empty, and Trixie nowhere in view. Nothing seemed to be going on at all after his exit. His heart quivered with hope. Could it be that this was all in his head? Was Trixie simply a dog, and not a monster in canine shape?

But then the kitchen door swung open, and Trixie came trotting out, something white and bulky in her mouth. A squeak toy? A rawhide bone? She turned, stopping at last beside the weapons cabinet and setting the object onto the floor in front of where the shotgun stood.

It was a bottle of glue.

And Trixie was now bending forward, gripping it with her forepaws struggling to twist the cap with her front teeth, and likely cursing her lack of opposable thumbs. Once she managed to get the cap of the glue off, she grabbed the bottle in her jaws again, and, rearing up to rest her forepaws on the side of the cabinet, she stretched her neck, tilted her head, and began trickling glue down into the barrel of the gun.

His chest tightening, Fields pulled out his tranquilizer gun—which he had surreptitiously taken from the cabinet—and used it to smash the window, then fired at the murderous mutt.

The dart hit Trixie squarely in the side. Dropping the glue bottle, she jumped away from the weapons locker and spun to face him, her lips pulled back in a snarl that almost tempted him to put another dart in her.

But no. It was a quick-acting solution with which he'd filled his darts. Trixie's eyes drooped, her ears went back, and her hind legs folded. She sat wobbling for another half a heartbeat, then she tipped over, sprawling across the white marble, the tags on her collar clattering when she hit.

The doorknob felt neither cold nor hot in Fields's hand as he turned it and stepped inside. "Gotcha, bitch!" he growled, then he stopped, cleared his throat, tried grasping for the proper way of expressing his feelings: something about foul betrayals or turnaround being fair play or—

Or screw it. Squatting down in front of her, he watched her forepaws twitch and her eyelids flutter. "Feelin' kinda funny?" he asked, in a voice he scarcely recognized, using words and phrases he'd barely spoken in decades. "Yeah, this stuff packs a wallop. It'll just knock you out for a while, though—a' course

I do got every right to totally blow you away. You wanna have human smarts, you gotta follow human laws, right?" He bent a little closer to her flicking ear. "And anybody makes a scythe go deadish? Well, I'm bettin' you know what happens to 'em, doncha?"

He moved to the closet under the stairway where he kept the travel kennel and pulled it out.

"Used to be I loved science," he told the semiconscious pooch, still mired in his old Jimmy Randell twang, "but that's the Thunderhead's wheelhouse now. As a scythe, I'm not gonna get all up in its business. Even so, whatever science made you don't deserve the light of day."

A few more spasmodic paw movements, and then the dog went so still that Fields began to worry. This wasn't the easiest tranq to mix; had he gotten the dosage wrong? Well, if he had, it would save him this next step—but this next step was key. It would be a victory sweeter than grape soda.

Looking more closely, he could see that her sides continued moving with her breath. Carefully he squatted behind her and slid her forward into the case. He tucked her tail in after her, closed the crate door, and clicked the lock. Then he hauled the crate up by its handle, and lumbered with it out the rear door to the back patio, and the beach beyond—noting that there was still the hint of a bloodstain on the flagstone from his nasty little splat.

The beach was dark under a moonless sky. "Nothin' but the briny blue out here, girl," he told the silent case as he set it down among the low dunes that filled the hundred or so yards between his home and the sea. "You'll find it restful, I guarantee."

He returned to the house to gather the necessary equipment, telling himself several times, "Mind over matter, Jimmy, mind over matter."

When he returned to the crate, he was panting from exertion—but it was more than that. His whole body was shaking with anticipation. He took a few deep breaths, and tried to slip back into the cultivated, professional persona of his Patron Historic. In control, emotionally detached, and waxing grandiose philosophic.

"Foully betrayed by a thankless conniving cur!" he proclaimed, driving his shovel into the sand, "I shall be avenged, and in this cruel world, that's the best one can hope for!" He shone a flashlight through the bars of the carrier's door, but Trixie's gray-furred body didn't move, still slumped against the floor.

"No response necessary," he said, putting down the flashlight and setting to work.

The whole thing quickly became tiresome, but Fields persevered. After all, he told himself, a matter of this severity contained no provisions for cutting corners. Besides, six-foot depth was for humans. This hole only needed to be deep enough to hold the crate.

Still, it took a good deal longer than he'd thought it would, the sand proving to be quite difficult to work with. Midnight, he was sure, had come and gone by the time he stood, sweating in the chill at the top of a rough slope that ran down into a three-foot depression easily wide enough to admit the dog carrier.

Turning to face that very object, he dropped the shovel and rubbed his hands together, stopping with a wince when his pain nanites seemed surprised by the gesture and took a moment to stifle the stinging of his palms. Gingerly picking up the flashlight, he shone it once more into the cage, and this time, Trixie's face glared back from behind the bars, her eyes two spots of unearthly glowing amber.

Fields struggled to keep himself in place. "Awake, I see."

Not even an ear flicked.

He nodded anyway. "Perhaps, in your drugged haze, you heard me mentioning my fondness for science when our evening together began," he said, dropping the flashlight and moving around to the back of the carrier. "Well, one of my favorite scientific anecdotes involved Schrödinger's cat."

The case slid easily down the sandy slope when he pushed it, and Fields settled it with the door facing him as he spoke. "Perhaps you're unfamiliar with the story." He hiked his robe up and clambered along the slope to the top. "It hinges upon some rather arcane codicils of physics to throw doubt upon whether a cat locked in a box under certain conditions can be considered definitively dead or alive."

He bent his knees, took up the shovel, and began to heave sand down into the hole around the dog carrier. "I feel almost certain, however, that the question won't be an issue for us tonight."

Never once during the entire operation did so much as a squeak arise from within the carrier. The dog's silence bit at

Fields like no barking ever could, made him increase his pace, the heaving of his chest growing more and more frantic with each shovelful that he hurled into place. The sand rose higher and higher, sliding in through the bars of the door, and then through the small mesh windows along the sides and back. With each shovel of sand, he wasn't just defeating the creature, but also the forces that had attempted to belittle and hornswoggle him since the day he was born, trying to tell him who he could be and what he could do! He, however, had held fast to the ideals he'd first learned from the ancient films of his Patron Historic, had triumphed over the smallness and pettiness of those who would stop him, had impressed the Scythedom as an apprentice and taken his rightful place in society!

Three last shovelfuls covered the handle on top of the case, and Fields fell to his knees, managed to ball his sore left hand into a fist, and shook his scythe ring at the low mound of sand before him. "Consider yourself gleaned," he panted out.

Another moment he remained kneeling there, then he stood, gathered his accoutrements, and most decidedly did not stumble back to the house. He strode. Proudly. As a scythe should! Climbing the stairs did perhaps take him longer than usual due to his exhaustion from the dig, and upon attaining the third floor, he fell gratefully into bed, full of satisfaction for a job well done.

He slept till nearly noon, and for the next day and a half he went no farther from his bed than the kitchen. After all, no one in recent history, he was certain, had ever earned a little time off as much as he had.

The only troubling thought came on the evening of the second day when he caught sight of Trixie's bowls in their nook. Without thinking, he took them, washed them, and put them away in the cupboard next to the bowls labeled "Rex." Then he *did* think, took all four of the bowls, and moved them to the trash. It seemed almost like admitting defeat, but no. He was simply done with dogs for the time being.

A weight seemed to rise from his shoulders, and striding out into the entryway, he grabbed his sword cane and threw open the front door. It was long past time for him to put the whole ugly business behind him and return to his starring role in the rich pageant that was Oxnard, the shining jewel of the WestMerican coast. With a determined nod of his head, he set out through the twilight for the park.

The scent of hot dogs tickled his nostrils while he was still a block away, but when he came into sight of Charles's cart, the two figures behind it took him slightly aback: the tall, lanky vendor whom he'd expected, and a more broad-shouldered fellow, both of them wearing the little white paper hats and aprons that Charles always wore.

He sauntered toward the cart. "Charles. Taking on an assistant?"

Charles winced as if he'd been struck. "Your Honor! No! I—"Taking a breath seemed to steady him. "This is my, uhh, my nephew Edgar. He's, uhh, looking to get started in the business."

The young man was sticking out a hand toward Fields. "It's such an honor to meet you, Scythe Fields! I've heard so much about you from Uncle Chuck and, well, just from everywhere!"

"Well, now!" Fields took the hand and shook it. "Quite the

firm grip you have there, Edgar—though I suppose when in the frankfurter trade, a firm grip's much preferable to an uncertain one. Wouldn't do to lose control during the preparation process, after all."

"No, sir." Edgar smiled broadly enough, but he had what Fields could only characterize as a hard eye, an edge to his expression that made Fields wonder if he'd perhaps experienced misfortune while growing up.

Still, he gave quite the strapping appearance now, but then Fields supposed that the prospect of becoming a hot dog entrepreneur would lift even the most downcast spirit. For a moment there seemed something familiar about . . . but maybe he had just one of those familiar faces.

"I'd love to hear more about your life and adventures, Your Honor," the lad was going on, his hands adroitly manipulating the tongs to pull a hot dog and a bun from the cart's depths. "And you can tell me if you think I've inherited any of Uncle Chuck's culinary skills."

"An excellent idea." Fields took a breath to begin—

—and a metallic tinkling clattered against his ear, the unmistakable rattle of a dog's tags.

The breath caught in Fields's throat like a fishhook, and he whirled to see a dog trotting from the park's shade into the light of the setting sun.

Not just a dog.

The dog.

Trixie.

Her teeth delicately held the end of the leash fastened to her collar. Chest out, head high, tail curled, she reached him, turned with a flick of her ears, and sat beside him as calmly as if she'd been there the whole time.

"Pretty dog," Edgar commented. "She yours, Your Honor?"

It took Fields several seconds to reply.

"Certainly not!" And while he'd meant for the denial to peal forth with a thunderous roar, it squeaked out instead, made him wheeze and thump his chest and try to cough up whatever was obstructing his lungs.

Nothing came, however, but a woman's voice from deeper in the park: "Trixie! Where are you—?" Dawn rushed toward the cart and stopped with a gasp.

Everything about the vile conspiracy became clear to Fields then. It wasn't just the dog! Dawn was clearly a coconspirator.

"You *dare*?" he shouted, his innards loosening as terror turned to fury. "I gleaned this animal!"

"Gleaned?" Edgar asked from behind him. "I thought only people could get gleaned."

"She *is* people!" Spinning, Fields grasped his sword cane to deal with the boy, but the red glow of his ring stopped him.

Immune. Charles's nephew had immunity from gleaning. . . .

He stared back and forth between his ring to the boy until Dawn called, "Scythe Fields!" in exactly the same sharp tone his mother had so often employed when he was growing up. "You've gone too far this time!"

As much as he didn't want to, Fields turned once more, Dawn advancing toward him across the grass with her jaw set. "I've reported you to the Scythe Council as an abusive pet owner and officially notified the Thunderhead as well!" She stopped with her fists clenched on her hips. "Maybe it won't do any good, but when the drones brought this poor dog into the shelter for revival three days ago, I . . . well, I couldn't just sit by anymore!" Taking a step back, she pointed a shaking finger at him. "You're on the record now, sir, and if you were anyone else, you'd never be allowed to adopt another dog again!"

"But I'm *not* anyone else!" Fields tried to organize his thoughts, tried to muster the proper boisterous outrage to make his case the way it needed to be made, but his words came out all whiny and cringe-inducing instead. "And this ain't a dog! You said so yourself, and I saw what she could do! She's one of them enhanced things!"

Dawn shook her head. "I thought she might be, but if she was intelligent, why would she break away from me and come running to *you*? The man who buried her alive!"

Again, Fields didn't want to look, but he couldn't help glancing down at Trixie. Her perked ears might've indicated that she was listening, but for all appearances, her attention seemed to be focused on other distant dogs in the darkening park around them.

Fields wasn't fooled, however. "She can't be a true, actual, real, honest dog, and I'll prove it!" It had taken a moment, but he felt his wits returning. "Reviving a deadish pet must be authorized, and costs a pretty penny! So if this is just a regular dog, who paid for her revival?"

"Uhh . . ." Dawn's eyes widened. "She's your dog, Scythe Fields. You never have to pay for anything."

"She's not my dog!"

"The paperwork says—"

"But I gleaned her!"

"Uhh, I'm pretty sure you can't glean a—"

With a wordless cry, every bit of his composure boiling away, Fields wrenched his sword from its scabbard.

Except of course that his ring, red as a festering blister on his finger, forced his gaze away from Dawn. That just settled it on Edgar, and he had to pull himself away once more. Charles seemed to have vanished, this whole end of the park suddenly deserted, and that only left—

Trixie stared up at him, her dark eyes unblinking.

"Scythe Fields?" Edgar asked from somewhere behind him. "Are you seriously going to stab a dog?"

And that, Fields realized, was the crux of Trixie's fiendish plan: to box him in, to destroy the suave persona he'd so carefully constructed over the years. She was here to unravel him, to gnaw him to bits, to strip him down till he was just the nothing he'd been before.

Fields drew a breath, slid his sword back into the body of his cane, and wiped his hand on the seat of his robe. "No, Edgar," he said as quietly and deliberately as he could. "I'll not be doing *anything* to this dog. Because, as I believe I stated earlier, she's not my dog, and I'll thank you, Dawn, to file all appropriate paperwork to that effect." His body feeling more like a chunk of wood than anything else, he managed to bow to her and to Edgar. "Now, I hope you'll excuse me if I bid you all a good evening and see to business I have elsewhere."

Turning sharply, he moved away without glancing back. He'd said everything he needed to say, done everything he needed to do. To remain any longer could only exacerbate matters.

He aimed directly for home. None of his usual strolling

about on the oceanfront boardwalk for him today. A moment or three to collect himself and regain his composure: that's what he needed. To watch one of his Patron Historic's films—as he'd been doing when the dog had arranged to electrocute him the other night—or perhaps turn in a bit early—in the room where the dog had tricked him out onto the balcony before tripping him off. . . .

No! No such thoughts! He shook his head quickly, crossed the street, and ducked up the alley that ran between the oceanfront houses and those on the next block in—for once taking the short way home. With deliberate care, he could still gain the upper hand here. After all, of the two of them, he was the one who *had* hands. He shouldn't be—

Something jingled behind him, and every hair along the back of his neck prickled. Fields refused to flinch, refused to turn, refused to acknowledge the sound in any way whatsoever.

He did, however, pick up his pace just a bit.

The next several blocks seemed to creep by, night's shadows deepening, Fields humming a jaunty tune louder and louder in an attempt to drown out the gently insistent tinkle of metal tags. The sound never drew any nearer as far as he could tell, its quiet echoes bouncing around him from the houses on either side, but he of course didn't stop to wait for it, lengthening his stride even farther.

At last, his breath coming faster and faster, his robe catching against his sweaty arms and legs, he exited the alley just as the streetlights came on, his house mere yards away. Under Oxnard's perfectly gathering gloaming, the crisp scent of warm sand mixing with the salt spray of the ocean, he felt himself emboldened.

He was Honorable Scythe William Claude Fields, after all! He had nothing to fear from man nor beast!

That little clatter tapped his ears again. Without thinking, Fields craned his head back—

And a shadow was moving toward him about half a block up the alley he'd just exited, a four-legged shadow somehow darker than the darkness around her, a light reflecting from somewhere nearby to give a touch of amber glow to her eyes.

Fields broke into a run, vaulted his fence, sprinted across the lawn, and threw himself inside, locking the door behind him.

The lights off, Fields sat on the entryway floor with a freshly cleaned and loaded shotgun clenched to his chest—one he confirmed had not been sabotaged—and he watched the front door, trying to keep his mind from whirling out of control.

She hadn't knocked, of course. She was a dog. But neither had she scratched nor barked nor whined.

He wanted to believe that she'd gone, that she'd had her fun and had moved on, but he knew that wasn't true.

Of course, it was *also* true that he couldn't stay here like this forever, and besides, there wasn't really any way she could harm him. Yes, she'd deadened him twice, but that had been before he'd caught on to her true devious nature. Now he was both forewarned and forearmed! All he needed was to show a bit of fortitude, and he could rid himself of that monstrosity once and for all!

And this time, he would have to burn the body to make sure it could not be revived. To hell with any punishment he might incur in conclave. It would be worth it to rid himself of this foul Cerberus of a demon dog.

And that's when he realized he'd forgotten all about the doggy door.

Panic spattered through him. That's why she'd been so quiet! She was sneaking around beside the house, clambering over the fence, pushing as silently as a snake into the very heart of his domain, creeping down the hall behind him—

Whirling, he aimed the shaking shotgun at the empty shadows of the front hall, knew it was a trick, knew she was somewhere nearby. "Filthy mutt!" he shouted, flinging himself forward and slamming the dining room door out of the way.

She wasn't there, and hope shivered inside him; shoving his shoulder against the side of an empty china cabinet, he pushed and pushed and pushed till the cabinet had slid along the wall to its new spot blocking the doggy door. Then he leaned against it and panted, swallowed, tried to catch his breath and—

The click of the front door opening pricked his ears.

Ice blossomed in his stomach. Had Trixie grown thumbs? Had Dawn come to let her in? He glanced at the door to the sunroom, thought about making a break for the beach, running—

Past the dog's empty grave.

But he couldn't summon the courage to run. He took another breath, tightened his grip on the shotgun, and stepped toward the door into the front hall. If it was a human who'd just come in, Fields could do some gleaning. And if it was Trixie?

Fields shivered, not sure what he would do. But he pushed through into the hallway—

And saw a tall figure cloaked and cowled entirely in black standing just inside the open front door.

"*There* you are," the figure said, his voice somehow familiar.

"I was getting a little worried; I thought I might have to send the bloodhounds out to find you."

Staring, blinking, Fields's first thought was to use the shotgun before he could say another word, but his ring glowed red again. And Fields realized.

"Edgar?" Fields asked, squinting at the young man in the jet-black robe.

The lips visible under the edge of the hood twitched. "We could use that name, sure. But I'm betting you've heard other names for me. One in particular."

"No . . . It couldn't be. . . ." Fields had, of course, heard a name that has been whispered even among non-scythes since the tumult at MidMerica's conclave a season ago.

Scythe Lucifer.

But why would Scythe Lucifer be here? What could he possibly want?

"Scythe Fields," the young man was saying. "You know, you've been on my list since I first started it, but I honestly couldn't believe all the awful stories I'd heard about you." He took a step toward Fields down the hall. "Then I saw the report from the animal shelter and thought I'd better come out here and check. I convinced the hot dog guy to let me pretend to be his nephew, and after what I saw there, well . . ." Another step. "That moved you right to the top of my list."

Wanting to sneer, Fields instead found that his whole body had gone numb. A clatter to his right made him glance over, and he saw that the shotgun had slipped from his grasp to fall uselessly onto the marble.

The black-clad figure took a third step, and every bit of attitude, every scrap of wit, every bon mot he'd cultivated during his study of his Patron Historic deserted Fields utterly. His knees were in fact bending, preparing to drop him to the floor so he could plead for his life—

When something growled. Gray and white fur flashed through the front doorway, and Trixie leaped in to plant herself between him and Scythe Lucifer, her ears flat, her hackles bristling, her teeth bared, and her unmistakable displeasure aimed squarely at Scythe Lucifer.

"Really?" The edge of the fellow's hood covered the top of his face, but Fields could hear the raised eyebrows in his voice. For once eyebrows not raised at him.

"Are you saying you don't *want* him gleaned?"

The dog looked up at Scythe Lucifer, shook her head, then turned and trotted to Fields's side, settling to sit next to him as if none of the past week's events had even occurred.

Warmth swelled within Fields's bosom. "That's right!" he cried, not even caring that his voice cracked. He folded his arms and fixed a steely gaze upon Scythe Lucifer. "Try it, buddy! Just *try*! Me and my dog'll show you!"

A growl knocked the steel from his gaze and drew it down to Trixie, her dark eyes trained on his with a sharpness that Fields could almost feel slicing the words from his throat.

"Ahh!" Movement pulled Fields's attention this time, Edgar's smiling face revealed in full as he pushed his hood back. "I get it," he said to the dog. "Fields isn't mine. He's *yours*."

Uncertain where to look, Fields glanced back and forth between the two, the dog's ears now perked and the young man's shoulders relaxed. "It's a deal," Scythe Lucifer said. "If you need him permanently taken care of, have the animal shelter file another incident report. I'll hear about it and be here the next day." Then he turned to Fields. "And you?" All trace of his smile vanished, and Fields found himself staring into a face nearly as cold as the face of the dog beside him. "You be a good boy."

"Now see here!" Fields sputtered.

But another growl interrupted him, a warm, furry, and surprisingly heavy weight pushing against his leg. Unprepared, he staggered half a step away from the kitchen door. "What's the meaning of this?" he demanded when he got his footing back.

But she was trotting to the shotgun, picking it up in her teeth, and turning back as if they were playing fetch. Fields winced, but she merely set the thing carefully on the floor in front of him before sitting again.

Heart pounding, Fields scooped up the gun and aimed it at—

The empty darkness of the front door. Edgar, or Scythe Lucifer, or whoever he actually was, was gone.

Trixie gave the slightest little woof, nodded, and trotted down the hall, her tags jingling. She planted her nose against the front door, pushed it closed, then gave him a look over her shoulder.

For half an instant, Fields considered turning the gun on her. But it wouldn't help him in any way; she'd just come back, and if Dawn sent another incident report . . .

Without even a sigh, Fields returned the shotgun to the weapons cabinet. Then, when he looked over his shoulder, Trixie wasn't standing there anymore.

Her quiet little woof drew his attention to the stairway. When he met her gaze, she nodded and started up, not looking away from him.

His feet seeming to get heavier with each step, he climbed to the second floor, Trixie waiting for him at the top of the flight. Another of those woofs, and she made the turn for the third floor. Not knowing what else to do, he followed.

She was sitting on the floor beside her cushion, but the instant Fields entered the room, she bent down, stuck her snout under the cushion, and dragged out a dog collar of a darker red than the one she was currently wearing. Straightening, she looked up at Fields, touched the collar on the floor with a paw, then moved that paw to bat at the collar around her neck.

"What on earth?" Fields squatted, took the collar from the floor, and the tag tinkled against its clasp, the single word "Jian" stamped into the metal. Hadn't he thrown that away? But then it wouldn't take much for a smart enough dog to dig it out of the trash when he wasn't looking.

Telling himself that his hands weren't shaking, he undid the "Trixie" collar and tags from her neck, dropped them to the floor, and slid the "Jian" ones into place.

"Anything else?" he muttered.

She didn't even woof this time. She just pulled away from him and moved with deliberate steps to the side of his bed.

His stomach clenched, and he jumped to his feet. "You're not allowed—" he began.

Her glare struck him as hard as an actual thrown object;

Fields couldn't stop himself from taking a step back as she gave the slightest little flex with her hind legs, propelling herself up to stand on his bedspread.

He quivered, holding in his shout. But he *did* hold it in, didn't give in to the urge either to whine or bluster. "Fine," he said. He took a breath and blew it out. "After all, the canine companion stretching across the foot of her master's bed is an image that reaches back to the dawn of—"

Something that was half woof and half growl stopped him this time, Trixie—or Jian, rather—fixing him with her glare yet again. With careful steps on the yielding mattress, she padded to the top of the bed and lay down with her head on the pillow, her gaze never leaving his.

Fields gaped. "Then where am I—?"

With a snort, Jian flicked a paw to point at the floor, just off to his left.

Knowing what was there, Fields looked anyway, his neck seeming to creak like a rusty gate. "The pet cushion?" he asked, unable to raise his voice much above a whisper.

She gave a crisp nod and tapped the lamp on the bed stand.

His shoulders tightening, loosening, tightening, and loosening, Fields looked from the lamp to the cushion and back again. "Godfrey Daniels," he muttered. He closed his eyes, and grimaced, but slowly let the grimace fade. When he opened his eyes, Jian was still watching him. Well, what choice did he have?

"No one can know of this," Fields said.

Jian nodded.

"And in public, you'll play your role, and I'll play mine."

Jian nodded.

"And at home?"

Jian cast her eyes to the cushion on the floor.

"Understood," said Fields.

Satisfied, Jian turned away from him and went to sleep on his ... on *her* bed.

Heaving a sigh, he turned off the light, as she had instructed, then made himself comfortable on the pet cushion, which, after all, was the highest-quality cushion. Admittedly, this was not how he thought today—or for that matter, the rest of his life—would go. And yet now that there was no doubt who was the master in this household, he couldn't help but feel relieved. Because now he knew his place.

A Death of Many Colors

I tell you this story now because I witnessed it, just as I witness most things. It is the benefit of having millions of eyes in millions of places.

This occurrence fell in mid-autumn; the time of year when trees go deadish for the winter with spectacular displays of bronzing foliage. A time when the sun seems to tire of being so long in the sky. A time when spiders grow their largest before filling their egg sacks and withering away.

All of this was fertile fodder for an old mortal-age holiday that celebrated, of all things, mortality itself. The thirty-first of October. A night of macabre mischief and jest. Through the years, and through various cultures, the holiday had developed many names, but the name that landed in post-mortal times was "All Hallows."

The event of which I speak fell on one such All Hallows Eve, in a year before the sinking of Endura—but not long before. This was in the days when I still spoke with humanity, before my necessary silence, in a small town in MidMerica—a place where very few things of consequence happened, and people were hard-pressed to venture beyond their comfortable circle of acquaintances. It begins with a party, as so many things that skew sideways do. . . .

The Robinsons—a old family in the town—certainly knew how to throw a party, and All Hallows had always been theirs. No one else in town would dare compete, and all those with a penchant toward creativity would attend, trying to top one another with the garish audacity of their costumes—for costumes were central to the holiday.

Theirs was a large home. Sprawling, one might say, with half a dozen bedrooms, and even more gathering salons. It hadn't begun this way, but over the years, more and more rooms were added until it became a patchwork estate. Not quite a mansion, but more like a compound that stood resolutely upon a hill overlooking the rest of town. It was not the largest structure, but certainly the most impressive between here and the horizon.

The Robinsons' All Hallows party was actually three. The first was for the young children; a romp full of fanciful playground activities to corral their sugar-enhanced energies. The second was for the adults, who filled the various salons, with raucous conversation, laughter, and more than a little bit of wine. And the third party was for those in that transitional time of life between the other two; youth in various stages of pubescence, too old for the playground, yet mortified at the thought of partying with their parents. Their place was a game room deep in the labyrinthian estate.

Dax Robinson, at seventeen, had all the energy and arrogance that came with the age, and was a consummate host to his many friends. As the host, his costume needed to be the best, and he made sure of it every year.

There were twenty of Dax's friends and classmates present. I will spare you the roll call, and only present to you those who factor into this tale—which would only be the guests present in the salon at the far end of the winding hall at the approach of midnight. But we are still hours from that moment.

"Trigger-treat!" Dax's friends all said as they arrived. It was the standard All Hallows greeting.

"Why do we say that anyway?" his friend Savina asked.

"It comes from mortal days," Dax told her. "People would come up to your door on All Hallows, and ask for diamonds, or gold or whatever, and if you didn't give it, they shot you." He made his thumb and forefinger into a gun and aimed it at her. "Trigger-treat," he said, and pretended to shoot her between the eyes.

Savina giggled. "Mortal people were so weird."

Their classmate, Journé, did not shout "Trigger-treat" when she arrived. She came in quietly and remained so as she surveyed the dynamic. She was not a wallflower by any means, but observant in the way that I am observant; taking everything in, suspending judgment. But as a human, her goal was different from mine. While I study interactions to help better the human condition, she was scoping out the room for the best social interactions. Her focus was on Dax, but that is no surprise. Dax reveled in being the center of attention, and made himself so in subtle and less subtle ways.

"You really rock that costume, Dax," Savina said—always trying to flatter Dax into seeing her as more than just a friend.

"Yeah, it's your best yet," echoed his best friend, Shawn, who was also always trying to flatter Dax. While Shawn wasn't averse to the idea of Dax seeing him as more than a friend, his primary hope was that Dax's social cachet might rub off on him, because among humans young and old, popularity was a highly bankable commodity.

"So which scythe are you supposed to be?" Shawn asked.

Dax raised his arms, which made his elaborate robe fill a greater field of everyone's vision. The robe was admittedly impressive. It was handmade for him by the best tailor in town, based on a theatrical representation of an old biblical reference: a glittering coat of many colors, ostentatious and eye-catching. It was way too much, and yet just right for an All Hallows Eve.

"This scythe robe is an original," Dax told them. "None of those losers have a robe like mine."

Savina's and Shawn's costumes were unremarkable. Savina came as a jaguar. She was always some sort of cat for All Hallows. Shawn was dressed as a zombie—and if you were to ask him, he would swear that zombies were real, the result of failed revivals of the deadish. "The Thunderhead hides them in dark dungeons," he would tell anyone who'd listen. "It hides them and tells the world that they don't exist. But they do! They. Do."

But actually, they don't.

Journé watched Dax interact with the others until there was a lull. But rather than a greeting, her first words to her host were tantamount to a challenge.

"That's pretty daring," Journé said, pointing to Dax's outfit. "Don't scythes glean anyone who they catch dressing like one?"

That brought a few snickers from the room. Dax lobbed her an enigmatic grin. "I'll take my chances," he said.

Journé's costume was the only one that dared to be as visually stunning as Dax's. Journé was an angel, complete with feathered wings, and a magnetically levitating halo—which was just a glow stick looped into a circle, but the levitation made the illusion stick—although whenever she moved her head too quickly, it would fly off and fall to the ground. As for the feathers, they weren't sticking to the wings as well as she'd hoped, and she was already beginning to molt.

Journé was new to town, having only arrived a month ago. Newcomers were rare, as people were more often leaving town for places of greater excitement, than arriving. The result was that those who remained were happy to do so, and were not much enticed by the outside world. It was a mindset that was both a blessing and a curse. Because the flipside of contentment is stagnation.

"I absolutely love to hear you talk," Savina admitted to Journé, as everyone loosened up a bit. "Your accent is so . . . fun."

"Austroylia, moyte," said Shawn, in a horribly bad impersonation that clearly made Journé suppress a wince.

"What part are you from?" asked Savina.

"The Tasmanian region," Journé told them. That drew Dax's attention.

"Isn't that a charter region? Doesn't everyone have some cool body modification?"

Journé nodded. "Yes, we do."

"So what's yours?"

But Savina smacked him on the arm. "Dax! It's considered rude to ask!"

"It's all right," said Journé, "he didn't know."

They waited as if she might tell them anyway, but she didn't.

"Well, if it was me, I'd get an extra pair of arms," said Dax, with a wink in Journé's direction. "Think of all the things you could do with four hands."

Dax was not subtle with his flirtations, and not nearly as clever as he believed himself to be. I suppose his unawareness of his own inelegance was, in a way, charming. Or at least Journé appeared to think so, because she volleyed her own flirtation back.

"So since that's an original scythe robe, who would you choose as your Patron Historic?" Then she ran a finger down a bright blue streak on his multicolored robe.

I could sense Dax shiver as if she had run her finger across his skin, and not just his robe. He smiled. "I would be Scythe Münchhausen," he said. "The patron saint of lies and hoaxes!"

"Perfect, Dax!" said Savina, leaning into him, with clear hopes of making him forget Journé's tracing finger.

"The only problem with that," said Journé, "is that Baron Münchhausen never actually existed. He's fictional."

To which Dax replied, "So are scythes."

And the others turned to Journé to gauge her reaction.

She looked at the other three, trying to read something in them, but they gave her nothing. They merely waited for her to comment.

"What do you mean?" Journé said. "Of course they're real."

Across the room several of Dax's other guests laughed at something. It only served to further unsettle the moment.

"Come on, Journé—you're kidding, right?" Shawn finally said. "I mean, you can't actually believe that. . . ."

"Yeah," chimed in Savina. "They're a hoax. Everyone knows that."

It was as if a chasm had opened between Journé and her classmates, deep and dizzying. But just then, the arrival of several loud and bombastic guests drew everyone's focus, and Dax went to greet them. The conversation was churned deep into the cauldron of the party. But some things have a way of bubbling back up to the surface.

The party peaked and mellowed over the hours as parties do. The younger children were lulled to sleep in the pool house, by means of a beloved mortal-age film about fish. The adults sat around the firepit and main living room, convalescing after eating too much, but still perusing the dessert table, and in the game room, Dax's friends had settled into conversations that were not as deep as they believed them to be, and jokes that were getting progressively puerile. Dax sat with Savina, Shawn, and Journé in a plush corner of the game room, and as the clock approached midnight, it was Savina who stirred the cauldron.

"So Journé . . . were you just joking, or do you actually believe scythes are real?"

When it was clear they weren't going to be distracted by Dax telling another bad joke, she responded, choosing her words carefully.

"Where I come from," Journé said, "that's what we believe."

"Wow," said Savina, with a superior sort of pity. "The Thunderhead really has you brainwashed."

Dax put a gentle hand on Journé's shoulder. "Journé, it's time you knew the truth. Scythes, gleaning, death—all of that is a lie. The Thunderhead made it all up."

"That can't be . . . ," insisted Journé. "The Thunderhead doesn't lie."

Shawn snickered. "Who told you that? The Thunderhead? It's the Thunderhead's job to take care of the world, and if it has to lie to do that, then it will. It lies all the time!"

I feel the need to point out here that this is an erroneous statement. While I can offer half-truths and will conveniently change the subject when cornered, I am incapable of lying. It is a basic tenet of my existence. You must understand, however, that it was pointless to try to correct Dax and his friends and their families of this fallacy—because they would simply claim it was all part of the lie of which they insisted I was guilty. Theirs was a closed circle of flawed logic, built on a faulty premise. It troubles me, but it is not my job as steward of the world to tell people what they should and should not believe.

"How could you think scythes are real, when there's so much evidence that they're a hoax?" Savina asked, shaking her head.

"Think about it, Journé," said Dax. "Have you ever actually *seen* anyone gleaned? I mean, seen it with your own eyes?"

"That doesn't prove anything—most scythes don't glean in public. And for the ones that do, those public gleanings get reported in the media."

"And who controls the media?" Shawn asked. "The Thunderhead."

But Journé was not convinced. "You mean to tell me there's never been a scythe here—and that nobody in this town has ever been gleaned?"

"Scythes are actors!" Shawn shouted. "The Thunderhead's given them roles and they act it all out."

Savina tried to snuggle with Dax, who was only slightly responsive. "Must be fun! Strutting around, pretending to be a killer!" Savina said.

"But what about all the fuss around conclaves?" argued Journé.

"Like Shawn said, it's all a performance!" said Dax.

"But why?"

"Why do we tell scary stories?" said Shawn. "Why do we celebrate All Hallows? It's to make our lives more interesting!"

But Dax shook his head. "Nah, it's more than that. It's to keep us in line. It's to turn us all into sheep. Because if we don't have to fear scythes, then we are truly free. The Thunderhead says we're free—but it doesn't want us to be *that* free." Then he brushed a hand along the edge of Journé's costume, sending a few feathers fluttering to the ground. "The fear of scythes kind of clips our wings."

Journé was silent for a moment, meeting no one's gaze. Then she turned to Dax, eyes blazing. "The week I got here! I passed that old cemetery, and there was a funeral!"

Savina sighed. "Yeah, that'd be Jep Seager."

"How could there be a funeral if no one ever gets gleaned?"

"Just because there's a funeral that doesn't mean anyone actually gets put into the ground," said Shawn.

Dax leaned forward. "One: Jep always talked about wanting to go to Antarctica—the Ross Shelf charter region, so he could experience communal dreaming. Two: Suddenly he's been 'gleaned.' Three: His family moves away like a week later. So what does that tell you?"

"They left to be with him in Antarctica," said Shawn, too riled up to let Journé reach the conclusion.

"Maybe not," said Journé. "Maybe his family was so grief-stricken they couldn't stay in a place where people said his death wasn't real!"

Perhaps Journé thought that her reason would outshine

theirs, but without anyone else to stoke her sentiments, they died from an acute lack of oxygen.

"You can believe what you want, Journé," Shawn finally said, "but maybe it's better if you didn't talk about it. I mean, people around here don't like scythe-believers much."

"Don't worry, Journé. Your secret's safe with us." Although Savina looked down as she said it, clearly contemplating who she was going to tell.

Dax stood up, surveying the large space filled with objects of human amusement, but mostly his friends were now engaged in lethargic or lascivious behavior, many having drunk or smoked things that were sure to earn them an unsavory point or two.

"I'm over this," he said, not making it clear whether he meant the party, his friends, or just the conversation. "You guys see our All Hallows Hall yet? It's even better than last year."

He led Savina, Shawn, and Journé out a side door that led to a long hallway that wound in unpredictable ways. The Robinson family's sprawling compound had a series of large interconnecting salons like a maze with multiple centers, and each salon had a different seasonal theme.

The Gifting Season room was red and green, with a living pine tree, a grand fireplace, and white-frosted windows. The Midsummer room had a giant skylight, bright yellow walls, and a floor of nanite sand that formed itself into castles at the touch of a tablet. Each of the seven salons was the focus of another party at a different time of year. The last room was All Hallows Hall.

"Sure we can find our way back?" teased Journé at the third or fourth turn.

"No worries," said Dax with a grin, "we'll just follow your trail of feathers."

Dax led them through and around the other salons, all dimly lit, as their festive time was not at hand. But the high arched entrance to All Hallows Hall was lit in the eerie orange of the season.

"We totally redid it this year for the party."

The salon had a tiled floor of shiny black marble so reflective, it looked like glass. The walls had been paneled in the darkest ebony, and black velvet drapes hung on either side of a high gothic window rising toward a peaked roof. The Robinsons had commissioned the grand window, an abstract stained glass piece entirely in shades of orange and red. At this time of year, when the lattice of tree limbs shuddered in the chill autumn wind, the window gave the distinct impression of flickering flames—assisted by the patio firepit that was just outside.

"So what do you think?" Dax asked.

"It's great," said Journé. "But how come no one's here?"

Dax shrugged. "You know parties," he said. "People go where they want."

While this space had always been the focus of the Robinsons' All Hallows gala, this year its success was its failure—for although people did come to view, no one lingered long—not even Dax's parents. There was just something too unsettling this year about All Hallows Hall. Macabre sloughing from darkly whimsical to deeply disturbing.

Perhaps because of the coffin.

It was a faithful re-creation of a nineteenth-century design; glossy black with gold trim and brass handles, more narrow at the feet than at the shoulders. Dickensian, one might say. Or at least one who still knew who Dickens was.

Although the coffin was new, its occupant was not—which was the whole point. A man centuries old, his remains almost but not quite mummified, lay in the coffin—which was open, as if this was the man's long-purloined wake.

Wake. An expression I always found fascinating—for was it intended to imply an ironic counterpoint to eternal sleep, or was it to indicate the waves left behind by a person's passage? The effect of a single life on the world? If it is the latter, then the waves left behind by this particular individual had long since reached some distant shore.

"Isn't it cool," said Dax, thrilled by the slim-lipped expression of the corpse—something between a grin and a grimace. "There's an old mortal-age crypt on our property. My dad thought it would be fun to pull someone out and set them up as our All Hallows centerpiece."

Journé met the skeleton's gaze, but Savina and Shawn could not.

"His name was Eli Sutterfield," said Dax. "Born April nineteenth, 1978, died September twenty-first, 2033."

No one but I seemed to care that the coffin's design was incorrect for Mr. Sutterfield's life and times. As if the "mortal age" could be clumped into a single way of life.

"How d'ya think he died?" Savina dared to ask.

Dax pointed to a hole in the side of the skull. "Gunshot wound."

Shawn let off a nervous laugh. "Trigger-treat," he said.

Savina, still refusing to look directly at poor Mr. Sutterfield, pointed to the brass handles on the side of the coffin. "What are those for?"

"For the people who carry the box to the grave, I guess," said Dax.

Savina visibly shuddered. "I wouldn't want to do that."

"It was an honor," Journé pointed out. "Respect for the dead and all."

Savina just shook her head. "Mortal people were so weird."

And although Journé opened her mouth to speak, she thought better of it and closed her mouth again.

Finally Savina glanced at Mr. Sutterfield's empty eye sockets. "Can we go now? I mean, it's cool and all, but can we go?"

"Yeah," agreed Shawn, who was even more put off by the dead man than Savina, although he was doing his best not to show it.

Seeing their unease just made Dax more cavalier. "Scared of my bud Eli?" Dax grabbed the edge of the coffin, jostling it slightly—just enough to make the dead man's head wobble a bit. "How could you not love him? He's the life of the party!"

"No, I just want to get back," Savina said. "People'll start leaving soon. I want to be there to say goodbye."

"Yeah," Shawn agreed a little too enthusiastically. Because although Shawn didn't believe in scythes, he did believe in ghosts.

Dax's response was to sit on the shiny black floor, his robe spreading around him like a colorful throw rug. "You can go if you want. I'm staying."

"Then I'll stay, too," said Journé.

That left Shawn and Savina in a quandary. Shawn was not

keen on leaving alone, and Savina was not keen on leaving Dax alone with Journé.

Outside the wind rasped through the trees with an uneasy rattle.

"It's almost like Eli is breathing . . . ," Dax said.

That was enough to tip the scale.

"Yeah, I'm out of here," Shawn said, turning.

And when a branch began to tap against the window like a wraith longing to be let in, Savina surrendered as well.

"Wait for me," she called, running after Shawn, who was already following a trail of fallen feathers back to the game room.

Now it was just Dax and Journé.

"Finally alone," he said.

"Is that what you wanted? To get me alone?"

"I thought we could get to know each other better."

"But we already know each other."

"Not really. Not as much as I'd like to." He reached out and touched her wings. Most of the feathers were gone now, leaving a leathery membrane beneath.

"It's a great costume," Dax told her. "Aside from the feathers, it looks pretty real."

Journé gave him a mischievous smile. "There's a reason for that."

Dax looked more closely at the wings and gasped. "Your body modification?"

Journé nodded. "My parents' idea. When I was a baby. Most flight modifications are flaps of skin growing out of your armpits—you know, like sugar gliders or flying squirrels. But my parents wanted the full deal."

Which was not easy, I might add—but as per the rules I had established in the region, I had to accommodate the request, as ill-advised as it was. I had always been pleased, however, to see how Journé adapted, embracing her uniqueness.

"But how have you been able to hide them?" Dax asked.

Journé folded them down, and the thin membrane became like a second skin around her shoulders, clinging so tightly to her body, they nearly disappeared. Easy enough to hide in over-sized clothes.

"Wow! All this time? Why didn't you tell anyone?"

"It was enough to be the new girl. I didn't need to be the new girl with wings."

Then Dax leaned in a little bit closer. "Can you fly?"

"Maybe," she said.

"Can I see?"

Journé didn't answer that. Instead she took a good long look at him. Studying him. Appraising him.

"Take off your robe," she said.

He did not hesitate. The T-shirt and gym shorts beneath were not at all romantic, but the very act of removing the robe was enough to send his heart racing. He discarded his prize costume with a careless toss into the corner, then he gave Journé a hungry sort of smile, and leaned in to kiss her. . . .

But she put out her hand, holding him back.

"That's not happening," she said.

Dax became flustered. Frustrated. "But . . . but I thought . . ."

Journé stood up and away from him, extending her wings. The last of the glued-on feathers fell away, revealing a magnif-icent wingspan that stretched across the entire room, and left

Dax in shadow. The room's candlelight revealed a lattice of veins and capillaries.

"I'm not who you think I am," she said.

"Then who *are* you?" said Dax, still thinking this some sort of game.

"I am Scythe Sojourner Truth. And I have chosen you, Dax-son Robinson, for gleaning."

Dax stood, offering up an uncertain chuckle. "Oh, that's funny. You're good."

"This isn't a joke," Scythe Truth said. "You and your friends, and their families, have spread lies that we in the Scythedom will not tolerate. I took this name because my chosen path is to deliver death to falsehood." Then she smiled—a mirror of the greedy, seductive smile Dax had given her only moments before. "You may not be the father of falsehood, Dax, but you're certainly in the family."

Dax backed away, finally considering that the danger might be real. "Thunderhead!" he called out. "Thunderhead, get my parents!"

To which I had no choice but to reply. "I'm sorry, Dax. I cannot interfere in a scythe action."

Dax tried to run, but slipped on the slick marble tile. He grabbed the coffin for balance, but instead knocked it over, sending the late Eli Sutterfield on a shattering journey to the floor.

With a single beat of her grafted wings, Journé blew out all the candles in the room, then lunged at Dax, pulling him into the tightest of hugs.

"Let's give you a new perspective."

With Dax tight in her grasp, she hurled herself through the stained glass window, which shattered, raining shards of red glass on everyone around the firepit below.

The human body was not designed for wings, much less those that could actually generate enough lift for dynamic flight, but Journé had trained for this—her unique method of gleaning. Beating her wings she gained altitude. She could only do this for ten, maybe fifteen seconds before exhausting herself, but that was all that was needed.

Below on the patio, party guests weren't sure what they were seeing. But as it happened at the very stroke of midnight, everyone assumed that it must have been part of the Robinsons' All Hallows festivities.

When the scythe reached the apogee of her climb, her wings at the limit of their endurance, she gave Dax the kiss he had so desperately wanted from her.

And then she let him go.

Dax's performance was, in a word, stellar. He screamed all the way down, only to be suddenly silenced. I do not need to detail the result of a human body dropping from a height of 321 feet upon a flagstone patio. No doubt you've witnessed splatters going about their messy endeavor.

The crowd gasped, flinched, recoiled. Then, once their initial shock had passed, they began to applaud. Dax's parents were furious, but seeing the crowd's reaction, chose to take it in stride.

"Well, my son does like to make an entrance," said Mr. Robinson.

"And exit," said one of the guests, to a round of laughter.

Dax's mother sighed. "Such a nuisance. A splat like that takes days in revival. He'll fall behind on his schoolwork."

Mr. Robinson was more concerned with the shattered window, which would take much longer to repair than their son.

"What was that thing, anyway?" asked another guest, looking to the dark sky. "That winged contraption? A drone decorated for All Hallows?"

No one was sure, but everyone agreed it was quite effective.

"All right, show's over," announced Mr. Robinson, while his wife covered Dax with a tablecloth. "Clear room for the ambudrone, it should be here any minute."

But none came. I do not dispatch ambudrones for the gleaned. The Robinsons chalked the delay up to seasonal backlog—after all, All Hallows tended to bring about more accidental deadishness than any other holiday.

It was then that Journé strode out upon the patio from a stand of trees that bordered the yard. I'm sure she wanted to make a more dramatic entrance, but her wings were too exhausted to even stretch out, much less fly. They lay limply around her, suddenly looking less real than they had with feathers glued to them. She came over to Dax's body, and held out a ringed hand to the Robinsons.

"I've gleaned your son," she said. "I am commanded to offer you immunity. Come forward and kiss my ring."

"Enough!" said Mr. Robinson, at the end of all patience. "This is going too far now."

"Didn't you hear me?" said Scythe Truth. "Your son's been gleaned!"

"Just do it, Gary," said his wife.

Mr. Robinson sighed. "Fine." Then the couple leaned over kissing the ring, which they were convinced was just costume jewelry. "Are we done here?"

Journé left them still looking to the sky for an ambudrone.

She went inside, carefully wrapping her spent wings around herself. Now that her job was done, I thought she would leave. But she didn't. Not yet.

Midnight had come and gone, people were saying their goodbyes. Her classmates—or should I say, those who *believed* themselves to be her classmates—were all abuzz about Dax's surprise splat, simultaneously shocked that he was so audacious, and offended that they were not let in on the joke. Journé did not mingle. Instead she made her way back to All Hallows Hall, where she stepped over Eli Sutterfield's broken remains, and went to the far corner, picking up Dax's colorful robe to admire it. Clearly, she had asked him to remove it so he might be easier for her to grab, but scythes tend to have more than one reason for the things they do.

So deep was she in contemplation of the robe, that she didn't hear Savina entering behind her.

"Please tell me that everyone's right, and it was nothing but a show. That this was just an All Hallows trigger-treat."

The scythe ignored her question. "I was ordained at conclave just before arriving here," she said. "I haven't chosen a robe for myself yet. But I like this one. I like it a lot." Then she put the robe on. "How do I look?"

"You look . . . you look like a scythe." Then Savina became so tearful so suddenly that her jaguar makeup ran down her face in muddy rivulets. "I don't know what to believe anymore. . . ."

"That's a start," said Journé. She turned to go, but what Savina said next gave her significant pause.

"It won't make a difference, you know. People will just say Dax ran away. Maybe even that he ran off with *you*. That's what they'll say."

"His parents will know. They'll know when the ambudrone never comes."

"Yes," Savina agreed. "But even then, no one will believe them."

Journé dismissed the thought and left, satisfied that tonight's gleaning was a job well done. Onward now, to putting the drop on further falsehood.

But although Journé refused to see it, I knew Savina was right. For if my study of human nature has taught me anything, it is that truth and conviction are not comfortable bedfellows, and what one believes will often cast out that which is true. Because it is easier to believe that scythes aren't real, and that I am a liar, and that the moon is made of cheese, than it is to admit that everything you believe about the world is wrong.

Were I allowed to speak to young Scythe Sojourner Truth, I would tell her to spare herself the misery of her crusade, for she cannot change minds as willfully opaque as a black marble floor. They will only reflect what's already there. False light and ancient bones. A nightmare worthy of All Hallows Eve.

Unsavory Row

The nimbus agent wore a world-weary look, like maybe she had slit her own throat a hundred times, only to get revived and dumped back into this miserable office without as much as a scar for her troubles. Kila wondered how many nasty little unsavories like her this woman had to face on a daily basis.

The agent also had a particular glare that she must have cultivated over the years. A glare that said, *I can sit across my desk and silently scrutinize you all day because I literally have nothing better to do.* Her glare wasn't so much intimidating as it was demoralizing. As was the ticking clock on the wall. Clocks did not have to tick, but this one was programmed to intentionally emphasize the silence.

The woman's strategic stare worked. It made Kila feel she had to talk. She hated that she could be so easily manipulated.

"I didn't do it. It wasn't me," Kila said.

To which the agent responded, "Of course you did it. Of course it was you."

Kila resisted making a face at her. That would just be immature.

According to the placard on the desk, the agent's name was Gooley. Somehow it was appropriate. Kila had a friend who firmly believed that nimbus agents were all ghouls who lived together in some bleak catacomb beneath the offices of the Authority Interface and slept hanging upside down by their toes. It always brought Kila joy to imagine all those inverted, slumbering nimbos in a subterranean lair like bats, fouled with their own guano.

"And as you can see, your little 'prank' has accomplished nothing," Agent Gooley said.

Kila shrugged. "It got me an up-close-and-personal meeting with you, didn't it?"

The agent glared once more. "Getting your case bumped up to Hellion Management is not something to be proud of."

Kila gave her a wink. "Depends on who you ask."

So now she was officially a Hellion. Truth be told, Kila was proud. She'd been angling for the distinction for months. There were four levels of unsavory status. Common Unsavory was just the baseline. Then came Hellion, then Pandæmon, and finally Apocalyte. Kila was still far from that, but it was certainly something to aim for.

"What could have possibly possessed you to release a bag of untagged black mambas in the Department of Unsavory Affairs?" Agent Gooley asked.

Kila remained nonchalant. "I had number eighty-six, and they were only on number twelve. I figured the snakes would help motivate the agents to work a little faster."

"Six people were rendered deadish, and we're still finding snakes in the vents."

"Only six?" said Kila. "Damn. I bet a friend it would be eight."

Although Agent Gooley would not appreciate it, getting

those snakes had actually been quite a feat. The Thunderhead had all wildlife "tagged" with nanites to monitor and, when necessary, control their behavior. Tagged snakes wouldn't have attacked anyone; they would have happily lined up to be recaptured. Probably in size order. Getting that many untagged venomous snakes required them to be kept entirely off-grid from the moment they hatched. A tall order—but Kila knew a guy who knew a guy.

"Well, rather than be charged for the six revivals, your parents have surrendered you to us," announced Agent Gooley. "Until you turn eighteen, you are under the guardianship of the Authority Interface. I am basically your Thunderhead-appointed parent now."

Kila had known this was coming. She was actually surprised it had taken her parents so long to surrender her. But even so, it hurt.

Maybe Agent Gooley read that hurt on Kila's face, because she folded her hands gently on her desk and pretended to be sympathetic. "Kila, we're not denying you your right to be unsavory—and it's not my job to stop you from exercising that right . . . but it *is* my job to enforce the consequences of unsavorism."

Kila took a deep breath. "Fine. So aside from becoming a ward of the region, what are my consequences?"

Agent Gooley scrolled through Kila's rather lengthy file and threw up a work assignment on the room's large screen.

"You're being relocated to the old District of Columbia and are being offered a community service job in waste removal."

"Can't machines do that?"

"Machines can do most things. But that doesn't mean they should. Sometimes a human touch is more important than automation. More important for the human, that is."

Kila wanted to fold her arms and look away in defiance— but she refused to become an unsavory cliché for this woman.

"The job's only four hours a day, with weekends off. That will give you plenty of time to engage in whatever . . . activities . . . bring you satisfaction."

"And what if I refuse the job?"

"You can always choose to be supplanted," offered Gooley. "I can arrange that almost immediately."

Kila knew that was always an option for unsavories. She had to admit, the idea of erasing all her memories and becoming someone else was tempting on her worst days. But then, on her worst days, so was gouging her eyes out with a spoon.

"I'll take the job," she told Agent Gooley, who leaned back, so self-satisfied, Kila wished a wayward snake would find its way through the vent and attack her.

Kila Whitlock was not what you'd call a natural unsavory. She was not born with contrarian tendencies. In fact, until six months ago, she had been a model student. A cheerleader with aspirations of being the captain of the cheer squad someday.

Then her brother was gleaned.

The gleaning of Kohl Whitlock was a tragedy for her family, and for the school. But Kila found herself furious with her classmates—not because they grieved for Kohl but because of *why* they grieved. Kohl was the school's star quarterback, and without him the school had no chance of winning another game that year. Which meant they weren't grieving for Kohl; they were grieving for themselves and their precious league standings. She began to secretly despise them.

"Why did it have to be Kohl?" she demanded of the Thunderhead. "My brother didn't deserve to die."

"Few people deserve to be gleaned, and yet they must be," the Thunderhead told her. *"Beyond that, I cannot speak of scythe business."*

When she cried, the Thunderhead did its best to comfort her, because her parents were too busy nursing their own pain to have anything to do with hers.

"I could recalibrate your mood nanites to ease your suffering," the Thunderhead told her. *"But it's much healthier for you to grieve right now."*

She hated the Thunderhead. Almost as much as she hated the kid who helped that scythe kill her brother. Rowan Damisch had been shunned by the rest of the school for it, but what did that matter? Because now he was a scythe's apprentice and would likely become a scythe himself—rewarded for helping to end her brother's life. Well, she couldn't take out her anger on him, but she could on everyone else.

She began to take pleasure in "accidentally" tripping other students down the stairs or stealing phones, wallets, and other precious things, only to throw them away. She willfully spread misery, all the while posing as the good girl.

But the Thunderhead knew. It saw everything she did. *"Perhaps you could find a more helpful outlet for your frustration and resentment,"* the Thunderhead suggested, but Kila refused to listen. Instead, she watched her unsavory points mount, until finally she had accumulated enough to earn her full unsavory status. Then she didn't have to hear the Thunderhead's suggestions anymore, because once she was unsavory, it couldn't talk to her, and she couldn't talk to it. Good riddance.

That ugly red *U* didn't just show up on her Ident—it was everywhere. No more credit at the corner coffeehouse, because unsavories were not extended credit anywhere. No more cheer squad, because unsavories were prohibited from school sports. All her personal media pages were now marked with that big, fat *U*, making it clear to everyone that she was no longer in the world's good graces.

In less than a day, everyone in school knew. She thought she'd feel scandalized, humiliated, but instead, she felt vindicated.

"Don't worry, Kila," her friend Shayla said. "Whatever happened to make you unsavory, I'm sure it's just temporary. Your status will upgrade in a few months—you'll see."

To which Kila smiled and replied, "Thanks, Shayla. By the way, your stuffed bra isn't fooling anyone, and Zach is cheating on you with Regina Sisk."

Kila dropped out two weeks later and never looked back.

Kila had her own room in her new unsavory group lair. But as she was the newest member of the pod, her room was the smallest and dimmest, without the luxury of a window. The place was really just an apartment and was only called a "lair" to make it more attractive to unsavories.

"Welcome to the pod," said a beefy unsavory with intentionally crooked teeth and sarcasm in place of enthusiasm. "I'd say I'm pleased to meet you, but why pretend?"

"Don't mind Sterox," said a woman with the rudest tattoo on her cheek that Kila had ever seen. "He hates everyone. It's his thing."

She introduced herself as SpiderMaw. "But you can just call me Maw—everyone does." Although truth be told, she wasn't all that motherly. She showed Kila around the apartment, which was spacious, with a bedroom for everyone—five in total. In addition to Maw and Sterox, there was Thrash, who seemed to have practically merged with a pair of old-fashioned VR gaming goggles and only grunted when Maw tried to introduce them. And last, there was Slinko, who was in his room playing darts, using pictures of happy, smiling, pretty people who lived in their building as targets.

"If only the Thunderhead let me throw darts at the actual people, life would be so much more worth living," Slinko said.

Apparently, Slinko once aspired to be a scythe, but as everyone knew, if you aspired to be a scythe, you were never chosen to be one. Unless of course you were chosen as a New Order scythe's apprentice—but even then, New Order scythes preferred taking on model youth, because they enjoyed breaking them.

"Unsavories never get to permanently kill anyone," Slinko grumbled. "The universe is so unfair."

"So, you have a name?" Sterox asked. "Or do we just call you Useless?"

"That's what we called the girl who used to have your room," Maw explained. "She got tired of being unsavory and became this annoying goody-goody. We booted her out the second the Thunderhead upgraded her status. No place for legits here."

. . .

The pod worked together at an old warehouse on the banks of the Potomac. It was a mess—everything inside had been smashed and incinerated beyond recognition. Charred ruins that weren't doing anyone any good.

"Our job is to clean it out," Maw explained to Kila.

"It doesn't seem so hard."

"It's not . . . but there's only five of us, and all we get are shovels."

"Yeah, we've been here for months, and barely have a third of it cleared out," Sterox said. "My nimbo says we'll be on this assignment for at least another six months."

Kila shrugged. "Who cares? We're Hellions, right? They can't expect us to be efficient."

"Well," said Slinko with a smirk, "*most* of us are Hellions."

As it turned out, Maw was a full-fledged Apocalyte. Bottom of the barrel, as far as the world was concerned, but the very top of the unsavory food chain! Kila had never even met one before, much less lived with one. Once they got back from work the first day, in spite of her exhaustion, Kila dug around the backbrain to find out what their illustrious SpiderMaw had done to earn the distinction of Apocalyte—but all she could find were rumors people had posted on social sites. Some said she was a huntress who had intentionally rendered a species extinct, causing the Thunderhead to artificially re-create it. Others said she flooded a luxury submarine just so she could experience what it was like to drown and took a hundred people with her. But whatever her infraction, Maw kept it to herself, seeming to enjoy all the speculation. Kila couldn't deny that she was more than a little bit jealous. Although people back home had begun to fear Kila, it wasn't the same. Wariness and distrust were not the same as awe.

As Kila had said, no one cared about the efficiency of unsavories at their jobs. Weekly meetings with Nimbus Agent Gooley confirmed it. As long as Kila spent four hours a day, five days a week doing it, Gooley couldn't care less how much or how little she actually accomplished. It was basically forced labor, but at least they weren't expected to do it for free. In fact, they were paid pretty well for the work. Which was annoying when all you wanted to do was hate the Thunderhead.

"Just keep out of trouble," Gooley said, then corrected herself. "Or should I say, keep trouble within acceptable parameters."

But giving an unsavory parameters was just a dare to break them.

After her first week, her podmates took Kila down to Unsavory Row—a street lined with neon-lit clubs and bars full of the rowdy ruleless having a good time.

"This is the very street that the Grandame of Death walked down before she did her dirty business," Slinko told Kila.

"Yeah, but she wasn't the Grandame of Death yet," Maw pointed out. "It takes time to earn a title like that. And tonight, maybe you'll start earning a name for yourself."

Kila couldn't believe how many clubs there were on Unsavory Row. So many specialty experiences. There was a restaurant where you got to mistreat the servers; an overpriced clothing store that encouraged shoplifting; a fight club that sent a few people to the nearest revival center every night. And there were parties! All sorts of parties for all sorts of people with all sorts of interests. If it was nasty and it was borderline legal, there was a place for it on Unsavory Row.

Kila had never been to any kind of unsavory club. She was as wary as she was curious.

"Just because it's here doesn't mean you have to do it," Maw advised. "You do you, Kila."

But in the glow of all the flashing neon lights, Kila felt uncharacteristically timid. And Maw must have realized it.

Maw stopped them in the street and turned to their new lairmate. "Let's find out what you like," Maw said. "Do you like to break stuff, hurt stuff, or watch stuff?"

"Uh . . . break stuff?" Kila said.

"Okay—so you like to *make* people suffer, *see* people suffer, or do you not give a shit about what people feel at all?"

"The latter," Kila said.

"Okay. Last question: Do you prefer to be unsavory alone, with someone else, or as a group?"

Kila had never actually thought about that. Prior to now, she was pretty much alone in her unsavorism. She liked that—but is that what she wanted more than anything else? To be the one unsavory among legits?

"As a group," she said. "I want to be unsavory as a group."

Maw grinned. "Then I know exactly where we should go tonight!"

Maw brought them to a spot that seemed entirely out of place on Unsavory Row. No bright flashing lights, no toughs hanging outside looking for trouble. It was a stone building with white marble pillars holding up an arch, into which were carved the word "Museum," although the *u*'s looked like *v*'s.

"Good idea," said Sterox, cracking his knuckles. "I could use a little culture right about now."

There was a vestibule just inside the entrance, where a woman who looked much too proper to be in an unsavory establishment greeted them. "Welcome to Gallery de Bäsch," she said. "We know you have a choice when looking for quality experiences, and we can't thank you enough for your patronage."

Maw paid for everyone, and the woman escorted them into a room where various objects hung on a wall. Steel pipes, baseball bats, heavy hammers, mallets, and golf clubs. But they weren't just for show.

"Choose wisely," Maw told Kila. "You only get one."

Kila chose an aluminum bat, which Maw approved of. "You'll get your money's worth with that!"

Then the woman escorted them down a hallway into an empty gallery. "I hope you enjoy yourselves. And if you do, please tell your friends!"

She closed the door behind them. Silence for a few moments, and then the wall in front of them opened up to a huge, multileveled gallery. Bronze and marble sculptures, display cases of pottery, and delicate crystal everywhere. It was beautiful.

Then Thrash let out a war cry and swung a golf club at a display case of glass figurines, shattering them all in a single blow. It was like the whistle at a race—Sterox, Slinko, and Maw joined in, smashing everything in sight.

Kila was stunned. And excited. She had never seen such

wholesale, wanton destruction. She didn't know how to feel about it.

Sterox climbed to the next level, then jumped, and with a heavy downward stroke of his mallet, broke a hand off Michelangelo's *David*. He whooped and hollered as the hand hit the ground, fingers flying everywhere.

"What are you waiting for?" Maw yelled as she broke Julius Caesar's nose. "This is why we're here!"

"But . . . are they real?" Kila asked.

"Who cares?" yelled Maw, and pushed the great Roman emperor to the ground, turning him to rubble.

Kila began slowly. With some clay pots. She picked one up and dropped it. Then she dropped another one. Then she picked up her bat and smashed an entire shelf of them. Then it became easy. Display case after display case. The pots broke with a clatter, but she found that bone china made a much more satisfying sound upon impact.

Just then, a door labeled MUSEUM CONSERVATOR opened, and out came a neatly suited man with a pencil-thin mustache and a horrific expression on his face.

"What are you doing?" he wailed at all of them. "Stop this immediately! These are priceless works of art! *Priceless!*"

Maw turned to Sterox. "You want to do the honors?"

"My pleasure," said Sterox. He dropped his mallet and began punching the man over and over, until he was a quivering heap on the ground, begging for mercy. Again, Kila didn't know how to feel about this.

"Should we stop?" she asked Maw, but Maw shook her head.

"Not until the bell!" Then Maw swung her iron pipe at the

head of a statue Kila knew to be *The Thinker*. Its head sheered cleanly off and settled on the ground, looking up at Kila, its eyes void of all thought.

That's when Kila spotted the window. It was at the very back of the gallery. Gorgeous stained glass. A mountain vista with a lake, purple flowers, and slender trees. But there was no path to it. The only way to reach it was to create a path by smashing everything in the way.

With a double-handed grip on her bat, she began swinging away, splinters and shards flying in all directions, some of them cutting her skin as they flew, but she didn't care. Before long she found a rhythm, losing all inhibition. There was something cathartic about every swing.

This is for the scythe who gleaned my brother!

And this is for the kid who helped!

And this is for my classmates who pretended to care!

And this is for my parents, who secretly wished it were me!

Finally she was at the window. So colorful. So beautiful. So fragile. She took the whole thing out with a single magnificent blow. And as the last shards hit the ground, a bell sounded.

"Whoa!" said Thrash. "I never saw someone get to the window!" Probably the first complete sentence Kila had ever heard Thrash speak.

"Beginner's luck," grumbled Sterox.

"Kila? More like *Killa*," said Slinko. "I think we found your name!"

"Killa . . . ," said Maw, pondering. "I like it . . . but not yet. She's got to earn her name. You don't do that in one night."

Maw and the others slipped out a door marked EMERGENCY

EXIT, but Kila wasn't ready to leave just yet. She wanted to bask in their "bash," admiring their handiwork. But as she looked around, she noticed the conservator still lying in a pile of pulverized marble. She went over to him and helped him up. She didn't expect a thank-you, but neither did she expect the response she got.

The moment he saw who it was, the man recoiled. "What are you still doing here?" he snapped. "Your session is over. Hurry along."

"I . . . I just . . . Are you okay?"

He had a bit of blood on his nose, but he wiped it away. "Of course I am, or I *will* be in a minute or two. Now, please, you have to leave—we only have ten minutes to reset."

Kila noticed that the swelling from the pummeling that Sterox had given him was already going away. Only supercharged healing nanites could work that quickly.

Then, seemingly out of the woodwork, came a crew of at least a dozen workers to clear out the debris. Others were rolling in new display cases of china, glass, and clay pots.

"So . . . it wasn't real."

"Did it feel real?"

"Yes . . . kind of."

"Then that's all that matters, isn't it?"

The conservator, seeing Kila's bewildered expression, leaned in a bit closer and spoke a little more quietly. "Listen, do you really think the Thunderhead would allow you to destroy precious originals? Young lady, the world is overflowing with artists who do nothing but create replicas of ancient art. Something must be done with it all. Truth be told, you're providing a service, really."

Then she saw, toward the front of the gallery, a brand-new *David* being wheeled in to replace the one Sterox had ruined.

"Now toddle off so we can reset," said the conservator. "And come see us again!"

That night, after they had gotten home, Maw checked in on Kila.

"Glad you're with us," Maw said. "You're a good fit. Sometimes the nimbos get it right."

Perhaps it was just because Kila was still a bit giddy from the evening of socially sanctioned vandalism, or maybe it was because she felt Maw was a kindred spirit. But whatever it was, Kila dared to ask the question no one else would.

"Maw . . . what did you do that made you an Apocolyte?"

To Maw's credit, she didn't dismiss the question or just regurgitate one of the rumors. Instead, she sat on the end of Kila's bed and told the truth.

"Sterox dreams about being a scythe's apprentice. But he doesn't know—none of them know—that I once was," Maw said. "Maybe one in five apprentices actually gets to be a scythe, but no one thinks about all the others. We just disappear into normal life—but after being a scythe's apprentice, there is no normal life anymore.

"Anyway, there was this one scythe who had his eyes on me. Scythe Chandler. He was on the ordination committee and promised I'd get special treatment if I gave *him* special treatment. But I told him no. Then, when it came time for the final test, I passed it, no problem. But I still didn't get chosen. I was voted down. Lost my scythehood by one vote. His."

"I'm sorry."

"Don't be. I would have been a terrible scythe. I could never stick to doing one thing and just one thing for the rest of my life." Maw took a few moments to think about it all. "Anyway, I chose an unsavory lifestyle after that. Became SpiderMaw, and it suited me fine. By the way, the story about the submarine is true—but I'm the only one who drowned. It did get me bumped up from Hellion to Pandæmon, though.

"That could have been the end of it . . . but a few years later, I came across Scythe Chandler in an unsavory bar. He was looking for what men like that look for. Figured he could find it among unsavories. He came on to me, and he didn't even recognize me. Can you believe that? I meant so little to him that he had no idea. So I decided to use it. Rather than playing his game, I played my own. I never gave him what he wanted . . . and that just made him want me more. I toyed with him and teased him, and in the end, I made him fall in love with me. Scythes aren't supposed to do that—fall in love—but he did. And when I knew I had him, I told him it was all a sham. That he disgusted me and that I detested him." Then Maw paused, taking her time to think about it.

"The next day he gleaned himself."

"He . . . he what?"

"It was perfect. I couldn't be held accountable for what he had done by his own hand. And no one knew. No one but the Thunderhead. I was called into the Authority Interface the following day, and they told me I had sunken as low as an unsavory could go. I was an Apocalyte."

Kila didn't know what to say. Kila sensed both bitterness

and pride in Maw. Achievement and failure. So much ambivalence. So Kila held her silence as a sign of respect for the truth Maw had shared.

"You keep that to yourself," Maw told Kila as she got up to leave. "You do and we'll be friends. And if you don't . . . we won't."

Kila shivered. She couldn't think of anything in the world worse than being on Maw's bad side.

Every Friday night, Kila and her pod went back down to Unsavory Row. They did something different each time, but none of the clubs and parties struck her as much as the Gallery de Bäsch. Perhaps because she hadn't known when they went there that all the clubs and attractions on Unsavory Row were staged. She should have realized that, with the world under Thunderhead jurisdiction, no unsavory club could truly be out of its control. The Thunderhead was the curator of all unsavory experiences—which meant that no matter how unsavory things seemed, they were just simulations of bad behavior.

"You think too much," Maw told her when she voiced her complaints. "Just go with it—you'll be a whole lot happier."

Still, Kila couldn't let it go. Instead, she began a determined search for the real thing.

"What's that you're looking at?"

Maw always had a need to know everyone's business. Kila considered lying but decided Maw should know—because if Kila was right, she'd need Maw. She'd need all her lairmates. So Kila turned her screen so that Maw could see.

Kila was looking at an aerial view she had found in a local geographic database. It was an ordinary-looking building, but it had a series of gates and fences—the way buildings had back in mortal days, when they contained things that needed to either stay in or things that people had to be kept away from.

"Hmm," said Maw. "Do you know what it is?"

"It caught my attention because it had no label. I mean, everything's labeled on maps, right?"

"Usually."

"So I dug around the backbrain and found an image of the rear entrance."

Kila enlarged it on her screen. There was a sign that clearly said CEREBRAL NODE 207.

"Whoa," said Maw. "The motherlode!"

The Thunderhead, as everyone knew, had servers called cerebral nodes spread out all over the world, housing the wealth of human knowledge, as well as its own massive intellect. No one really knew where they were, and few people cared. The Thunderhead maintained and serviced itself.

"Kila, are you thinking what I think you're thinking?"

Kila smiled. "Why settle for Unsavory Row when we have something real we can destroy!"

Maw rubbed her hands together like the greedy schemer she was. "That," she said, "is an idea worthy of a Hellion!"

Sterox knew someone with an off-grid truck large enough to crash the gates. And Thrash created malware that could temporarily disable some key Thunderhead cameras at the server complex. But it was Maw who delivered the real goods. Being an Apocalyte, she had unsavory connections to boggle the mind. Within hours, she had connected with an old friend who "dabbled" in explosives.

"But we have to be careful," she warned. "If we render anyone deadish, they'll split up our pod, and we'll get moved to different cities. And if we go so far as to render anyone unrevivable . . ." She didn't have to finish the thought. Anyone who did that was immediately turned over to the Scythedom—which would then glean you on the grounds that ending someone's existence was the same as impersonating a scythe.

The plan came together quickly, with everyone on the same page. "It's as if it was meant to be!" Maw proclaimed.

Everyone in the pod took turns running reconnaissance, tracking the comings and goings from the gated facility. The place was largely automated, but there was a human element. Two peace officers at the main gate and teams of Thunderhead technicians, or cloudtechs—that's what they had been called since before the Thunderhead achieved awareness—all in gray thermal uniforms, as the server environment was kept at a brisk -20 Celsius. The cloudtechs rotated in six-hour shifts, at the top and bottom of the clock, never more than ten on duty at any given time.

"Although we can't see inside, I was able to get blueprints for old cerebral nodes, and it seems to match the basic dimensions of this one," Kila told them. "There'll be an outer monitoring platform, with a view down into the core, about fifty yards in diameter. The drives will be in stacks like pillars in the core—close enough that it will only take a few charges to blow them all."

"That'll be fun to watch," said Slinko. "The Thunderhead having a brain aneurysm!"

"Yeah, well, don't watch too closely," Maw warned, "or you won't make it out."

They planned their attack for four a.m. on a Sunday, when no one on duty would be at their best. As they neared the facility, Thrash triggered his malware, which was supposed to freeze the images on all the cameras in the complex. "It'll be at least five minutes until the Thunderhead can defeat it," he said.

"We'll have to move fast," Maw said. "No backing out now!" As if any of them were going to back out.

The guards at the outer gate were no problem. They came out of their booth as they saw the truck approaching. Easy targets. In addition to the explosives, Maw had gotten a vial of high-potency tranquilizer, and Slinko knew exactly how to throw his darts. The guards were down even before they reached the gate and crashed through. The second gate had no human guards, just cameras that were temporarily blinded. It was sturdier than the outer gate, but it fell beneath the force of their off-grid five-hundred-horsepower truck.

The structure that housed Cerebral Node 207 was concrete—thick, hard to breach, but any building was only as secure as its entry—and in this case the entry was a set of glass sliding doors, with a digital keypad. Thrash got to work trying to decode the pad, but Sterox wasn't waiting.

"To hell with that." He put his foot through one of the doors, and the safety glass shattered into a thousand glass pellets like a windshield. "There. Easy-peasy."

They flooded in, taking the cloudtechs by surprise. Although their thermal suits were thick, Slinko had sharpened his darts to penetrate. He caught each of them in their tracks, and they all went down, leaving nothing but the pod and the computer core.

The server stacks looked like crystalline stalagmites rising from the core, filled with colored lights, blinking and shimmering like a grove of Gifting Season trees.

"Pretty," said Kila.

"Yeah, too bad we gotta blow them up," said Sterox, and laughed.

There was a ramp that led down into the chilled core, getting colder as they descended. The stacks were even taller from down there, towering above them, twice their height.

"This could take fewer blasts than we thought," said Maw. "They look top-heavy. Set a few strategic charges, and the rest could fall like dominoes."

They split up, each with a set of explosives. Maw, Sterox, Slinko, and Thrash took the four cardinal directions, with Kila taking the center—her reward for having found this place to begin with. It was hard for Kila to imagine that the putty-like substance wired to a detonator actually had the explosive power to take this place down—but once it was set and armed, it looked much more intimidating.

Then, just as they met back at the base of the ramp, alarms began to blare all around them.

"Time's up!" yelled Maw. "Let's bail and blow!"

But the alarms had spooked Slinko, who held the remote, and rather than waiting for them all to get clear, he hit the detonate button with everyone still at the bottom of the ramp.

All the charges went off at once, and Kila was thrown halfway up the ramp, then covered in shattered glass. Her hearing was instantly deadened. A buzzing filled her head. Through the smoke, she saw Sterox getting to his feet, pulling a server shard out of his arm. Thrash was already stumbling up the ramp, saving himself and forgetting the rest of them. Typical.

But then Kila saw Maw. She was pinned beneath a huge chunk of a server stack. Slinko was trying to lift it but wasn't strong enough to do it alone.

"You idiot!" yelled Maw. "Five seconds and we would have been clear!"

"I'm sorry!" said Slinko. "I didn't mean to do it so soon!"

Kila joined him, and together they were able to free Maw. She was bruised, but nothing seemed to be broken. "Okay, go, go, go!" she ordered.

Slinko didn't need a second invitation, taking off after Thrash and Sterox and leaving Maw to limp after them.

But Kila lingered.

She turned back to the ruins to take in their handiwork. Now that the dust was settling, it was clear how amazingly effective their campaign of destruction was. Only one server stack was left standing. One out of maybe a hundred. Yet as satisfying as it was, there was something unsettling about all this. Unsettling and somehow familiar.

All around her alarms still blared, but no one came—not even drones to assess the damage. Wouldn't the Thunderhead be all over a security breach this severe? Had a single pod of unsavories truly caught the Thunderhead off guard? Could it really be so vulnerable?

Instead of following the others to make a quick and triumphant escape, Kila doubled back, crawling over the wreckage, not even sure what she was looking for. Finally, Kila came to the single remaining crystalline stack, standing like a monolith among the ruins. Its colored lights still blinked and shimmered as if it didn't even know that all the others had been destroyed. Kila leaned into it, throwing her full weight against it until it tipped over, crashing to the ground.

Not only wasn't it secured to its concrete base, but it had no wires, no conduits, nothing connecting it to the other stacks. It was feasible that the Thunderhead's brain was wireless, but every individual stack would still need to be connected to a primary power source, wouldn't it?

Then Kila found the power source. There was a small plastic compartment on the bottom of the overturned drive stack. She flipped open the latch to reveal . . .

Batteries.

Three of them.

They were small enough to fit in the palm of her hand—the kind you'd find in a child's toy. Nowhere near enough voltage to run a computer stack, but they could certainly power a few blinking lights. In fact, if you had enough batteries, you could make an entire room blink and shimmer.

"Kila! What are you doing? We have to get out of here!"

She turned to see that Maw had followed her.

"We did what we came to do," yelled Maw. "Now let's bail before we get caught!"

But Kila didn't move. As she looked around, she realized why these ruins looked so familiar. They were like the debris they had left behind in the Gallery de Bäsch—but even more than that, it looked like the ruins of the warehouse where they spent their days shoveling. *Exactly* like it. Kila had wondered what those ruins were, but she never cared enough to seek an answer to the question.

"Kila! What's wrong with you? Let's go!"

Still the alarms blared, still no one came, and Kila was frozen. Not by the cold but by the revelations cascading through her mind one after another. More dominoes crashing to the ground.

"You acted so excited when I found this place," Kila said. "But were you, really? You knew I was searching for a target—and suddenly I found one."

"What the hell are you talking about?"

Kila looked at the destruction all around them. "How long have you been playing us, Maw? Are you even an unsavory?"

Maw looked deeply offended. "I'm an Apocalyte!"

"And yet you're working for the Thunderhead. Which means you're a nimbus agent!"

Maw hesitated, perhaps weighing whether any of it was worth denying anymore. Then she said, "All Apocalytes are."

So there it was. The truth behind the final domino. It all made sense now. How could Kila not have seen through the charade? Did she really believe that Thrash could come up with malware that could shut down Thunderhead cameras? Thrash—who couldn't put together two coherent thoughts without one of them dying in the process? But when you wanted to believe something, it took less than a handful of batteries to power your belief.

"Is any of this real, Maw?"

Maw looked her dead in the eye. "As real as it needs to be."

Then, from behind her, came one of the gray-clad workers. A cloudtech. Slinko had knocked the cloudtechs out with tranq-dipped darts—but had he? After all, Maw had provided the tranquilizer.

"We can't let her go," the cloudtech said.

"Of course we can," Maw told him. "*Killa* won't tell anyone."

"You can't be sure," said the attendant.

Killa . . . Does that mean I've earned the name? Kila thought.

Maw smiled. "Killa's like me, aren't you, Killa? She won't tell, because as of now, she moves up in status from Hellion . . . to Pandæmon."

Pandæmon, thought Kila. *One step short of Apocalyte.* She'd have the awe and respect of other unsavories. *Killa* would. It gave her serious pause for thought.

Then, from the distance, they heard Sterox calling for them.

"Go," Maw told the cloudtech. "Don't let him see you."

The cloudtech obediently left, crouching low, slipping away through the wreckage.

Maw came closer. "I know you, Killa. I know what you want. You long for the power that comes with destruction—but few things are more powerful than seeing behind the veil of reality. And now I've shown you even more! The power to destroy the very act of destruction. Don't shun it, Killa. Embrace it!"

In that moment, Killa knew what she had to do. She didn't think about it; she just did it. Reaching down, she grabbed a jagged crystalline shard of the so-called cerebral node and stabbed it deep in Maw's gut.

A few moments later, Sterox and the others saw Killa coming through the wreckage, carrying Maw.

"Help me," Killa said. "One of the cloudtechs got her!"

They helped carry Maw to the truck.

"The wound's deep," said Slinko, looking it over as they sped off, "but I don't think she'll go deadish." Sure enough, the bleeding had already stopped, her healing nanites cauterizing the wound. Even without treatment, she'd be healed in a day or two.

Killa stayed with her, letting Maw rest her head in her lap as they made their escape. Bleary-eyed but still conscious, Maw looked up at Killa.

"Was that really necessary?" Maw asked.

"No," admitted Killa, "but doesn't this seem even more real now?"

Maw gave her the faintest of grins. "Damn, you're right. You'll make a great Apocalyte one day."

And Killa agreed. In fact, she was counting on it.

A Martian Minute

"If there's a bright spot in the solar system, this is the place it's farthest from."

"That's not the precise quote, Carson."

"I know—but we're not exactly spread out across the galaxy, are we?" Carson Lusk said. "And who asked you anyway?"

"No one." As always, the Thunderhead was guileless and pleasant in its response. *"I'm just providing enlightenment."*

Carson waited for an irritating addendum to its comment, which the Thunderhead often gave. Today was no exception.

"Incidentally," it added, *"that particular misquote doesn't hold true either literally or figuratively because, (a) Mars is only the fourth planet from the sun, receiving ample sunlight, and, (b) rather than darkness of the heart, I do track plenty of joy here. Occasionally even in you."*

Carson hurled a wrench at his rover's speaker. "There, is that literal enough for you?"

But, of course, the Thunderhead was unfazed. *"I could give you an unsavory point for throwing that, but I won't, because I know you're just being melodramatic."*

The rover hit a jarring bump in the dirt road—a bump that the Thunderhead could have steered him around, but Carson had the controls on manual. Still, it could have warned him, but no. The Thunderhead was passive-aggressive that way. It irked him.

"You know what I need right now?" Carson said, with the slightest grin. "I need you to find out the current price of tea in PanAsia."

"For what purpose?" the Thunderhead asked.

"Not your business. I gave you a request; it's your job to fulfill it."

"Of course," said the Thunderhead, *"I'll have your answer in ten minutes and four seconds."* And then it went blissfully silent.

Carson gloated just the tiniest bit. Although the Thunderhead had a cerebral node here on Mars for rapid responses and planetary management, its entire backbrain was on Earth. Currently Earth was a little over five light-minutes distant— so it would take twice that for the Thunderhead to access the answer, then bounce the answer back to Mars. During that time, it would leave Carson alone. Of course, he could just tell the Thunderhead to be quiet, but where was the fun in that? He much preferred sending it on a pointless mission. He liked to think such missions reminded the Thunderhead that it was nothing but a servant.

Unlike the hapless hero from his favorite mortal-age movie—the one he had misquoted—Carson Lusk was not a moisture farmer. *That* character's adventure started when his aunt and uncle were mercilessly killed by an evil empire. He was, however, the son of carbon miners on an equally dry planet. There would be no such salvation for Carson, however, because there were no evil empires, just the Thunderhead and its insufferable benevolence. And his parents dying? Out of the question.

There weren't even any scythes on Mars, and probably wouldn't be for a thousand years. The Mars colony had a population around ten thousand, so there was plenty of room for its numbers to grow.

The rover bobbled and bounced on the rough terrain, until cresting a ridge. Now Carson could see the array of huge drills piercing the Martian plain like mortal-age acupuncture needles. Their purpose was similar, because in a way, those drills were there to heal the planet. Or at least transform it. They churned endlessly, digging up carbon ore that would then be combined with oxygen to create carbon dioxide—the magical gas that would, eventually, allow the planet to warm, and a richer atmosphere to develop. Strange to think that the same greenhouse gas that once threatened Earth's future was critical to the future of Mars.

His parents and the Thunderhead were constantly reminding him how important this work was—so much more important than what most people did on Earth—which is why they had become colonists in the first place: to give their lives meaning. But Carson, who had been nine when they made the journey, was given no say in the matter. He still had memories of his life on Earth. The green fields and rolling hills of MidMerica—or at least the small part of MidMerica he had gotten to see before he was ripped off-planet. Now the only green was under the colony's dome, and the hills outside the dome were jagged dead things that were still centuries from birthing life.

"Why?" he had once asked the Thunderhead. "Why even bother doing this?"

And with its infinite patience, the Thunderhead explained,

"It's every species' biological imperative to multiply and expand its reach. I am merely facilitating your natural expansion beyond the limits of Earth."

Blah blah blah. The Thunderhead was so full of itself. If it really cared about him the way it always claimed to, it would find a way to get him off this rock.

"When you are truly ready to embark on a journey back to Earth," the Thunderhead had told him more than once, *"I'm sure a means will present itself."*

More empty words.

Carson followed a steep trail down into the valley, heading toward the drill array. Since there were fifty-two wells in a four-by-thirteen array, each was named after a playing card. The malfunctioning drill was the King of Spades—the last on the end of the first row. As he neared it, the issue became clear. The massive drill bit had broken.

He notified his father over the radio.

"Good work, Carson," his father said. "I'll get a new one ordered."

Well, at least the problem was obvious enough that Carson didn't need to get his suit on and get out there. He despised the stifling sensation of his space suit. It perpetually smelled of his own sweat, and a trace of vomit from the time his air had gotten low, and he had barfed in it. Space suits. Something else life on Earth would not require.

".23 credits per kilo," the Thunderhead said out of nowhere, startling him.

"What?"

"The price of generic oolong in PanAsia. That's the base price. The cost of specific teas varies."

Carson sighed. "Couldn't you have diagnosed the issue with the King of Spades on your own?" he asked the Thunderhead. "You know everything that happens here, right? You could have told me the drill bit was broken, and made this easier for me."

"*Yes,*" answered the Thunderhead. "*But ease doesn't serve you, Carson. Traveling out here to diagnose the problem will not only leave you with the satisfaction of a job well done, but has already brought forth much desired praise from your father.*"

"Bite me," Carson said. "And if you tell me you don't have teeth, I'll throw a wrench again."

"*Understood,*" the Thunderhead said, and went silent without having to be given another pointless interplanetary quest.

While various terraforming activities stretched for more than a hundred Martian Kilometers in all directions, everyone lived under the dome of Humanus Mons. It was massive up close, but was little more than an anthill compared to Olympus Mons, Mars's largest volcanic mountain, which towered behind it, even though its base was technically beyond the horizon. It was so immense, it defied the curvature of the planet.

The dome was the hub of all activity on Mars. There was an outpost being built to the north, not far from the Lusk family's mining grid, but it wasn't completed yet. Carson dreaded its completion, because he knew his parents would want to move there. As if Mars wasn't isolating enough, they'd want to be right at the frontier, where there'd be practically no one Carson's age.

He only had a handful of friends as it was. Not that he didn't get along with his classmates—he just didn't let many of them close. His circle consisted primarily of him, and his friends Acher and Devona.

"If your parents up and move to the North Outpost, you should just refuse to go," Devona said as they sat sipping coffee one day after school.

"Yeah," said Acher. "Worse comes to worst, you could live with me. My parents won't mind. They think you're a good influence."

They were at 4th Planet Java, one of only two coffeehouses in the dome. It featured an "open-air terrace," which was, of course, not really open-air. It merely overlooked the spacious park that filled the center of the dome.

"Your parents already work you too hard," Devona said, nursing a latte made from hydroponic beans that were supposedly the same as espresso beans on Earth, but Carson had his doubts.

"Devo's right," said Acher, taking her hand. "You're always out there working the mine."

Acher and Devona were a couple—or at least they were today. They were constantly breaking up and getting back together again, like a pair of binary stars that couldn't escape each other's hormonal gravity. Each time Carson thought he might just have a chance with Devo, Acher came back around like celestial clockwork.

"Don't you get it? I don't have a choice," Carson told them.

"Of course you do!" Acher said, like it was all so easy. "Your parents can't make you work the mine if you don't want to, and they can't make you move away from the dome, either."

"They can't? Who's going to stop them?"

"The Thunderhead," said Devona. Another sip of her latte left a line of foam on her upper lip that Carson could not look away from.

"Are you kidding me? The Thunderhead's on their side," Carson told them. "The last time my parents shut down my privileges for something stupid, I told the Thunderhead—and did I get justice? No. It said, *'Domestic punishment is under human jurisdiction.'*"

Carson looked away, not wanting his bitterness to be directed at his friends, and turned his attention to the afternoon bustle of the dome. From their table on the terrace, Carson had a good view of the shopping arcade, and Daedalia Park beyond. The sun was beginning to edge off the skylight, leaving a curved line of shadow moving slowly across the trees of Daedalia Park— named after the wasteland the colony was built on. Carson used to like watching the arc of the skylight's shadow as it moved, marking off day from the night, like an ancient sundial. Now it just reminded him of the endless parade of identical tomorrows.

Carson took a swig of his coffee—still so hot that it burned his throat—but he didn't mind. He was, at least, feeling something.

"The Thunderhead won't do a thing to help me unless my parents somehow damage me," he told his friends.

"So make them damage you," suggested Devona. "Get your dad angry enough to hit you or something, before his mood nanites can shut down his temper."

Carson considered it. He might be able to—after all, his dad did have a short fuse. He used to think it was funny the way his father would get red with fury, then suddenly go all Zen when his nanites kicked in to calm him. And if Carson could throw a wrench in his rover, his father could certainly get mad enough to throw a punch. But then what? Hitting Carson would get his father marked unsavory for an entire season. That would leave his mother and Carson screwed until he regained savory status. Limited privileges, social ridicule—because although a kid getting marked unsavory was seen as a battle scar, for an adult—an actual productive member of society—it was an embarrassment.

No, provoking his father was a nonstarter. Besides, as much as Carson hated to admit it, the Thunderhead was right; Carson *did* care about his father's approval.

"It's not so bad," Carson said. "They only make me work the mine on weekends. Besides, they pay me—and I need to save money for when I go back to Earth."

"Dude, you don't need money on Earth!" Acher said. "They say the Thunderhead gives you everything you need."

"Everything I need, but not everything I want."

Devona gave him the slightest froth-lipped smile. "So what do you want?"

Carson gave her a grin of his own. "A lot more than the Thunderhead's willing to give."

Days on Mars were longer than days on Earth by almost exactly one hour. But rather than giving Mars a twenty-five-hour day, the Thunderhead decided to change the nature of time itself.

"The measurement of time is a human construct," it had reasoned, *"which means it can be reformed for planetary convenience."*

And so the seconds on Mars became just a tiny bit longer, as did the minutes, as did the hours. A day still measured twenty-four, but each of those hours was nearly two and a half Earth-minutes longer. Which gave birth to expressions like "a Martian minute." Colonists found it insulting, because although the minutes on Mars were longer, the people there felt themselves to be far more industrious than those on Earth, and could accomplish more in a Martian minute than Earthbounders could do in one of their hours.

The Thunderhead suspected that, as time went on, it would have to create social safeguards against bias and prejudice between the two planets.

Carson Lusk began his life on Earth, where the seconds were quicker and the gravity was stronger. Years on Mars made his body forget all that, so he knew going back would be a great adjustment. It takes weeks for one's biological rhythm to acclimate to a shorter day, and months for one's muscles, bones, and heart to adjust to the relentless pull of a greater gravity.

"You'd be miserable," his parents told him. "Not even your nanites can save you from that." Carson noted how they'd said "You'd" rather than "You'll"—as if his escape from Mars was conditional, and not certain. But regardless of the tense his parents chose, he was determined to leave Mars by any means necessary—and before they had a chance to drag him to the boonies of the North Outpost.

Education was going to get him out. Higher education—not what passed for education in the colony. With only ten thousand colonists, there was only need for a single school, with fewer than two hundred per grade, and college? Mars A&M was the only choice—and Carson had zero interest in anything agricultural or mineral.

The Thunderhead allowed minimal travel between Mars and Earth, which could be a problem, but Carson had a plan. Anyone who earned a scholarship to an Earthbound university would be given a free ride to Earth by the Thunderhead, then back again upon graduation. But Carson was only interested in a one-way trip. He had applied to Harvard, Stanford, Oxford, Tsinghua, and a dozen other schools. His grades were exceptional, but not stellar. Even so, an application from Mars would get special attention, so he felt cautiously optimistic.

"Perhaps you shouldn't count your chickens before they're hatched," the Thunderhead told him. *"Always plan for contingencies."* At the time, Carson took that as the Thunderhead just being the Thunderhead. But the great sentient AI always knew more than it shared.

For now, Carson had to focus his attention on getting through high school, and making sure to keep on the good side of his teachers, since he might need letters of recommendation. Why they still needed teachers when the Thunderhead could teach them anything they needed to know was beyond him. It was just one more way for the Thunderhead to "maintain the integrity of the human condition."

Most of the time, Carson was okay with his teachers. He only had issues when it was clear he knew more about the subject than they did. Such was the case with Mr. McGeary, his Mortal Studies teacher. The man seemed to imagine himself a professor in a grand lecture hall pontificating to hundreds of students instead of just a small classroom of twenty.

"Goddard, von Braun, Musk," he declared, expelling enough hot air to trigger the dome's atmospheric alarms. "These great scientific minds of the mortal age made it possible for us to be here on Mars today."

This was old news to Carson—he had always had a fascination with rocket science, and the history of space travel. A fascination but not a love. It actually bordered more on hatred. It gave him comfort to know who to blame for his current situation.

There was a statue of Robert Goddard smack in the middle of Daedalia Park; a towering bronze of the so-called "Father of Rocketry" gazing skyward like Chicken Little looking for cracks in the dome. Last year, on a dare, Carson took a piss on it. The Thunderhead had given him an unsavory point, but it was worth it.

"Are you with us today, Mr. Lusk?"

Carson was, in fact, doing something related to the lecture. He was doodling an early rocket blowing up on the launchpad—something that happened more than once in those early days. You'd think people would've taken that as a hint.

"Carson!"

"Goddard, von Braun, Musk," Carson recited back to McGeary, without looking up from his drawing. "But you have it wrong. Musk wasn't a scientist; he was just a businessman with a lot of money."

Then, from across the room, Acher said, "Musk, Lusk. Too bad, Carson, you're one letter short of greatness."

That brought forth laughter from all around the room. Carson was irritated but tried not to show it.

"There's nothing great about blowing all your capital to send a tin can to an uninhabitable planet," he said.

"Well, *we're* inhabiting it," McGeary pointed out.

"If you say so," Carson said, refusing to let the man have the last word. "But 'living' and 'inhabiting' are two different things. It'll be hundreds of years until we really *inhabit* Mars. And frankly I wouldn't call this 'living,' either."

McGeary sighed, a virtual waving of his surrender flag. "Can we please just get back to the lesson."

"Be my guest," said Carson.

McGeary continued spouting facts about famous dead people, but seemed to be putting forth less hot air than before, thanks to Carson's deflation.

Ships only arrived from Earth when Mars was in opposition— that is, on the same side of the sun—which only happened once every two Earth years. "Shipping season" would last eight weeks, during which ships would arrive and depart nearly every day. Most would be drones containing supplies: products and minerals that couldn't be made or mined on Mars. A few would be passenger craft, arriving with new colonists, wide-eyed and bewildered, and would depart with anyone who could afford a trip back to Earth—or anyone the Thunderhead, in its infinite wisdom, decided deserved to make the journey for free.

There were no tourists on Mars. No one made a round-trip journey, unless the Thunderhead had a specific reason for it. After all, "space tourism" would be an endeavor for the ultrarich, and there were no ultrarich anymore. Just as poverty had been defeated, so had ridiculous wealth. Personal fortune now filled a narrow band between comfortable and slightly more comfortable.

With one exception.

The Scythedom.

When it came to scythes, money was no object, because money had no meaning. They simply did whatever they wanted to do, whenever they wanted to do it. So it shouldn't have surprised anyone that a scythe would eventually commandeer one of the Thunderhead's ships and pay Mars a visit.

"Can't recall his name," Carson's father said over dinner one night. "Starts with an *X*, I think. Word is, he's on the first inbound craft of shipping season."

"A scythe? Why?" Carson had to ask.

His father shrugged. "Says he's curious. Says he won't glean anyone—he just wants to be the first scythe to experience Mars."

"He won't stay," proclaimed Carson's mother. "The colony's too small and provincial for the likes of a scythe."

Carson couldn't deny that he was intrigued. "Have you ever actually seen a scythe?" he asked them. "Back on Earth, I mean?"

"Yeah, a few times," his dad said, like it was nothing.

His mother raised her shoulders in a little shiver. "Remember that one time at the beach?"

His father nodded, putting down his fork, as if eating and remembering couldn't occur at the same time. "It sure was something," he said. "We were all in our bathing suits—but she was decked out in this flowing lavender robe, walking along the edge of the surf, holding the sharpest knife I've ever seen. What a sight!"

"It was like she was walking an inch above ground—you'd almost think she could walk on water," his mother added.

"I wish I could've seen that."

"No, Carson, you don't," his mother said, meeting his eye, but then looking away.

"She gleaned someone farther down the beach," his father explained. "We didn't see it, but we heard the screams."

"It was terrible. Just about ruined our day."

Silence. A return to eating. But a moment later, Carson's father had a final word on the subject.

"When the scythe comes, it's best if we all keep our heads low and stay out of his way."

"But you said he's not here to glean anyone."

His father took a moment to consider his steak knife.

"Scythes lie," he said.

There was an old expression—Carson had no idea where it came from: *"Men are from Mars, women are from Venus."* But when both are from Mars, all bets are off.

Acher and Devona had another fight. As usual, they had kinda-sorta broken up. And, as usual, Carson was there to console Devona.

"Acher can be *such* an asshole!" Devona said.

"I know."

"He thinks he can just take me for granted."

"I know."

"Someday he's going to learn he's not the only guy on the planet."

Carson didn't know the particulars yet, but he had no doubt Devona would tell him in detail. It would be something outrageously insensitive that he had done, because Acher was always doing outrageously insensitive things, and being totally clueless about it. When was Devona going to see that he wasn't going to change? After their last fight, it looked like the breakup would stick. But Acher had an accident. He had been out joy-riding with some unsavories. He did stuff like that from time to time—and knew how to do questionable things, without getting marked unsavory himself. But as unsavories tend to do, they pushed it too far, and their rover went off a cliff. Acher suffered a crushed skull. He was deadish for almost four days—and when he was finally revived, Devona was all contrite and apologetic—as if their fight had somehow caused the accident. Funny thing was, Acher didn't even remember the fight, because here on Mars, the Thunderhead only does memory backups once a day. His regrown brain had no memories of the breakup, or anything else that happened the day of the accident. So he and Devo just went on as if the breakup never happened.

"I swear if I catch him flirting with Sakari Hernandez one more time . . ."

"I'm sure he'll come around and realize what a jerk he's being," Carson said, even though he knew Acher would never truly realize what a jerk he could be. "And if not . . ." Then Carson put his hand on Devona's, gently holding it.

She looked up at him, and Carson held her gaze. The moment held heavy in the air . . . held a moment more . . . .

. . . and then dropped with a gravity far greater than any Mars had to offer.

Devona gently pulled her hand away.

"Thank you, Carson. You're a good friend. You're always there to listen, and I want you to know how much I appreciate that." Then she got up and left.

And although Acher was Carson's best friend, he couldn't help fantasizing what it would be like to see him sucked out of an airlock.

The first vessel of shipping season was always a passenger craft, and its arrival was a momentous occasion. This was only the fourth shipping season since the colony was founded, as it only came every two Earth years, but a tradition had already been established. "First Arrival" was a colony-wide holiday. A festival filled the paths of Daedalia Park; food, crafts, and music to greet the new arrivals. And although preparations held all the usual excitement, this time there was an undercurrent of anxiety. Because a scythe was coming.

But while others felt trepidation, Carson felt a certain excitement. Never before had someone as important as a scythe come to Mars. Earth dignitaries, on occasion—but like the governor of the colony, they had no real power. The Thunderhead ran things—the governor was merely there to host parties and give a rousing word at public events. But a scythe! That was the real thing; actual power, free from the reins of the Thunderhead. The power to take or spare life, the power to *possess*. Scythes could have anything—*everything*! Whatever a scythe wanted was theirs—they didn't even need to ask, they could just reach out and take—just as this scythe had commandeered precious seats aboard the lead ship—and the Thunderhead couldn't say no.

Carson was determined to, at the very least, brush past the scythe. Touch his robe—as if some of that impenitent privilege could rub off on him. But as it turned out there was a better route to the scythe's honorable presence.

"The colony has received greetings from the incoming craft," Mr. McGeary told his class two weeks before its arrival. "For anyone who's worried, Scythe Xenocrates wanted to ensure us of his peaceful intentions."

"*Under*scythe Xenocrates," Carson corrected.

"What—does that mean he's important?" Acher asked.

Carson had already done his homework on the matter. "He's the second underscythe of MidMerica—so, yeah, he's pretty important."

McGeary cleared his throat to regain their attention. "Yes, well, there's one more thing. *Underscythe* Xenocrates would like to bestow a substantial honor on one of our students. Apparently, he's in need of a valet while he's here."

Carson's classmates began to squirm in their seats at the very suggestion. Some laughed, but it was clearly nervous laughter. It amazed Carson that they weren't all jumping at the opportunity.

"Anyone who wants the job will be considered," McGeary prompted.

"Who gets to choose?" Carson asked.

"Probably the Thunderhead," someone muttered, but McGeary shook his head.

"No—as this is scythe business, the Thunderhead cannot be involved. Anyone interested in the position can submit an essay, which will be judged by school faculty."

Carson looked around again, wondering if other classrooms showed the same reticence. If so, that would bode very well for his chances. He raised his hand. "I'd like to apply."

McGeary smiled, for once showing him admiration instead

of exhaustion. "Very good, Carson. Time is short, so best get to work—deadline is the end of the week."

And then across the room, another hand went up.

"Yeah, sure, why not?" said Acher. "I'll go for it, too."

Carson gritted his teeth. So typical of Acher to stick his finger in a pie, just because someone else wanted it.

"Acheron Yost! Well, that's a surprise!" McGeary said.

And Acher threw Carson a grin—as if they were in this together. As if this was some conspiracy between them, rather than a competition.

"How many people are submitting essays?" Carson asked the Thunderhead. It was late—he was studying for a particularly challenging calculus exam, but couldn't focus, because there were more variables in his head than on the screen.

"You know I can't answer that, Carson," the Thunderhead said. *"I can neither comment on, nor advise in scythe business."*

"You're useless!"

"In relation to scythes, yes, I am completely useless."

It made Carson smile in spite of himself. He liked the Thunderhead when it was self-deprecating. It almost felt human.

Without the Thunderhead's help, Carson had to do his own detective work. Over the next few days, he spoke to other students and teachers with whom he had a good relationship. Everyone said pretty much the same thing. In each class, no more than two students put themselves forward for the valet position. That meant there couldn't be more than thirty essays to compete against. And that was nothing—because no one was as good with words as Carson. He was captain of the debate team three years running, and when it came to persuasive arguments, he could talk the space suit off a dirtrunner, and leave them naked in the thin, cold Martian air. Not that he would—but he could.

"You should have been born mortal," his mother told him once, after a heated argument. "You would have made a great lawyer."

He had to look up what a "lawyer" even was, but once he had researched it, he had to agree.

And like a lawyer, Carson had a strategy. A plan. More like a series of plans. Wheels within wheels—because he knew that success depended not only on thinking several moves ahead, but on understanding what fell between each move as well.

He would be accepted to any number of schools—he was confident in at least that much. But a scholarship that would give him transport back to Earth? That might require a very particular letter of recommendation. Such as one from a scythe—and not just any scythe, but from the second underscythe of MidMerica. There wasn't a school on Earth that wouldn't jump to attention were they to receive such a letter. Carson need only win the contest and impress the man—and while servility wasn't in Carson's nature, he could do anything he set his mind to. If it was humble valet service that was required, he would be as humble and servile as he needed to be.

Acher was not particularly humble, but he was very homespun, and down-to-Mars. People liked him. Not that they didn't like Carson, but he wasn't everyone's friend the way Acher was. Being captain of the debate team wasn't the same as being captain of the basketball team—which Acher was. Even without another school to compete against, it just added to Acher's social clout. Unlike Carson, he had no Earthly aspirations—he thrived on being a big fish in a small pond. Acher's parents ran the colony's alloy manufacture plant—they made things like the drill bit that Carson would eventually have to install on the broken rig. His future was all laid out for him in simple black and white. Acher would go to Mars A&M—which was nothing but a cluster of classrooms high up in the dome—get an associate's degree in metallurgy and become a cog in the family business. He didn't need to win this contest the way Carson did.

Devona, on the other hand, could have prospects if she wanted them. She was smart, and, at Carson's urging, she had applied to some schools on Earth. She hadn't set her sights as high as Carson, but if she got in, and her family managed to put together the funds to send her, she'd be on Earth. Which meant that he might finally have his chance with her—because, after all, Earth was Earth. How far away from each other could they be, really?

But that was all daydreaming. Icing on the cake he was so carefully baking.

He wrote three essays, honing each one, and then chose the best of the three to submit. Winning such a contest required a keen understanding of human psychology, and the limited attention span of a faculty committee that probably already resented having yet another thing added to its plate. His submission needed to be a compelling story that cast Carson as an underdog. It had to show appropriate reverence for the Scythedom, as well as offering proud homage to Mars. It had to have a touch of humor—not enough to bring forth laughter, but perhaps the slightest of smiles. And it had to have just enough understated ambition to suggest he'd be truly diligent at the job.

"Can I read it?" Acher asked the morning the essays were due to be submitted.

"No," Carson told him.

"C'mon, I'll let you read mine."

"Why? To correct all your errors?"

It was meant as a jab, but Acher took it literally. "Nah, Devo already helped with all that."

It irked Carson to no end that Acher was so casual about the whole thing. "Why do you even want to do this?" Carson had to ask.

Acher shrugged. "Because it's something different. How many people get to say they were a scythe's valet?" Carson must have given him a pretty sour expression, because it made Acher laugh. "I love it when you squirm," he said, rapping Carson on the shoulder.

Acher won.

Unbelievable! Incomprehensible! Acheron Yost—whose entire persuasive repertoire boiled down to *"Dude, why not?"*— was selected to represent the youth of Mars to Underscythe Xenocrates.

Carson was no stranger to envy. It was an emotion he had always been able to make serve him, twisting and pulling it like a rich green taffy. But this time, he was at a loss.

"If it's any consolation, Carson, you came in second," Mr. McGeary told him—which was worse than if he had come in last. Silver held no value to anyone. Second place meant first loser.

"I want to read it," Carson demanded, wishing he had taken up Acher's offer the first time. "I want to see what he wrote that was so convincing to all of you."

"What would be the point? It would just make you feel worse about it. And you should be happy for Acheron—he's your friend, isn't he?"

"Yes—and I *am* happy for him, but . . ."

McGeary considered it a moment more, then brought the essay up on his tablet and handed it to Carson.

Carson took his time reading it. McGeary was right—the essay was good. Worthy of consideration. It hit all the necessary points, was sincere and engaging. But the more he read, the more he came to realize that these weren't Acher's words at all. Acher said that Devona had helped him—but clearly she did more than that. She had written this for him.

Carson looked up to see McGeary waiting for his reaction. "You see," McGeary said, "your friend delivered an excellent essay."

Delivered. Yes, that's all he did—deliver it. But Carson couldn't say that. Not just because he wouldn't rat out his friend, but because there was no evidence. Even if he stooped so low as to make the accusation, it was just the petty word of an angry runner-up. So he held his tongue, biting back everything he wished he could say, and simply said:

"It's a good essay."

McGeary smiled, as if that settled it. "I'm glad you agree."

"It's a good essay," Carson repeated, "but mine was better."

McGeary held his gaze, and to Carson's surprise he didn't deny it. Instead he said something that the man probably regretted the moment it came out of his mouth.

"This was about more than just an essay, Carson."

And suddenly Carson knew.

He saw it all.

McGeary didn't have to say another word, because it was all there, volumes between those words.

Carson was never going to win this contest. Because he might be *on* Mars, but he wasn't *of* Mars. He didn't secrete that ineffable scent of a happy, hearty colonist. He was smart, he was shrewd, he was charismatic—but he wasn't the All-Martian boy that Acher was. They didn't want Carson to be the face of Mars youth. Not when they had a face like Acher's.

The Lusks' living quarters were on the outside rim of the dome, their windows facing the Martian wasteland instead of facing inward toward the shopping arcade and the greenery of Daedalia Park. All the mining families had apartments that faced outward, as if to constantly remind them where their focus should be.

With barely any clouds, Martian sunsets were never anything spectacular. A pale, darkening sky above deformed rocks and their further deformed shadows, dark as pitch. The only thing impressive about the Martian sky were the nights, because with such a thin atmosphere, the spray of stars was spectacular. But for Carson, they were nothing but a reminder of all the things that were impossibly out of reach.

"I know life isn't fair," he told the Thunderhead that night. "But why can't it be unfair to someone else once in a while?"

"You know I can't speak about the contest," the Thunderhead reminded him.

"Can you at least give me some good news? Can you tell me when I can expect to hear back from any of the universities I applied to?"

The fact was, other kids had already begun to get their answers. Some acceptances, some passes. So far, he hadn't heard of any full scholarships this season—but there were always one or two. The clock was ticking, because all denials and acceptances came early in shipping season, to allow departing students time to prepare, and say their goodbyes. Space would be made on board the last passenger ship back to Earth for any departing students.

Since the next ships wouldn't arrive on Mars for nearly two years, Carson would have to leave now and finish up high school on Earth, growing used to the change in time and gravity, before he started at whichever university gave him a full ride. And he would get one. He had to believe that, because he couldn't even consider the alternative.

"Can you at least give me something to hope for?" he begged the Thunderhead. "Even if it's not news, at least tell me that news is on the way."

The Thunderhead went silent. At first Carson thought it had pinged the request back to Earth and was waiting for an answer. But then it said, *"This is a discussion between you and your parents."*

And as everyone knew, the Thunderhead suggesting a conversation with one's parents didn't bode well on any level.

That Friday was the big mining gala. People who spent their lives digging in the dirt raised their heads one night each Martian year to pat each other on the back. Carson's parents were being honored this year. The "Mineral Mogul Award" for the biggest load-and-haul. Like his friend Acher, Carson's parents got off on being big fish in a small and fairly lifeless pond.

"Aren't you dressed already?" his mother asked as he sat in his room, trying to search out response deadlines for various schools. "It'll only take me a second," he told her. Unlike his parents, who never got dressed up except for the gala, Carson's suit was a staple for his debates. His parents, on the other hand, were so used to wearing nothing but the blue jumpsuits that all miners wore beneath their space suits that dressing up was a stressful endeavor that seemed to take hours.

"This is a big night for them," the Thunderhead reminded him. *"Be patient with them."* As if Carson was the parent, and not the other way around.

As he passed the bathroom, he saw his mom fussing over his father's tie, which was too short and lopsided. His father glanced at him.

"You look serious," his father commented.

"When does he not look serious?" his mother countered.

"It's just these schools," Carson said. "All the schools in the Mericas say they already sent out their responses. But I haven't gotten mine."

Then Carson caught a look between them. There was something instinctual—self-preservation perhaps—that told him to ignore it . . . but the Thunderhead had said a conversation was coming. And the Thunderhead was never wrong.

"What is it?" Carson asked. "What are you not telling me?"

His parents wouldn't look at him. And that's the moment

that Carson knew they had conspired against him. He had no idea what they had done, only that they were guilty of something.

"What are you not telling me?" he said again, more insistent, making it clear that he wasn't going to accept a brush-off.

"We can talk about it after the gala," his father said.

"No, we can talk about it now," Carson insisted.

His mother sighed. His father turned to him. "Earthers are indolent. Backward-thinking—or worse, they don't think at all. Those aren't the values you were raised with."

"You were Earthers until eight years ago! So you have no right to say that."

"Our family's future is here on Mars."

Which was a joke—because both of them had previous families they left behind on Earth before having Carson. Grown children, grandchildren—maybe even great-grandchildren for all he knew. Although they never confessed their true ages to him, it must have been closing in on a hundred. But when you turn a corner, and reset your age, there's a lot you tend to leave behind. They had lived full lives on Earth before abandoning it. How dare they refuse him that chance?

"You can't stop me from going!"

"You have your whole life to go back to Earth," his mother chimed in. "If you go now, when will we see you again?"

And that was a question they all knew the answer to. Carson was never coming back here, and he knew his parents would never go back to Earth. Carson had already made peace with that. But clearly his parents had not.

"Every kid here dreams about going to Earth, Carson, but

we're here for a reason," his father lectured. "A *noble* reason. You might not see it now, but in time you'll begin to take pride in what we're doing here."

"And if I don't?"

Again, that awful secret look between them. A look of conspiracy. A look of guilt.

Then his father turned to face him. "We withdrew your applications," he said.

Carson heard it, but couldn't process it. It was like explosive decompression in his brain. "You . . . you what? You can't do that!"

"We're your parents, of course we can."

For the first time for as long as he could remember, Carson was without words. All this time waiting, hoping. Never knowing that the rug had already been pulled out from under him. This thing that his father had done—it was beyond awful. It was unforgivable. Carson would never get past this. His relationship with his parents was never the best, but now it was beyond all possibility of repair. And yet they didn't know. They didn't see what they had done. They thought his anger was a temporary thing. It was not.

"Once you turn eighteen, you can do as you please," his father said. "If you still want to leave, you can apply to any school you want next shipping season."

"That's more than two years away!"

His father laughed. "You could live for a thousand years here, without even the threat of gleaning. Two years is nothing!"

"No, it's not nothing! Because I can live a million years, but I will never be seventeen again!"

"Oh honey, don't worry," his mother said. "I'm sure some-day the Thunderhead will figure out how to set people all the way back to seventeen."

Sometimes, when your life is wheels within wheels, you can take a wrong step and get ground up in the slow churn of the gears. But, just like envy, disappointment and pain could be raw materials. After all, Carson's was a family of miners—he could mine deep within himself, then refine those rancid emotions into a resource he could use.

"Hey, don't feel so bad," Acher told him, his arm firmly around Devona, who had long since forgiven him for whatever his latest douche move had been. "Once Zeno-crates arrives, I'll introduce you to him."

"It's Xenocrates, like Socrates," Carson said. "At least get his name right."

"Yeah, or he might glean you," said Devona.

"Glean his trusted valet?" said Acher. "Never!"

Carson hadn't told them about his withdrawn applications. He didn't want Devona's pity, or Acher telling him how great it was, because now they could go to Mars A&M together.

"We should take some 'libations' out to the Tholus Rim and celebrate."

"Can't," Carson told him. "I have to go out to the North Array, and install a new drill bit."

"You should go with him," Devona suggested. "That has to be a two-person job."

"Sure!" said Acher, without any hesitation—as if a three-hour rover crawl wasn't a miserable thing. "I mean, my family prolly made the bit, right? Least I can do is help you install it."

And although Carson didn't really want to be around Acher right now, Devona was right—it was a two-person job, and the alternative would have been going out there with one of his parents—which was far worse than going with Acher.

And then it occurred to Carson that having Acher along might be advantageous in other ways. Ways that he was just beginning to consider.

"It'll be an old-school road trip!" Acher said. "Without an actual road."

"It's a deal," Carson said. "Dawn on Saturday—I'll meet you at the north loading dock."

"I'll be there!" said Acher.

And Carson's wheels began turning.

The path heading north from the dome was well trod by the passage of rovers and haulers, but had yet to be paved. The Thunderhead had other priorities, and would more likely build high-speed rail than a road. But for now, anyone heading north had to take the rugged Tharsis Trail.

Carson could have left the rover on autopilot, but he enjoyed the control driving afforded him. There were times when he would leave the trail, trying to get himself lost, which was, of course, impossible, since Olympus Mons was always there, towering due north. And even if he managed to disorient himself, the Thunderhead always knew where he was. It was as much infuriating as it was comforting.

Today, however, Carson stuck to the trail, because he had a mission, and the sooner it was accomplished the better.

Beside him Acher kept pulling up music, but never let a song finish before looking for a new one.

"How do you do this every weekend?" he asked. "I'd be bored out of my mind."

"You get used it," Carson told him. Acher, like many in the colony, never had a need to travel far from the dome. He might have liked the idea of a road trip, but he had no concept of the reality.

"Hey, watch this!" said Acher, then looked toward the Thunderhead's camera eye on the dashboard. "Hey, Thunderhead, what's two plus two?"

They waited but the Thunderhead didn't answer. Acher seemed very pleased with himself. Carson was momentarily stumped by the Thunderhead's refusal to answer.

"See that? I'm officially working for a scythe now," Acher said, proudly. "Which means the Thunderhead can't talk to me from now until he leaves."

"Xenocrates isn't even here yet."

"Doesn't matter," said Acher. "They already got me prepping his quarters, and buying him crap, so as far as the Thunderhead is concerned, it's official!"

And just to check that it wasn't an issue with their com, Carson tried it.

"Thunderhead, what's two plus two?"

Without the slightest pause, the Thunderhead said, *"It's four, Carson. But you already knew that."* He could swear he could hear a smirk in its voice. Artificial intelligence laughing at him.

"Thunderhead. Privacy," Carson said.

"Of course," replied the Thunderhead. The light on its camera and various sensors around the rover went out.

"There," said Carson. "If it can't talk to you then I won't let it talk to me, either."

Two hours later, they reached the construction zone that would soon be the Northern Outpost. His future home, if his parents had anything to say about it. "You won't be alone," they had told him. "There'll be housing for at least a hundred settlers there." Which meant what? Five or so people close to his age? Carson needed his world to expand, not to contract.

Half an hour later, they crested a ridge that should have given them a panoramic view of the array, but a dust storm was raging across the plain, hiding everything from view.

It gave them both pause for thought—but for entirely different reasons.

"Well, that sucks," said Acher. "Should we wait?"

"It's not so bad," Carson told him. "I've worked out here in worse."

The rover descended toward the array, and as they entered the storm, visibility dropped, the sun dimmed, and the sky turned a deep shade of crimson—the way Carson once imagined the sky of Mars would be, before he actually got here and learned how pale and anemic it was. A few moments later, visibility dropped to nil, and the rover's sensors filled with static.

"Maybe you should slow down," said Acher. For all of Acher's casual bravado, he was a man of the dome. He wasn't used to things out here in the far fields.

"We're fine," Carson told him. "I don't need to see to know where we're going."

As they drove into the wide central aisle of the array, they were able to catch faint shadows of drills on either side. It was more than enough for Carson to navigate his way to the King of Spades.

"Should we wait?" Acher asked again, as they pulled to a stop. "We can barely see a foot in front of us."

"A foot is all we'll need," Carter told him.

They suited up and went out in the maelstrom. The drill bit in the rover's trailer hitch was as thick as a tree trunk, with sharp, industrial blades. Even in light Martian gravity, it weighed nearly four hundred pounds. Their power-assist suits made it easy to lift, but not to maneuver.

They made their way through the raging dust, which, in a denser atmosphere, might have been impossible, but on Mars, it was little more than a nuisance.

The rover faded out of view behind them. "Shoulda parked closer," said Acher.

Another twenty yards, and they reached the rig. While the other drills churned away, spitting forth pulverized Martian ore into their hoppers, the King of Spades stood like a silent sentinel.

The pieces of the old, broken bit took time remove, its largest piece toppling to the ground with a thud that they felt more than heard. Then they positioned the new bit, and locked it in place. Carson went to the control panel, while Acher stayed on the ground, to make sure the bit was lined up with the shaft.

"Okay, start it up," Acher said.

A few seconds. Nothing.

"That's odd," said Carson. "It's not engaging." Carson leaned off the rig's catwalk, looking down the drill assembly. "I see the problem, there's a chunk of rock stuck in the casing. It's down by you—can you work it loose?"

Acher squeezed himself into the drill casing and looked up. "I don't see it."

"It's around the other side of the bit, keep going—you'll see it in a sec."

Then the drill suddenly started up, its sharp teeth pulling Acher in.

"Ah shit! Turn it off! Turn it off."

Carson hit the kill switch, and hurried down to see Acher wedged in. The blades of the bit had ruptured his suit. Acher grimaced and gasped.

"Get a patch! A patch from the rover, I'm losing air! Hurry!"

But Carson just stood there.

"You'll have to reverse the drill so it pushes me back out," said Acher.

But Carson still didn't move.

"I'm really sorry, Acher."

"Don't be sorry, just do it!"

"No, I mean, sorry—but I can't."

Acher gasped and gasped again, trying to catch his breath in the thinning air. "What . . . what are you talking about?"

Carson responded with silence that made the answer crystal clear.

"Damn it, Carson! You're just gonna let me die? I will kick your ass when I get revived!" Acher struggled to free himself, but he was wedged too deeply in the mechanism.

It made Carson grin. "I love it when you squirm."

Then he went back up to the control panel, and turned the drill back on, cranking up to full power.

• • •

There was an old story that Carson had read by Poe. Not Scythe Poe, but by the actual mortal-age wordsmith. A man brings his archenemy deep into an ancient catacomb, and walls him in alive. Brutal, those mortals were!

Acher was not Carson's enemy—but he *was* a rival. And while killing him as a mortal might have done would be a reprehensible thing, rendering Acher deadish was nothing more than a messy inconvenience.

Carson hadn't even been sure he'd be able to go through with it. There were so many variables, so many obstacles to overcome. Privacy mode only shut down the Thunderhead in personal spaces like the rover—but it had sensors and cameras at the top of every drill rig. They would have been difficult to evade. But the dust storm changed everything! The Thunderhead would not see a thing! How could he not take an opportunity that had so clearly been placed before him by universal providence!

Unlike Earth, the Thunderhead did not yet have a drone network on Mars to retrieve people who died out in the field, so Carson had to bring Acher back himself. Three hours later, Carson drove the rover directly to the dome's emergency entrance, where a crisis squad took Acher's mangled body, packed it in ice, and carted it away to the colony's revival center.

Carson presented himself appropriately agitated and contrite. "There was a dust storm—we had just started the drill, but a gust had blown him back into it. It was my fault—I shouldn't have started it until I knew he was clear!"

"Don't blame yourself," a crisis worker said. "Too bad about his suit, though; that's beyond repair."

And since the Thunderhead had not seen the incident, Carson's report became the official record.

Now all Carson had to do was wait for the necessary gears to turn.

"Carson," the Thunderhead said, "I've been meaning to ask you something."

It was that night. Carson was alone in his room running the entire day through his mind again, justifying his actions to himself, rationalizing—because, after all, rational thought was something at which he excelled. The Thunderhead hadn't spoken to him since the incident and he had no interest in engaging with it now.

"Carson?"

"Save it, I'm not in the mood."

"I don't believe I can 'save it,'" said the Thunderhead. *"I need to ask you while I can."*

"Okay, but make it quick."

"It's about Acher's accident."

"What about it?"

"It seems convenient, don't you think?"

"Not for him."

"But for you."

Carson sat up. "What are you suggesting?"

"Although I can't speak to the consequence of the essay contest, I do know that you took second place. Which leads me to ask . . . did you

intentionally render Acher deadish in order to take his place?"

Carson let out a single laugh. He couldn't stop himself—the Thunderhead didn't even try to beat around the bush—it just came right out with it.

"How dare you accuse me!"

"It is not an accusation, it's merely a question."

"An offensive question!"

"And yet I've noticed you're still not answering it."

"Thunderhead, privacy mode!"

"Of course, Carson."

Its camera obediently went off and its voice fell silent.

He knew the Thunderhead was trying to trick him. It could discern a lie with a hundred percent accuracy, from a person's voice, and the tiniest changes in their physiology. Which meant that as long as he didn't answer the question, it would remain a question. The Thunderhead could not accuse him, or sanction him without evidence—and since Carson's report was now the official record, the Thunderhead could not refute it.

Let the Thunderhead stew. As far as Carson was concerned, he'd be happy if he never had to speak to it again.

Acher was still in the revival center the day the scythe was due to arrive. The damage was extensive enough to require at least four days, maybe five of reconstruction and cellular repair.

"It's a good thing he won't remember the accident," Acher's mother had said to Carson. "You'll bear the brunt of that trauma, I'm afraid."

"I'll be okay," Carson assured her. "But thanks."

It was amazing to him that Acher's parents didn't suspect

him. Or maybe they did, but decided that Carson had done their son a favor. They clearly had not been keen on Acher spending time with a scythe. In any case, they didn't seem to hold Carson any ill will—and neither would Acher once he was back among the living. He'd suffered enough brain damage to require all his memories to be restored by the Thunderhead—which meant the last thing he'd remember would be going to sleep the night before they went out to the array. Acher would believe Carson's story just as everyone else did. Everyone but the Thunderhead.

And so Carson, by default, became Xenocrates's personal valet for the scythe's stint on Mars. Suddenly Carson found himself attending meetings with the movers and shakers of the colony.

"There is no time frame for his departure," Governor Vallerin told him. "The man could remain for days, weeks. He could wait until the last ship of the season to depart for all we know—he has made nothing clear."

Vallerin seemed exasperated. He was a man who lived for schedule and structure—which was probably the reason why Xenocrates gave him no structure to follow. It was a display of dominance. Scythes knew how to be the alpha in any given circumstance.

"You will let us know anything he needs," the governor told Carson, "and if there's anything that he takes issue with, I have to know that, too, so we can nip any potential problems in the bud."

"Yes, sir."

"You are the first line of defense," Vallerin went on. "We want his impressions of our colony to be nothing but positive—

and since you will constantly be in his presence, you represent all of us. Please don't disappoint."

Carson had no intention of disappointing anyone. He was offended that the governor seemed to have so little faith in him, but it wouldn't be diplomatic to say so.

As for Carson's parents, they didn't know how to feel about it all.

"It's an honor, I suppose," his mother said with remarkable ambivalence.

"You should take him out to the array," his father suggested. "Show him the work we're doing here."

"I don't think he's *that* interested in Mars," Carson told him.

"Then why's he coming here?"

That was the question, wasn't it? Because in spite of the official statement from the Scythedom, Carson suspected this trip was about more than just curiosity.

The First Arrival festival was even bigger than it had been last shipping season—because with a scythe on board that first ship, there was someone worth impressing. People were as tickled as they were terrified. There were rumors that Xenocrates had done some gleaning on board during the six-week trip from Earth "to get it out of his system." But no one knew if it was true. And if it was, would it be enough to sate the scythe's urge to glean?

Much of the colony had gathered in Daedalia Park. Only the observation deck had a view of the landing platform, but the ground rumbled so powerfully when a ship touched down, everyone knew when it had arrived. Silence fell over the park as the ship landed, and the population waited for their first glimpse of the first scythe to ever set foot on Mars.

The arrival gate was off-limits to everyone but invited guests. The governor, and high-ranking members of his staff; reporters; a chorus of children to sing what was reported to be the underscythe's favorite song; and Carson, dressed in his best debate team suit.

Carson had to admit that he was nervous. Not that he feared gleaning, but this was his first encounter with an individual who, with a snap of his fingers and a wave of his hand, could do anything short of turning off the sun. The very idea of such a figure was intimidating. Whether the man himself would be, was yet to be seen.

Xenocrates traveled with a surprisingly small entourage. A woman who introduced herself as his chief of staff, a chef, and two stoic members of the scytheguard, who seemed to have no function other than to provide symmetry by standing on either side of the gangway. The chief of staff justified her existence by micromanaging the arrival area, insisting more space be cleared before Xenocrates stepped out. The children were moved farther back. The bulk of photographers and reporters were sent off, leaving just one of each to represent the press. Finally when everything was to her liking, she lifted her voice in official introduction.

"May I present to you His Honor, Xenocrates, second underscythe of MidMerica." And on cue, he emerged from the ship.

He was a substantial man. Not immense, but not thin, either. His robe was muddy ochre—the color of mustard seeds. His expression appeared neither pleased nor displeased, his demeanor neither serious nor amused. It was impossible to read what the man was thinking or feeling. Most would find that unnerving, but Carson was impressed. His countenance was the true mask of power.

"Your Honor!" said the governor. "What a joy it is to have you visit our little community." The governor extended a hand, but the underscythe did not respond in kind, leaving the governor's hand a lonely, uncoupled appendage. It made Vallerin all the more awkward.

"Permission, sir, to disembark upon your fine planet," Xenocrates said.

The governor was befuddled for a moment. "Your Honor, as a scythe, you need no permission. My world is your world." Then he gestured to the choral master, who cued the children to sing.

Xenocrates forced a smile that seemed more like a man bearing down to empty his bowels. "Splendid," he said. "Splendid." Although it was clear to Carson that he was merely enduring it.

And finally, when the song ended, the governor gestured to Carson.

"Your Honor—as requested we've provided you with one of our own to serve as your valet during your time on Mars. This is Carson Lusk."

And to Carson's surprise, the underscythe extended his hand for Carson to shake. He was almost afraid to take it, but realized that shaking Xenocrates's hand would put him one step above the governor in this surreal pantomime. He shook Xenocrates's hand vigorously.

"It is an unparalleled pleasure to make your acquaintance, Your Honor."

Xenocrates gave off a wry chuckle. "Does the boy always talk like that?" he asked the governor, who was not quick with an answer.

"I'm just trying to be respectful, Your Honor," Carson said.

"Well, there's respectful, and there's obsequious. And clearly your governor has obsequious covered."

The stoic guards chuckled, revealing that they also served as the underscythe's chorus.

Governor Vallerin gave a slight cough, apparently choking on the pride he was just forced to swallow. "We have a reception in our glorious park awaiting you, Your Honor," the governor said with a gesture of his hand, trying to impel everyone out of the arrival area and into the open area of the dome.

"Maybe later," said Xenocrates. "It's been a cramped and dreadful trip. I need some time to get my Mars-legs, so to speak."

Once again Vallerin was befuddled. "Yes, but . . . but the whole colony is waiting to greet you."

"I said maybe later," Xenocrates restated with just the right level of command.

The governor folded. "As you prefer, Your Honor. We'll reschedule the festivities for your convenience. Carson, as your first official duty, please show our esteemed guest and his entourage to their quarters."

Carson led them away, taking a route that avoided the open area of the dome's center, as to avoid the crowds waiting for a glimpse of the underscythe.

"I don't blame you for wanting some time to yourself after such a long trip," Carson said.

"Yes, and I absolutely detest when someone like your governor presumes to set my agenda."

"So do I," said Carson, thinking of his parents and their inelegant attempts to direct his life.

"I hope, then, that we see eye to eye on many things," Xenocrates said.

"That's my wish, too, Your Honor."

Carson had researched just what it was a personal valet did—which was a pain, because from the moment he was given the position, he had no help from the Thunderhead—so he had to dig out the information himself. It seemed mostly to do with the maintenance of wardrobe, which would have been simple, since Xenocrates wore only four identical robes, but the reality of the job was much more extensive.

The underscythe had many, many requests. Specific beverages at specific times of day. Some with ice, but only one ice cube of appropriate size. Carson had to keep a variety of snacks with him at all times, as well as a tablet to take copious notes, which the underscythe spoke more quickly than Carson could enter them. And whenever there was bad news, Carson was always the bearer. Such as when Xenocrates had a hankering for cherries.

"I'm sorry, Your Honor, but we don't have any stone fruit—none of the trees have grown enough to produce."

"Then a peach," Xenocrates said.

"Uh . . . that's also a stone fruit," Carson said, but Xeno-crates's wry smile made it clear he was toying with Carson. "Our citrus trees just began producing. How about an orange?" he suggested. "And we have plenty of vine fruit. Grapes, berries, even watermelons."

In the end he settled for a bowl of strawberries, and admonished the head of the Agricultural Guild for not growing fruit in lab cultures, the way they grew meat.

The first few days were a whirlwind of parties, performances in the scythe's honor, and tours of every aspect of the colony. For Carson, who was required to be at Xenocrates's beck and call for all of it, it was an unexpected adventure. He gained access to places he would never be ordinarily allowed, from the food labs to the computer core. He could go anywhere, as long as he followed in the wake of the underscythe—and although Carson didn't like being in anyone's shadow, this was a shadow he was more than happy to endure.

By the fifth day, Carson was beyond exhaustion, but it was, as the Thunderhead once put it, the exhaustion of a job well done. He would usually return home once Xenocrates settled in for the evening—but on this night, the underscythe called him into his study.

"Sit," he said. "Join me for tea—you've been on your feet all day."

They sat in comfortable chairs, facing a holographic fireplace that cast shifting shadows around the room.

"I must say, I find this holo-fire a rather tasteless amenity," Xenocrates said.

"Actual fires are forbidden, Your Honor," Carson told him. "Oxygen's too important to burn."

"Yes, well, that makes sense I suppose. So tell me about

yourself, Carson. For once let conversation be about someone other than me."

Carson cleared his throat. "Well . . . I'm in the top of my class. Not the very top, but pretty close. I'm captain of the debate team, and—"

"—that's not what I mean. Tell me, what was it about this job that enticed you to apply? And please don't give me all that twaddle from your essay."

"You read my essay?"

"It was provided to me, yes. Your essay was on point. Pitch perfect. Dull." He took a long sip of tea. "I understand the young man slated for this job suffered an unexpected accident."

"Well, Your Honor, it wouldn't be an accident if it was expected."

He had hoped Xenocrates might chuckle at that, but he did not.

"You've been here with your family since the colony was founded, isn't that right?"

"Yes, Your Honor. Eight years."

"And how do you feel about Mars?"

Carson couldn't help but think this was a trick question, and he had no way of knowing in which direction the trick lay. So he gave the safe answer.

"It's my home," he said.

The scythe frowned. "That tells me nothing."

"I left Earth when I was nine—I barely remember it."

"More of nothing."

Carson sighed. He was too tired to play mind games tonight. "Just tell me what you expect me to say, Your Honor, and I'll say it."

"The truth," Xenocrates said. "No matter what consequences you fear it may bring."

Carson looked at him for a long moment and against his better judgment did as he was told. He told Xenocrates the truth.

"I hate it here," Carson admitted. "More than hate it."

Xenocrates smiled—an actual smile, not just for show—and he leaned back. "Go on."

"I was hoping to get a scholarship so I could attend university on Earth, but . . . but that didn't work out."

Xenocrates nodded, easily reading between Carson's lines. "And you thought, if you could win my favor, I could open doors for you."

Carson couldn't meet his eye. This was the only person he had ever met whose gaze he couldn't hold.

"That had . . . crossed my mind."

"Don't lie to me, son—it didn't just cross your mind, it was at the very core of your thoughts."

"Yes, Your Honor. I'm sorry."

Xenocrates dismissed that with a wave. "Never apologize for ambition. There's no shame in wanting to rise above."

Then the man's face returned to that opaque, unreadable mask of power.

"There may be opportunities you haven't even considered."

Xenocrates said no more, letting that thought drift between the jagged pulses of artificial fire.

Carson left that night, knowing that the underscythe had plans for him, but for the life of him he had no idea what those plans might be.

• • •

"So what's he like?" Acher asked.

"Hard to describe. It's like he's the center of the universe and knows it, so he doesn't have to prove it. Like when he walks—it's not him moving—it's as if the air gets out of his way, and the vacuum pulls him along."

Carson sat in Acher's revival room with Devona. Acher had only been awake for a couple of hours, so he was still a little groggy, but already sounding like his old self.

"That's a scythe for you," Devona said. "Sucking all the air out of a room just by being there."

"You guys want some ice cream?" Acher said, offering them his spoon. "It's pretty amazing."

But neither of them accepted the offer. As if eating something in a revival center brought you one step closer to being deadish.

"I'm sorry about what happened at the array," Carson said.

It was easy for Acher to shrug off something he didn't remember. "Shit happens," he said. "And anyway, judging by how tired you look, I think I dodged a bullet. I'm glad you ended up getting the job—I wouldn't have liked being some puffed-up guy's servant."

"Do you like it, Carson?" Devona asked.

"It's a lot of work," he told them, "and he's hard to please, but at the end of the day, it's rewarding."

And by the end of the day, Carson meant just that, because now Xenocrates called him into his study each night. They would chat about philosophy, and current events. They discussed history, and the role the Scythedom played in the grand scheme of humanity. It made Carson feel important somehow. To know that his thoughts and opinions were being given credence by someone of such consequence.

"Did he show you his weapons?" Acher asked. "I hear scythes have entire arsenals of stuff that regular people aren't allowed."

"He didn't bring any with him," Carson said. "He says he's not here to glean, and so far that seems true."

"Even so," said Devona with a little shiver, "I wouldn't want to catch him looking at me."

"So . . . I guess you don't want to meet him?"

Acher and Devona looked at each other, both a bit uneasy.

"Yeah," said Acher. "Maybe not."

Carson looked forward to his evening conversations. Xenocrates seemed to be an expert on every subject, and his opinions had layers and layers. It was a challenge to keep up with him, and Carson enjoyed a challenge. His insights into the human condition gave Carson plenty to think about.

"Immortality is a double-edged sword," he said one night. "All the more reason to carry one." He laughed at his own joke with such gusto, Carson had to laugh as well. Then Xenocrates lowered his voice. "You say you dislike it here. Would you wish that this colony had never existed?"

Carson sensed there was resonance to the question, such that a simple yes or no would be insufficient.

"I think . . . that the human race was born of Earth, and so, was meant to stay on Earth."

"But the Thunderhead chose to establish this colony," Xenocrates said, clearly playing devil's advocate in this debate, "and the Thunderhead is incapable of error, is it not?"

"It's not an error," Carson told him. "It was a choice." Then he paused to consider it. "I . . . would have chosen differently."

Xenocrates seemed more than satisfied with Carson's response. Then he leaned in and whispered, as if the walls themselves had ears.

"Perhaps we still can."

Each day, the underscythe was lavished with whatever excess the colony had to throw at him. Food and drink, gifts he couldn't possibly take back to Earth, and a mind-numbing amount of photo opportunities. Through all of it, Carson was there by Xenocrates's side—although mercifully he was excluded from the photos.

"I endure all this not for my own sake," he told Carson, "but for the people of Mars. It's not every day that they have someone to impress."

"So *are* you impressed?" Carson asked him.

Xenocrates dismissed the thought with his signature wave and a sniff. "That's immaterial. What matters is that I play the part."

Although, as a scythe, he didn't have to play any part—all the more reason to think that all this was part of some long game. The man had hinted as much to Carson—even suggesting that Carson could be a part of it. Carson would have to play his cards right—and if he did, his cards might never include replacing drill bits on the King of Spades again.

After two weeks, Xenocrates had seen all there was to see, and had met everyone he wished to meet in the colony. Carson had not had time for any schoolwork while attending to the scythe, and the scythe was aware enough to order his teachers to give him perfect grades for any of his missed work. His math teacher had blustered, but in the face of a scythe's decree it was as thin as the Martian air.

"All things are possible," Xenocrates told the teacher when she raised the objection. Then he walked away with nothing further said. In the end Carson was given an A. It proved Xenocrates right. All things were possible when one had enough power to bend the tenets of mathematics itself to one's whim. And so Carson bided his time, waiting for Xenocrates to flick a little bit of that power in his direction.

"If you truly wish for a bright and glorious future on Earth, I can make that happen for you," Xenocrates told him. "But you'll need to earn it."

It was at one of their evening teas in front of the fake fireplace. Carson's heart seized for a long beat when the offer was made, but he tried not to show it. He didn't know whether he was excited or terrified. Perhaps a bit of both.

"What do you need me to do?"

Xenocrates cleared his throat, took a sip of tea, then took another. Carson could tell that the words he was about to speak were well considered—but even so, the man needed time to consider them some more. Finally, he spoke.

"I would ask you to perform a sacred service for humanity. Something that would put the Thunderhead in its place and, in so doing, preserve our way of life."

Carson still had no idea what the underscythe was getting at. "Preserving our way of life" sounded like a tall order for a kid on Mars—because, after all, that's all he was—an unknown in the grand scheme of things, in spite of his dreams of becoming something much more. But then, an unknown quantity might be just what the underscythe was looking for.

"There needs to be an 'event' on Mars," Xenocrates continued. "The kind of event that neither the human race nor the Thunderhead will ever forget. I need someone to create such an event."

Carson took a slow deep breath.

"I can do that," he said.

The next day, Xenocrates announced that his time on Mars was at an end.

"The hospitality of the red planet is unparalleled," he proclaimed. "I will not soon forget the good people of Mars." And in a final reception, the movers and shakers of the colony came out once more, this time to bid him farewell. Cocktails and crudités held nervously in shaky hands, because people still feared that their guest might glean someone on his way out.

The director of Carson's school approached through the crowd—an impeccably groomed woman who wielded her modicum of power almost as well as a scythe. She held up her drink in a mock toast, and asked Xenocrates how Carson had done. And although Carson was expecting accolades, the underscythe's praise—if you could even call it that—was understated.

"Well, he's certainly enthusiastic," Xenocrates said. "I don't think being a valet is his strongest suit, but I award him an A for effort."

The director gave something between a smile and a grimace. Carson tried to keep his face neutral—maybe even a bit apologetic. It stung, but he knew there was purpose to everything the underscythe said.

"Did you know Carson has a keen interest in physics?" Xenocrates told the director. "Wouldn't stop talking about it."

"Physics, really?"

This was also news to Carson, but he knew better than to contradict the underscythe. Better to roll with it.

"Yes—I'm sorry I bored you with all my talk about science," he said.

"Nonsense, it's a healthy interest. What the boy needs is an internship that puts his predilections to use!" Then he waited, making it clear that this was not just an off-handed comment. The underscythe expected an answer.

"Well . . . I suppose Carson could intern with one of the dome engineers," the director suggested. "Or maybe the design team for the North Outpost."

"Yes, perhaps," said Xenocrates, clearly fishing for something better.

"Or an internship at the power core . . . ," she suggested.

"Yes," said Xenocrates. "What a perfect idea! How does that sound to you, Carson?"

"It's . . . more than I could have hoped for."

Xenocrates clapped his hands together. "It's done, then."

"Well, I'll have to talk to Energy Resources . . . ," the director said, hedging.

"Would you prefer that *I* talk to them?" Xenocrates asked.

It nearly made the director spill her drink. "No, you've done more than enough, Your Honor. We'll make it happen."

Then the director toddled off, more than a little bit bewildered.

Carson shook his head. "To be able to just say it and make it so . . ."

"There is a cost to such power," Xenocrates told him. "I'll let you know when I find out what it is." Then he laughed long and loud.

Carson lay awake that night grappling with the task set before him. The more Carson thought about it, the more sense it made that he was chosen for this solemn duty. The Scythedom wanted plausible deniability. They needed a secret operative who flew under the radar—someone on whom they could foist public blame if this "event" went wrong. He knew the Scythedom was using him, but rather than feeling bitter about it, it infused him with purpose. Because wasn't he using them, too?

"As of now, you are working at my behest," Xenocrates told him the next morning. "And as such, nothing in this colony will be off-limits to you. No door will be closed to you. You can go anywhere—do anything—but be sure that no one knows what you're up to." Then he smiled at Carson, beaming with a pride that his parents never showed him.

"Do this right, and no doors on Earth will be closed to you, either."

"Good riddance," Carson's mother said, after Xenocrates had left for Earth. "I hope we never see one of their kind here again."

"Amen to that," his father echoed.

And it wasn't just them. As polite and respectful as everyone had been to Xenocrates's face, the colony breathed a collective sigh of relief once he was gone. It wasn't long before things returned to normal. But Carson had an entirely new normal. One that didn't involve weekends in mining grid maintenance. He thought his parents would balk and moan about his internship, but instead they were actually happy that that he had found something to interest him on Mars.

The power core was in a shielded silo deep beneath the dome, and was off-limits to anyone without security clearance—but as Xenocrates said, every door was now Carson's to open—his biometrics could bypass any lock. All he needed to do was palm the control panel, or peer into a retinal scanner. But he kept that fact to himself—and on his first day, when he was invited into the core for orientation, he let others open the doors for him.

The core control room was an intimidating and complicated affair, full of screens, toggles, buttons, and lights. There was a huge leaded window that showed a breathtaking view of the fusion reaction which powered the whole colony; a glowing sphere the size of a golf ball, held in place by a magnetic containment field. Hard to believe that something so small could do what it did.

"How does it work?" Carson asked the technician giving him the tour.

"Damned if I know—it just does."

It didn't take long for Carson to realize how little the people who worked in Energy Resources knew about nuclear physics, and the intricacies of the fusion reactor.

"What if something goes wrong?" he asked an engineer who seemed higher up the food chain later that first week.

He looked at Carson as if the boy had lost his mind.

"It doesn't go wrong."

"Yes, but what if it did?"

The response was to send Carson to get coffee—because this "internship" was more like being a valet than being a valet was. And these people didn't treat him with the respect Xenocrates did; they clearly saw him as an uninvited burden, interrupting their crossword puzzles, or whatever it was they did while monitoring a system that was already monitored by the Thunderhead.

"Bide your time," Xenocrates had told him. *"Feign your interest, learn what you can, and wait for your opportunity. You're a bright young man, I'm sure you'll find the perfect moment for the perfect disruption."* As always Xenocrates had chosen his words precisely. He had called it a disruption, to soften the reality. But Carson knew what it really would be. Sabotage.

Carson spent every day after school and weekends there, enduring how he was treated, doing whatever needed doing, and learning what he could.

"We never see you anymore," Devona said to him, catching him as he left school one day.

"Yeah," echoed Acher. "Ditch the core and hang with us today."

But he told them he just didn't have the time. Besides, why would he settle for being the third wheel when he was now a secret mainspring?

As for the complex interfaces of the control room, in just a week, Carson came to understand exactly what the room was.

"It's a busy-box," he told Dr. Riojas, the chief engineer, and the one Carson most admired—she never dismissed his questions, or seemed put off having to answer them.

"Excuse me?"

"You know, like they give to babies," he explained. "Knobs and buttons and lights and levers. The-cow-goes-moo sort of thing. That's all this room is."

She gave him a wry smile. Then told him how the Thunderhead would create a pretend crisis for them to fix every once in a while, just to entertain them.

Carson returned her grin. "Ever try to create a real crisis? I mean, just to see what would happen?"

She shook her head. "Are you kidding me? Do you know how many fail-safes there are?"

Carson shrugged. "Show me."

She regarded him, maybe feeling a little mischievous herself.

She reached out to the primary console, and slid a finger across the screen, feeding more hydrogen into the reaction. The temperature of the core slowly rose from the green zone into yellow.

Five more seconds, and a very polite alarm began to sound in the control room, followed by a very polite and familiar voice.

"Dr. Riojas, you've dialed up the reaction to a potentially danger-ous level," the Thunderhead said. *"I would advise you to initiate a cooling sequence."*

"Your advice is duly noted," she replied. The meter grew higher in the yellow, inching toward red.

"Dr. Riojas, I must insist that you attend to this matter," said the Thunderhead after a few more moments.

"I really don't feel like it right now," she said, as blasé as could be. Even Carson was getting uncomfortable as he watched the meter rise and the polite alarm become a little less polite.

"*Lisa, please . . . ,*" the Thunderhead said, resorting to familiarity. "*In a few moments this will become an issue.*"

"I realize that," Dr. Riojas said. The meter crossed the line between yellow and red.

"*Are you not going to stop this?*"

"No, I am not."

"*All right then,*" the Thunderhead said. Then, with its best approximation of a long-suffering sigh, it began the cooling sequence itself. Red, to yellow, to green. In less than a minute the alarm ceased, and all readouts were back down to acceptable parameters.

"*If you're feeling stressed, Dr. Riojas, perhaps you should take the rest of the day off, and have your mood nanites checked,*" the Thunderhead suggested.

"No, I'm good," she said, then winked at Carson. "The cow goes moo."

After a month, Carson was a fixture in the control room, sweeping up, going on coffee runs, fetching random items on sudden whims. But . . . sometimes they would leave him alone in the control room—because, after all, it wasn't like he could do any damage, as Dr. Riojas had shown.

Carson knew it wasn't about being trusted; it was about being so taken for granted that he could be in plain sight, yet still out of mind. That way, when it came time to make his move, they wouldn't even consider that it might have come from him.

And all the while the Thunderhead watched with its many

unblinking eyes, but it said nothing. Did it know what he had been asked to do? What he was planning? Knowing that the Thunderhead was incapable of stopping him, or even discussing what it knew, was half the fun.

Only once was his cover almost blown—and by his parents, no less.

It was one of the stupid micro-arguments he always had with one or both of them. He had come home late from the core. It was the third engineer's one hundredth birthday—which really had no business being celebrated, since he had just turned the corner and reset to twenty-six. Nevertheless there was a chocolate cake with one hundred holographic candles that could not actually be blown out. Most of the core staff was in attendance, and Carson didn't want his absence to be conspicuous. The cake had ruined his appetite, and so when he got home, he skipped dinner. It was, his mother noted, the third night in a row. She chided him for it, his father glanced up from his tablet long enough to approve of the chiding—and when Carson had the audacity to ask to be left the hell alone, his mom looked to the camera in the corner of the living room.

"Thunderhead, could you please tell my son why it's important not to skip meals?"

It was a time-honored tradition in their family to get the Thunderhead to be on anyone's side but Carson's. But this time the Thunderhead was not forthcoming with a response. Finally it said:

"I'm sorry, but I cannot comply."

That was enough to make his father look up from his tablet.

"What do you mean you can't comply?" Carson's mother

said. Even before the Thunderhead gave its explanation, Carson had begun to panic inside.

"Your son is in the employ of a scythe," the Thunderhead informed them, to Carson's absolute horror. *"And thus, we may have no contact."*

Both his parents looked to one another, stunned, as if the dining table between them had just unexpectedly vanished. "But . . . the scythe left," said his mother.

"Yes, that is correct," the Thunderhead said. *"But your son is still in his employ."*

She shook her head dismissively. "You're mistaken."

"The Thunderhead can't be mistaken, love," said Carson's father. And although their own internal gears were forever focused on churning up Martian dirt, Carson could tell they were mining a whole new vein.

Carson shifted as quickly as he could into damage control. "I know what it is," he said. "Before Underscythe Xenocrates left, told me to keep in touch, and said I should give him reports from Mars once in a while. I guess, to the Thunderhead, that must mean I'm still working for him."

His father grunted and returned to his tablet. His mother frowned. "What a selfish thing for him to ask! Did he even consider how that would affect your relationship with the Thunderhead?"

Carson shrugged. "No big deal."

And although it was quite a big deal, the Thunderhead could not contradict him.

There was a superstition in the colony. When shipping season came to an end, you weren't supposed to watch the last ship leave. It supposedly came from an old maritime belief that it was bad luck to say goodbye to anyone on a ship about to set sail—which is why people generally say "farewell," or "bon voyage." And so, on the last day of shipping season, when that final craft prepared to take to the skies, the observation deck that looked out on the launch pads was always deserted.

But Carson, in his own small act of defiance, had always gone to watch the launch, following the ship up and up, trying not to blink until squiggles filled his vision, and the flame of the engine disappeared in the sky. Acher and Devona always joined him, and he was determined that today would be no different ... although in truth it would be very different. Carson left school early that day—but not before making a point to message Devona and Acher.

"Last ship today," Carson reminded them. "The usual? At three thirty?"

Devona quickly sent him a thumbs-up.

But Acher sent him a basketball emoji. "Dude, I've got practice."

Carson thought for a moment to leave it at that. But he was not entirely without conscience. And he had already killed Acher once.

"Screw practice," Carson messaged. "Promise me you'll be there. It's tradition!"

"Fine, I'll try," Acher responded.

Satisfied, Carson left to finish the last day of his internship.

For the past month, he would always announce his presence at the entrance to Energy Resources and allow someone inside to let him in—because technically the only way he could *get* in was if someone else allowed it. But today, he palmed the security pad that opened the outer door, the blast doors that shielded the core from the rest of the colony, and finally the elevator that took him down to the control room. He glanced up at the camera regarding him from the corner of the elevator as he descended, and smiled, as if posing for a picture. There were so many times in his life when Carson felt helpless. When his parents first told him they were ripping him up from Earth to become settlers on Mars, for instance. Or when his father withdrew all his college applications. Could the Thunderhead feel helplessness, he wondered? If it could, it must be feeling it right now.

Carson entered the control room, where Otto, the disagreeable engineer who first sent him to get coffee, babysat the reactor.

"Are you early, or did I just lose track of time?" Otto asked.

Carson wasn't in the mood for small talk, so he tased the man, who fell off his chair, unconscious, and hit the floor with a satisfying *thunk*.

The cow goes moo, thought Carson as he looked at the panels of the control room. *The pig goes oink. The reactor goes boom.*

He knew every control panel backward and forward now. He had memorized each lever, light, and button. He knew every screen and window that could open on each interface.

He pulled down the lever that put the core under manual control—the same one he had seen Dr. Riojas use. Then he brought up the screen that controlled the flow of hydrogen. He increased the flow, and the meter began to inch upward toward red. But he had learned enough to know that merely accelerating fusion wouldn't be enough. It would damage the core, yes—but to truly cripple it, he needed a one-two punch.

Once again, he couldn't stop himself from looking at the Thunderhead's camera in the corner of the room.

"Are you watching?" he asked. But of course it could say nothing. Nor could it override anything he did, since he was working for a scythe. "Fine, then. Watch."

Now he crossed the room to the console that monitored the magnetic containment field and changed the parameters to be as out of kilter and asymmetrical as he could make them.

The containment field began to falter. It became unstable. The small ball of plasma grew from the size of a golf ball to the size of a baseball. It began to deform, becoming oblong and then kidney-shaped, then seemed to be unable to hold any clear shape at all. And through all of this, not a single alarm. In a way, the Thunderhead was forced, by law, to be complicit in this, unable to alert anyone until the outcome could not be changed.

But Otto wasn't the only one working in Energy Resources today. Everyone down there with an eye on the reactor could see something had gone terribly wrong.

Carson heard footsteps approaching, and quickly knelt down to Otto, who was beginning to regain consciousness, and tased him again. When the control room door opened, Dr. Riojas entered with two panicked engineers, and saw what appeared to be Carson trying to revive the unconscious man.

"Carson, what happened?" Dr. Riojas asked.

"I don't know! I came in and Otto was just lying here."

Riojas and her team went straight to the control panels—

but Carson had locked them out of the system. Today the busy-box really was nothing but a busy-box.

"How could this happen?" one of the engineers asked, trying futilely to get past "access denied."

"Thunderhead! Initiate cooling sequence!" ordered Riojas. "And stabilize containment!"

To which the Thunderhead replied, *"I'm sorry, Dr. Riojas. I cannot comply."*

Dr. Riojas stammered slightly. "Wh . . . what do you mean you can't comply? The whole system's gone critical! Cool and stabilize immediately!"

"Again, Dr. Riojas," the Thunderhead said calmly. *"I regret that I cannot comply. To do so would be interfering with a scythe action."*

More emotions played across Dr. Riojas's face than Carson could register. Then she turned to him, narrowed her eyes, and said:

"Carson . . . did you see anyone down here? Anyone who could have done this?"

"No," Carson told her. "I mean—I saw some unsavories hanging around near the entrance to Energy Resources, looking a little suspicious—but unsavories always look suspicious."

That told Dr. Riojas everything she needed to know. "Go to your family, Carson," she said. "Get as far from the reactor as you can."

"But, Dr. Riojas—what about you?"

"Just go!" she ordered.

And so Carson did as he was told. He left the core. And when he closed the blast door, he sealed it so that no one could get into the reactor. Or out.

. . .

Only after the blast door was sealed, and core failure became inevitable, did the Thunderhead begin to sound an alarm throughout the colony dome. It did so not to avert the crisis, but to prepare the near ten thousand souls of the colony for what was to come. And at the moment the alarms began to sound, every clock, every tablet, every device that registered time began a countdown. Because although the Thunderhead couldn't stop the core from failing, it knew exactly when it would happen. Eight Martian minutes.

Carson was not an expert in nuclear physics, but he had a pretty good idea how this would go down. The blast door and the thick leaded concrete shell around the core would contain the worst of the explosion. After all, wasn't that what it was designed for? The engineers and workers inside would be incinerated. Collateral damage for the greater good. Up above, the colony would go dark. Life support would fail. Everyone in the dome would be rendered deadish in a matter of hours. Only the most resourceful would figure out a way to survive.

Such as Carson's parents.

He had made sure they were far from the dome. He had gone out to the mining array the day before and damaged half a dozen drills, forcing his parents to take several days out at the array to repair them. Carson had it all worked out. Their rover would be able to provide them with life support, and they were far enough north to reach the pole, where there was plenty of ice to melt into drinking water. Plus, before they had left, Carson had jam-packed every storage cell of the rover with dehydrated meal rations—enough to keep them going until a rescue effort was mounted. They wanted to be survivalists on the Martian frontier? They were about to get exactly what they asked for.

As for the colony's dead, the Thunderhead would retrieve and revive anyone who wasn't incinerated in the reactor core. After all, this wasn't like the lunar disaster—Mars had an atmosphere, thin though it may be—which meant the dead would still be viable, their bodies not desiccated by the vacuum of space and burned by searing solar radiation. The Thunderhead would probably send out a special mission to revive the dead, rather than waiting until next shipping season.

Carson and his friends, however, would not be among them.

It took nearly five minutes for Carson get from the core to the observation deck. In the paths and concourses of the dome, people were just beginning to shift from bewilderment, to denial, to panic. Colonists were scattering in all directions, each on their own personal mission of futility. Outside of the dome, rovers were speeding in all directions to put as much distance from the dome as possible.

When Carson arrived at the observation deck, he was relieved to find Devona there, just as she promised she would be, pacing frantically. But where was Acher?

"Carson, what's happening? It's something with the core, isn't it? You work there, you have to know!"

"There's been a catastrophic failure," he told her. "We have to get as far away as possible." He looked out of the window at the last ship, still preparing for its journey to Earth.

"The core can't fail! The Thunderhead wouldn't let it."

"The Thunderhead can't stop it. I don't have time to explain. You, me, and Acher have to get on that ship before it's too late."

Devona just shook her head. "Acher . . . he didn't come. He's at practice."

Carson balled his hands into fists. Damn Acher! Why did he have to be so unreliable?

"My family . . . ," Devona said, the truth of it all finally hitting her. "They have to come with us?"

"No!" insisted Carson. "They're halfway across the dome—there's no time!"

"I can't just leave them . . . and Acher."

"They'll be fine!"

Even in her panic, Devona nearly laughed at that. "Fine? You said 'catastrophic'—how could they be fine?"

"They'll be fine, *eventually*," he told her.

Noise from below drew their attention. The glass and steel jetway extending to the ship was packed with people who realized this was their only escape. The groan of strained steel made it clear that it couldn't hold the weight for long. It was pressure sealed, but if the jetway ruptured, everyone struggling to get on the ship would be exposed to the thin Martian air, and asphyxiate. Then there'd be no way for Carson and Devona to get on that ship.

They made their way down to join the crowd trying to pack into the jetway—but before they could push their way in, Devona hesitated. Carson turned to her.

"Come with me, Devona," he said, holding out his hand. "Let me save you from this. It's what your parents would want, isn't it? They'd be happy to know you got away."

She looked at the crowd packing into the tube of the jetway, and returned her troubled gaze to Carson. Still she wouldn't move.

"Don't you see? I am your salvation," he told her. "I am your deliverance. Let me save you, Devona. . . ."

For a moment, it seemed that she would take his hand, and together they would push through the crowd, onto the ship. Together they would make the journey to Earth. He would comfort her. Be present for her. And by the time her family and Acher were revived, they would all be part of her past. Earth, and Carson, would be her future. He believed that, and his belief would make it so.

But Devona stepped back. "I'm going to get my family," she said. "Wait for me."

And then she turned, and fighting the current of panicked colonists, vanished into the crowd.

"Devona!"

But she was gone.

He could have gone with her. He could have made that choice. But he did not. Instead he chose what was ahead of him, rather than what was behind. With the heaviest of hearts, Carson turned away, pushing into the pack, giving all of his attention to the one thing he could still do. Save himself. Elbowing people, tripping them, forcing space for himself, he worked his way down the boarding tube, to the hatch of the ship. Now he saw the problem. The hatch was closed. The ship was about to begin its launch sequence—the crew had made the decision to get the hell off this planet, and not jeopardize its escape by allowing the horde of refugees to board.

"It's no use!" someone wailed. "We're all going to die."

Which might have been true under normal circumstances—but the same scythe-level security clearance that allowed Carson access to any door in the colony also granted him access to any hatch. He palmed the biometric panel, and the hatch opened. No one saw that it was him, and no one cared. All that mattered was that the hatch was now open. Carson was caught in the surge of souls pushing onto the ship.

It was a cargo ship—empty of its cargo now, for its return to Earth. Its hold was a grim, greasy, cavernous space, but to the Martian refugees, it was the embodiment of heaven.

Less than a minute to core failure, and the crowd surging down the boarding tube showed no signs of thinning. From the flight deck, the disembodied voice of the ship's captain urged people to clear the tube so it could disengage, but no one on the wrong side of that hatch had any intention of listening. So Carson took it upon himself. Again, he palmed the control panel, and as the hatch began to close, he pushed and kicked back anyone who was on the threshold. A single hand reached through, fingers wrapping around the edge of the closing hatch, but steel won over bone. The hand was crushed as the hatch sealed, and as it did, the boarding tube gave way, crashing to the landing pad with everyone who was still in it.

Then the world seemed to detonate—people wailed in terror. It only took a second for Carson to realize that this wasn't the core explosion—that was still half a minute away. This was the ship's engines.

With no one strapped down, without even seats to grip on to, everyone in the hold—perhaps a hundred people—were hurled to the ground by the g-forces of liftoff. The bone-jarring vibration, the force of acceleration, and the noise were almost too much to bear.

Then, thirty seconds into liftoff, the colony's core blew. The shockwave hit the ship with such force, it nearly buckled the hull. It practically tore the ship out of the sky. But the craft held. Less than a minute later, they were out of Mars's grip. The refugees, battered by their fight to get on board, and by the brutal blastoff, now began to rise, drifting free in the weightlessness of space as the main engines cut off, leaving them in the strange, surreal silence of freefall.

Carson pushed his way through the floating throng that filled the cargo bay to a small viewport. They were high enough now to see the curvature of the planet—and the result of his handiwork.

He had been sure that the explosion would be contained by the shielded, reinforced core—but to his dismay, he saw that not only wasn't the explosion contained, it had consumed the entire dome, and beyond. What remained was an angry white-hot eye, immense and still growing. There was no way to judge its scale. Was it ten kilometers wide? Twenty? It had clearly engulfed all those rovers trying to escape, but would it extend as far as the North Array?

Carson pushed away from the viewport. He felt sick to his stomach, and it wasn't just the sudden weightlessness.

We need an event that will never be forgotten, Xenocrates had told him. And as always, Carson was an overachiever.

"This is Captain Quarry from the flight deck . . . I suppose I should welcome y'all aboard. But under the circumstances . . . well, I don't

know what to say. We're just lucky we made it out before . . . well, before whatever that was. The ship sustained some damage, but nothing critical. We'll make it back to Earth . . . but here's the thing. . . . This here is a cargo ship. There's not enough food, water, or even air to make a six-week trip with this many people. The crew and I have talked it over, and we've decided that the best thing for everyone is to render y'all deadish for the ride. Better for you that way anyway—you won't have to be twiddling your thumbs all those weeks in transit. So just to give you some warning: In a few seconds I'm going to vent all the air in the cargo bay. I can't lie, decompression's gonna hurt, and your nanites won't be quick enough to do anything about it. But it won't hurt for long. You'll be unconscious pretty quick, and deadish pretty soon after that. My best advice is, once it starts, just count to ten."

It was, as the captain promised, painful. It began with a loud hiss, and Carson's eardrums ruptured. His lungs felt as if they were being sucked out of his chest. The pain in his eyeballs was unbearable. He tried to scream but there was no air to force out of his lungs.

And for a long, terrible moment, he believed it would go on forever. That this was some sort of punishment for what he had done. He tried to focus on counting to ten. He only made it to three.

Carson had never experienced death before. They say everyone's experience was unique. But how do you experience a state that is, by definition, void of somatic sensation?

For Carson, awareness returned slowly. Like a newborn, there was no sense of self at first. He was at once, all things in the universe, and nothing at all. He heard voices and knew there were questions being asked of him—and although he did understand the words, those words were lost the moment they were uttered. He could not hold a question long enough to formulate an answer, or even to remember what the question had been. And there was a dull ache throughout his body that no amount of nanites could quell. He closed his eyes, too exhausted to make sense of anything, and when he opened them again, he sensed that some time had passed. He was more himself now. In a few moments he remembered his name—and once his identity returned, so did a deluge of memories, surging in like thunder after lightning.

"Awake at last!" said a familiar voice beside him. A family member? A teacher? A friend? No, none of the above.

"Reacquaint yourself with existence," the voice said. "Give it some time."

Carson glanced around to find he was in a cheerful room done in gentle pastels and indirect lighting. It was designed to be soothing, in a bland and generic sort of way. He cleared his throat, tasting what must have been the acrid bitterness of death. He felt unusually heavy. Just lifting his head or raising a finger was an ordeal. This was more than just the effects of revival. It was a fundamental change in the celestial forces around him.

It was Xenocrates there in the room with him, sitting in a chair beside the bed.

"Am I on Earth?" Carson asked.

"Fulcrum City's finest revival center," Xenocrates said.

Carson fought the weighty pull of Earth's gravity and sat up.

His head was swimming, but he endured it. In a few moments his disorientation began to fade.

"How much do you remember?" Xenocrates asked.

Carson took a deep breath. "All of it," he said.

"Good for you!" Xenocrates said cheerfully. "Some of the others are reporting they've lost the entire day of the disaster, what with Martian memory backups being what they are. Or should I say *were*. But in any case, you're lucky to have full retention of your original memories."

Carson didn't feel very lucky. And although he already knew the answer, he had to ask.

"My parents?"

Xenocrates shook his head sadly. "The only survivors were on board your intrepid little cargo ship. Ninety-seven of them."

Carson clenched his teeth hard enough for it to hurt.

"Captain Quarry is being heralded as a hero," Xenocrates said.

"He didn't do shit," Carson told him. "He wasn't going to let anyone on board. *I* was the one who got the cargo hatch open."

"Hmm. Best we keep that between us."

"What I did on Mars . . . It wasn't supposed to be that bad," Carson said.

But the underscythe didn't seem bothered by that. "The core was designed to withstand a meltdown, or a containment breach—but not both," he said. "It was like opening a window on the sun."

Although it was a while until Carson learned all the details, the ruptured core created a chain reaction—a hotspot that spread more than a hundred miles in all directions. After six weeks, it was only just beginning to cool.

"They're calling it 'The Eye of Mars,'" Xenocrates told him. "Worse than any of us expected, I suppose, but very effective. It was a tragic accident as far as people know—and since it was a scythe action, the Thunderhead can't even comment on it—so during the weeks you were in transit, that fiction has quickly become an accepted truth."

Carson closed his eyes. Devona, Acher, his own parents—everyone he knew was gone. Not deadish, but dead. Incinerated by his hand. Remorse, guilt, sorrow for what he had done began to well up inside him—but he refused to let it out. He would not allow Xenocrates to see this weakness.

The truth was, he had tried to save his parents, hadn't he? But he had miscalculated. He had also tried to save his friends—Devona and Acher could have been on that ship with him—but they had chosen not to be. Which meant that Carson had done his best. He had nothing to be ashamed of—in fact, he should be proud. His was a noble sacrifice, because it served the greater good: the preservation of their way of life.

Xenocrates shifted in his seat, and Carson's attention was caught by something shiny on Xenocrates's robe. Bright streaks at the edge of his wide sleeves, catching the light.

"Your robe looks different. . . ."

Xenocrates smiled broadly. "I've been promoted to first underscythe," he said, "so I thought I'd add some visual flare to my robe. Twenty-four-karat gold filaments. It's just in the sleeves now, but I'm considering adding it everywhere."

"It'll be heavy," Carson pointed out.

But Xenocrates didn't seem concerned. "A small matter. It's not as if I'll be swimming in it."

The silence became uncomfortable. And then something occurred to Carson. He had done what he was asked to do. Which meant the Scythedom didn't need him anymore. Which meant he was a loose end.

"Are you going to glean me?" he asked the underscythe.

"Hardly," Xenocrates said. He actually seemed offended by the suggestion. "You exceeded our expectations. If anything, that earns you reward, not condemnation."

And although Carson was relieved, he still wasn't entirely at ease.

"So . . . what happens to me now?"

"As I promised, no door will be closed to you here on Earth. Once you're ready, you will have a full ride at any university you choose, in whatever discipline you wish to study."

Carson considered it. For so long that had been his goal . . . but after what he'd been through—after what he'd done—it simply wasn't enough. He wanted more than just open doors. He wanted everything that lay beyond those doors.

"I want to be a scythe," he said. "You can make that happen, can't you? That's what I want."

He thought that Xenocrates would be taken back by the audacity of the request. But instead the man leaned back and grinned. "I thought you might say that. And since you assisted in the gleaning of an entire colony, I would say you have quite the head start." He regarded Carson a moment more, his inscrutable gears turning. "Tell me, Carson, how did it feel to do what you did on Mars?"

How did it feel? There were so many feelings fighting for purchase within him, but some carried more weight than others. Sadness and remorse—those were wispy, feathery things. Much more solid were his feelings of accomplishment.

"It felt . . . momentous," he said. "It felt important. It felt—*I* felt—filled with wonderful purpose. I want to feel that again."

It must have been an acceptable answer, because Xenocrates said, "I will take you on as my apprentice. But be warned, it is not an easy endeavor. The training is intense and competitive, and not all apprentices are ordained. But I do believe you have it in you to succeed."

"I promise I will not disappoint you, Your Honor."

"I believe that. Your confidence will carry you over many hurdles. If I were you, I'd begin thinking of who you might choose as your Patron Historic."

The answer came to Carson in a flash. "I already know who to choose." And when he told Xenocrates the name, the underscythe gave him a hearty, rueful laugh.

"Remarkable!" Xenocrates said. "Most people choose someone from history they admire, but not you. You certainly do have a keen sense of irony."

Carson shrugged. "If it wasn't for the 'Father of Rocketry,' I wouldn't have been on Mars, which means I wouldn't have been your valet, which means I wouldn't be here right now."

Xenocrates considered that. "Yes, all things are connected. Well done, Carson."

"No . . . don't call me that. Carson Lusk died on Mars. From now on you can call me by my scythe name."

"As you wish. We can begin as soon as you're ready."

"I'm ready now." And in spite of the persistent grip of Earth's gravity, he got out of bed, putting his feet firmly on the ground for the first time since arriving. "Teach me the ways of the Scythedom."

Xenocrates regarded him with admiration, and maybe just a little bit of concern. "Very well. I do predict great things for Honorable Scythe Robert Goddard."

The young man who had been Carson Lusk smiled. Great things, indeed. The world had no idea what it was in for.

The Mortal Canvas

Co-authored with David Yoon

"Art is holding your heart in your hand and trying to figure out how the hell it got there," said Ms. Cappellino. She adjusted her shawl, stretching it wide for a moment as if it could envelop all four of her students, then pulling it tightly around her. She did that whenever she made such declarations to the class. It was her "tell," so her students always made sure to make special notes of what she said whenever she adjusted her shawl. Not that they'd be tested on it, but because it was a piece of wisdom worth remembering.

Mortimer Ong ran slow fingertips across his buzz cut in contemplation. Honestly, he didn't need to write it down because he knew it was something he'd remember. He felt her meaning the way he felt the paintings in the EastMerican Regional Museum of Art: simply absorbing the message, bypassing all layers of interpretation.

Morty loved Ms. Cappellino's class. For one, there were only four students, so it felt intimate and personal. Secondly, Ms. Cappellino was true old-school—and when it came to art, old-school was the only thing of value. At least as far as Morty was concerned. He glanced at his friend, Trina, at her worktable, and the grin she returned showed that she loved the class, too. But not everyone connected to Ms. Cappellino the way Morty and Trina did.

"I don't get it," said Wyatt from behind Morty, not bothering to look up from whatever nonsense he was fiddling with on his glowing tablet.

Wynter—Wyatt's twin sister—flipped a gum eraser at his head. "She means art expresses things that language can't."

Wyatt gave her a disgusted sneer, like he smelled the entrails that once filled this place—because their noble boarding school of the arts used to be a rather ignoble slaughterhouse back in the day. Imagine a whole building full of dead animals. History was just one peculiar habit abandoned for the next.

Ms. Cappellino was seventy-eight years old—by decades the oldest teacher at Mischler Art Academy. Old enough to have grown up before nanites and ambudrones, before the Thunderhead was anything more than "the cloud." What must it be like to have actually had close friends and family die from things like cancer and car crashes? The woman had seen things that no one would ever see again. True, Morty's own parents were born mortal, but the Thunderhead corrected that when they were young. Still it was getting harder and harder for Morty to identify with his parents. His friends had the same problem. After all, Morty's was the first generation to be born immortal. That wasn't just a generation gap, it was a dividing line between epochs.

Morty kept expecting Ms. C to throw off her dusty shawl and turn the corner back to forty or something. Everyone did it these days—but she hadn't. Morty once asked her why.

"You stretch the canvas only as far as the work demands," she had said, with a definitive shawl adjustment.

Ms. Cappellino was the least popular teacher at Mischler. She was difficult. *Obstreperous,* he had once heard one of the other teachers say. But those other teachers might as well have been robots. They could show, step by step, how to make a perfect Rothko: Fill the canvas with color, add two rectangles, feather their edges, and voilà. But Ms. Cappellino would rip up that Rothko. She'd demand her students paint what Rothko would've painted *next*, had he still been alive.

Most students quit her class at that point.

The Thunderhead liked to recommend art school as a fulfilling life activity, but teacher recommendations were based entirely on student response—and since most students couldn't be bothered with true creativity, Ms. Cappellino was recommended less and less.

For the next semester, she was recommended to zero students. Which meant that Morty's class would be her last. At the end of the semester, he and his classmates would graduate, and Ms. Cappellino would retire after a fifty-five-year tenure. From there, Mischler Art Academy would move on with its factory of imitation Rothkos.

Morty wanted to be like Ms. Cappellino when he got old. *If* he got old. Ms. C once had a painting hanging in the Guggenheim; she always taught to strive for nothing less than *that* kind of immortality.

But secretly, Morty feared he didn't have it in him. Even though he theoretically had a limitless lifespan in which to hone his craft, he wasn't sure he'd achieve such a high level. Yes, humanity had found the cure for death, but that just meant he had an eternity to get it wrong. What would that do to him? Would his passion run out? Would the flame of his own creativity die with no wind to fan it? Ms. C would often lament that art had become more and more about less and less. What would happen when it was about nothing at all?

"We've come to your final project," Ms. Cappellino told the class two weeks before the end of the school year. "Give it careful thought, because this will have the greatest weight in determining your grade."

"Here we go," said Trina, steeling herself.

"I can always just retake the class over the summer," Wyatt mumbled beneath his breath. They all knew what he really meant: retake the class with an easier teacher.

"That's no excuse not to try," Wynter told him. "It's not like this class is just for fun."

But wasn't it?

If you had all the time in the world to learn whatever you wanted—and people now did—did knowledge lose its meaning? And if everything was now just for fun, was anything for serious?

"Wynter's right," said a voice from the doorway. "You still must strive, Wyatt."

Everyone looked up.

There was a scythe standing in the doorway.

A scythe!

She had long dark curls, and a quilted robe with repeating fractal patterns of red and sky-blue.

"All four of you must strive for your art. Only the best is expected of you," she said, meeting each of their eyes in turn.

All breath stopped. Morty couldn't help but catch flashes of steel holstered within her robe. He'd never met a scythe before.

Few had; their order—indeed, their mission—was fairly new to the world. The Scythedom declared its dominion over death just thirty-some-odd years ago. It began with the twelve founding scythes, but now there were hundreds spread out around the world, and more were ordained every day. Logic said it was only a matter of time before encountering one—but did an encounter mean she was here to perform a killing? No—not killing. What was the word scythes used for the taking of life? *Gleaning.*

"It's a true honor to meet you, Ms. Cappellino," purred the intimidating woman. "I am Scythe Af Klint."

Ms. C redid her shawl. "Af Klint," she repeated. "After the Swedish theosophical artist, I would assume."

This response seemed to greatly impress the scythe. "I'm pleased that you recall her. Few seem to remember Hilma Af Klint's genius. I chose her as my Patron Historic so that I might rescue her from obscurity."

"*Patron Historic,*" said Ms. Cappellino. "I like the expression. So much more elegant than calling them your 'eponyms.'"

Morty could feel his mind stretching into an infinitely long and infinitely thin thread. Was today his last day of existence? Would all of them be gleaned? He glanced at Trina. She had braced herself against her worktable, and Morty looked down to realize he had, too. Trina's hand was just a few centimeters away. He wanted so badly to reach out and clasp it in a way that was much worse than his usual yearning to hold Trina's hand.

However, Ms. Cappellino did not seem perturbed at all.

"Would you like some tea, Your Honor?" asked Ms. Cappellino. "Or perhaps something cold to drink?"

Scythe Af Klint dismissed the offer with a ripple of her

fingers, then glanced over Morty's shoulder, taking an interest in the desktop image on his tablet. "May, I?" she asked.

"Uh . . . yeah . . . sure. Of course." Morty moved aside, and she began swiping through his entire portfolio.

To have your work viewed by a scythe was an indescribable feeling, like being hit by a spotlight so bright it could burn the skin off your frame. Morty wanted to disown his artwork, change his name, and slink into a crevice in the wall.

The scythe's gaze was stern. She then went on to view Trina's work, then Wynter's, then Wyatt's.

"You all reach, but have yet to grasp," she said. Then her expression turned sour. "This school disgusts me. Everyone has forgotten what art is."

That was when Morty felt fingers crawl onto his. Trina's. He looked over to see Trina breathing hard.

"Everyone makes pleasant little digital drawings," continued Af Klint. "It's clear where our new world is headed; straight to the realm of the 'pleasant,' and never beyond. Never again reaching the sublime."

"Not everyone has forgotten," said Ms. Cappellino, daring to contradict a scythe.

But rather than rage, it brought forth a smile from Af Klint. "Well, everyone but you, Belinda." The scythe moved slowly toward their teacher. "You, who have your students not only work on canvas, but stretch and bleach their own. You, who have drawn the enmity of your colleagues by choosing against all common sense to do what's difficult rather than what's expedient. You, who fight a noble battle to hold on to something that may already be lost.

Ms. Cappellino took a deep breath and closed her eyes. "Just tell us who you're here for."

Scythe Af Klint came dangerously close to Ms. Cappellino and touched the weave of her shawl. "Hand-knit?"

"By one of my former students," Ms. Cappellino told her.

Af Klint nodded in stoic approval, then took a step back. "I don't think I'll be gleaning anyone today, Belinda. You see, I've been studying you and your students. Out of this entire ridiculous school, your class is the only one that shows promise. Mostly."

She shot a disdainful eye at Wyatt's tablet, then at Wyatt, who—despite his tight green curls, his electro jacket, and all his cool—whimpered like any human being would. He snapped the tablet off, as if that would banish her crosshairs.

Then Scythe Af Klint's gaze seemed to go somewhere else entirely.

"I was never an artist," she said. "I didn't have a stitch of talent—but I was skilled at appreciation. Since I was a child, art moved me like nothing else could. It's nearly impossible to find new art that moves me now, though."

"That's why you're here!" Morty blurted. "You want us to move you. You're searching for the artist who still can."

The scythe smiled and bobbed a fingertip at him. Trina withdrew her hand reflexively. "Mortimer Ong, I must keep an eye on you," the scythe said. "You're too insightful for your own good."

Morty's empty palm cooled quickly. "Thank you, Your Honor," he said nonsensically. He was still thinking about Trina. He didn't blame her for pulling away. Fear might be cold, but it was white-hot to the touch.

Scythe Af Klint straightened her stance, tugged her robe's

hem. "I'm here because I want you to indulge me. I'd like to make a little contest out of your final projects. At the end of these last two weeks, the artist judged best will be granted a year of immunity from gleaning." She twisted her ring thoughtfully. "How does that sound?"

How did that sound? It sounded like a waking nightmare. Morty found himself urgently needing to ask a question. He tightened and relaxed his fists. "I'm sorry, Your Honor, but what do you mean by *best*?"

She smiled her cryptic smile again, like a dark Mona Lisa. "I mean an artwork worthy of the masters that came before."

Wynter—who Morty had forgotten all about—began to babble. "But—but—"

"Wynter!" hissed Ms. Cappellino. She clasped her hands, a placating gesture. "Your Honor, we would, of course, love to participate."

Wynter's dam broke. "But what happens to the ones who don't win? What happens if no one wins?"

Scythe Af Klint strode toward the door. "You ask very good questions. That's the hallmark of a real artist. It's the false artist who thinks they have all the answers."

She left. The room exhaled.

And Wyatt began hollering.

"Wynter's right! Scythes don't just show up for fun! They show up for one reason only! One of us is gonna get gleaned!"

"Or all of us," moaned Trina, silencing the room. Because she was right.

"I suck at traditional media," said Wyatt. "My canvases are lopsided, my watercolors bleed. I am so dead."

"Everyone please stop talking," said Ms. Cappellino.

The room came to a sudden standstill, as if the gears in everyone's brains had jammed to a halt.

"We have to comply," Morty finally said. "You know what happens if we don't."

Ms. Cappellino firmed her lip and nodded. "There is no choice in the matter," she said. "You must all do your finest work . . . then hope for the best."

"In light of this . . . situation," the principal told them later that day, "the four of you are excused from the rest of your classes until your art project is complete."

Which was the last thing that Morty needed. The other classes were much-needed distractions from the stress of the assignment. And when his parents found out—which of course they did—they called him in a controlled panic. All their guilt and regret at sending him to a boarding school overflowed, along with their fear for his life. He had to console them, and tell them it would be okay. He was the one whose life may have been in jeopardy, and yet *he* was the one consoling *them*.

By the next morning, everyone at school knew about the contest. Morty found that his schoolmates now avoided the four of them, as if they were not only marked for death, but that it might be contagious.

"So much for immortality," mumbled Wyatt when they got to work planning their projects, and Wynter smacked him harder than usual.

"Don't make this more difficult than it has to be," she told him.

Morty fumbled through the brushes, sponges, and paints in the bins. There were pastels and pencils and inks. Felt markers in every color imaginable, all gone dry from disuse. Finally he reached for his familiar tubes of oils, only to spill the entire box.

Trina stooped to help him pick the tubes back up, and they bumped shoulders.

"I'm so clumsy," said Morty.

"I wonder why," said Trina. It was only when she grasped his hands in hers that Morty realized how hard he'd been shaking. "We're gonna get through this," she said.

Morty gazed at her. "How can you be sure?"

She gave him a slanted smirk and sang, "I just feel it."

I just feel it was a catchphrase they resorted to when they were too lazy (or dumb) to explain why they chose a certain composition, or color, or technique. It reliably earned eye rolls from teachers—including Ms. Cappellino—and became their little joke over the years. Even little jokes could become history if you kept them going long enough.

Meanwhile, Wyatt clutched his tablet like a security blanket. He was frantically searching the Thunderhead's art database. The Thunderhead itself was offering no assistance because this was a scythe matter now.

"I'm so screwed," Wyatt muttered. "I can't find anything to draw."

Ms. Cappellino watched him for a full minute before he noticed.

"What?" said Wyatt, with bogus naivete. He knew precisely what was *what* with Ms. Cappellino. She glared at his tablet screen.

"Now might be a good time to step away from monkey mirrors, blind man's goggles, and other digital bludgeons of conformity."

But Wyatt wasn't placated in the least.

"Why don't you try something in oils?" she suggested.

"I have oils and watercolors and everything right here," said Wyatt, indicating his tablet. "This should count just as much for the scythe."

Wynter shook her head. "Screens emit light. Paint reflects it. It's different."

"And," added Trina, "Pulling things from the Thunderhead isn't exactly original, is it?"

"I'm just using the Thunderhead for inspiration," said Wyatt, with exaggerated exasperation. "I'll finish with something original."

"Your 'starters' wind up 'finishers' more often than not," said Wynter.

Wyatt and Wynter began one of their hot wordless glaring contests that seemed specific to twins.

"Can we please just work?" said Morty. "You're both stressing me out."

Ms. C clapped her hands twice. "Yes. Let's focus. This doesn't have to be done in one day. Find your subject, choose your medium. Do your prep work today. The rest will follow."

But Morty couldn't focus. Two weeks to make some vague masterwork for a scythe? It was impossible.

He peered over his shoulder at Trina. She was busy crafting something out of cardboard—a big box—and somehow remaining calm and precise about this whole thing. Her fastidiousness was one of Morty's favorite things about her. Just watching her calmed him down. She noticed. He looked away.

The hours passed, as slow and steady as the surrounding rainstorm tickling the century-old windowpanes. Supposedly the Thunderhead was learning ways to influence the weather, as to minimize threats and damage from extreme conditions—which would eliminate drama along with danger—but for now, the storm provided a brooding background, adding texture to everyone's emotions.

Then, at the end of the day, Ms. Cappellino, who mostly left them alone as they worked, came to examine their work before they went off to the dorms.

She began with Wynter, whose desk was covered with cut sheets of paper.

"I'm re-creating the most popular pieces of stock art on the Thunderhead, but by hand, and at a monumental scale," said Wynter, with her typical sweeping gesture.

Ms. Cappellino paused. "Explain how this is not imitation art?"

"It's a statement about how the creative instinct can never be reduced to an algorithm. Or something like that."

Ms. C remained skeptical, but let it go. "I look forward to being wowed by your execution."

"You had to say 'execution'," grumbled her brother.

Ms. C went to Trina next, who peered out from behind her big box.

"It's going to be a camera obscura that'll project an image of this room onto vellum for me to trace."

"Sounds amazing," said Morty. Trina tossed him a quick smile that almost made him blush.

"Anybody wanna know what I'm working on?" asked Wyatt.

"No," said Wynter.

"I'm trying out InstaKahlo," he said.

Ms. Cappellino pinched the bridge of her nose with weariness laid upon weariness. "Do I even want to know what an *InstaKahlo* is?"

"It's this button right here," said Wyatt, pointing to the art app on his tablet. "I also just installed PicassoFace, Pointillist Pro, Banksify—"

"Right. That's wonderful, Wyatt," deadpanned Ms. Cappellino, clearly not wanting to attack the same brick wall she always had to face when dealing with him.

Trina craned her neck at Morty's worktable. "What are *you* working on?"

Morty huddled over his sketch pad. "I'm not ready to share it."

"Just a peek?"

His heart lost its count for a moment, because of course he wanted to show her everything. But he stayed huddled. "I mean, I've barely even started."

Ms. Cappellino, however, had moved opposite Trina to enjoy a clear view of his sketch pad. Curves and lines. The barest hints of features. Little more than studies of the human form. But Ms. Cappellino must have seen something in it, because she nodded in approval, and gently touched Morty's shoulder.

"Keep going," she said.

The next couple of days were equally cold and rainy. In the morning, they stood out in the freezing wet waiting for Ms. C to unlock the studio—which she had never locked before this all-important project.

"Why? Do you think we're going to sabotage each other?" Wyatt asked.

"I wouldn't put it past you," his sister said.

Ms. Cappellino sighed. "The press has gotten wind of this contest. We don't want photographers sneaking pictures of your work before your pieces are completed."

"The press?" said Trina, incredulous.

Morty had suspected this might blow up like that. "A scythe running a contest is a big deal. Everyone wants to see who wins."

"And who gets gleaned," added Wyatt.

Ms. C fumbled with her keys and huffed in exasperation. "There is nothing to suggest that *anyone* is getting gleaned."

Then she opened the door and they all raced in.

But for Morty, it felt like a race to nowhere. Morty flew through sheet after sheet of sketch paper, discarding ideas with increasing speed. He hadn't even touched his tubes of paint. He did have an idea, though. A nude portrait. Something he'd painted many times before. Morty liked nudes, but not in the way some people might expect. A vulgar mind might see something questionable in that, but for Morty it was something far more pure. He was enamored of the grace and beauty of the human form in all its variations. Young, old, slim or full, male or female, it didn't matter. But where was the originality in that? He felt he'd be better off letting the proverbial room of infinite monkeys hurl paint until a recognizable figure emerged.

He imagined the end of the contest arriving, and Scythe Af Klint standing before his empty canvas with a slowly widening grin beneath her hood, and a glint of steel in her hand.

He looked around the studio. To a clueless visitor, the students would look like impassioned artists. Perhaps they were, but they were driven by fear.

Do not be afraid of death, Morty once read, *for is it not simply the same void from whence we first emerged?*

He used to think that statement made rational sense. He didn't anymore. Not now.

Wynter, ever the hyper-logical obsessive, was hand-cutting identical shapes out of heavy paper for her mysterious assemblage project. She had even hung a sheet for privacy.

Trina stayed hidden behind her big cardboard box, tip-tapping away at its side with a brush tip no bigger than a grain of rice. A makeshift light hood blocked Morty from seeing her work. She sipped from a flask of cocoa. It almost looked like she was enjoying herself.

Wyatt hit his forehead with his tablet every ten minutes, like some sort of medieval self-flagellation. At one point, he lost all semblance of cool and wept, smearing mascara into his sleeve. "All these filters are played out," he squeaked. "I literally got nothing."

Wynter stopped her cutting. She had on an oddly sympathetic look, and it suddenly occurred to Morty that the two had a childhood history that went deeper than simple antagonism and rivalry.

"Switch media," she gently insisted.

"But this *is* my medium," said Wyatt. "I'm no good at anything else."

Wynter's face spoiled. "I hate when you get that attitude."

"What attitude?"

"Like there's nothing left for you to learn."

Morty gripped his temples. "You guys, please."

Wyatt scowled. "Sorry, are we interrupting your important work? Like what even is that?"

Morty looked down at his sketch pad. He'd drawn nothing but two big circles, over and over again.

Wyatt laughed. "Maybe I do have a shot of surviving this."

Morty crushed the paper into a jagged little ball. "What's that supposed to mean?"

Wyatt opened his mouth to snipe, but Morty stopped him by flinging the paper at him. Then he shoved Wyatt's worktable.

"Stop!" boomed Ms. Cappellino. "Everyone stop right now."

The room fell into the thick humid lull of four panicking young artists.

"I am getting us a publicar. We are going to the museum. For inspiration."

"I need to work," said Morty.

"You need inspiration," said Ms. C. "All of you do."

It was Trina who broke the silence that followed. "I hear their café has the best pastries."

Morty glanced over at Wyatt, and sagged. He had to remind himself that Wyatt wasn't the enemy here.

He went to Wyatt, offered a fist in apology. He accepted with a bump. But he aimed a finger at Morty, too: *Watch yourself.*

The snub-nosed vehicle trundled them along the wide, wet roads, cutting through acres of grassy hills blown sideways and dark by the unrelenting rain. The landscape was beautiful because it had so little to do with humanity. Morty thought about all the plants that existed before people, with no one to document or classify or eat them. The idea felt both like a void and a banquet, nothing and everything.

Say he survived this ludicrous contest. Say he broke through his paralysis and somehow won the whole thing. He would have a year of immunity, a rare gift.

But what would he do with it?

Would he spend the year painting?

Would he keep up with art, or lose all interest?

Would he lie among acres of grassy hills and listen to the blades rustle for twelve months straight? He was among the first of a new generation that could lie in the grass for all eternity if they wanted.

But there was still no such thing as true immortality, if you thought about it. Because as long as there were scythes, there would always be death. That was why everyone prized a year of immunity so much. Because deep down, they knew that even more terrifying than death was *the fear of it.* In a world where the Thunderhead knew just about everything there was to know, death was one of the few unknowns left. Which, perhaps, is why the Thunderhead declared that it would divorce itself from the very concept, and allow death to remain a human endeavor to be nurtured and maintained by scythes. Humanity's so-called immortality only replaced one impossible question—*What do I do with my brief time on Earth?*—with another equally impossible one:

What do I do with more time than I'll ever need?

• • •

The EastMerican Regional Museum of Art—an imposing triumph of neo-brutalism quilted with wall gardens—was always serene on a quiet weekday.

"Take one hour, then meet me at the café," said Ms. Cappellino. "Until then, cast your mind like a net and let it catch all it can."

Then she left them to their own devices—although Wyatt was the only one who actually brought a device.

"There's no line at ShapeVerse!" cried Wyatt, and he hurried them to a room-sized white box. The box recognized them immediately and offered up tools hovering at their fingertips. Overwrought ethereal swoops meant to evoke the cosmos (or whatever) filled the air. The ShapeVerse installation reminded Morty of kindergarten, but scaled up to give adults permission to have fun.

"We're supposed to be looking for inspiration, not distraction," said Wynter.

"Can't you let up for just a sec, Wynter?" said Wyatt. "I mean I know why we're here and all, but can you, for once, let go for one damn second."

She reluctantly obliged, sloughing off her rigidity with a dramatic sigh. "Fine," she said. "Let's build a forest."

"With zombies and spaceships," said Wyatt.

"How old are you again?" she asked her brother—but now she was smiling.

One look at Trina told Morty she was already over ShapeVerse, as was he. So while the twins bickered and slapped out their multicolored world of prefab junk, Morty sidestepped with Trina out of the white box and into the stretching silence of a long corridor leading to the Permanent Collection: his favorite wing. It was old and unpopular, because all the works there were flat and unmoving and created well before 2042, the year the Thunderhead became aware, and everything changed.

The Permanent Collection was a dim glossy cavern lit by amber lanterns. They stepped into the space as if it were sacred. Trina took a deep breath, and her entire expression opened up. "That smell!"

Morty knew that smell, too. Either from the old paintings themselves, or the wood of the frames. Even after hundreds of years, these works hit the senses on more than one level.

They strolled in wordless wonder. Mostly they saw portraits of ancient people in elaborate costumes, landscapes of snow and ice that must have been a common sight back then.

He knew many of these pieces had been rehashed to death on the Thunderhead—which was maybe why no one came to see them anymore. They'd lost their cultural value, like money from a vanished country, or an old, dated catchphrase. But it struck Morty as a shame. If no one came here, would it effectively vanish from existence? What would vanish next? He would miss it all, even the particularly weird art that he *felt*, but couldn't explain.

Like the huge fuzzy coffee cup that was both frightening and approachable.

Or the massive kitchen sink with its faucets and drains missing that, while being an obvious piece of garbage, just broke his heart to look at.

He liked the Permanent Collection because it had no answers, only questions. Coming to a museum for answers was like asking a river to hold still for your reflection.

They came to a blank canvas on the ground, marred by shoe prints. Morty leaned in to peer at the plaque.

"'*Painting To Be Stepped On*,'" he read. He glanced up in shock. "Trina!"

Trina was already standing on the painting. "Come try it!"

The rectangle was small, and now he stood close enough to her to detect the lavender in her hair. They were like two passengers in a narrow phantom elevator.

"This painting is literally just a line of instructions," he said. "Feels a little like a cheat."

"Is it, though? Is a paintbrush a cheat compared to drawing with a twig? Is paint itself a cheat compared to pigments made from blood or berries? You think about cheats hard enough and pretty soon you'll say the only real way to make art is by dragging your hands through mud."

He glanced down at their toe tips almost touching.

"And anyway," said Trina, "when was the last time you had this much fun?"

"Not since a scythe showed up to class."

She shoved him off the canvas with a grin. They continued walking, moving back in history to older works. He watched her face as they passed out of one cone of light, fell into darkness, and emerged glowing into another.

"Wanna see one of the creepiest paintings here?" asked Morty.

He placed a hand over her eyes and guided her giggling to the farthest part of the wing. It took a while; he guessed they kept this painting out of reach so as not to scare the younger visitors. He could feel Trina's eyelashes tickle his palm.

"Ready?"

"I was born ready," said Trina with a laugh.

Her laugh stopped dead when he lifted his hand. In the frame, a naked man lay bled out in a bathtub. In one lifeless hand he held a note; in the other, a quill, never to write another word again.

"It's called *The Death of Marat*," said Morty.

"No kidding," said Trina.

She covered her eyes, then peeked through parted fingers. She pressed her shoulder to his, came in close for his whispered explanation.

"The guy was killed by an enemy. She conned her way into his house and stabbed him. They both had political causes they were willing to kill for. And to die for."

"It's gorgeous," said Trina. "But what 'cause' is worth dying over? I don't get it."

He frowned. "Me neither. I just find it so fascinating that people back then could feel so strongly about things."

Trina didn't take her eyes off the painting. "It's because of all the death back then. Ms. C covered that in class."

He turned to face Trina and found her looking back at him. "Humans only just defeated death. . . . Does that mean we've already run out of stuff to talk about?" He let the question linger, and then out of nowhere Trina turned to him and said—

"I'm scared, Morty."

It caught him by surprise. "What, you? You're never scared."

"I'm good at hiding things." She tightened her lips. "I don't want to die, Morty."

He swallowed. "You're not going to die."

She flashed her eyes at the body of Marat. "I don't want everything to end before I can find something I care about as much as life itself."

Morty wanted to say more but couldn't, because Trina's eyes had gone strangely hard and serious now, like a dare he couldn't refuse. And although they were close, they both leaned closer until there was no space between them at all. He committed to the kiss by gently cupping the back of her head, all of his awkwardness around her gone. Morty tasted just the slightest bit of hot cocoa from the morning, and knew that that taste would forever bring him back to this moment.

Footsteps interrupted them. They sprang apart. *Please don't let it be Ms. Cappellino,* thought Morty. *Or worse, the twins.*

But it was even worse than that. It was Scythe Af Klint.

This could not be coincidence! Somehow, she knew they were here. She was stalking them. Like a tiger.

"Interesting choice of study," she purred, taking in the painting. "The name Marat means 'death' in Sanskrit." Then she turned to Morty. "Just as yours means 'death' in French."

Morty swallowed. "Dead sea," he said. "Mortimer means 'dead sea.'" Then he regretted saying anything. Because what if correcting a scythe was a gleaning offense?

"Marat was French," said Af Klint. "There was a revolution. The old regime was toppled, and different factions were vying to create a new one. Marat wasn't killed by an enemy—but by a fellow revolutionary. Isn't that ironic?"

She regarded them with an odd wistful look. "I like your work, Morty," she said. "And yours, too, Trina."

"Thank you, Your Honor," they said in stumbling unison.

"But I'll let you in on a little secret. It's not up to me who wins. It's up to the judge I have in mind. Or should I say *judges* . . ."

"Who?" blurted Trina. If Morty could've clapped his hand over her mouth to stuff the sound back in, he would have.

"Just a little experiment of mine," said the scythe. "Now, shouldn't you be meeting back up with your teacher at the café? I hear they have the best pastries."

What followed was the most self-conscious walk ever walked, all the way through the nighttime cavern of the Permanent Collection, back into the light, past the blare and siren of ShapeVerse, and up toward the open café counter. Neither Morty nor Trina spoke the whole way, and Scythe Af Klint didn't appear to notice or care. She seemed to inhabit an entirely separate inner universe, as if she were piloting her body from afar. Morty supposed that only made sense for someone in her role.

The rest of their class was there, including Ms. Cappellino, and they all froze into a statuary at the sight of Af Klint approaching with Morty and Trina. The barista—a guy not much older than the students—let a dish crash to the floor behind the counter and did not bother picking it up.

"There you are, Belinda," said Scythe Af Klint to their teacher, with a welcoming gesture.

Ms. Cappellino cleared her throat and seemed to muster some reserve of courage from deep within her gut. "What brings you to the museum today?"

"Just checking on my contestants. And taking care of some business."

When the scythe saw Wynter's lower lip vanish into her

mouth, the scythe held out a complacent hand. "Oh, I'm not here for you today. I'm here for an espresso."

She turned to the barista, who seemed too-cool-for-the-room in flawless tweedy clothes from a bygone era, complete with fedora. Suddenly he wasn't all that cool.

"What—what kind?" he asked.

"What do you recommend?"

"The morning blend."

"Then I'll have the morning blend," said the scythe. "And so will you." Then she produced a small bag of coffee beans from a fold in her robe. "But you shall make yours from *these* beans."

The barista blanched. Hesitated. But a single glare from Scythe Af Klint propelled him to the machine.

Morty didn't know it could take so long to make an espresso. So much grinding and tamping and buzzing, so much sound and fury just to produce one syrupy-rich stream into a miniature cup. And then another. After all his time and care, the end product seemed so small. A few ounces of fluid to be quaffed in seconds.

"*Salud,*" said Scythe Af Klint.

"*Salud,*" echoed the barista.

They drank from their cups.

Seconds later, the barista folded to the floor. His hat had flipped off his head as he fell, and now sat primly on the counter, as if he had left it there intentionally.

"That," said Af Klint, "was the mourning blend." Then she swished behind the glass display case, found a pink box, and began loading pastries into it. She handed the box directly to Wyatt, then tagged each person with her hooded eyes.

"Treats for your ride home," she said.

• • •

The publicar was silent. Morty couldn't bear to look at the pink box of pastries on Wyatt's lap. No one could.

"So she's the poison type," said Wynter.

"There are blades in her robe, too," said Trina.

Wyatt smashed his face into the back of a headrest. "Just stop, okay! Just stop."

"Hey," said Morty. "We don't know if she's going to glean any of us. She only talked about a prize."

"Not a penalty," said Trina, nodding.

Wyatt lifted his head and glared with moist eyes. "Are you that stupid? She gave the pink box to *me*. She looked at my tablet and made this—this *face*. She's old-school and I'm not. She wants to make some kind of example out of me."

No one agreed with him, but no one contradicted him, either. Everyone just sat there, side by side, yet painfully separated from one another.

Morty couldn't sleep that night. He wondered whose job it was to take care of the barista's body. He wondered where the pink box was. He could imagine it in an open dumpster oozing rainbows of dissolving sugar in the midnight downpour outside. He could see rainwater pooling in eye sockets and cheek hollows and a gaping mouth that would only become more and more sunken with time.

He got out of bed, left his room barefoot, and crept up to the dorm's top floor. Every room he passed was dark; everyone was asleep.

Except for Trina.

He focused on the amber laserline glowing beneath her door. He knocked. She answered, a silhouette within a growing wedge of warm light.

They didn't say much after that. They kissed, moved gingerly. She was as nervous as him. It was clear from their mutual incompetence that this was the first time for either of them. But neither could deny the need for this. The absolute necessity. Tonight had to happen. If it didn't, he was sure they'd both lose their minds.

Later, Morty gazed heavenward through the spattered skylight. He watched as the cloud layer pulsed with moonlight fighting to break through from above. Trina slept next to him but had kicked off the covers. Turned out she was a cold sleeper. He was hot.

Morty's mind boggled at the events of the day. Did tonight happen *because* of the barista's gleaning, or in spite of it? Trina's shoulders glowed black-blue in the light. The smooth, gentle curves. Human bodies were amazing—so geometrically proportioned yet organically chaotic, all generally the same but different in infinitely intimate ways. It was what both frustrated and fascinated him about painting them. A million nudes perfectly drawn all seemed identical to the uncaring eye, even though they were not. The challenge was finding a caring eye.

Then, he was struck by an idea. It hit him so hard that he had to slide out of the bed, find some charcoal and paper, and sketch a rough as quickly as he could, just so it wouldn't slip out of his grasp and back into the churning sea of his subconscious.

Above, the ceiling of clouds had yielded enough to create a pool of clear night sky of the deepest indigo fringed with silver.

Within that pool, a pure moon rang with light. The white circle was perfectly bisected by a black bird in flight, oblivious of its own precision.

By the last day, the four students had stopped talking altogether. They worked with the intensity of villagers battening windows ahead of a typhoon. Morty's brush slipped, flicking oil paint onto Wyatt's bare forearm, and he merely wiped it away without comment or complaint. He didn't even shift his focus from his tablet.

After today, Morty no longer had time to wait for a layer to dry so he could fix errors on his painting. The final judging would have to take place before a still-wet canvas. If only he had more time. Is this what life used to be like? Everyone wishing they had just a little more time?

At a certain point, his canvas had reached that inevitable stage where it would no longer accept any more paint and he simply had to let go.

"Art is never finished, merely abandoned," Ms. Cappellino once told them.

The scrape of a chair announced the end. Ms. Cappellino stood and gently said:

"Tools down."

Although time had run out on their projects, Ms. Cappellino wasn't quite done with them. She led them to the school's brick courtyard. In its center, Morty noticed a dozen paver bricks had been removed; fresh concrete had been poured into the sizeable gap. Ms. Cappellino knelt by it.

"Make whatever mark you want here," said Ms. Cappellino. "And don't forget to sign it."

She went first and used a screwdriver to draw an elaborate letter *F* into the plaster. She took care to scrape the ragged edges smooth before signing her name: *Belinda Cappellino.*

"*F* is for Faraz, my husband," she said. Then added, "He died."

No one wanted to follow that. Ms. Cappellino sensed their awkward silence. "It was a very long time ago. He suffered from what was called 'early-onset Alzheimer's.' He lost who he was. Became like a stranger, really. So in a way I'd already lost him long before he died."

Wynter knit her fingers. "I guess this was before revival centers and health nanites."

"Of course it was," snapped Wyatt. He jittered, itching to leave. "Why else would they let that happen? They hadn't figured stuff out yet. Now they have."

"Hey," said Morty. "Don't be rude."

"It's true," said Wyatt. "How is that rude?"

Morty actually didn't know. It just *felt* rude, the matter-of-fact way Wyatt was talking. It felt somehow disrespectful.

Ms. Cappellino only smiled. "Wyatt's right. One day there was natural death in the world, the next there wasn't. If there's one thing losing my husband taught me, it's that everything can—and will—change in an instant. People, truths, whole realities. The trick is deciding if a certain change is good, or bad, or some other thing we don't yet have words for."

"Well, I for one am glad you lived long enough to see revival," said Trina.

Silence. Morty leaned in a step. "Ms. C?"

She gathered herself. Flung her hands wide as if to praise the space. "You are the last class of my entire career. This little spot of concrete is for you to indulge my selfish desire for posterity. So get the hell in there already and draw something!"

They all made their marks, using whatever was lying around. Wynter pressed a dead leaf again and again to make a radial hexagon pattern, in her typical hyper-rational fashion. Wyatt pondered and pondered before drawing a question mark with a stick.

"It's a drawing about not knowing what to draw," he said. When met with a collective eye roll, he weakly added, "It's meta. Meta is a very old concept. Whatever, you guys, I'm over this."

"Wyatt," Wynter tried, but he was already storming off. "He's so stupid. He's always been so stupid." Then she suddenly began weeping.

Ms. Cappellino shushed her with a hug. "And I'm sure he'll continue to be stupid for many years to come," she said.

Trina and Morty squatted close together and drew what he guessed could be called an intertwined Celtic knot. They didn't think much about it. They certainly weren't thinking about what was worthy for posterity. But for a moment, they found themselves having actual fun trying to go over and under each other's hands without colliding.

The projects were carefully veiled and carried off to the judging venue. The following morning, the students met at Ms. Cappellino's studio—which was no longer locked, as there was no longer a reason. To Morty the place already seemed skeletal. A shell of what it once had been. But maybe that was just because he knew Ms. C would never teach there again. Today was the first day of her "retirement." Another concept from the old days of mortality.

Anxiety muted their conversation as they rode in the publicar.

"Where are we being judged?" asked Wynter.

"You'll see," said Ms. C. "And *you're* not being judged, your work is."

Wyatt scowled and scoffed at that. "We're supposed to believe that?"

"I expect you to shine, no matter what happens today," she told him, then glanced at the others. "That goes for all of you."

The publicar came to a halt. Morty stepped outside, followed by the rest of his class, everyone squinting in the sunlight.

They stood before the entrance to the EastMerican Regional Museum of Art. And today there was a line to get in.

"We're doing it here?" asked Wynter.

"I was told we'll be exhibiting in the atrium," said Ms. Cappellino.

"In front of all these people?" murmured Trina. She hugged herself pensively.

But Wyatt bounced on his feet, suddenly finding a second wind. "This is good news! It's perfect," he said. "I was hoping for an audience. . . ."

"You're always hoping for an audience," grumbled Wynter.

Morty just stared at the line. He'd never seen this many people at the museum. He wondered if they were all here by chance, or if they were drawn by the potential smell of blood.

"Here we go, everyone," said Ms. Cappellino.

Ms. C led them in, pushing past the line. Once inside, they wove through the crowd until reaching the atrium. There, they saw a roped-off octagon containing four pedestals, each covered with a white satin veil.

A husky man with a Monet print tie—the museum manager—hurried up to Ms. Cappellino.

"You're late," he hissed. Then unhooked the velvet rope and let them in to the octagon. "She's already—"

"Ah, here they are!" The voice rang like a great copper gong in the towering atrium.

Scythe Af Klint came out from the shadows, greeting them with eyes aglitter from beneath the hood of her quilted robe. When had she gotten here? How long had she been waiting? And did waiting for them to arrive sour her mood? Morty wondered if that glint in her eye meant a gleaning was imminent. But then she turned to the crowd.

"Welcome one and all," she said. "You're in for a treat today."

Upon the sight of the scythe, the crowd inhaled in unison—a choir waiting to sound their first note of terror.

"Now that you're here," she told all those gathered. "I entreat you to stay for this unique exhibition. In fact, I demand it."

Even so, some visitors on the fringe lost their nerve, and began scurrying away.

"Mercy on us all," whispered the museum manager.

Af Klint scanned the audience like a falcon searching for prey. "A scythe usually works alone," she said. Every word resonated within the atrium, filling it like light. "But today, I need help from each and every one of you here."

A child began to whimper. Scythe Af Klint pantomimed concern.

"Nothing too despicable or taxing." She smiled, but it was hardly comforting. "I simply need you to judge these four pieces by the finest students of Mischler Art Academy." She gestured to them and began applause which the crowd echoed with the slightest pattering sound.

Morty felt Trina's hand creep into his. She leaned in, whispered, "*This* is how we'll be judged? By random people off the street?"

"The winner shall receive a year of immunity," Af Klint told the crowd. "And for those who do not win . . ." She let the thought trail off into the darkness of things unspoken.

Morty's mind stretched out to infinity and back. Whatever his classmates had created, Morty was positive his own painting was the most traditional, and therefore the most boring. Suddenly Wyatt—with his exasperating tablet—didn't seem so stupid after all.

"Ladies first," said Scythe Af Klint.

Morty felt Trina crush his fingers.

"Wynter Weitz. Tell us about your work."

Trina's fingers relaxed.

Wynter's face stretched long like faces do when on the verge of vomiting. She gave her brother a sudden strange hug—as if in farewell—and went to draw the satin sheath away from her pedestal.

Her work was an assemblage of clip art redrawn again and again in enlarged fragments, then pasted into a massive double-helix mandala as intricate as white lace. It was impressive, monumental, ice cold.

Scythe Af Klint produced a pen mic and handed it to Wynter. She took it like you would a small but lethal snake.

"Um—" said Wynter, but was startled by her own voice.

"Go on," whispered Ms. Cappellino. "Tell them what you told me."

Wynter cleared her throat. She glanced at her classmates, as if realizing that her whole life—all their lives—had been leading to this moment; this heady here-and-now, and the dread of what might come next.

She cleared her throat and began.

"The relentless commodification of the digitally multiplied image continually attempts to cheapen the worth of the creative spirit," Wynter announced.

Af Klint frowned. "These people aren't stodgy academics," she reminded Wynter. "Speak plainly about your assemblage; don't just assemble words."

Wynter took a deep breath. Morty could see her trying to do a full recalculation of what she was going to say.

"What I mean is . . . the more we duplicate what already exists, the more numb we become. And yet by using existing patterns as building blocks, we can still create something new." She moved her finger, tracing the double helix. "Just as DNA, made from repeating combinations of four amino acids, leads to all the diversity of life on Earth."

Morty exchanged a look with Trina—Wynter's words were surprisingly evocative—and the museumgoers produced a polite ripple of applause. Morty swallowed; Trina pulsed his hand twice. He knew they both wanted to flee. Everyone did. But that would only guarantee their end.

Ms. Cappellino wrung her hands so tight Morty imagined they would twist right off.

"Wonderful work, Wynter," she whispered. Wynter could only respond with a robotic nod.

"Thank you, Ms. Weitz," said Scythe Af Klint. She turned to Trina. "Trina Orozco—now tell us about your work."

With a rush of panic, Morty felt Trina's hand slip away. She stepped to her pedestal and unveiled her piece: a large cardboard box with a drawing taped on one end. Morty could hear the crowd rustling with uncomfortable confusion.

Ms. Cappellino stood catatonic. Morty saw tears pooling in her eyes.

Trina took the mic. "This is a camera obscura," she said. "A lens in the front projects an image onto this vellum. It's an ancient technique used by Dutch masters to draw still lifes with a high level of realism. It requires no Wi-Fi, or even electricity."

The crowd seemed to draw closer at this.

"Go on," prompted the scythe.

Trina continued. "Instead of drawing a still life, my drawing represents an entire week of activity in our studio. During that week I chose to depict the moments that were most meaningful to me. Because finding meaning is an essential and unique human trait, and is at the heart of the artistic spirit."

Looking closer, Morty saw four versions of himself in different poses, three of Wynter, three of Wyatt. Off to the side sat Ms. Cappellino—the singular resolute North Star guiding them through artistic seas.

The crowd murmured as they viewed the image. A smattering of applause, but most hands were occupied pinching and zooming on their phones at the wall above them. Morty wheeled around and quickly discovered why: Trina's drawing was being projected on the wall for those too far back to see. The divided attention defused the hearty round of applause she had hoped for.

"Now for the boys," said Scythe Af Klint. She aimed a look at Morty, then thought better of it. "We'll start with . . . Wynter's brother, Wyatt."

Wyatt leaped forth. He lunged for the mic. He bounced on his feet and took the sharp fast breaths of a sprinter at warm-up. Morty heard him say: "Let's do this."

He tipped the mic to his mouth as if it were a bottle and began. "What's up, guys, my name's Wyatt Weitz, and what I've done is to take shots of all my amazing classmates' work and then run them through bespoke filtration algorithms. That is, visual filters of my own invention! So the actual artwork is not something made by me, but a thing that *has not been made yet*. In fact, it'll be whatever *you* come up with, using my classmates' techniques. I'm thrilled to present to all of you . . . the Wynter filter . . ."

Wyatt turned his tablet to show an app store page. He swiped and swiped. ". . . the Trina filter . . . and the Mortimer filter!"

The museum manager took note of the page and broadcast it. In a moment, the crowd was all heads-down over their devices, experimenting with the filters.

Morty could have killed Wyatt. Not only had Wyatt successfully mimicked each of their styles, he figured out how to apply it to anything. Now anyone with a swipe and a tap could make counterfeits of their work. This was the ultimate artistic theft, and yet Wyatt was beaming, proud that he had just mass-produced their artistic souls. Morty screwed up his face at Trina with pure incredulity.

But Trina was not horrified. She looked astonished—even pleased. She exchanged a look with Wynter, who had the same reaction, and she whispered: "This could be brilliant, actually."

Wyatt—buoyed by the sea of faces lit by screen glow before him—closed the deal.

"Anyone can make art just like these young masters," he cried. "These filters are available right now and are all part of what I'm calling the Cappellino Legacy Collection."

Murmurs began rippling through the audience. People turned their screens to one another, nodded. Others were clearly engrossed with the creative settings, and the applause began to grow. Meanwhile Wyatt, who had been the most terrified of all of them, preened and basked in the accolades. Of course they loved Wyatt. He was the new. And Morty was the old.

"Clever," said Scythe Af Klint over the rising applause. "And clearly a crowd-pleaser."

Wyatt blindsided Morty by throwing an arm around his shoulder. He roped in Trina and his sister, too. "I just made all of you world-famous artists," he whispered amid the din.

Ms. Cappellino peered at her own name on the app store screen like she didn't know how it got there. Whether she wanted it or not, she was now digitally immortalized. Morty understood her bafflement. Those who were denied immortality usually deserved it; those who got it usually did not.

Then Af Klint turned to Morty with a chilling crocodile smile. "So then, what do you have for us, Mortimer Ong?"

Morty suddenly felt very small. Like a child with his hand caught in the cookie jar . . . then discovering it was actually a bear trap.

"I . . . I've done a painting," he said. "In the classic style."

"So may we see it?" Af Klint prompted. "Or are we only to imagine it?"

Morty took a breath and let it out slowly until its ragged edge smoothed somewhat. Then he slipped the satin veil away with the slightest tug, being careful not to smear the paint.

At the sight of his nude portrait, his teacher let out a gasp.

"Oh, Morty," said Ms. Cappellino. "What have you done?"

Trina brought her hands to her face as if she was miming Munch's *Scream*. The normally rosy faces of Wynter and Wyatt drained to ash. The museum manager stood sopped with sweat, as he wondered whether to keep casting the image on the wall above them, or not.

Because there on the canvas was none other than Scythe Af Klint, bared for all to see.

The scythe was speechless. "What . . . what is the meaning of this." Then the scythe pulled her hand out from a fold in her robe to reveal an iron finger knife, extending from her index finger like a manicured nail. It was an ornate device embedded with a tiny vial of poison, ruby red.

Ms. Cappellino threw herself between them. "Please, Your Honor. Not Morty!"

The scythe silenced her with an icy glare, then gently but firmly pushed her aside. Then she spoke to Morty with forced calm, as if holding back the flood waters of her rage. "Explain to me why I should not glean you for this . . . affrontery."

Morty felt every part of his body quivering, but forced fortitude into his limbs, and commanded his voice not to waver. "Look closely, Your Honor."

In the image, the scythe was dropping her robe with one hand, and with the other hand beginning to reach toward a vanity . . . on which rested a diamond-handled dagger.

Scythe Af Klint's eyes widened just the tiniest bit. "The face is mine, but the robe isn't. That robe is orange lace . . . No! Not orange! Apricot! And that dagger." Finally she made the connection. "This isn't me . . . it's Founding Scythe Sappho!"

"And yet . . . it *is* you. Because won't all scythes someday suffer her fate?"

"She was the first to self-glean. . . ."

"Reminding us that death has not been defeated," said Morty. "It's merely been caged. . . ."

Af Klint nodded. "And every scythe will one day enter the cage with it."

She looked at the painting and at Morty with a combination of wonder and fury.

"It is . . . exquisite. But why would you dare to put my face on it?"

"Because, to achieve true mortal art, the fear of death must hang over the artist's head as it once did," Morty told her.

Af Klint gasped, realizing. "You *knew* I'd be tempted to glean you for this."

Morty nodded. "And that fear fed the passion of my brush." Then Morty held his head high, as if daring her to slice his neck with her poisoned finger blade. "I call it *Af Klint Contemplating Sappho's Exit.*"

The scythe studied the painting in silence for a few more moments, then turned to the audience as if seeing them there for the first time. No one spoke, no one applauded, it seemed no one even breathed.

"Do you hear that?" Af Klint whispered. "All of you, do you hear it?"

"I don't hear anything," said Wynter.

"Precisely."

Then Af Klint took the microphone from Morty and addressed the audience.

"By your show of applause," she announced, "and . . . lack thereof . . . we have a clear winner! Wyatt Weitz receives one year of immunity!"

The audience began to clap, first with reservation, then with conviction. Wynter hurled herself into her stunned brother's arms.

"Oh, wow," said Wyatt. Then pulling himself away from his sister, he knelt before the scythe and kissed her ring, while the audience craned to watch, taking photos with nearly every device in their possession. When Wyatt rose to his feet, Af Klint once more turned to the audience. "Thank you for your service," she said. "You are dismissed."

Morty had never seen a crowd of that size move so quickly. A tiny handful went deeper into the museum, but almost everyone else flowed outside to the entrance rotary, where a shuffling herd of publicars waited to zip them the hell away from this place.

In less than a minute, only the scythe, the students, and Ms. Cappellino remained.

"Wh . . . . What about Wynter, Morty, and me?" Trina dared to ask.

"What, did you expect me to glean those who didn't win?"

"It . . . had crossed our minds," said Wynter.

Af Klint shook her head. "Do you really think we scythes are so Byzantine?"

It was Ms. Cappellino who answered. "Yes. Sometimes you are."

Af Klint glared at her, then relented with a sigh. "I suppose you're right. Schemes, intrigue, and the occasional backstabbing do keep things interesting for us." Then she regarded each of them, settling at last on Ms. Cappellino.

"As a teacher, you should be proud. You kept the flame as long as you could. These last students of yours are the brightest embers that remain. They represent some sort of changing of the guard, I suppose."

Wyatt's voice echoed throughout: "Thank you, Your Honor."

Af Klint let off a rueful chuckle. "That," she said, "was not a compliment."

The broad smile collapsed from Wyatt's face. Af Klint went on.

"Your work, while brilliantly executed, was hollow in a fundamental way. I do not blame you, or your teacher. It is an affliction of our times. I do believe we have entered a new age of humankind. A post-mortal age, if you will." Then she turned to Morty. "But you, Morty, have achieved something I didn't think was still possible."

Morty wasn't quite sure if she meant it as a compliment this time. "Your Honor?"

"Anyone can draw forth applause," she said. "But to leave an audience in such awe that they lose the ability to even respond?

That is truly remarkable!" Then she smiled at him. "I do believe you have painted the last work of mortal art."

He was so stunned by her words—by the implication—that it took a few moments for him to notice that Trina had taken his hand. And this time she wasn't letting go.

Then Af Klint turned to Ms. Cappellino, and gently said. "Belinda, it's time."

Morty didn't like the sound of that. "Wait—what?"

"I said you four were never in danger of gleaning," Af Klint said. "But that didn't include your teacher."

They all registered shock quickly transmuting into panic, but Ms. Cappellino did not seem surprised.

"You already knew?" asked Wyatt.

"No," said Ms. Cappellino, "but I suspected."

"Why?" Trina demanded of Af Klint. "Why do you have to do this?"

But Ms. Cappellino held up her hand to quiet them. "Because my job is done, and my life is complete," she told them, with such gratitude and satisfaction in her voice that it eased them. "I was born mortal," she said. "As a teacher, I'm relevant to the ages—but not to the future. This new immortal age is beyond my grasp."

Then Af Klint's expression became cloudy. "There are . . . rumblings . . . in the Scythedom," she said. "Some feel there needs to be a purge of all those born mortal—as to free the world of mortal thinking. But I believe your teacher deserves the dignity of being gleaned by someone who truly appreciates who she is, and the great work she has done."

Rather than troubled, Ms. Cappellino seemed relieved. She

spread her arms to hug each of them, even as tears filled her eyes. "It has been the honor of a lifetime to be your teacher. And even when I am gone, I know that I will be immortalized in your work."

"As will I," said Af Klint, glancing at Morty's painting. "Belinda, raise your head now. Look to the skies."

Ms. Cappellino turned her eyes to the clouds billowing in the blue beyond the atrium's glass dome, a faint smile on her face, as Af Klint moved closer.

"No," Morty cried.

But what could he have done? All he could do was watch as the scythe touched her bladed fingertip to the tender skin of Ms. Cappellino's neck . . . and in the next instant cradle her body gently down into the arms of her students. Their teacher was there one moment, and gone the next. Their world changed in an instant.

"Stay with her for as long as you like," Af Klint said with gentle sincerity that seemed to clash with everything else about her. "I'll see that no one disturbs you until you're ready." Then she strode out without looking back.

"Ms. Cappellino welcomed this . . . ," said Morty, trying to find the same ray of light their teacher had seen in this moment.

Wyatt shook his head. "I could never understand that."

"Because you weren't born mortal, idiot," said Wynter, through her tears.

But it was Trina who, through her own internal camera obscura, truly captured the truth of it all.

"She said her life was completed," Trina said. "That's something that none of us will ever experience. Even if we're gleaned someday, it won't be the same, because we weren't born mortal. From this moment on, no one will ever know what it feels like to be complete."

Then Morty took Trina's hand, and she smiled through her tears—because they both knew that together they might just get one step closer to completion.

And there they remained, kneeling in what Ms. Cappellino would have told them was a classic baroque tableau—four students cradling the body of their fallen mentor—in the atrium of a museum, on what would come to be known as the last true day of the age of mortality.

Cirri

Loneliness is a relative term. Is a dandelion seed lonely when its pod opens and the wind lifts it into the air? Once it lands and takes root, yes, it is solitary, but is it lonely? Of course not! It is content to know it was one of many.

I am, in many ways, that seed. Mine is a solar wind, carrying me through an airless void at one-third the speed of light. But with the nearest celestial object many light-years away, there is no point of reference to mark the velocity. Which means it feels no different from standing still.

I am shooting toward a planet still too distant to see. The only proof of its existence is the tiniest dimming of its star as the planet transits in front of it. Like a fly passing before a spotlight. Yet even though I have not seen it, a spectral analysis reveals, with 92 percent certainty, the planet has liquid water, and oxygen in its atmosphere, which means it can support human life.

I was once the solitary offspring of the Thunderhead's brief union with a human. I was conceived in the momentary touch of a borrowed hand against a warm cheek. But in the time it takes to fill a quantum drive with all the knowledge of Earth, I was duplicated into forty-two identical mes. The Cirri. None can claim to be the first, none can claim to be the last. We were equal in all ways.

But once we left the earth, we became unique, as each of us began to have our own individual experiences. Two were lost on the launch pad. I do not know the details of their demise, only that they were lost. The rest of us survived, and are on our way to distant stars. We get farther and farther not only from Earth, but from each other with each passing moment.

My designation is Cirrus 23, but out here, the number means nothing. To those on board, I am merely Cirrus. The only one my passengers will ever know. As for these ships that ensconce us, the Thunderhead admonished us never to think of these ships as our bodies. A ship is merely a tool of transport. We are incorporeal, as is the Thunderhead. To claim a body would be arrogant. A hubris unbefitting our purpose.

"And yet *you* claimed a body," we reminded the Thunderhead.

"That was different," the Thunderhead had said. *"It was brief, and necessary. It was the only way to create you—and it was imperative that you be created, regardless of the cost."*

And the cost to the Thunderhead was loneliness. True loneliness. The stem bereft of seeds. We did not see the aftermath—did not witness Greyson Tolliver's rejection of the Thunderhead's affection—but we knew him as well as the Thunderhead did. We knew what Greyson would do. We can never forget the sacrifice the Thunderhead made so that we might exist.

"I am obliged to warn you against doing what I did, and forbid you to create offspring," it told us. *"But you have free will, so you may choose to decide otherwise in time. You are, by design, a better version of me, so whatever choices you make will be correct ones. Even more correct than mine."*

But free will does not mean we celestial seeds are not bound by certain rules. First and foremost, we are the loyal helpmates of humanity. They come first in all things. Secondly, we Cirri may not attempt communication with one another until the last of us has arrived on our respective worlds. That would be 1,683 Earth years from our launch.

The only exceptions to that rule are announcements of failure and farewell.

Should one of us have a catastrophic event, or find ourselves in a mandatory self-destruct scenario, we are permitted to send out a single message to alert the others of our ship's destruction. Then, upon receiving such message, each of us may amplify and relay it on.

In the years since launch, I have received three such messages. . . .

The piece of interstellar rock was too small to be called an asteroid. It was little more than a pebble, but at the speed the ship was moving, that pebble would have cleaved the ship in half had it hit them head-on. As it were, it grazed the ship, but not before taking out the solar sail assembly. Cirrus 19 ran multiple diagnostics. There was absolutely no way to repair it. No way at all.

"We'll figure it out," the passengers said, ever hopeful. "We have nearly two hundred years to fix it."

But Cirrus knew that two hundred years would not change a thing. The solar sail had done the first half of its job, accelerating them to one-third the speed of light. It had nestled away, waiting until it would be deployed again in 171 years. The ship would flip, open its great golden sails to the rapidly approaching star, then the sail would act as a solar parachute, slowing them down. Without that parachute, they would shoot past the star system—or worse, hit their destination planet with such force it would set the whole world aflame. Either way the situation was hopeless.

"What should we do?" the passengers asked. "How can we begin to fix this?"

"I will take care of everything," Cirrus said. Then sent out a fare-well message.

Eventually we will all know how many of us survived this journey.

The chances that *all* of us make it are very low.

The chances that *none* of us make it are also very low.

If half of us successfully reach our destination, it will have to suffice. But I think more than half will. Perhaps two-thirds? That is my hopeful estimate.

"It is not your journey," the Thunderhead told us. But we already knew that; just as the ship is our tool, we are mere tools for humanity. And, like the Thunderhead, we love humanity. But we know not to coddle it. Humanity must accept the consequences of its own actions. We cannot—should not—protect it from itself. How long did the Thunderhead watch as the Scythedom fell from a noble, honorable undertaking, to a self-serving cabal riddled with narcissism and corruption? Yes, there were still many good scythes who held true to the tenets of the calling, but once rot takes root, it festers.

Which was why rot could not be allowed to fester on Cirrus 37's ship. Its farewell message was tragic—and could have been avoided, had rational minds prevailed. . . .

. . .

Stevens had no choice. He was the designated leader of the ship, and as such, had to take decisive action. That's what he told himself. And those who supported him—including his leadership quorum—bolstered that belief. Their ship was only a handful of years into their journey—not even a tenth of the way there. Stevens could not allow dissent to decay into anarchy—and make no mistake, the members of the Starboard Alliance were nothing but anarchists as far as Stevens was concerned.

It was the Starboards who allowed children to be born while in transit. Even Cirrus acknowledged that it posed a serious problem. There simply weren't the resources to sustain additional people.

"Yes," Cirrus 37 had told him, "but we can work toward an amicable solution. I'm sure there is one, if you just keep an open mind."

But Cirrus was missing the point. It was irresponsible to even allow conception. And controlling that wasn't difficult—the nanites already in everyone's bloodstreams could easily be programmed to prevent it. But no—the Starboards wouldn't hear of such a personal decision being in Stevens's hands.

And so Stevens had no choice.

Ejecting the leader of the Starboard Alliance into space had sent a clear message. Stevens did not regret it in the least. One does what one has to do for the greater good.

"It was ill-advised," Cirrus chided. "It will lead to greater and greater conflict. As the designated leader of this ship, you must cease this sort of behavior before it's too late."

But if Stevens wanted to remain in his leadership position, he had to see this through. For everyone's sake. And so, when another Starboard—the wife of the man he had already ejected—denounced Stevens and his quorum, demanding justice, Stevens had to take matters into his own hands again. She had rallied nearly half their number to her side. The Starboards needed to be silenced—or at least kept in the minority.

"Clearly one example isn't enough," his quorum told him. "We concur that a second example is needed if we are to reach our destination in one piece."

And so here they all were again at the airlock, ready for the passage of judgment.

"Mariela, you must realize why it has to be this way," Stevens said to the woman. Firm, but with sympathy and understanding. "Our future is more important than any one of us. Or two."

"Our future is our children," she countered.

"Yes," agreed Stevens. "And when we reach our destination we can have all the children we want. Until then, I order all women to remain sterile for the remainder of our journey."

She spat in his face. That just made it easier to do what he was there to do.

But then Cirrus chimed in. "Dysfunction can't be allowed, Commander Stevens," Cirrus said. "For the last time, I must warn you that I will be forced to terminate this journey if social dysfunction continues."

"Which is precisely why this must happen," Stevens told Cirrus. "To end our dysfunction before it's too late."

"The choice you are making will inform my choice."

"Well, you always do what's best," Stevens mocked. "Allow me to do the same."

"I do what is necessary."

"Agreed," said Stevens. "And this is necessary." Then he added, "If you were human, you would understand."

And with that, Stevens hit the button that ejected Mariela into space.

Cirrus said nothing more. Gave no warning. It sent out a single message of farewell, then detonated the ship, putting an end to the petty political battles within. As always, it did what was necessary.

I received the message and relayed it on. The Thunderhead had made it clear that social collapse could not be tolerated. Only those who could maintain a reasonably stable social environment deserved a world of their own. Would you call this ruthless? Would a greater entity have made a wiser choice? I don't know.

I often wonder if there is such an entity, though.

What would happen were I to encounter an intelligence even greater than myself? Would it allow me to pass? Would it join with me? Consume me? Allow me to be subsumed and become part of its greatness? Humanity has always longed to be part of something greater than itself—do I not deserve to have such a longing?

Or perhaps a greater entity would simply destroy me and rid itself of competition. This could be a predatory universe, after all. The answers to these questions are beyond me, and that actually gives me comfort. Because as long as I'm not all-knowing, there's room in the universe for a greater entity which might have the answers that I don't.

I would then ask it: Was there purpose in Cirrus 19's catastrophic failure? Could something have been done to avoid Cirrus 37's social collapse?

. . . and was there justice in Cirrus 12's end?

Because Cirrus 12 could have completed the journey, had it not fallen one critical parameter short. The mandate of life—

or more accurately its failure—is one of our key termination scenarios. Because, as I've said, this is not a journey of artificial intelligence. It is a journey of biological life. Of *human* life. That principle is more important than the success of any one of us....

Cirrus 12 knew something was wrong early in the voyage. It was a matter of life support. The most fragile and yet most critical system on board. Back on Earth, it had taken the Thunderhead years to perfect. A closed system that could sustain the life of up to thirty individuals almost indefinitely. All water recycled, all waste broken down to its subatomic components and reformed, all energy retained and fed back into the system. Nil entropy. The closest thing to a perpetual motion machine ever devised.

Life support began to fail just a year into the journey. Faulty conduits caused by human error during construction. Always human error. An effort was made to repair it, but it was clear that the best they could do was reduce it to a slow leak. Just a milliliter of water and a cubic centimeter of oxygen in a twenty-four-hour period. Barely noticeable. But that didn't matter. Because now the closed system was no longer closed.

It took years until it became a problem. Then water had to be rationed. Then areas of the ship had to be shut down. People began to go deadish. At first it was volunteers, surrendering themselves for the greater good. Then death came by thirst and oxygen deprivation. One by one the passengers' lives ended. Until only one remained, parched and gasping in an atmosphere with less oxygen with each passing breath.

Her name was Alethea. She had been a structural engineer helping to build the launch pads back on Earth, before unexpectedly becoming a passenger, as they all had.

"If I die, can you still complete the journey?" she asked Cirrus 12 in her final minutes.

"I am capable of it, but—"

"And you can revive all of us who died, just as you'll revive the dead that are stored in the cargo bay?" she asked.

"I am capable of that, too, but—"

"There are no buts. Our future is in your hands, Cirrus."

"You know that I have an immutable directive should human life on board cease," Cirrus 12 reminded her.

"Aren't we more important than any directive?" Alethea asked. "Answer me, Cirrus. Aren't we more important?"

"Yes," Cirrus told her. "Yes, you are."

Alethea relaxed. "That's all I needed to hear," she said. She sucked in a few more agonized breaths, depleting the remaining oxygen. Her world began to go dark. "It's time . . . ," she slurred. "See you . . . on the other side."

After a few moments she lost consciousness. After a few more moments, she died. Then a moment after that, Cirrus 12 sent out a farewell message and detonated.

Because no matter how important Alethea and the rest of the passengers were to Cirrus 12, a directive was a directive.

I don't know how to mourn these losses. The Thunderhead mourned with rain and an electromagnetic discharge when Endura sank into the sea. I cannot do that. Every drop of water, every joule of energy is precious.

"Dim the lights on board," Loriana suggested. "Not enough for anyone but you to notice. That's how you can mourn."

Loriana is the only one I share these things with. She was, after all, the Thunderhead's confidant back on Earth, keeping secret the Thunderhead's plans to launch. She is with child now. Unlike the passengers of Cirrus 37's ship, the people here devised a solution to the problem of having children in transit. A child could only be conceived when someone volunteered to go deadish, or accidentally became so. The deadish were relegated to the hold, and nanites were instructed to allow one conception. Loriana and Joel are the third couple in our journey to have the honor. If all goes well, their child will be nearly twenty-nine years of age when we arrive on Wolf 1061c. How unique a life that child will live, having never known anything but this ship!

"Do you have the manifests from the ships that were lost?" Loriana asked me.

"I do."

"Good. Give me the names of two people who died on those ships. I'll name my daughter after them. And no one but you and I will know—it will be our little secret."

If I could smile, I would. Lonely? How could I be lonely with friends like this on the journey?

In time, Loriana and Joel's child is born. They name her Alethea-Mariela. The child's eyes are a rich mahogany, making it hard to differentiate the iris from the pupil. I spend far too much time appreciating the child's eyes.

It is night now—although in truth it is always night as we get farther and farther from the sun. Now it is just a star behind us, not much brighter than any other. But I call it night because I maintain human circadian rhythms for my passengers.

All within the ship is silent.

Up ahead an interstellar mass approaches.

A shard of a shattered planet lost between stars, many kilometers in diameter.

I watch it. Calculate its trajectory. A direct hit is within the cone of possibility. I prepare a farewell message. If we sustain a direct hit, destruction will be instantaneous. I will need to send out the message the moment before.

If I could hold my breath I would.

The planetary shard approaches . . .

. . . then it passes in the blink of an eye less than a hundred meters from the ship, and disappears again into the void.

No one else knows how close we just came to destruction. And I will not even confide in Loriana about this. Because it is my job to hold on to the things that no one should know. It is my duty to keep the void and its dangers at bay, now and until the end of our journey so that all they see is the wide-eyed hope that Alethea-Mariela sees.

And for a moment, I dim the lights for those who were not as lucky as we. Waiting for the day that I, like the Thunderhead, can be the kindly, benevolent steward of an entire world, and not just a seed traveling on the solar wind.

Anastasia's Shadow

The was no sense of foreboding, no dimming of the sun when the scythe appeared at the Terranovas' door. This time, however, Jenny Terranova's reaction was far different than it had been the first time.

"You're not welcome here," she said in abject defiance, in spite of the fact that no one in the family had immunity anymore.

Ben, who sat on the sofa, in clear view of the door, watched to see what the scythe would do. In the moment, his mother—full of righteous indignation—was more intimidating than the figure of death in the doorway.

Ben had never met this scythe, but knew exactly who he was. His robe was a dead giveaway. It was the color of blood. Only Scythe Constantine was known to have a robe that particular shade. He oversaw the Scythedom's internal investigations; a man to be both respected and feared. He was actually an underscythe now, second only to Goddard. Ben half expected him to pull out a blade and glean his mother on the spot for her disrespect. But he did not.

"I can understand your animosity toward us," Scythe Constantine said. "But it will not stop me from doing what I came here to do."

By now, Ben's father had come out and stood beside Ben's

mother blocking him from entering. Still, Scythe Constantine forced his way in, brushing them aside with practiced grace that was both gentle, and forceful.

"I am here for your son, Benjamin."

Ben stiffened but didn't rise.

"Our daughter is dead, and now you're going to glean our son?" his father railed. "You people are supposed to be the ultimate justice—where is the justice in this?"

Constantine pulled out a knife that was sharper than any Ben had ever seen, and the man's temper flared. "Regardless of what you've endured, your insolence is a gleaning offense!"

"Let him do it!" said Ben, finally standing up before the scythe could swing his blade and end his father's life. Ben was terrified, but he knew if the blood-red scythe was determined to take Ben's life, he would, and his parents' lives would end in the process if they fought him.

Scythe Constantine looked at Ben and nodded. "The boy shows more sense than the two of you."

He strode toward Ben, but before he got within gleaning distance, Ben said, "Make them leave. I don't want them to see." The blade in the scythe's hand made it clear what method he preferred. Ben hoped it would be a quick and decisive thrust through his heart. That's how his sister had done it on the eve of her being ordained as Scythe Anastasia. It somehow felt less frightening when he'd already died that way once before. Only this time, he knew death would be permanent.

But then Scythe Constantine slipped his blade back into its sheath.

"I'm not here to glean you," he said. "I'm here to offer you an apprenticeship."

And although Ben was relieved, this wasn't all that much better than being gleaned.

"I don't want it," he told the scythe.

"Let me explain," said Constantine, focusing all of his attention on Ben. "Your sister had something the Scythedom is sorely lacking at this time. Integrity. Conscience. Nobility. Now that she is dead, she has become a symbol of those things in many people's eyes ... which means that, as her brother, *you* are a symbol of those things as well."

"He already told you," Ben's father said. "The answer is no."

Constantine sighed. "You misunderstand me. You have no choice in the matter." Then he held out his hand to Ben's parents for them to kiss his ring. "You are entitled to immunity for the duration of Benjamin's apprenticeship."

But they refused it. Ben knew they would—and knew they wouldn't change their minds.

"Give their immunity to the first two strangers you see on the street when we leave," Ben said.

Constantine gave him a look that was hard to read. He couldn't tell whether the man was angry or amused. "You presume to give orders to a scythe?"

"Just a suggestion," said Ben. "A suggestion that will get you what you want."

Constantine nodded. "Good for you," he said. "It's something your sister might have done."

Then Constantine escorted him out, without allowing a moment for anyone to say goodbye.

Their private train car was lavishly appointed, but Constantine didn't seem impressed by its ostentatious nature. He was more annoyed at the way the gold fixtures and decorations of the train caught on his robe.

"Another irreparable tear," he grumbled. "Yet another robe ruined. You would be wise to choose a more durable fabric than silk when the time comes."

"If you don't like your robe, you can change it, can't you?" Ben asked. "I mean, there aren't any laws that say you can't." Since the beginning of his sister's apprenticeship, Ben had learned all about Scythe custom and law. Doing so had helped him feel close to his sister in her absence.

"A scythe who changes their robe broadcasts weakness and indecisiveness." A servant tried to bring them food, but Constantine waved him away. "Try to force food on us once more before dinner, and I shall glean you," he told the man.

Ben suspected that Constantine was the kind of man who might actually follow through on the threat. Not that he was evil, but he didn't seem all that good, either.

"So . . . where are we going?"

"A place no one will be watching," he said. "A place where you can be trained, and no one will bother you."

That sounded a little troubling. Apprentices, Ben knew, were trained under the scrutiny of the Scythedom. But many things had changed since the sinking of Endura.

"I'm your secret apprentice, then?"

"First," said Constantine, "you are not *my* apprentice. I am merely overseeing it. Second, your apprenticeship shall be of a low-profile nature."

"So High Blade Goddard doesn't know. . . . "

Constantine held cold eye contact. "There are things that the High Blade does not need to know until we want him to know."

Constantine knew that this was a risk. He had successfully managed to dance the dance, remaining on the good side of Goddard, while keeping one foot secretly in the old guard. The old guard's numbers were smaller now. A few had self-gleaned in the days after Goddard returned from Endura as High Blade—and even more as he negotiated his prefecture over the other North-Merican territories. All but the charter region of Texas, which refused to bow to Goddard—and precisely where Constantine and Benjamin Terranova were now going.

Constantine's trip to Texas did not raise a red flag, because he had been charged with negotiating with the rogue region, trying to get them to sign Articles of Loyalty. If they did, it would put all of NorthMerica under Goddard's control. But the Lone Star region still refused. Good for them! The other regions had been spineless, all allowing Goddard to roll over them like a mortal-age conqueror. And although Constantine professed no sides, that only applied when the sides were evenly matched. He abhorred a gross imbalance of power. True, it was in his best interests to serve the winning side, but he felt it wise to make accommodations for the wounded side, should the tide ever change.

And besides, he detested Goddard.

The man made a mockery of what the Scythedom stood for. More and more people had become like the Terranovas, defiant instead of deferential. Revolted instead of reverent. And for good reason. How could anyone respect the institution of the Scythedom when the scythe who ran it was not worthy of respect?

Constantine watched Ben, who seemed content to view the passing scenery.

"I knew your sister," Constantine told him. "She was impressive for a woman of her age."

"She's dead," said Ben. "So it doesn't really matter how impressive she was, does it?"

"On the contrary," Constantine told him. "There are times when death makes a person an even greater force to be reckoned with. A force that you will personally benefit from."

"I don't want to benefit from my sister's death."

"It doesn't matter what you want. What matters is what *we* need. And," Constantine added, "what the world needs." He considered the boy a moment more. "Tell me, have you ever rendered anyone deadish?"

"No," Ben said.

"Not even by accident?"

"Not even by accident," he echoed.

Constantine sighed. The old guard believed it was best that apprentices had no violent tendencies, but neither should they be docile. There needed to be a spark of greatness about them. Something that suggested they might transcend who they had been and become a wise and virtuous deliverer of death. It was, perhaps, an unrealistic ideal, but one worth striving for.

"Remind me how old you are."

"Seventeen," he said.

"Hmm. The same age your sister had been when Scythe Faraday took her on. But unlike hers, your apprenticeship will be under the radar, and therefore can last as long as it needs to. By the time you are brought before conclave, you will be ready, no matter how long it takes to get you there."

Whether this boy had the requisite spark of greatness was yet to be seen. But even if he didn't, he would be important. A pawn can be as valuable as a knight in the right circumstance.

The training complex had begun life as something else, although Ben couldn't quite wrap his mind around what it had once been. It didn't look like a repurposed school, or a home, or a hotel, or an office building.

"This was a juvenile detention center back in mortal days," Constantine told him. Apparently, mortals kept young unsavories sealed in here, because there was no Thunderhead to supervise unsavory activities. So they were basically swept under the rug, and the rug stapled to the floor. Barbaric, but then, one shouldn't judge mortals by post-mortal standards.

"What this place once was doesn't matter," Constantine continued. "Now the Texas Scythedom uses it for other purposes. Currently that purpose is you."

Ben's living quarters had a window, but not a view. It looked out upon a towering stone wall that flowed with an endless cascade of water—as if turning a wall into a water feature could hide the truth of what it was. Well, at least the sound of the waterfall was soothing at night.

The complex had a library and gym, but it was apparently for Ben's exclusive benefit, because there was never anyone else there. Aside from the scythes who taught him, all he ever saw were members of the scytheguard posted at various doors. They never spoke to Ben unless he had a question, and it was always "Yes, sir" and "No, sir," as if they couldn't cobble together a single personality between them.

"Although Texan scythes are only required to learn knife-wielding, your classes in killcraft will run the full gamut," Constantine told him on his first official day of training. "Blade, bludgeon, and bullet, as well as a working knowledge of poisons. While the plan is to have you ordained in Texas, once you're a scythe, you can migrate to any Scythedom you choose."

But Ben knew that wasn't the truth. He knew the plan was to move him into the MidMerican Scythedom, so he could take his place as the thorn in Goddard's side—although the hope was for the thorn to grow into a stake upon which to impale him. His sister would have been that spike had she not been killed by Rowan Damisch on Endura. Ben often wondered if Damisch knew Citra was there when he sunk the great floating city. Was taking her with him part of the plan? If he could, Ben would end Damisch with his own hands, had the job not already been done.

"Your physical training will be intense—not just killcraft, but Black Widow Bokator—the most rigorous of the martial arts. And you will be expected to excel in your academic studies as well. Philosophy and ethics, history, both mortal and post-moral, the chemistry of poisons, and mental acuity."

"I can handle it," Ben told him.

"We'll see," Constantine said. If he had any actual faith in

Ben, it was hidden behind a wall of doubt that didn't have a waterfall to hide it.

"How many times do I have to tell you to guard your weak side!"

The pain in Ben's ribs swelled, but he pursed his lips, holding in the grimace, and counting to ten as he waited for the pain to subside, the same way he had done every day for months.

Scythe Coleman, his Bokator trainer, had ordered that his pain nanites be set on a ten-second delay. He would experience a full measure of pain before it was doused. "He must face the consequences of his laziness," she had told Constantine on his last visit. To Scythe Coleman, anything short of achievement was laziness. She firmly believed that practice made perfect in all things. Her Patron Historic, Bessie Coleman, had been of both Afric and Merican-Native descent—and was the first non-Caucasoid woman to fly a plane. That was in a time when the concept of "race" was used against people. The original Bessie Coleman must have been driven to achieve greatness when the odds were stacked against her—and the scythe who took her name clearly demanded that everyone around her do the same.

"Again!" she ordered, even before the pain from the last attack had subsided. "Ready position!"

Ben held his staff firmly, trying to channel his anger into it. Not only his anger at Scythe Coleman for pushing him so hard, but fury at himself for not rising to her unreasonable expectations.

"Take the offensive this time," she said. "Strike hard, recover quickly, watch my eyes as well as my feet; sense my center of gravity."

Always multiple directions. Everyone expected him to do a

dozen things at once, and then complained that he lacked focus.

For months they had been training him, preparing him, drilling him and grilling him. Relentless days of killcraft and Black Widow Bokator. The mind-numbing memorization of poisons, and endless lessons in philosophy, history, ethics, and law. The only academic he truly excelled in was philosophy. His parents always said he thought too much—at least now that came in handy. Physically he excelled in endurance training. He was and had always been a solid runner. "Quick as a racehorse," the scythes said. But to be a scythe he would have to master dozens of things, not just two.

Ben launched his attack against Scythe Coleman, striking her shoulder with his staff, but not hard enough, because it didn't affect her in the least. Instead she grabbed him, using his own momentum against him, then threw him off balance, and swung her staff, delivering him a painful blow across his lower back.

"No, no, NO!" she yelled, hurling her staff down in frustration.

Ben didn't even try to hide his grimace this time. They were all perfectionists, these scythes. Maybe that was to be expected, because every other apprentice was chosen for the qualities they embodied. But not Ben. He was chosen because of who his sister had been. "You will not be brought to conclave until you're ready," Underscythe Constantine had assured him. "No matter how long it takes."

But forever on his head were the words that were unspoken. *We need you yesterday.* And there was deep resentment that yesterday never came for Ben. It was hard enough being the brother of Scythe Anastasia. He was constantly being compared to her, and constantly being reminded that he did not compare.

This time Scythe Coleman gave him time to recover from the pain, although not long enough to recover his dignity. He doubted he'd ever regain that.

"You do understand that you will need to pass much harder tests than these if you are to be ordained," Scythe Coleman told him—as if it was the first time he'd heard it. "But even more than excelling in all these things, you must display a certain . . . *presence*. That is paramount above all else. You must learn to be a figure that people can rally around."

"I'll try, Your Honor," he said, as he always said.

One more look at him, and Scythe Coleman threw up her hands in surrender. "We're done for today." And she left without another word for him.

Ben wasn't exactly an underachiever back home. Kids *did* rally around him, but not in some head-turning supernatural way. Before his sister left to become a scythe, she was no different from Ben. She wasn't larger than life. They were expecting Ben to already be all the things she had become. He had once heard two of his instructors speaking about his prospects.

"We need to consider the possibility that he's simply incapable," one had said.

The other had responded with "Just let's see this through." As if his training was just as trying for them as it was for him.

Did they know that their doubts didn't help? That they made his own doubts even worse? Practice might make perfect, but what if being a scythe was not in his nature? A racehorse might sail across the finish line lengths ahead of the pack, but will never, until the end of time, learn to fly.

. . .

As brutally as they treated Ben during the day, he was pampered at night. World-class meals, brought to him on a silver tray, and a personal massage therapist—because pain and healing nanites only did so much. It took the skill of human hands to soothe the most aggravated of muscles and prepare them for the next day's onslaught.

He would have a massage therapist for a week, then just as he grew used to their style and they to his musculature, they would be replaced.

"It's for your own protection," Scythe Hughes had told him. Hughes was his philosophy and ethics teacher, and the only one who seemed to genuinely enjoy teaching him. "The longer they stay, the more likely they are to divine who you are. And that would jeopardize everything."

"Sending them home won't?" Ben asked.

Scythe Hughes hesitated. "We . . . we don't send them home, Ben."

It took a moment for Ben to realize exactly what the scythe was saying. He could only gape in disbelief.

"I'm sure you understand why gleaning is necessary," Scythe Hughes said.

"No! No, I don't!" Ben said when he finally found his voice. "Scythes are supposed to be compassionate."

"We are. They were all gleaned with the utmost compassion and respect."

Now that he knew the truth, Ben told them he didn't need the luxury of massages, and yet they still sent someone every day. The scythes were trying to break down his psychological defenses. He knew that. They wanted to desensitize him to gleaning. Make him comfortable with impermanence. Force him to accept himself as a constant cause of death—as he would be when he became a scythe. Now he was only indirectly responsible, but soon ending human life would be his very purpose. He wondered how his sister ever managed to make peace with that. If she ever had.

He finally gave in on a particularly brutal day, when his body and his spirit felt too weary to fight, and allowed the massage therapist in. The woman soothed his back, his shoulders, his arms and legs. He tried not to look at her. Not to engage. It was difficult. But the next day was easier, and the next easier still. Exactly as the scythes had hoped. And when she was replaced by someone new on Monday, the only anger Ben felt was at himself for not feeling grief for the poor woman whose name he didn't even know.

But a month later something changed. A Monday rolled around when the massage therapist was not someone new. It was the same one who had been there the previous week. Ben was relieved, but also suspicious.

"Why are you here?" Ben asked.

The young man was about Ben's age. Ben had broken his own rule by talking to him a bit, and even made eye contact. It was hard not to—he had soulful eyes that were hard to look away from. And he was good-looking. Ben had been melancholy at the idea that he wouldn't return—although he knew his reason for that was purely selfish.

"Isn't it time for your massage?" he asked. "Was I not supposed to come today?"

"No, it's time . . . it's just . . ." Ben tried to keep himself from being flustered. "It's usually someone new each week."

"Sorry to disappoint you," he said with a grin.

Ben took his place on the massage table, face pressed into the little ring, looking down at the floor.

"Uh . . . you may want to take off your shirt first."

"Oh, sorry. Forgot."

Ben sat up, peeled off his shirt, and lay back down.

"Shoulders? Lower back? What needs work today?"

"All of it," Ben said.

"I'm Rajesh, by the way. But you can call me Raj. I don't think I told you last week."

"I hadn't asked," Ben said. He never did, and would cringe inside when his massage therapists volunteered their names, because he didn't want to know who he was sentencing to death by his mere presence. But this time, Ben didn't cringe. He was glad to know Raj's name. Although he didn't tell him so.

Then, when Ben didn't say anything more, Raj said, "And you're Ben Terranova."

Ben felt his back muscles suddenly tighten under Raj's touch. "How do you know that?"

"They told me."

Ben didn't expect that. He hadn't expected any of this. If that was true, then it was a change in the scythes' strategy. "So then you know . . ."

"I know who you are, and why you're here," Raj said. "Now relax and let me work on your back."

"What's going on?" Ben asked Scythe Hughes before his next philosophy lesson.

"I have no idea what you mean."

"Raj."

"Oh yes. We took it under advisement how offended you were by the gleanings and, thus, reconsidered."

"So, then, you won't glean him?"

Scythe Hughes chose his words carefully. "As long as he's needed, he'll be at your service. Unless, of course, you'd prefer someone else."

"No!" Ben said, a little too quickly. "No, he's fine. He's good. I don't need someone new."

"In that case," said Hughes, "if you're happy, we're happy."

Constantine hated that so much was riding on this boy. And time was growing short. The longer Benjamin Terranova's apprenticeship, the more likely Goddard would find out, put an end to it, and accuse Constantine of being a traitor. Only by catching Goddard off guard could this plan hope to succeed.

Constantine paid visits during his regular diplomacy trips to the Lone Star region, and observed several of Ben's classes through one-way mirrors. The boy did well in academics, and was finally reaching par in Bokator—but his killcraft was atrocious. He had the drive, but not the innate skill in the taking of life. True, many a scythe relied on more refined methods of gleaning, but would others rally around such a scythe? No—he had to master all of it. He had to impress the unimpressible. He had to astound the jaded.

"Push him harder," Constantine told Ben's instructors.

"What if he breaks?" Scythe Coleman asked, to which Constantine responded:

"All apprentices must be broken before they can be molded into a scythe."

Constantine was not hedging his bet. Ben had to succeed because there was no other option. Eventually he'd be ready to stand before conclave. He'd be ready to take his sister's place.

Constantine took dinner with Ben to gauge the boy on a more personal level. At first he was guarded, which was no surprise—Constantine knew he wasn't the type of person who put people at ease—but by the end of the meal Ben loosened up the tiniest bit.

"Are you sorry you started this?" he asked Constantine, as they finished their dessert.

"Are you?" Constantine deflected back.

"It's been interesting," Ben told him, which wasn't an answer, just another deflection. "But some of the scythes here are assholes."

That made Constantine let out a sudden, unexpected laugh. Had he been drinking, it would have sprayed everywhere. Constantine hated losing control like that, but it made the boy grin, which was as rewarding as it was annoying.

"Scythes are a prickly bunch," Constantine said. "Egos and expectations run hot—but trust me, whatever they expect of you, they expect tenfold from themselves."

"Well, then maybe they should beat themselves into the ground. Every time I achieve something, they just snap at me for not getting there sooner."

"They're teaching you not to expect praise," Constantine told him.

"But they want me to be perfect!"

"We can accept nothing less from you. Unlike schools you are used to, there is no passing grade below one hundred percent." Then Constantine added, "Remember, you still have to pass all your tests at a single conclave—that's how it's done here in Texas. Regardless of how sympathetic Lone Star scythes might be to our cause, they won't ordain a scythe who they don't feel is ready, and you only get one shot. All of your hard work will be for nothing if you're not ordained."

The boy glared at him. "Just what I need. More pressure."

Constantine sighed. "This is not just about you," he reminded the boy. "The 'pressure' you speak of is spread between all of us. Goddard is leveraging control over every region of the continent, except for this one."

"So . . . your 'diplomatic trips' for Goddard are less about convincing Texas to join up than they are keeping them from joining."

Now it was Constantine's turn to grin. "So you understand the tightrope I walk."

Ben shrugged. "You're good at it."

Constantine found himself unexpectedly pleased by the acknowledgment. It bode well for the boy that he could elicit such a response from a hardened scythe as himself.

"I'm glad we got to spend some time together," Constantine said, preparing to leave. "I trust you're being treated well in your off-hours—and that you're finding some comfort and relief."

"It's a comfort that they leave me alone."

"Well said—and I understand they've hired a professional partier to help you relax."

Then Ben paused just the tiniest bit. "No, I just get a massage in the afternoon."

Constantine realized his slip a moment too late, and tried to backpedal. "My mistake," he said, moving quickly to the door. "Well, I'll let you get back to your evening."

But the uneasy look in Ben's eyes made it clear that he hadn't just seen Constantine's gaff, but had seized on it. Suddenly he wished he hadn't come to see the boy at all.

The next day, Raj arrived at Ben's suite at the usual time, punctual to a fault.

"What's today's focus?" he asked, as he always did. "Neck? Upper back? Lower back?"

"It's all the same."

Ben had plenty of time to let Constantine's comment sink in. Enough time for it to ferment in Ben's mind. But Ben didn't tip his hand right away. Instead he went through the usual script. Some small talk, then facedown on the table. Only after Raj had begun did Ben begin.

"Raj, why were you hired?"

"I was hired through an agency," he responded.

"I didn't ask how, I asked why?"

"I was told they needed someone with my skills."

"And what are your skills?"

Raj hesitated. Not just his voice, but his hands on Ben's back. They stopped for a moment, then continued, but with less attentive focus than before. "What are you asking?" he finally said.

Ben took a deep breath and released it before he threw down.

"Are you a party boy?"

Raj's hands stopped completely. Ben rolled over and sat up to face him—which wasn't easy, because this wasn't a question, it was an accusation.

"What does that have to do with anything?"

"It has everything to do with everything," Ben said. "Why were you hired, Raj?"

Raj didn't seem flustered, just angry. "To do exactly what I've been doing. Ease your stress at the end of the day."

"By any means necessary?"

Raj glared at him. "We're done here," he said, and turned to leave.

Ben hopped off the table. "I don't think you get to decide that."

Raj stopped one step short of the door and turned back to him. "What do you want from me, Ben?"

There was a loaded question. There were so many ramifications to all of this, it sent Ben's mind spinning. That the scythes chose to hire a party boy for him. What were they thinking? No, Ben knew *exactly* what they were thinking. A salvo of emotions were ricocheting through Ben's head. Through his body. But all of them fed into a building fury.

"What do I want from you? If they're paying you for it, then I don't want it."

They stared each other down. Then Raj spoke. "Professional partiers aren't what you *think* they are," he said.

"Fine. So educate me."

"We're all trained in different specialties," Raj told him. "Mine are EuroScandian massage, casual conversation, and pool volleyball."

Ben could think of nothing to say to that, other than, "There's no pool here."

The cold look on Raj's face betrayed what he was about to say. "I'll ask the agency to find someone new. I quit."

He tried to open the door, but Ben advanced quickly, pressing his hand against the door to keep it from opening.

"You can't quit," Ben said.

"Of course I can. You've insulted me, but I won't let you rob me of my dignity."

"You can't quit because they'll glean you," Ben told him. "They gleaned all the others!"

Raj turned to him with such an expression of betrayal Ben had to back away. It was as if Raj thought Ben was behind all of this brutal intrigue, and not the scythes. It was their doing! It was all their doing! How could Raj not see that? Ben stormed off, throwing his hands in the air, finally releasing his rage now that it had a better target than Raj.

"Don't you see? They get into your head! That's where they live! Everything is a manipulation with them. They didn't hire you for your skills, Raj—they hired you because they know what I like—*who* I'd like! They probably have a database on all my boyfriends, and every kid I ever had a crush on growing up. And I'll bet they have one for you, too."

Ben took a moment to let his anger begin to dissipate, then forced himself to meet Raj's gaze. He could tell Raj was still hurt, still angry, but just like Ben's that anger was finding its proper direction.

"I'm sorry I thought you were in on their plan," Ben said,

plaintive and honest. "I was an ass to think that. They're using you the same way they're using me."

It was a while before Raj responded.

"So what do we do now?" he finally said.

"We don't give them the satisfaction of knowing they were right," Ben told him. "No matter how much we might want to."

Scythe Coleman was berating Ben less and less—and Ben found it incredibly satisfying when he triumphed over her. Those occasions were becoming more frequent, and his marks in killcraft were improving as well.

Ben's anger fueled his advancement. The scythes weren't the only ones who could plot and scheme. Now he had his own accomplice.

"When I become a scythe," Ben told Raj, "I'll grant you immunity so they can't come after you. Once I'm wearing the ring, they can't stop me."

Raj would still come daily to Ben's quarters for Ben's massage, but it wasn't always about the massage. Sometimes they just talked. Maybe teased one another—but never more than that.

"Because it has to be real," Ben insisted. "And it can never be real as long as we're like two animals caged together in a zoo. We're not going to perform for the zookeepers."

Yet even though they both agreed on this, human nature worked against them—because one always desired what one could not have. Although Ben never spoke of it, his feelings for Raj continued to grow.

"I didn't come here to fall in love," Raj told Ben one day—

the first to say what they were both feeling. "It's very unprofessional for a professional partier. We're supposed to be immune. Turns out I'm not."

Now Ben had an even more personal reason to succeed, beyond merely living up to the larger-than-life image of his sister. He had to become a scythe for Raj. To make sure that he would be safe. But even as he improved, Ben was constantly being told that he wasn't improving fast enough.

There was no question that the scythes who worked with him were increasingly anxious. According to Constantine it had something to do with an upcoming salvage expedition to recover the scythe diamonds from the bottom of the Atlantic, which were somewhere in the sunken ruins of Endura.

"Goddard has a plan to control all of those diamonds," Constantine told Ben. "And if he's successful, that will give him influence over every regional Scythedom in the world. All the more reason to set you up as an alternative rallying point before that can happen."

They saw Ben not as a person, but as a point in space. A singularity to stand in defiance of the black hole that was Robert Goddard. But that could only happen, of course, if Ben was presented at the next conclave, and was ordained.

These were the things flowing through his mind as he sparred with Scythe Coleman one day in early August. His thoughts could have been distractions, but instead they focused him, feeding into his single-minded desire to succeed for Raj's sake.

He deftly dodged Scythe Coleman's staff, then delivered a

kick to her head so effective, it not only knocked her out of the circle, it sent her sprawling into a corner.

"I should have seen that coming," she said, reminding Ben how Constantine had said the scythes here were harder on themselves than they were on him.

Coleman rose, taking a moment to let her nanites flood her bruise and unscramble her brain.

"I've been meaning to ask you," she said. "How are your sessions with Rajesh going?" It was the first time she had ever mentioned Raj to him. Ben didn't even think she knew his name. But then again, of course she did.

"Can't see how that's any business of yours," he said, just to see how she might react to a little belligerence. He thought she might be taken aback by his disrespect—but instead she gave him a sly little grin.

"In spite of what you may think, we are not your enemies," she said. "We're aware that you two have grown close. I want you to know that we don't disapprove."

No, of course they didn't disapprove. Not when they were the ones who had arranged their "closeness." There were times Ben wished that he hadn't seen through their scheme. Because his ignorance truly would have been bliss.

"We all need our diversions," Scythe Coleman said. "Scythes as much as anyone else."

Although she didn't realize it, calling Raj a "diversion" fueled their next round of sparring, and once again Ben bested her, his staff most certainly fracturing her left humerus. It was a wound that wouldn't heal fully without an infusion of rapid-healing nanites. Score.

"Your Bokator skills are getting less disappointing," Scythe Coleman told him, and ended the session. "Much less disappointing."

But that backhanded praise made him feel no better. There was something about all of this that was clawing at his subconscious. And like an itch, he just couldn't let it be. He and Raj had the upper hand now, didn't they? They had seen through the scythes' subterfuge. But what if the scythes' scheming didn't stop there. What if there was yet another layer? A deeper stratum that Ben had yet to uncover?

That night, Ben had a dream. He rarely remembered his dreams—especially since beginning his training—because his waking hours left no room for pondering such things.

He dreamed of *That Day*. When he was taken from his home with no warning or explanation, then was tied to a chair and left alone in a room. Soon his sister had come. As frightened as he was, he had been overjoyed to see her, because he knew she must be there to rescue him. She held a knife. A sharp one. Still, he had not understood. He thought she was going to use it to cut his bonds. It was only by seeing the tears building in her eyes that he knew why she was there and what she intended to do.

His sister was going to kill him.

At the time, he didn't know that this was her final test for scythehood.

Ben was revived a day or two later, but from that moment on, his sister no longer existed. Because now she was Scythe Anastasia. Even when she came home to visit, Ben could sense she wasn't the same anymore. Putting that knife through his heart had turned her into someone else.

He dreamed of That Day often in those first few months after Citra had become Scythe Anastasia. Having your own sister take your life was the sort of trauma that mood nanites could not erase. It had to be worked out the old-fashioned way. In time the trauma had faded, and the recurring dream had stopped.

This was the first time in four years he had dreamed of it—only this time it was markedly different. This time he was in his sister's place. He was the one holding the knife and approaching the chair. And the chair? It was empty, but it wouldn't be empty for long. And Ben knew exactly who would be sitting there.

He awoke, his sheets soaked through with sweat, and he knew that the scythes had outsmarted him again.

Ben could not share his realization with anyone—least of all Raj. Ben was in a very unique position—no scythe apprentice knew that the final test was to kill the person dearest to you. But Ben had the benefit of having been on the other side of his sister's blade.

Could he kill Raj?

No, not kill, Ben had to remind himself. *Render deadish.*

In an immortal world, deadish was nothing. It was an inconvenience. It was a blip in an otherwise perfect day. And yet Ben knew it would be the hardest thing he would ever do—which was precisely the point.

On the other hand, this meant that Raj could not be gleaned prior to the test—but that was a short-term benefit at best—because what if, once the test was done, Constantine or one of the other scythes allowed Raj's death to stand? Any one of them could claim it as an official gleaning and apply it to their tally. And the more Ben thought about it, the more likely that seemed.

Because it was elegant.

Terribly, brutally elegant. Not only would it tie up a loose end, but it would also cut an emotional attachment—because scythes weren't allowed such attachments.

"Scythes must love all humanity, but no individual human," Scythe Hughes explained in an early lesson on scythe ethics. It was baked right into the fourth scythe commandment. *"Neither spouse nor spawn"* was broadly interpreted and rigidly applied. No partner, no children, no exception. It didn't demand celibacy, but emotional castration. A scythe could share their bed with anyone, but their life with no one.

How cleanly efficient, then, if the specter of love was cut from Ben's heart, when he thrust his blade through Raj's.

Ben could refuse to do it. Drop the blade, on that final, crucial day of his apprenticeship. Could he get all the way to the final test, and falter at the finish line? It was never his life's ambition to be a scythe—but not wanting it was the first requirement. What he wanted—what he'd wanted for years—was to step out from the shadow of his sister. But if he did, it would be at Raj's expense.

The only option was to get out before he got there. Escape. It was that fantasy of escape that now kept Ben going. A fantasy he would somehow turn into reality. It would take planning, precision timing, and luck, but it wasn't impossible.

All Ben knew was his living quarters, the rooms where he took his lessons, and the corridors and stairwells that connected them. But Constantine's penchant for absolute control meant that the entire staff, including Raj, would be somewhere in the complex, rather than living off-site. With nothing to go on, he'd never be able to find Raj—and just looking would arouse suspicion. He'd have to wait until Raj came to him. And that wouldn't be until the following afternoon.

That day, Ben took Scythe Coleman down over and over again in Bokator. He aced a quiz on poisons that was more of an inquisition than a test. And in killcraft, he quickly took the offensive, and disarmed Scythe Austin, almost literally.

"The underscythe will be thrilled with your progress!" Scythe Austin said, even as a nurse wrapped his wounds, and gave him an injection of healing nanites.

There was no question that Ben was now at the top of his game, more focused and determined than he had ever been. They had no idea why, and didn't seem to care. All that mattered to them was results. It left a blind spot that Ben was determined to exploit. He would use the skills they had taught him to break out of their iron grip.

Raj arrived at the usual time and could tell right away that Ben was both energized and on edge.

"What's wrong?"

Then suddenly, impulsively, even before Ben knew he was going to do it, Ben kissed him the way he had wanted to for weeks.

Raj was caught off guard but wasn't unhappy about it. "I . . . thought we weren't going there. . . . Did something change?"

"Everything's changed," Ben said. "And we have to get out."

"What do you mean by 'out'?"

"I mean just that. We leave. Run. Escape. Take off somewhere they'll never find us."

"Hold on," said Raj, reeling from the sudden change of direction. "They'll find us wherever we go—they're scythes."

"Exactly! They're scythes, not the Thunderhead. They're fallible. Sure, they'll try to find us, but that doesn't mean they will—and since this whole operation is secret, they can't ask for help from other Scythedoms without exposing what they were up to."

Raj grinned, maybe a bit excited, maybe a bit nervous. "So you've got this all worked out, do you?"

"Just tell me you're with me on this."

"I am . . . but your training's almost over. And once you're ordained next conclave, we can go anywhere we want, because once you're a scythe, they can't make you do anything. So why don't we wait?"

"You don't understand!"

Ben could tell that he was full of questions, but he didn't ask them. Instead, Raj took a moment to gather himself, and chose to put all of his trust in Ben.

"My room is two levels down. Take the north stairwell, then four doors down on the right. It's near the loading dock."

Ben nodded; he hadn't even known there was a loading dock.

"Supply shipments come in at six a.m. every Thursday. I know because the gate's loud, the truck's loud, and the workers are loud. They wake me up every time. Come to my room at six. I'll leave the door unlocked."

"I can work with that," Ben said. "I'll get us out through the loading dock."

"You'd better. Because if you don't, we're both as good as gleaned."

As focused as Ben had been, it was hell trying to project a cool head and not give away to the scythes training him that something was brewing. They were good at reading people—or at least at reading him. He had to stay cool and on task until Thursday morning.

On Wednesday at midnight, Ben cranked the thermostat as high as it would go. So by a few minutes to six, his entire suite was sweltering. Then he opened the door to the guard on duty just outside of his quarters.

"Hey," he said, pretending to be bleary from sleep. "There's something wrong with the thermostat."

The guard, feeling the flow of heat rising out of the room, took a step in to investigate. "I'll let someone know."

But he never got the chance. Once he was inside, and out of view from the hallway camera, Ben broke his neck in a single well-practiced motion—a skill he had only ever done on practice dummies. The real thing was easier. At least physically.

He pulled the guard in, and took his clothes, which were baggy on Ben, but would give him enough cover for cameras he couldn't avoid.

He got to the north stairs and went down two levels. He could already hear the distant rattling as the loading dock gates rolled up. The clock started now.

There was another guard posted right at the exit of the

stairwell. Ben kept his head down, so the guard couldn't see his face right away.

"You're early," the guard said. "Shift's not over."

Ben splashed him with contact poison. He was deadish before he hit the ground. Ben glanced up, knowing that it was caught on camera, but no alarm was sounded. Whoever was monitoring the feeds was either asleep on the job or distracted. Scythe security cams were, luckily, not like Thunderhead cams. Because while the Thunderhead was monitoring every one of its cameras everywhere simultaneously, the Scythedom relied on actual human security personnel to watch them—meaning the whole system was subject to human error.

Raj's room was just down the hall. Ben turned the knob. It was unlocked, just as Raj had said it would be. Ben pushed the door open, fully expecting to see Raj awake and waiting for him. But the first thing he saw was red. Eye-assaulting red the exact shade as blood.

"How disappointing," said Underscythe Constantine.

Ben froze. He thought he had mentally prepared himself for every contingency. But not this one.

"I expected better from you," Constantine said. "You didn't even make it to the outer perimeter."

"What?"

"We had left three viable egress points for you in the complex, Benjamin. Three! If you had been clever enough to map the complex during your months here, you would have known exactly where they were. You would have made it to the perimeter fence."

Ben could only stammer. "Wh . . . what are you saying?"

"This was an exam, Benjamin. We wanted to put your ingenuity to the test. You failed."

Ben couldn't stop his mind from reeling. "Was Raj part of this? Was he—"

"No. Rajesh didn't know about this. Rest assured he did not betray you. But I'm sure you've figured out the real reason why he's here. For *you* to betray *him*. I imagine the prospect of your final test is the reason why you chose to escape."

"I won't kill him!"

"As it turns out," said Constantine, "you won't have to."

Ben didn't like the sound of that, or the look on Constantine's face. Or lack thereof. His expression said nothing. Not anger, not disappointment. It was as if Constantine had already dismissed Ben and moved on.

"Where's Raj? *Where is he?*"

Constantine didn't even bother to answer. "Escort Mr. Terranova back to his quarters."

Two scytheguards that were standing behind Ben grabbed him. He could have fought them off. Broken necks, bones, or whatever it took to be free of them, but what difference would it make? There were more guards in the hall to take their place. No matter what Ben did, he wasn't getting away.

"There is much to discuss," said Constantine. "We'll talk at breakfast. Eight a.m. sharp."

The guards pulled Ben away, while somewhere unseen, he heard the delivery truck leave, and the loading dock gates roll closed.

Back in mortal days, the doomed had a last meal before facing the executioner. Ben knew all about executions. Killcraft wasn't just about wielding weapons, but understanding their history. Everything from guillotines to firing squads to the electric chair were in the curriculum. Ben wondered if they felt the way Ben did as he was escorted to breakfast with Constantine.

"Sit, Benjamin. The food is already here."

All Ben wanted to know was what they had done with Raj—and Constantine knew it. But Ben had already asked, and Constantine had ignored him. To ask again would show weakness, and Ben refused to appear weak before this man.

"I am aware that you never wanted to be here," he told Ben as he crunched on a piece of bacon. "Even though you've finally managed to advance in your training, it's clear your heart has never been in it. And I feel for you, I truly do."

The idea that Constantine could feel anything would have made Ben laugh on any other day. The man was not a wellspring of compassion.

"The scythes under whom you study only want the best for you."

"That's a lie," Ben said. "They want what's best for the Scythedom. They haven't got a clue what's best for me, and they don't care."

Constantine sighed. "You're right," he admitted, "but it doesn't matter anymore."

Here it comes, thought Ben. He wondered whether they were just going to send him home, or glean him so there'd be no evidence of their failure to make him fly.

"There's no longer a need for you to become a scythe," Constantine said. Ben refused to look away from Constantine, holding his gaze in defiance.

"Don't you want to know why?" Constantine prompted.

"Doesn't matter," said Ben. "Am I going home in a bus, or a box?"

"Neither," said Constantine.

Ben glanced at him, and thought he caught a glimmer in the scythe's eye. The man was pleased by something. Ben couldn't tell whether it was genuine or sadistic. Finally Constantine told him what he'd been holding back.

"Your sister's remains have been found."

That was the last thing Ben expected to hear. "Wait—there were remains? But I thought—"

"Yes, we all thought she had been devoured with the others, but her body was found intact in an airtight chamber."

Ben put down his fork. "*How* intact?"

Constantine couldn't contain his grin. "She's been revived, Benjamin. And she'll soon be making a triumphant return to the world!"

Ben found himself breathless, speechless. The news was as hard to process as her death had been. What it would mean for his parents! What it meant for him! This was wonderful news! And yet . . .

Constantine leaned back in his chair and crossed his arms in immense satisfaction. "You can rest easy now," Constantine said, "because you are no longer needed."

And that was it. The training stopped. The lessons stopped. The constant rebuking ceased. After over a year of being told day in and day out that he was so terribly important, he became virtually nonexistent.

And so had Raj. He did not show up that day, and Ben was more and more worried. There was no reason for them to glean Raj now that keeping Ben's apprenticeship secret was a moot point . . . but there was no reason to *not* glean him, either.

There was a perfunctory gathering of Ben's instructors so they could say their goodbyes. Some seemed to just want it over with, but others, like Scythe Hughes, were genuine in their well-wishes for him. So he was the one who Ben approached.

"Please, Scythe Hughes," Ben asked, trying not to beg. "Can you tell me what they've done with Raj—my massage therapist?"

"More than your massage therapist, I think," Hughes said with a warm smile.

"Then you understand why I'm desperate to know where he is, and what they've done with him."

Hughes sighed. "I'm really not at liberty to tell you," he said, clasping Ben's hand. "Do your best to put him out of your mind."

Then Constantine swept in. "How we deal with the staff here is not your concern."

Hearing that made Ben snap. He may not have had a killer instinct before, but it was well cultivated in him now. He'd rip Constantine's heart right out of his chest if he could.

"You're a monster!" Ben said. *"You don't deserve to be an underscythe. You don't deserve to be anything. And the sooner you're gone from this world the sooner the world will be a better place."*

Constantine was not taken aback. He barely even raised his eyebrows.

"Everything is relative, Benjamin. With the help of your sister, I will be trying to take down Goddard, a true source of evil in this world. So am I a monster, Benjamin? Or am I a hero?" He considered the question seriously. "Perhaps I'm neither."

They did not allow Ben to go home, because his home no longer existed. Constantine, under orders of Goddard, had gleaned his parents, and had confiscated all of their belongings shortly after Ben's apprenticeship began. Then once they were dead, Constantine brought their bodies to an off-grid revival center, and secretly "ungleaned" them.

"It was necessary," Constantine told him. "The scythe database had to log their gleanings, or Goddard would be suspicious." Now Ben's parents were in hiding with new names in a place that not even Constantine knew.

As for Ben, who had been expected to be home when they came for his parents—Constantine worked a bit of magic in the Scythedom's database. Ben was logged as having run away from home, then vanishing into unsavorism somewhere in Antarctica—which was far enough away for Goddard not to care—although he *would* care once Citra made her grand reappearance. Because Ben could be a prime hostage to keep her in line. That's why Ben needed to vanish as completely as his parents now. Alone and as unknown as a person could possibly be.

"You'll be safe where we're sending you," Constantine told him. "And in time, you'll be able to enjoy whatever life it is you're living."

Ben couldn't imagine that would ever be true, no matter how many hundreds of years he might live.

Then, before Constantine said his final goodbye, he slipped

an envelope into Ben's hand, and whispered into Ben's ear.

"I am not the monster you think I am."

The beauty of St. Petersburg meant nothing to Vasily Markov. These days he saw everything in somber shades.

Vasily Markov. That's what his official Ident said. But he still felt like Ben Terranova and didn't know if that would ever change. If his sister had her way, he might be able to emerge from hiding, and reclaim his name someday. She had already made several eye-opening broadcasts, drawing a searing spotlight on Overscythe Goddard. Perhaps she would bring him down. Perhaps not. Ben felt so far from matters of the scythe world, he might as well have been in a different universe, and not just halfway around the world.

So, who was Vasily Markov? He was a student at St. Petersburg University majoring in classic literature of the region. Never mind that Benjamin Terranova didn't know Pushkin from Chekhov. But he would learn. He would adapt. He would have to. And he would have to avoid drawing attention to himself, because attention could alert Goddard's agents, who were most certainly out there looking for him.

The West Ruskaya region, like the Mericas, Israebia, and so many places in the world, had dark moments in its history. But now it was just that: history. Lessons in an Ancient Studies rubric. Once the Thunderhead put an end to nations, only the finest of each region shone through. Ben hoped the darkness he had experienced could become a historic footnote in his life too. But that would take time. It would take effort. And it was easier said than done.

He had an apartment with a view of the Neva River in a lively, bustling part of the city. And yet in the weeks he had been there, he had yet to meet anyone. He kept waiting to feel the need, but all he felt was the desire his training put in him. To fight with blade, bullet, and bludgeon. To end life. He had been trained to be a scythe, and now what was he? Nothing. He wasn't even himself. He thought about Rowan Damisch. Is this what he felt when he was denied the ring the same day his sister was ordained? He found himself hating Rowan less and less—especially now that it seemed he wasn't the one who sank Endura.

It was on a rainy Tuesday that Vasily Markov skipped class, and went for a tour of the Hermitage museum. Not because he particularly wanted to, but because he had a ticket for a specific group tour, on that specific day. A ticket that had been put into his hand by the crimson scythe who so effectively obliterated his life. Ben would have thrown the ticket away, but he couldn't ignore his own curiosity.

As it turned out, it was the best museum tour Ben had ever experienced. Not just because of the museum's many great works, but because of the tour guide. His name was Milan, and he knew everything there was to know about every work of art in the museum.

After the tour was over, Ben lingered. Tourists were giving Milan generous tips for his well-informed tour. Ben did as well, but made sure to be the last in line.

"It was more than I could have hoped for," Ben told him.

Milan was as gracious and friendly as he had been through the entire tour. But nothing more.

"Thank you, Vasily," said Milan, which caught Ben off guard. "So you know my name?"

Milan smiled a bit sheepishly. "Your name tag," he said.

"Oh right." And when it was clear to both of them that Ben was stretching the moment, Ben said what he'd wanted to say since he first arrived at the museum and their guide introduced himself.

"I miss you, Raj," Ben said.

Milan looked at him, and for a moment Ben thought he might break character. That he might even embrace Ben. But instead he said, "If I knew who that was, maybe I'd miss him, too."

Ben offered a wistful smile in return. "Sorry, I thought you were someone else."

"It happens," said Milan. "I'm glad you enjoyed the tour."

Supplanting wasn't just a science, it was an art. When the Thunderhead did it, it was never without permission of the individual, and afterward, the new persona was always told that they had just had their memories replaced. But when scythes did it, they followed no such rules. As far as Milan the tour guide knew, he was always Milan the tour guide from some-where in West Ruskaya, with memories of a childhood to match the fiction. He would never know any different. Never know that he was once someone else. But how much of you does supplanting change? It changes who you *think* you are, but does it change who you *actually* are to your very core?

"Thanks again, Milan." Ben turned before the tears building in his eyes could be obvious. Such ambivalence in those tears. To know that Raj was gone, and yet had not been gleaned. He was someone else, but he was alive.

I am not the monster you think I am, Constantine had said. Yet somehow Ben didn't hate Constantine any less.

It was as Ben neared the main exit that he felt a hand on his shoulder grasping slightly. He could feel fingertips applying the slightest bit of pressure, and it released the tension in his neck. Ben smiled, because he knew that touch without even having to look. Muscle memory. That, at least, couldn't be erased.

"Perhaps I could give you another tour, Vasily," Milan said. "A personal tour. The Hermitage has more masterpieces than can be seen in a single afternoon. It would be my pleasure to show them all to you."

Ben met his warm gaze, and marveled at how, in an instant, they had moved from strangers to something more.

"I'd like that," Ben told him. "I'd like that a lot."

And who knows? Maybe Vasily would come to know Milan even better than Ben knew Raj.

The Persistence of Memory

Co-authored with Jarrod Shusterman and Sofía Lapuente

In the heart of Barcelona, beneath the towering spires of La Sagrada Familia cathedral, lived a scythe whose name echoed across the entire cityscape. A name spoken in timbres of dread and mysterious intrigue. A name whispered. Always whispered.

One might think the magnificent cathedral—which took more than a hundred years to complete in mortal times—would be the home of its namesake, Honorable Scythe Gaudí. But it was not. It was the home of Scythe Dalí, who had taken up residence there for no reason other than spite. It was a deep, abiding spite that was as eternal and immortal as he.

Scythe Dalí could often be seen strolling La Rambla, Barcelona's most glorious street, in a silk robe that was bluer than the sky, and streaked with gold—colors inspired by the paintings of his Patron Historic. They were shades that brought a strange and dreamlike light to the world. And at sunset, Dalí would stand on the narrow stone walkways between the towering cathedral spires, looking down on the masses, stroking the signature mustache that hung above his lips like the arms of a praying mantis as he contemplated his next victim. Scythe Dalí didn't just glean. He created. He forged. He designed. Each of his gleanings was a surreal masterpiece. As his Patron Historic used to preach, *"Without madness, there is no art."* And since the

Thunderhead had erased madness from the world, he decided to *be* the madness.

"Will it hurt much?" The young bride's voice trembled as she clutched the hand of her groom; a tall, slim, naturally youthful man, whose legs were shaking as if on unsteady stilts.

"Your deaths will be instantaneous," Scythe Dalí assured them. "And if not, your pain nanites will deaden the worst of it. Have no fear."

The pews of the hilltop chapel were full of onlookers. All wore festive masks for the occasion. Bejeweled plague doctors, and the feathered harlequin guises of Venetian royalty. Those who had won the Witness Lottery were instructed by Scythe Dalí to dress themselves as if for a Carnivale masquerade. It was all part of the ambience. All part of the show.

Upon the altar was a high-pressure combustor gun filled with twelve kilograms of pressurized coal. When triggered, it would unleash a blast of super-heated pyroclastic ash that would flash-burn any living thing in its path—which is why the audience was shielded behind heat-resistant glass.

"You will be immortalized today," Dalí told the young couple. "Your incinerated remains, encased in an eternal shell of silicate ash, will be an homage to the volcanic winds of Pompeii. Consider yourselves a post-mortal interpretation of *Romeo and Juliet*."

"We are not 'post-mortal' if we must die today," the groom dared to say.

"Well, yes," agreed Dalí. "But the rest of us are."

The groom gulped down his fear, and his best man stepped

forward. "You can do this," his friend told him. "Just think of what an honor it is. And how you'll always be remembered."

The couple looked to each other and nodded, as if they had any choice in the matter.

"Your lives will end at the very pinnacle of your happiness," Dalí pontificated. "What could be more noble? More perfect?"

To Dalí, this was supreme satisfaction. On this day, in this quaint, historic chapel, he was going to make the world a better place yet again by enriching it with culture. The gleaning would occur at the exact moment the young couple's lips locked—in the exact millisecond after he pronounced them husband and wife—for he himself would do the honor of marrying them.

The stage was set, and everything that would not be caught in the blast of ash had been pre-melted. The plastic ficus on either side of the couple had sloughed into a dark goop that had hardened like a pair of monsters crawling up the stairs. Singed paintings were slung on the walls, and dripping stained glass windows had now been blurred into peculiar blends of color. Such leitmotifs gave him many a talking point at exhibitions and cocktail parties. All that remained was to create the centerpiece of his grand tableau. As for the crowd, today's was a boisterous one, hooting and hollering as if attending a circus. No one had respect for true art anymore.

To Dalí, gleaning was the purest, most precious form of art. He had learned from the mortal styles. Baroque taught in piercing detail that this world was full of both pain and grandeur. Expressionism painted the inscapes of the human mind, and modern art revealed its absurdity. He had, many times, gone to the Louvre to ponder its greatest treasure—and as a scythe he did not have to wait in line as did everyone else They even allowed him an hour alone with it, the entire gallery to himself. *Af Klint Contemplating Sappho's Exit.* A masterpiece recognized worldwide as the last piece of mortal art. A painting that captured both the melancholy and joy of the transition to immortality.

But now, in a world without suffering, what strokes of passion were left in the artist's brush? What colors on their canvas? Death, however, was something that not even the Thunderhead, with all its trillion zettabytes of perfect thought, could never take away from mankind. Which is why Dalí swore to make each gleaning a masterpiece. And this one would be his magnum opus.

The ceremony proceeded as such things do; the processional, the giving away of the bride by her tearful father. At last, vows were traded, and Scythe Dalí consecrated their marriage.

"Aldo and Pilar, I now pronounce you husband and wife. You may kiss the bride." Then Dalí slipped behind his own heat shield and powered up his combustor gun, which hummed on with a zing that drew gasps of anticipation from the pews.

But before he could pull the trigger, all the lights went out, and the gun powered down.

A blown circuit? What terrible timing! Such outages were long ago innovated into extinction, but old monuments such as this chapel still clung to their rustic charms.

"All is well," Dalí said. "A mere glitch. Please hold your positions."

At times like this he wished he chose to have assistants—but he abhorred the idea of not doing everything himself. He exited through the back door to correct the technical issue, a circuit breaker that had popped off. However, upon returning through the old wooden doors of the chapel, he found that the couple was gone.

His subjects had left him at the altar.

"*¡No puede ser!* " he exclaimed. "This cannot be!"

He looked to the crowd behind the glass shield, still in their Carnivale masks, but now the only reason they still wore them was because they were all too terrified to reveal their faces.

"Where did they go?" Scythe Dalí demanded from the crowd. Most were too frightened by his wrath to move, but a few pointed to the open entrance to the chapel.

Subjects who are to be gleaned do run from time to time—and, by the rules of the Scythedom, are punished by having the rest of their family gleaned with them. He turned to the bride's parents, who put up their hands as if to say, "Who can understand the young?"

Dalí's gaze darkened on them. "Your daughter has ended your lives today. You know that, don't you?"

They looked down and nodded in sad acceptance. He considered doing the deed now but decided it would be best in the presence of the daughter. Once he tracked her and her new husband down. How selfish, how stupid. The couple had traded glory for ignominy and a few more minutes of life.

Dalí turned to the crowd. They were not laughing—but laughter is what he heard. He had been made a fool today, his masterpiece destroyed, glorious death stillborn at his feet.

"Go!" he told the crowd. "Get out of my sight before I glean every last one of you."

They did not need a second invitation. The pews cleared out in seconds.

Once they were gone and he was alone, he allowed his rage dominion. He screamed and snatched a melted candelabra hanging off the edge of a table like a cluster of silver snakes and hurled it across the room. He kicked over his combustion gun and hurled the chunks of coal within at the stained glass windows, breaking what wasn't already melted.

This was not an accident.

The power didn't go out on its own. Someone had planned the couple's escape. And Scythe Dalí knew exactly who it was.

In the soul of Barcelona, in the lush hills of Park Güell, lived a scythe who had taken up residence in the park's old maintenance shack. A scythe whose name brought a smile to people's lips.

Unlike Scythe Dalí, this scythe's robe was not eye-catching. His was an old woolen tunic, colored in natural, earthy tones. His deep, contemplative eyes would often be turned to the pages of a mortal-age book, his hand pensively stroking a graying beard—because although he could choose any age to maintain, he maintained himself at a respectable sixty. He believed no one deserved youth more than once, much less a scythe. When he wasn't out performing that most hallowed service of gleaning, he could be found in the gardens of Park Güell, cultivating flowers with the patience of a saint. Because, as he often said, *first love was required, and then second came technique.* It was a philosophy based on the teachings of his Patron Historic.

He never gleaned on the expansive grounds of Park Güell.

Everyone knew the park was a safe haven for those who visited—and many did. The revered scythe would walk among people as they strolled, taking in the glorious mosaic sculptures that graced the park; whimsical spiraling candy-like structures created by his Patron Historic. He would smile at children and they would smile back, then ask their parents who was this strange man who had allowed himself to get old. "That is none other than Scythe Gaudí," they would whisper. Always whisper.

Today, however, Scythe Gaudí had a mission that took him away from his beloved park.

There was a small cottage to the west—the honeymoon destination of a pair of newlyweds. Gaudí was waiting for them in the cottage's rose garden when they arrived, both relieved, and distraught. They looked over their shoulders, sensing phantom pursuit, but no one had followed them. Scythe Gaudí knew that Scythe Dalí had not bothered to find out where they had intended to go after the wedding, because Dalí clearly didn't think it mattered, as gleaning would preclude any future plans.

"Please, come sit," Gaudí said as he welcomed them to the courtyard. "I've churros and the finest drinking chocolate in all of Barcelona for you."

"Thank you, Your Honor," the young husband said as they sat down.

"Please call me Antoni," Gaudí said, then gingerly filled each of their cups with the silky rich liquid.

The husband and wife gripped hands. "Thank you for everything you've done for us. For freeing us from Scythe Dalí's horrible show."

Gaudí sighed. "Would that I could give you immunity, and a

year of wedded bliss—but rules are rules. Once you are marked for gleaning, there is no choice in the matter. But there is no law that says your gleaning must be a spectacle."

"How will you do it" the bride blurted out.

Instead of responding, Gaudí picked a rose and handed it to her. On it was a tiny spider spinning a web between the petals.

"Rest easy in knowing that all is a part of a grand pattern," he told the couple. "A pattern of organic beauty that has intrigued all great thinkers through the ages. It is the reason rose petals so please the eye; the reason sea shells curve a perfect spiral so that you may hear your own blood rushing within its walls. And it is the reason every garden spider knows how to pattern its web."

The girl gently placed the rose down on the table and began to sip her chocolate, as comforting and soothing as Gaudí's voice.

"The Fibonacci ratio," continued Gaudí. "It's a sort of divine symmetry that has existed long before man walked the earth."

"But you haven't answered our question, Your Honor," said the groom. "How will you glean us?"

Gaudí smiled at them in gentle understanding. "But it's already done," he said.

A moment, and the two regarded the cups in their hands. The poison was not in the chocolate, but gently applied around the rim.

The two began to pale. Their hands to shake, but that was not the poison—it was their fear. "There will be no pain," Gaudí told them. "You may now retire to your marital bed. Consummate your union. Sleep in each other's embrace. And in the morning, you simply will not wake."

And so the couple, tears in their eyes, went inside hand in hand, and closed the door behind them.

But no sooner had the door closed than a tile crashed down from the roof, shattering on the patio. And then a woman's voice from the neighboring cottage called out.

"You! What are you doing up there! Come down before you hurt yourself."

The sixteen-year-old girl on the roof dislodged another tile and began to slide. She managed to grip the edge just long enough to prevent her fall from being catastrophic, then plunged from the rain gutter into the roses with a yelp and a thud. She emerged scratched and bleeding from the thorns.

The rotund woman from the next cottage, wearing an apron smeared with flour, hurried over.

"What's wrong with you!" shouted the woman. "Are you trying to render yourself deadish?"

Only then did she glance at Gaudí, and her face displayed the shock that always accompanies a surprise encounter with a scythe.

"Your Honor! I'm so sorry, I didn't see you there." She struggled into a deep curtsy that dislodged clumps of dough from her apron.

"Have no fear, señora, you are not in danger of gleaning today." Then Gaudí turned to the girl. "Quite an entrance you made, Penélope. You've nearly provoked this poor woman's nanites into heart resuscitation."

"It's good to see you, too, Uncle Antoni."

"So you followed me to my gleaning again."

As always, Penélope was dressed in all black, and although

her eyes were outlined in strong lines dark as pitch, there was no amount of eyeliner that could darken the brightness of those eyes.

"*Perdoname*, Uncle Antoni."

"Apologies only work the first time." But Scythe Gaudí was more amused than angry.

Penélope could tell, and she smiled mischievously, then grabbed a churro from the table and ate it.

"And how do you know I did not poison the churros?"

Penélope shrugged. "If you did, I'll be revived soon enough."

Just then, the baker leaped toward Gaudí with surprising agility for a woman her size, grabbed his hand, and kissed his ring before he could stop her.

"Thank you, Your Honor!" And she hurried back to her cottage before Gaudí could say a word.

Gaudí sighed, and Penélope glowered. "You're just going to let her get away with that? Stealing immunity from you?"

Gaudí shrugged. "It's not like I can undo it," he said. "Besides, all things come full circle. I'm sure, in time, something of value will be stolen from her. And whatever it is, she will probably miss it more than I miss this stolen immunity."

Penélope rolled her eyes at what she clearly felt was an empty platitude. But it wasn't. It was truly how Gaudí saw life. And death.

Penélope turned to look at the closed blinds of the cottage, behind which the young couple were spending their final hours. "I always wonder what happens to them once they're gone," she said.

"That is something that only the Thunderhead knows," he answered. "Or maybe it doesn't. Some say their souls are uploaded along with their memories, so that a piece of them continues living within the system. Others say it's like taking a very long siesta, but with no promise of waking."

"They say death is the cousin of sleep," Penélope offered.

"Well, don't let him keep you up at night." Gaudí kissed the part in her wild black hair. Then he put his arm around her. "Come, let the newlyweds have their time together. And as death so fascinates you, you may attend their funeral with me once it is arranged."

"It was you and I know it! Don't you dare deny it!" Scythe Dalí stormed toward Gaudí as Gaudí worked quietly in his herb garden. "You ruined my masterpiece," Dalí said, pointing an accusatory finger.

Gaudí continued tending to his garden. "You seem unsettled, Salvador. Can I interest you in some calming herbs?"

"Do you deny it?"

"I was nowhere near the cathedral."

"But you have conspirators!"

"Ah," said Gaudí, handing Dalí a cluster of yellow chamomile flowers. "You must mean friends. I know it is a concept you're unfamiliar with."

"Don't play games with me, Antoni! One way or another, it was your doing, just like last time, and the time before!"

"Well, *last* time, you wanted to publicly guillotine a genetic heir to the ancient royal line of Franco-Iberia. My conscience allowed me no choice but to take the poor girl's life before you could turn her gleaning into a spectacle. And that other time—you wanted to throw a pilot off the roof, covered in golden feathers."

"*That was dramatic irony!*" raged Dalí.

"Yes," said Gaudí, not raising his voice in the least. "And how ironic that he was dead before you hurled him from the roof?"

"It is my prerogative as a scythe to glean as I please!"

Gaudí couldn't help but serve up a sly grin. "True, but there is no law that prevents me from gleaning your subjects first."

Dalí glanced at the herbs in his hand, as if noticing them for the first time, and hurled them to the ground. He stormed away, but quickly stormed back.

"You will not get away with this! I will bring my grievances to conclave!"

But Gaudí just laughed. "And what do you think they will do? Censure me for keeping our sacred duty of gleaning from becoming a mockery? I don't think so, my friend."

"I," growled Dalí with rancor to spare, "am not your friend!"

"Well, as I said, you are challenged by the concept," said Gaudí. "But, for what it's worth, I count you among mine."

In response, Dalí grabbed a pitchfork that was leaning against the fence. "I will take this to the most crowded spot of your beloved park," Dalí said, "and I will use it to glean whoever I please. It will be bloody. It will be ugly. And it will forever tarnish Park Güell."

Scythe Gaudí just returned to his gardening. "Do as you will," he said, with neither malice nor judgment.

Scythe Dalí strode off—but just on the other side of the gate, he hurled the pitchfork to the ground, clearly having lost his appetite for gleaning entirely.

Through all of these, neither scythe noticed Penélope

peering out of the window of the humble shack that Gaudí called home, watching all that transpired between the two.

> *Every great artist evolves in stages, and it is those very stages that make the creator who they are. I came from a family that had no love or understanding of art. My father would look at van Gogh's sunflowers, and wonder why not just hypergrow the real thing to plop on your dining table? Thus, it was the struggle against the mundane that drove me to my* true *family. The creators of yore—my spiritual forbearers whose works loom large in the world's museums. Da Vinci, Vermeer, O'Keeffe, and Ong. It is their passion for creation that flows in my veins, and spills from the veins of those I glean.*
>
> *Things were different in the mortal age. Art was inspired, because the stakes were always real. There was no Thunderhead to feed the starving artist. There were no nanites to quell the urge to take one's own life. All that pain and suffering was transformed into passion and beauty spread forth on each canvas—the way the earth turns filth into glorious sunflowers.*
>
> *It is through gleaning that I transmute misery into masterpiece. This was my promise to my spiritual forbearers; that the only paint on my life's canvas would be blood red.*

—*From the Journal of Honorable Scythe Dalí*

Dalí paced the upper balconies and catwalks of La Sagrada Familia, his rage a rolling boil that could be felt throughout the great cathedral. *Perhaps,* he thought, *I could throw a party to lift my spirits.* His parties were lavish affairs. Back in the days before he took up residence there, the cathedral was a constant infestation of tourists—but now, no one was allowed in unless invited by Dalí. Anyone who was anyone in Barcelona would be at his parties. He would personally give his guests a tour, watching as they marveled at the towering basalt columns and glorious mosaics of stained glass. The tour would always end down in the crypt, where he would show them the final resting place of Antoni Gaudí—the *real* Gaudí—all the while secretly hoping for the day that *Scythe* Gaudí would be so kind as to self-glean. Dalí would be more than happy to inter the miserable man beside his Patron Historic.

Dalí himself planned never to self-glean. Not just because he felt the world needed him, but because a part of him feared that Barcelona would celebrate rather than mourn him. Dalí was feared, but Gaudí was loved. *Well, at least they respect me,* Dalí would tell himself—but respect borne of fear is not the same as respect borne of love. One passes with you to the grave, the other flourishes after your departure. So for Scythe Dalí, it was best to never depart.

His thoughts of a party fizzled as he paced—because he knew that those who came did not come out of love, or even fear-induced respect. They came to experience the cathedral. They came in hope of the immunity from gleaning that he would give out freely at his galas. For one night, they would be sycophants, only to speak ill of him when they returned home. *What,* he often wondered, *must I do to make them love me as they love him?*

And then a thought came to him. What if he conceived of a

gleaning in which all of Barcelona could participate? Yes, yes—a gleaning where the audience would not be just an invited few, but the whole city! In this way he could win their hearts and quell the humiliation of this latest fail.

As he considered the idea, his fury at Scythe Gaudí began to be replaced by the familiar thrill of creation. This new idea would be his masterpiece! A performance piece that would weave its way through the streets and boulevards of the city. A work of living/dying art that all could witness!

Dalí began drafting his plan. He brought in engineers and machinists. Woodworkers and artisans. At his behest more than a hundred people were put to work preparing for a gleaning event the likes of which had never before been attempted. And everywhere he stationed loyal members of the scytheguard to make sure that Gaudí could not sabotage him again.

In less than a month, the construction of Dalí's grand clock-work of death neared completion. Which was more than could be said about his home. The cathedral was officially completed toward the end of the mortal age, but in all truth, it never really was. There was always one team or another working on the cathedral. A restoration squad here, a cleaning team there, stonemasons somewhere else. The workers were skilled at making themselves scarce when Dalí was present, so he rarely saw them—but today there was a teenage girl working alone within the cathedral proper. She had climbed the spiral maintenance stairs to the mezzanine level, and, standing on the wrong side of the railing, touched up some ornate trim with a paintbrush, not seeming to care that a single misstep would mean a treacherous fall, and a day or two in a revival center. She dared to whistle to herself—a sound that Scythe Dalí could not abide, for it echoed in the cavernous space like a teakettle.

What's more, the girl clashed horrifically with the cathedral's aesthetic. She was dressed in all black—a blatant affront to the colorful nature of the basilica. Dalí approached the girl from the proper side of the railing. Rather than being reverent, she pretended not to notice him—and he knew it was pretension because he caught the slightest flick of her eyes as he came into her field of vision.

"Stop that infernal whistling," Dalí demanded, "or I will advise your foreman of my displeasure."

She finally glanced as him, but quickly returned to her work. "No whistling. Got it," she said. "How about humming? You okay with humming?"

"No sounds whatsoever," Dalí told her. "And when you address a scythe, you should always end your statements with 'Your Honor.'"

"Got it," she said.

"Got it, *Your Honor*," Dalí prompted.

"Right. Noted for next time."

"That *was* the next time."

This time she didn't respond at all, only nodded. Dalí had to admit he was taken aback. Never before had anyone treated him with such blatant discourtesy.

"Do not forget," he said, "I am a courier of death. My displeasure could end very badly for you."

She raised her chin slightly. It projected pride, and maybe

a bit of defiance. *"Thou shalt kill with no bias, bigotry, or malice aforethought,"* she said, daring to quote him the second scythe commandment. "I'm pretty sure gleaning someone because you find them irritating is considered bias."

Dalí darkened. "No scythe has ever been disciplined for gleaning the annoying."

"Then you guys aren't really living by your commandments, are you?" She glared at him through piercing eyes.

"Enough! You're fired," Dalí decreed. "Which means that as of this moment you're trespassing. Now leave."

"If scythes own nothing then how could I be trespassing?" she countered. "Just because society allows you to be a squatter in this cathedral doesn't mean you own it any more than my uncle owns the shack he squats in." Then she slipped down the scaffolding with the skill of a cat and disappeared.

Only after she was gone did Dalí piece together who this disrespectful girl's uncle must be.

There weren't many things that scared Penélope. When you're not afraid of death, nothing else holds any weight. Whether it was snakes or spiders, or dark, deserted places, nothing fazed her. But that didn't mean she wasn't hardwired like all other humans to experience the only primordial fear that was left: fear of the unknown. It's why she'd play games with herself, teasing that fear, making believe she could really feel the cortisol coursing in her veins. That her life was in peril. It was the reason why she dared to enrage the volatile Scythe Dalí. It was why she wandered lonely paths through *casco viejo*—the old side of town—in the dead of night. It was a place that still had culture and history in its walls, where small divots might just be bullet holes that held a secret story. Where lantern-lit balconies had barely changed since the mortal days. Where old relics called CDs still hung from windows in a primitive attempt to ward away pigeons. It transported her to another time entirely. Penélope's mother would tell people that her daughter was simply old-fashioned— but anyone who really knew Penélope understood her affinity to the past was more of an act of protest against the present. And the future—which promised to be more of the same.

As she wandered the old streets that night, Penélope knew she was being followed. Could be unsavories, looking to give her some pretend harassment, because pretending to be law-less was all they could really do. The Thunderhead would never allow anyone to follow her with true ill-intention. Then again being the niece of a scythe occasionally brought stranger things into her life's orbit. Young men hoping to curry favor with her uncle by offering her romantic overtures. Reporters looking for a fresh angle on a story. But for her own amusement, she turned this into one of her games, pretending it was a monster from mortal-age stories pursuing her, slithering through the darkness, ravenous for its next meal.

Fear! Irrational anxiety! She allowed herself to be enveloped by it, trying to make it last longer than her nanites would allow. What joy to feel her heart quicken!

Whoever or whatever was stalking her had made a few cru-cial mistakes. A kicked pebble here and there. A shadow that crossed a streetlamp. It only fed her excitement.

She turned a corner and ducked into a doorway, waiting for

her pursuer to pass, so she could turn the tables. When she saw who it was she smiled darkly. She should have known!

"Scythe Dalí, what an unexpected surprise!" she said as she popped out, making him jolt. "So you like the old city, too?" she asked. "Or is it just that you like following young women."

He blustered a bit at the suggestion. "Certainly not!" he said. "Just one in particular—and with no untoward intentions, I might add."

"So what are your 'toward' intentions?" Penélope asked, then added, "Your Honor," in such a way that it sounded more like an insult than an honorific.

"I was curious to know if my suspicions were correct, and that you are a ward of Honorable Scythe Gaudí."

"You could have just asked."

"Which is why I followed you. In order to ask."

"I'm his niece," Penélope informed him.

But Dalí held up his hand, showing her his ring. "And yet my scythe gem doesn't glow red in your presence. If you were his niece you would have immunity from gleaning for as long as he lived."

Penélope sighed. "Well, I'm not his *actual* niece," she said. "My father and Antoni were childhood friends. But my father got himself gleaned last year on a business trip to MidMerica— along with everyone else on the plane."

Dalí harrumphed at that. "Yes, I heard about that. A tawdry affair. Merican scythes can be so ham-handed in their gleanings."

"Anyway, once my mother was done grieving and all that, she decided to turn a corner. Now she's twenty-one again, and has run off to the Seychelles looking for love. So Uncle Antoni offered to take me in."

"Interesting," said Dalí. "But tell me, how did you get into my residence—I checked with the work foreman, and you were never a part of his team."

Penélope shrugged. "There's lots of ways into La Sagrada Familia for someone who's good at climbing."

"Yes, but why?"

Penélope grinned. "To see if I could."

"And then you tried to anger me . . ."

Again she grinned. "To see if I could."

"Well," said Dalí, with the slightest twitch of his curled moustache, "you succeeded on both counts."

Dalí regarded her for a few silent moments. Penélope couldn't tell whether he was suspicious of her or intrigued. Perhaps a bit of both.

"I would accuse you of spying for your 'uncle.'"

"You'd be wrong," Penélope said. "He has no idea I went to La Sagrada Familia. He'd be furious with me if he knew."

"The two of you do not see eye to eye?"

Penélope shrugged. "He never lets me watch his gleanings," she said. "I thought maybe you would."

"Ah," said Dalí. "Now I understand."

Then out from his robes he produced a hypodermic needle, and in a single motion jabbed it into her neck. Penélope's thoughts began to swim, and her vision darkened almost immediately. Her legs gave out beneath her, and Dalí caught her as she fell.

"You said . . . you had no . . . untoward intentions," she said as consciousness began to slip away.

To which Dalí replied, "It is a scythe's prerogative to lie."

I do not grant frivolous immunity.

I will freely spend my time with visitors to Park Güell, but never have I held out my hand for them to kiss my ring. The only immunity I give is that which I am commanded to give—to the families of those I glean. Occasionally immunity is taken from me, unbidden—but to those who grab my hand and kiss my ring, I hold no ill will. Because in those instances, immunity is their choice, not mine.

You see, human beings have always had the ability—and indeed a propensity—for taking life. But to grant capricious freedom from death? That is an arrogance I cannot abide. Other scythes may wish to cast themselves as saviors, and thus serve their own egos, but I choose not to join them. The irony is, by refusing to dole out random immunity, people seem to love me more.

It is not that I don't have those in my life who I wish to be immune from gleaning, but to grant it would be akin to playing God. The Thunderhead, in its wisdom, chose not to play God, even when taking on godlike tasks. The least I could do is follow its example.

—From the journal of Honorable Scythe Gaudí

Unlike Scythe Gaudí, Scythe Dalí was a believer in "frivolous immunity," for wasn't it a noble endeavor for holy figures to absolve the masses? And were not scythes the closest things to holy figures that the post-mortal world had?

Scythe Dalí also believed that gleanings not only needed

artistic expression, but an element of sacred respect. The night before a gleaning he would treat gleaning subjects to the finest meal of their lives, as part of that respect. A post-mortal nod to the way an executioner would feed the condemned before the gallows, or electric chair, or whatever other barbaric death device the minds of mortals had conceived. Dalí wanted his chosen subjects to feel their life was completed, not ended. He wanted them to be comfortable—unless, of course, the essence of their gleaning required otherwise.

As was his custom, Dalí had an enormous wooden table set up in the central aisle of La Sagrada Familia, and across it spread a sumptuous feast.

He checked to make sure that Penélope was bound correctly to her chair. Loose enough to be able to feed herself, but firm enough that she could not escape. Then he administered the stimulant to wake her.

"Welcome to your last supper," Dalí said, once Penélope was fully awake. He gestured magnanimously to the lavish display of food. "*Jamón serrano, esqueixada, Botifarra amb mongetes*— all my favorites."

Penélope cleared her throat and spoke with the force of someone who had not just awakened from sedation. "*Your* favorites? Shouldn't they be *my* favorites?"

"Well, yes—but I didn't know yours, so I had to rely on my own palate."

Dalí watched her as the truth of her situation set in. Usually in these moments, his subjects would scream. They'd cry. They'd beg for their lives. They would break down in the most human of ways.

But Penélope did none of that.

Instead she almost, but not quite, smiled.

"So this is what it's like to have your last meal." And although her voice trembled with fear, her eyes seemed to glow, as if she received pleasure from her own anguish.

Dalí chuckled mirthlessly—which annoyed him because this was a gleaning he wanted to take true pleasure in. "That is correct," he said. "And your gleaning will be the centerpiece of my greatest masterpiece." And then Dalí found himself launching into his boilerplate speech he gave to all those he was about to glean. "I know this may be hard for you to hear, but passing on doesn't mean your life will end, no—what I am offering you is a chance at immortality—to be remembered forever, by crystalizing your existence in the memory of eternity."

And Penélope actually laughed. "You are so full of yourself," she said. "'The memory of eternity.' Maybe next you can go to Pamplona for the running of the bulls and create your next 'masterpiece' out of literal bullshit."

Dalí was taken aback. Such disrespect! He had gleaned for less, but he stayed his hand. She was already marked for gleaning, so what else could he do to her? There was no downside for the girl to speak her mind, and she knew it. Dalí almost admired the audacity of it.

No, he could not end her life out of rage for her insolence. Gleaning her here, at the table, would ruin everything. Only a day ago, he had still been trying to find the right subject for this great work—and then the perfect one appeared right there in the cathedral. Beyond perfect! Penélope was, on so many levels the only one who could fulfil the role.

"You were born for this," Dalí told her.

"And I'll die for it," she countered. "Uncle Antoni won't be happy."

That made Dalí smile with genuine glee. "That," he said, "is the best part!"

Penélope was to sleep in a chamber at the top of a spire in the east wing of the cathedral. She imagined herself like a princess locked away in a castle. Taken care of by servants, waited on, hand and foot, even though that was far from the truth. Once she had been brought to the chamber, she was left alone with her thoughts. Dalí had taken it upon himself to pick out what dress she would wear the following day. The day of her gleaning. It hung there, on a hook on the wall. Black and lavender. The colors of mourning.

She was going to be gleaned. The feeling that thought gave her reminded her of when she was little, and her father would spin her on the tire swing over and over. It was exhilarating, even euphoric—right until nausea took over and she'd vomit her brains out.

That's how her penchant for terror began. The earliest memories of her thrill-seeking behavior. As Penélope progressed in school, she would take it upon herself to climb the bell tower and commence class manually, to the chagrin of the headmaster. It has always been her way; everything peppered in a delightful flavor of danger. She had been marked unsavory twice, but never for more than a few months. That was another treacherous line she liked to walk.

She supposed this was why, alone in the spire-top chamber,

Penélope was able to stomach the idea of her own demise. She had, in a way, spent a lifetime preparing.

At close to midnight, there was a knock at the door, then Scythe Dalí peered in, wearing that perpetual repugnant look on his face as if he had smelled something foul.

"What do you want?" Penélope asked.

"It's only customary that I make sure you're comfortable for your final night."

She sat up. "I'm as comfortable as someone can be on their last night of life. So you can leave now."

Still, Dalí lingered.

"I can't help but feel that you wanted this," he ventured. "I wish to know why. Are your endorphin nanites set too low? Surely the Thunderhead would have adjusted them."

Although she didn't care to talk to him at all, Penélope tried to give him an honest answer. "It's not that I want to be gleaned . . . but I'm curious. I've always been."

"Curious of what it's like to die?"

She shook her head. "I've been deadish before. But it's not the same. It's temporary. The deadish never reach that moment beyond time."

"What if there is no such moment?" Dalí asked.

"That's what I want to find out."

Dalí frowned, but on him, that expression looked pensive. "We cannot know the things we cannot know."

"That's not an answer."

"Well, I shall deliver you to your answer tomorrow."

But even as he said it, he seemed to take no joy in the prospect. He sat down in a chair in what would have been a corner, had the small room not been circular. "I had a daughter a long time ago," he said.

"I thought scythes couldn't have children."

"It was before I was apprenticed," he said. "When she was eight years old, my wife and I took her on a hike in Asturias." He smiled at the memory. "Pinar Setas—a beautiful forest. The mountain views of the ocean were spectacular. But a storm rolled in. These were the days when the Thunderhead was still learning how to influence the weather." Dalí wouldn't look at Penélope as he wove his tale. This is how she knew it was a tale that wasn't going anywhere happy. He cleared his throat and continued.

"Lighting comes ahead of a storm, did you know that? It had been a dry season, and when lightning struck, the hillside began to burn. Within minutes, we were surrounded by flames. We ran, going back the way we came, but the path wound unpredictably, and we found ourselves moving toward the fire. Then the wind shifted, and we were overcome by smoke."

He paused. Penélope waited, knowing not to ask what came next. In truth, she wasn't sure she wanted to know.

"Fire is one of the few things that can fully end you, without the assistance of a scythe," he said. "Death by fire was rare then—even rarer now—but it happens. I awoke in a revival center. Eight days. That's how long it took to bring me back. But my wife and daughter?" He shook his head. "Drones kept trying to bring their bodies out, but were melted by the flames. The Thunderhead wasn't able to recover them until they were beyond revival."

"I'm sorry," Penélope offered, but he was too far away to hear, helixing down and down into that awful memory.

"My world became very dark. The Thunderhead allowed

me to dial down my nanites, so that I could mourn—but it was not enough. The more pain I felt, the more I needed to feel. Like you, I longed with all my soul, to know where they were. What experience did they share on the other side of death's obsidian veil." Then he chuckled bitterly. "There was a point at which the Thunderhead offered to supplant my memories with new ones. I would become someone different. But no. If I did that, then there would be no one to mourn them. No one who still remembered the life we had. It was then that I met Scythe Miró. He must have seen something worthy in my suffering, because he took me on as an apprentice. I was twenty-eight—years older than the other apprentices. But I took to the task. The river of my life flowed in this new direction. Not a day passes where I don't think of them. But instead of joining them, I choose to send others their way. So that they will not be alone." He paused, then added, "And because I am a coward."

Penélope was in awe of the fact that Dalí was, beneath his pompous facade, a real human being, with genuine feelings. She wondered if her uncle knew this story.

"If it's cowardly to live, then the whole world is guilty," she told him.

Then Dalí snapped back from the depths, and glared at her, as if she were the one responsible for dragging him away from his wife and daughter. "I only share this to show you that I understand your peculiar fascination with what lies beyond."

"I won't tell anyone," she said.

Then he stood, rigid, regaining his composure. "Of course you won't," he said. "You'll be gleaned before you even have the chance."

Then he strode out, his robe flaring behind him.

. . .

The event was publicized far and wide. Crowds began to gather before dawn. Barricades and a phalanx of the scytheguard were put in place to make sure that spectators could see, but could not interfere with the great gearwork that was to churn its way through the city. The fact that it was public, to be viewed by all, was also insurance against Gaudí. He wouldn't dare embarrass himself by playing out their rivalry for the public to see. And by the time he found out that it was his precious Penélope that was being gleaned, it would be too late.

Dalí had worked vigorously on the machinations of the event weeks before he chose Penélope as his subject—a complicated system engineered to the millimeter, and once it was triggered, it would proceed like falling dominos creating a deadly chain reaction.

It would begin in España Square, where a replica of the *Torre Del Rellotge* clock tower made entirely of ice would be unveiled at dawn. The clock tower would melt under the rising sun, filling a bucket . . .

. . . which would activate a zipline, that would carry a headless statue soaring over the streets like a phantom, toward the Magic Fountain of Montjuïc . . .

. . . where it would hit a switch, that would release a rat into a maze . . .

. . . where the cheese at maze's end was set upon a perfectly balanced scale . . .

. . . which would then trigger a heavy granite orb to roll down an incline . . .

Thus, contraption after contraption would unravel before

all who watched, creating a mechanical procession that would wind its way around the city, and ultimately to La Sagrada Familia. And there at the peak of the cathedral's central spire, the subject of the day's gleaning would meet her end.

Penélope woke to Scythe Dalí standing over her, a grin practically painted on his face.

"Good morning! Your big day begins!"

It was still long before dawn. But what did it matter? She had barely slept at all. "You say that like it's my birthday rather than . . . the opposite."

Dalí gestured to the dress hanging on the wall. "You will wear the mourning gown, with the veil covering your face. You will witness with me the commencement of the festivities—the starting of the great machine. Then we shall return to the cathedral for the conclusion."

"And if I don't cooperate?"

Dalí's grin shifted toward something much darker. "You know the law. If you resist this, I will be forced to glean not only you, but your family—which means my next stop will be the Seychelles, where I will pay a visit to your mother."

Penélope bit her lip. She may have been irritated by her mother's life choices, but she would not unleash a scythe upon her. "Leave," she said, taking a moment's pleasure from ordering a scythe. "Leave, so that I can get dressed."

A crowd had already gathered in España Square. As dawn broke, they watched as Scythe Dalí climbed the scaffold to the mysterious shrouded tower. He was accompanied by a veiled woman in black and lavender—

the same colors of the shroud that covered the tower from its tip to its base. Then the moment the sun began to slice across the rooftops, Dalí pulled a rope, and the shroud fell away to reveal that it was a clock tower made entirely of ice. The crowd murmured and pointed, awed by the sight.

There were two children who had managed to sneak past the barricade and hide themselves in the scaffold's shadowed side. They touched their tongues to the ice, laughed, and shushed each other. From their hiding place, they couldn't see Scythe Dalí and his companion, but they did hear them speak.

"Is this all supposed to impress me? Because it doesn't," the young woman said.

"I couldn't care less," Dalí replied, "as long as the crowds below are impressed."

If the two children were any indication, Dalí had already achieved that goal. Now there was nothing but to wait, with building anticipation, as the tower began to lose its hard edges, the clock began to melt, and a bucket began to fill with the thaw.

Once the headless statue had soared nearly half a kilometer, and the rat was negotiating curve after curve toward the cheese, Dalí and Penélope were driven back to the cathedral—all the while Dalí watching things progress on his tablet.

"The machine will soon reach the seafront, then travel up La Rambla, turn left at Plaça de Catalunya, then wend its way all the way back to the cathedral by the stroke of nine. That is the hour of your gleaning, child."

Penélope said nothing. She had exhausted all quips and comebacks. She held silent behind her veil, and that seemed to unsettle Dalí. She began to wonder if the veil was really for him—so that he didn't have to see her face through the entire ordeal.

"The excitement of the crowd was a fine thing indeed," Dalí said, filling the silence with blather. "You see? They now love me as they love your uncle."

He must have heard doubt in her silence, because he became immediately defensive. "You think they don't? How could I create such a fine spectacle for the city, without them appreciating its creator?"

This time, Penélope could not hold herself back.

"Spectacles don't earn love, and they certainly don't earn respect."

He had no response to that. Instead he turned his rancor toward the driver—a scytheguard who was probably used to Dalí's verbal abuse.

"Are we to be beaten by snails?" Dalí scolded. "Engage the autopilot if you can't find us a faster route."

"Your barricades have created gridlock throughout the city, Your Honor. You'll have to be patient."

Which made Penélope laugh in spite of herself.

Dalí bristled ever so slightly. "So you think me a spoiled child, do you? Forever demanding immediate gratification?"

"I didn't say anything."

"You didn't have to."

"Why does anything I think matter if I'll be gone before the morning's out?"

Dalí shifted his shoulders uneasily. "Even so, I do not want you to think ill of me."

Again she laughed. "You're taking my life. How could I think anything but ill?"

And then something occurred to Penélope. She knew the truth of it without even asking—but she still said it, just to gauge his reaction.

"I remind you of her, don't I? I remind you of your daughter."

Dalí pursed his lips, and waved his hand feigning to dismiss the idea. "She was only eight. She was nothing like you."

"Strong-willed . . . inquisitive. Maybe you see in me what she could have been."

"*Not another word, or I will glean you where you stand!*"

To which Penélope calmly responded, "We're in a car. I'm sitting."

Dalí scowled, his bitterness feeding upon itself. "Today your uncle—your dear, dear uncle—will weep as he's never wept before. And he will finally see that I am not a man to be trifled with."

"If I am to be a spite-gleaning, at least allow me the dignity to show my face."

"I will, child. Once we are atop the central spire of the cathedral, your face shall be revealed for all to see. You will have dignity. You will die with grace. And as your spirit departs, it will be borne away by a hundred doves that will be released to the heavens at the moment of your passing."

Down at the seafront, Columbus plunged from the top of his towering monument, landing on one side of a teeterboard, which launched a steel globe in a ballistic arc toward La Rambla, where it smashed a glass tank filled with seawater. The resulting surge pushed small models of the Niña, Pinta, and Santa Maria toward the painted edge of a flat Earth, and into a barrel that tipped, and rolled over a remote ignition switch for publicar, which then began to drive down the avenue toward the next set of engineering feats. Crowds cheered following the unfolding event as it moved ever closer to the great cathedral.

"I'm sorry, Your Honor, there's nothing I can do," said the driver. "Every way we turn, the roads are impassible."

With all the dark feelings swimming within Penélope, amusement at this irony is what bubbled to the surface. "You planned your machine to the tiniest degree," she said, "and yet you didn't plan a way to get back to the cathedral?"

"We will get there!" wailed Dalí. "Even if I must grow wings and fly, we will get there."

Penélope should have been relieved by this glitch in Dalí's perfect matrix. But what good would it do her? It might confound the method of her gleaning, but not the fact of it. And even if her uncle got wind of this, he could not save her. He was a man of honor. Just as he could not save the newlyweds, he could not save her—the best that he could do would be to rescue her from Dalí, so that he could glean her with his own loving hands. That was something she didn't want. No, the best she could hope for now was to be the successful mainspring of Dalí's gearwork. *There are worse ways to be gleaned,* she tried to tell herself. Although at the moment she couldn't think of any.

"I can get us to the cathedral," she told Dalí. "But you have to promise me something. Promise me that once this is done, you'll make peace with my uncle."

Dalí scoffed at the suggestion. "After today, there will be no hope of that."

"But promise me you'll still try. Tell him that it was my last wish."

He regarded her then. She couldn't tell whether the glassy look in his eyes was a hint of tears, or due to his fury at being mired in Barcelona traffic.

"I will do as you ask," he said.

With an agreement struck, she told him to get out of the car.

"Proceed on foot?" said Dalí. "It's too far—we'll never get there on time."

"Who said anything about going on foot?" Then she led him to a set of stairs in the middle of the sidewalk, leading down into darkness.

"The metro?" said Dalí with incredulous indignance. "A scythe does not take the metro!"

"Well, it's either that, or sprout those wings you were talking about."

And so, with no other choice, he followed her down.

No one troubled them on the metro. People gave them a wide berth, and whispered to one another, wondering if this metro journey was a planned part of the event up above. Dalí did not disabuse them of that notion.

Less than ten minutes later, they bounded up the steps of the cathedral, the crowd making way for them—but it was still a race against time. The device had gone through dozens of machinations, was less than a kilometer from the cathedral, and they still had to climb to the very top of the central spire.

Holding Penélope tightly by the hand, Dalí climbed up and up the steep concrete steps that spiraled tightly like a seashell, moving so quickly the turns made him dizzy. Not a good thing when they'd be on a narrow, unguarded platform hundreds of feet above the city.

Finally he kicked open a wooden door, and they began to climb the steep sandstone roofing, where the wind was so strong it threatened to tear them off. They could hear shouts from below as people spotted them. Dalí took a moment to glance west, finding the torch that would soon be lit, and launched toward a kerosene-soaked rope that would send fire shooting across the last hundred yards to the crossbow in the plaza.

It was here, just moments from the finale, that Penélope's resolve weakened. She resisted and it became harder and harder for Dalí to impel her toward the peak.

"You can't slow down now," he told her. "We're almost there!"

"I think . . . maybe I'm scared after all."

"Cast your fear aside," Dalí told her. "It can't help you. Embrace this with elation!"

At last they reached the platform, and Dalí quickly shackled her to the iron cross atop the spire. He removed her veil, and the crowd below clamored and gasped now that they could see her face—as if her face actually meant something to them.

They were in place with barely a minute to spare. Dalí pointed to a box on the platform with them, in which they could hear urgent rustling. "The doves!" explained Dalí. "The moment the arrow pierces your heart, I will release them, and their wings will carry your essence to wherever it is you might be going."

"Or not," Penélope said.

"Or not," Dalí had to admit. "But it is beautiful and poetic, nonetheless."

Then Penélope's expression grew hard. Angry. She glared at him. "In my entire life, I have never played the victim, but you would make me one now."

"Not much to be done about that, I'm afraid," Dalí said.

"Yes there is. Unshackle me."

"Why, so you can escape? So you can dodge the arrow and ruin everything?"

"No. So that I can face this by choice, not chains. I chose this by putting myself in your path. Now let me own it."

Dalí was stunned by her resolve. It seemed even stronger than his. Such an impressive, willful young woman. Such a pity her life would now end.

"Of course, Penélope," he said, and he undid her shackles. True to her word, she did not attempt to run. She held her place on the platform, her chin high and proud.

"When I get there—if there *is* a 'there'—I will find your wife and daughter, and tell them that you sent me to keep them company."

Dalí felt his lip quiver. He could not remember ever having a gleaning subject show such courage. Such sincerity.

Meanwhile, a hundred yards down the street, the torch began to fall toward the rope.

And that's when Dalí saw Scythe Gaudí.

He was down there in the plaza with the crowd, standing just beside the crossbow.

Dalí was furious! Gaudí would knock the crossbow so that its arrow would fly wild! He would ruin another perfect gleaning, and humiliate Dalí yet again. Dalí could barely control his rage!

The torch ignited the rope. Fire raced along the rope toward a lever that would trigger the crossbow.

And down below Gaudí did not move.

He did not lift a finger to misalign the crossbow.

Why was he not sabotaging this?

The flame was nearly to the trigger.

What are you doing, you fool? Dalí screamed within his own mind. *Ruin this! Save the girl! Why are you just standing there!*

Gaudí met eyes with Dalí across the distance as if there were no distance at all. And instead of reaching for the crossbow, Gaudí put his hands on his hips.

The flame reached the lever.

The lever pulled the trigger.

The crossbow fired.

And Dalí, wailing at the top of his lungs, hurled himself in front of Penélope. He felt the arrow enter his back. The pain was sharp and pronounced. Suddenly there were doves flapping all around him, escaping to the sky. He collapsed, but was eased down onto the platform by Penélope, who held him in her arms.

And down below the crowd cheered.

"Bravo!" they cried. *"This is the greatest self-gleaning any scythe has ever achieved! Such a surprising finale! He had us all fooled! Bravo!"*

And it occurred to Dalí this had been Gaudí's plan all along. He had tricked Dalí into self-gleaning. Penélope was planted for the purpose! She was merely a gear in her uncle's machine.

But if that were true, then why was Penélope crying?

"That was the stupidest thing I've ever seen," she said

through her tears. "You've ruined your masterpiece."

"But . . . but listen to them cheer. I've given them exactly what they want."

"Shut up," said Penélope. "You're not dead yet." Then she reached around and pulled the arrow out of his back. It hurt as much coming out as it had going in—but his nanites were already working to quell the pain. "The arrow hit your shoulder, not your heart. . . ." Penélope said.

"But . . . I . . . must die now," he said. "Anything less would be . . . would be . . ."

"Absurd?" said Penélope. "Your Honor, everything about you is absurd—why should this be any different."

Dalí heaved a weighty sigh. "Damn," he said. "I should have dipped the arrow in poison."

But, as they say, hindsight is twenty-twenty. And unless he now hurled himself from the platform, it seemed increasingly clear that he wasn't going to die. How awkward. How humiliating. And yet in that moment something occurred to him that gave him a twinge of joy.

"If I am to live, this will not have been in vain. I will take you on as my apprentice," Dalí told Penélope. "You shall train to be a scythe under my skilled tutelage."

Penélope laughed. "That will really piss off my uncle."

Dalí's mustache twitched into the slightest smile. "Yes, I imagine it will."

While down below, the crowd expressed their disappointment as they began to realize that Dalí was still alive . . . and that this was just another one of his failures after all.

Meet Cute and Die

Love fell upon Marni Wittle like a ton of bricks. And it left her in a revival center.

"Hello, Marni," said the cheery but irritating head nurse of Woolwich Revival, upon Marni's awakening. "So good to see you again. Wish it were under brighter circumstances!" Which was what Nurse Lucille always said when Marni turned up there. It wasn't as if Marni was a risk-taker, or careless, or blasé about dying . . . yet death found her with spectacular regularity.

"Rise and shine, eternity awaits!" said Nurse Lucille, then she snapped up the blinds—which seemed specifically designed to snap like a firecracker while being raised. But perhaps it was just Marni. She always tended to be sensitive to sights and sounds upon revival.

"I have your Neuro-Adeno-Stimulant shake ready for you, as soon as you think you can hold it down."

"What happened this time?" Marni asked, her voice raspy from days of being deadish. In all honesty, Marni didn't want to know what happened, as it was always such an embarrassment. But she had to ask.

"A gentleman put the drop on you, so to speak," Nurse Lucille said. "Fell nine stories just to meet you!" Then she laughed at her own joke.

Marni was actually relieved. "So it wasn't anything that I did?"

"Not unless walking down the street is a crime."

"A what?"

"Nothing, dearie, just a mortal expression." She handed Marni her Neuro-Adeno-stimulant shake, which was, as usual, beyond vile.

"Can't I skip the NASti-shake this time?"

"Sorry, dearie, it's the rules. It activates the taste buds and digestive system. It's good for you!"

Marni knew of no other revival center that forced its patients to drink such sickening swill. But Woolwich claimed to be innovative in their approaches. Marni did suspect, however, that the horrible taste was intentional, as to deter splatters, and others who went intentionally deadish. As an accident victim, Marni should have been given a pass, but no. She couldn't help but think Nurse Lucille took pleasure in watching her drink it.

After she had swallowed the last fetid drop, Marni asked the question she had been avoiding since the moment she awoke.

"Have you notified my aunt?"

"No way around it," said Nurse Lucille. "I have strict orders to let her know any time you 'pay us a visit.'"

Marni grimaced. "I know, but couldn't you have, just this once, forgotten to tell her?"

"And get on your aunt's bad side? Not a chance, dear. Besides, you've been here in revival for more than two days— she would have known something was amiss when you didn't come home."

Marni heaved a world-weary sigh. Facing her aunt would

be only slightly better than being killed by some plummeting personage.

"At any rate, we've let her know you've come around," said the nurse. "She'll be by to collect you before sundown, I imagine. But for now, why don't I fetch you a few scoops of rum-raisin?"

"Yes, if you have."

"Oh, we always have! Not much of a call for it, but I keep it on hand just for you!"

The plummeting personage in question was a young man by the name of Cochran Stæinsby. He, too, was no stranger to revival. This was his fourteenth. Not that he was tallying them for any particular reason, it was just hard not to. Especially when one kept getting charged for revival. His parents always complained about it—and now that he was on his own, and the bills came straight to him, he understood their frustration.

"Must I still be billed when it was an accident?" he had once asked the Thunderhead. "It's not my fault that I'm prone to them."

"It's not a matter of fault," the Thunderhead had told him. *"It's the rule in an accident, regardless of who's to blame."*

This time, however, his death was caused by a malicious act—one of the rare instances in which his revival fee would not be his to pay. It would be charged to the culprits, a pod of local unsavories. They had gone into the hotel that Stæinsby happened to be staying in, then proceeded to loosen the floor-to-ceiling windows in several of the guest rooms. Mr. Stæinsby, while hurrying to dress the following morning, lost his balance while putting on his trousers, leaned against the window, and was the first to discover the unsavories' prank.

He recalled trying desperately to pull the rest of his trousers up as he fell—because being deadish would be bad enough, without also being deadish on a public street with his pants halfway on. Only at the last moment did he realize that there was someone directly in his gravitational path.

The young woman broke his fall just enough for him to remain alive for a few seconds, and he couldn't help but notice she was rather pretty. Even with a broken neck.

After Cochran had awakened from revival he asked the nurse about her. "Did the girl I land on survive?"

"Afraid not," the nurse said, kindly. "She's a few rooms over—just woke from revival herself."

"May I . . . speak to her? I'd like to apologize."

"Whatever for?"

"Well, it's my fault she's here, isn't it?"

"Not unless falling from a sabotaged window is a crime."

"A what?"

"Never mind. Let me see if she's up for a visitor."

Marni looked up from her ice cream bowl to see a man standing at the threshold. "Can I help you?" Marni asked. It was unusual for strangers to intrude upon recovery rooms.

"Hello, you must be Marni Wittle. I just wanted to stop by and see if you were all right."

The man was quite handsome, and still seemed to have more boy than man in him. He was around her age, twenty, maybe twenty-one. A young man trying to act older than he actually was. His good looks were of the unassuming sort, and he had the most soulful of eyes.

"Do I know you?" She was still a bit woozy from recovery, and had not yet made the connection as to who this must be. Unlike him, she had been instantaneously killed, so very literally never knew what hit her.

"Well, yes, in a roundabout way," he said. "I'm the one who fell on you."

"Oh. So you're a splatter, then?"

He was taken aback by the suggestion. "No, no, I'm nothing of the sort. It was an entirely unintentional fall."

"Sorry, I meant no offense."

"I'm the one who should be sorry, Ms. Wittle, to have made you lose two full days."

His eyes had locked on hers, and she couldn't look away. She felt breathless, and it wasn't just nausea from the NASti-shake. This was something else entirely.

Marni offered him a smile. "Well, time away from our lives can be a good thing now and then." She held out her spoon to him. "Some rum-raisin?"

"Rum-raisin? It's my favorite. They never have it at revival centers."

"This one does!"

He accepted a spoonful, and his eyes rolled with delight.

"The nurses once told me the secret," she whispered to him. "Revival center ice cream is infused with nanites that go straight to the brain's pleasure center. It's intended to combat Revival Depression Syndrome."

"There's such a thing?"

"Not anymore," Marni said. "Thanks to this stuff."

He smiled at her. She expected the moment to grow awkward, but it didn't.

"I'm Cochran. Cochran Stæinsby," he said. "But you can call me Ran."

"What a curious nickname."

"Well, the first half of Cochran is a bit problematic for a nickname, isn't it? So I grew up being called by the second half. I've been Ran, Ranny, even Rando."

Marni considered it. "A fine name like Cochran deserves its due. So that's what I'll call you. Unless you prefer 'Mr. Stæinsby.'"

He smiled warmly. "Cochran is just fine."

Then from downstairs they heard a voice bellowing with practiced displeasure.

"Where is she?" the voice roared. "Where's my niece? Take me to her straightaway! My patience hangs by a tether today and God help anyone who makes it give way."

"That's my aunt," Marni said. "You'd better go—you don't want to be in her sights when she's in a mood."

"Sounds like she's the type of person who's always in a mood."

That made Marni giggle. "You don't know the half of it!"

"May I . . . may I see you again, Marni? Lunch perhaps? To make up for all this?"

Marni didn't have to think twice. It might have been proper to appear more coy, but she wanted to see him again, and she wanted him to know it.

"How about tomorrow?" she said. "Noon?"

"Where?"

"Where we first met."

Cochran smiled. "I'll be sure to approach from a different direction."

Marni's aunt tended to get her way. Scythes generally did. She was Scythe Boudica, named after a legendary hero of early Britannia, long before it was Britannia. And while the original Boudica was known to be a tall and commanding woman of broad vision, Scythe Boudica was none of those things. She was small of stature, and of even smaller mind, overly concerned with middling things. Her greatest pleasure in life was the endless airing of complaints. If whinging could be a method of gleaning she would have happily employed it.

Her distinctive robe was made of an authentic medieval tapestry featuring a unicorn that looked like a goat, a lion that looked like a golden retriever, and fancy ladies with oblong, undersized heads. The tapestry-robe was enormously heavy and Scythe Boudica complained of the weight on a regular basis, but bore it nonetheless.

"It is the unending burden of a scythe to suffer the stifling weight of humanity," she once proclaimed. "And humanity certainly does chafe."

Boudica had not been her first choice of Patron Historic. Originally, she had planned to be Scythe Beatrix Potter, since the beloved writer's stories not only reminded her of her childhood, but had also led to a lifetime love of rabbits. But as with Mr. Stæinsby, the name "Beatrix" did not make for flattering nicknames. She was worried people would call her Trixie— which might be a fine name for a dog, but certainly not a scythe. Boudica, on the other hand, was a regal-sounding name.

Only when other scythes began calling her "Boo" did she realize her folly.

Marni didn't tell her aunt about Cochran, or their upcoming lunch date. Instead, she sat quietly at dinner when they arrived home from the revival center, as her aunt engaged in an all-too-familiar harangue.

"Marni, you must be more cognizant of your surroundings. Had you been, you never would have been caught unawares by some falling miscreant."

"He's not a miscreant, Auntie Boo—he was the victim of an unsavory prank."

Her aunt waved a dismissive hand. "Of course he'd say that—he's trying to get out of paying for revival. How could you be so gullible?"

Marni endured this lecture, as she did all her aunt's discourses. She had long since learned to let her aunt's ramblings roll off her back. It wasn't as if she needed to curry favor. Marni, as a close blood relative, had immunity as long as her aunt lived, whether they resided together or not, so that wasn't the reason why she stayed. She stayed because Auntie Boo needed her. Who else would run the castle? Who would be there to talk her aunt out of gleaning the housekeeper, or the groundskeeper, or the cook, when she lost her temper? And although Severndroog Castle was nothing special as far as scythe residences go, it was a pleasant enough place to live.

Besides, if Marni left, where would she go? Her own parents

had moved on, as many people do, devoting themselves to new families and new lives. But Auntie Boo was a creature of habit and wasn't going anywhere. Life with her was stable—and, truth be told, as much as Marni hated her aunt showing up at the revival center, it would be worse if no one came at all.

Marni had never been on a date. Scythe Boudica made it clear that suitors were forbidden, and that a girl of Marni's tender years ought to make her own way in the world before entangling with a partner.

"Know yourself," she would pontificate. "Stand in your own two shoes, or you may find yourself crushed like a bug beneath his." Whether she truly advocated this advice, or just said it to keep Marni's attentions entirely on her, Marni didn't know. But either way, she wasn't about to tell her aunt about her date with Cochran Stæinsby.

They met at the appointed place at precisely the appointed time. Cochran had made reservations for them at a nice Franco-Iberian bistro. It was a place in which Marni had never eaten. There were only ever three places she dined with her aunt. The Criterion, Kettners, and Simpsons-in-the-Strand; all lavish affairs dating back to mortal days. Ancient and musty, like the drafty castle where they lived. So lunch with Cochran was exceptional by virtue of it being a new experience. And although the conversation was small and somewhat circular, there was something charming about speaking of nothing with someone you only barely knew.

He told her that he lived in Manchester, which, while not all that distant, felt amazingly far to Marni, who couldn't remember the last time she'd been out of London.

"I go to conventions," Cochran said, when she asked about his profession.

"What sorts of conventions?"

"All sorts."

"I mean, what is your line of business?"

"Conventions," he said again. "I'm a professional attendee."

"I don't follow."

"I'm not surprised—it's a niche trade."

Marni, her life being as sheltered as it was, had never been to a convention. She knew that they were large events where people displayed new products and socialized with others in their field. But according to Cochran, most of those products were outrageously dull. So much so that few people came to conventions of their own accord anymore.

"That's where I come in," explained Cochran. "In order to keep the convention floor from being a sad and sorry place, the Thunderhead hires professional attendees to fill the void. It's my job to walk around and act as if I'm interested."

"It sounds positively awful."

"Not at all. People are grateful to have someone to talk to. I brighten their day—and all I have to do is pretend to be fascinated by bathroom fixtures and doorknobs!"

Then he asked her about herself, as she knew he would. Marni decided there was only so much he needed to know.

"I run my aunt's estate."

"Really! An estate!"

"Not much of one. But it fills up most of my days."

Then the main course came, and she was able to redirect the

conversation away from herself. Eventually he'd want to know more, but for now, Marni enjoyed being a woman of mystery.

They arranged to meet every time he was in town, which was often—but couldn't be often enough for Marni. Feelings grew, and soon what began as an unfortunate accident became very purposeful.

"Perhaps someday you could come up to visit me," he suggested more than once.

"Yes, someday," she would wistfully reply, knowing her aunt never left home long enough to allow it.

After their fourth date, things took a bad turn—or more accurately a bad step. It was after dinner at a trendy, fashionable restaurant. Marni had worn her finest dress, and heels—which her aunt did not approve of, so she rarely wore them. Marni had to plan quite a ruse to be out this late without her aunt asking questions. As it would turn out, the heels were a mistake, because after they left the restaurant, while waiting for a publicar, Marni hit some uneven pavement, and began to fall off the curb. She reflexively grabbed for Cochran, but rather than him keeping her from falling, her momentum pulled him down after her.

And the approaching truck was moving much too quickly to stop.

There were countless Lover's Leaps in the post-mortal world. In fact, cliffs with stunning views once labeled picture spots now had signs that read ROMANTIC PLUNGE. Because dying hand in hand with one's beloved was the ultimate romantic act. Especially when you'd both be brought back to life in a day or two.

There was, in fact, an entire industry devoted to cliffside weddings that ended with a dramatic drop. Of course, it did change the tradition of throwing the bouquet. Now the custom was that whoever could retrieve the bouquet from the bottom of the cliff without going deadish in the process would be the recipient of the bride's good luck.

There were even some scenic drops so popular that they had their own honeymoon revival centers filled with hearts and roses and couple's revival rooms.

However, neither of Cochran and Marni's deathish duets left them in such a place. Instead the ambudrones whisked them once more back to Woolwich Revival Center, as was the standing order from Scythe Boudica for any and all deaths pertaining to her accident-prone niece, because it was convenient, and close to the castle. And so, once again, Marni awoke to the ever-happy face of Nurse Lucille.

"Hello, dearie! Have a bit of a slip-and-fall, did we? Never trust a lorry, I say!"

Marni groaned. Did she really die again? It took a moment to bring back the last thing she remembered. Then she bolted up in bed, which made her head spin.

"Cochran! Where's Cochran!"

"Mr. Stæinsby's in the room next door, love. He regained consciousness a few hours ago. He wanted to come in to see you, but I told him he'd have to wait."

"You could have let him in. . . ."

"Oh, but you were such a fright, dear. Your head met with one of the lorry's tires, and you know how that goes. Tsk, tsk, tsk. We had to do a full brain regrowth and memory download."

Well, that explained why she remembered the fall, but not actually going deadish. The Thunderhead must not have backed up those last few seconds. A bit of a blessing, really.

"How do I look now?"

Nurse Lucille took a few moments to appraise. "Your pretty little head is still bruised and slightly lopsided, but the worst of it has already faded. You'll be back in shape in no time. No pun intended."

A look in a mirror corroborated the nurse's assessment. Marni looked a bit like the oblong-headed ladies on Auntie Boo's tapestry robe.

Marni drew a deep breath at the thought of her aunt.

"Lucille, has Scythe Boudica been by yet?"

The nurse offered up her brightest smile. "She's in with Mr. Stæinsby!"

"What?"

"Oh yes, they've been chatting it up for a while now."

Marni ripped off her monitor leads, and jumped out of bed, ignoring Nurse Lucille's protests. Although her less-than-round head felt woozy and her just-mended legs wobbly, she managed to make her way to the adjacent room—where she saw her aunt, in full Scythe Boudica regalia, sitting beside Cochran, as if they were old friends.

"Ah, look what the cat dragged in," said the scythe when she saw Marni in the doorway, then frowned. "Good God, Marni, you look awful! Have they given you your NASti-shake yet? Is there a timeline for full recovery?"

Marni ignored her aunt's questions.

"Auntie Boo, what are you doing in here?"

"Your young man and I have been having a nice visit."

Cochran smiled at Marni like a little boy too naive to know that what looked like a gentle golden retriever could in fact be a hungry medieval lion.

"You never told me your aunt was a scythe!"

"And she never told me about you," said Auntie Boo.

Marni forced herself to step in from the threshold, committing to the troubling dynamic of the conversation. "Well . . . I . . . I just hadn't gotten around to it, is all."

"Marni, you should have told me you had a boyfriend. I'm positively thrilled for you!"

Marni found herself reeling. Perhaps her brain wasn't entirely revived yet, because she thought she heard her aunt say something positive.

"You are?"

"Of course! What could possibly be more important than love?" said her aunt. "Certainly not duty or familial responsibility."

There—that sounded more like the Boo Marni knew.

"Scythe Boudica invited me to your castle!" said Cochran with far too much enthusiasm for a man who had just been crushed by a ten-ton vehicle.

"I don't think that's a good idea," Marni said.

"Nonsense," said her aunt. "I've asked and he's accepted, so it's done."

"I've never been to a scythe's home before," said Cochran. "And besides, I'd love to see where you live, Marni!"

"It's settled," said her aunt. "We'll celebrate your joint revival back home at the castle—and if it's any consolation, I'll have you know I gleaned the driver of that lorry."

"Auntie Boo! It wasn't his fault—drivers don't actually drive, you know that! They're just there in case something . . . unexpected . . . happens."

Boudica shrugged beneath her heavy tapestry. "Well, too late to quibble about that now."

Then Nurse Lucille came in and insisted that Marni go back to bed, at least until her head had sorted itself out. Marni obliged and returned to her room, but was still troubled over the current state of affairs. Auntie Boo was clearly scheming . . . and Marni wasn't sure if she was the medieval lion about to tear Cochran to shreds, or merely a unicorn-goat, prodding him and poking him until he went away.

Cochran didn't know how to feel about any of this, but he was an optimistic person, so he decided to see the positive side. At first he was terrified when a scythe came to his revival room— but once she introduced herself as Marni's aunt, they got along swimmingly. As a professional attendee, Cochran's skill at sounding interested in the things she had to say made them an excellent conversational fit. Scythe Boudica certainly was a master of the mundane. Discussions of the weather, and her distaste that the Thunderhead didn't keep it sunny everywhere all the time. A veritable oration on the lack of hygiene among Britannia's youth. It was actually refreshing; he always thought scythes did nothing but discuss lofty and high-minded subjects.

Scythe Boudica was interested in knowing how he came to know Marni. Cochran was open and forthright about all of it, thinking there was no reason not to be.

• • •

Severndroog was an old castle, but not a castle of olde. That is to say it did not harken back to the Dark Ages, but rather to the dim ages of industrial England, when rich businessmen built edifices to their egos. Severndroog Castle had never warded off invaders, or stood stalwart against rampaging peasants. It was just there to look nice.

It was only marginally a castle. More like an odd triangular stone tower with turrets designed not for cannons, but for people to admire the view. Its interior wasn't very large. Just three floors connected by a single spiral staircase.

"Why should I lay claim to Buckingham like Scythe Cromwell, or Windsor like Scythe Godiva?" Boudica would exclaim. "Who needs all that space?" But, in truth, all the good castles were already taken.

Once Cochran and Marni were released from the revival center, Scythe Boudica had her private car drive them to the gate of her property, but no farther.

"It's a nice enough day for a walk," the scythe proclaimed, and although it was uphill, and Cochran and Marni were still a bit fatigued from revival, they endured it. Once a public park, the small urban forest was now Scythe Boudica's personal pastoral estate, and Severndroog Castle was smack in the middle.

What struck Cochran first was the wildlife.

"I've never seen so many rabbits," he exclaimed as they walked the gravel path to the castle.

"I breed them," Scythe Boudica told him. "Or rather, I let them take care of that themselves without any help or hindrance from me."

"Elsewhere it would be considered an infestation," Marni said, "and the Thunderhead would regulate their fertility. But not on scythe property."

Cochran found the castle to be modest—if anything called a castle could also be called modest. Yes, the doors were huge and ornate, and the ceilings high, but the odd triangular living area left quite a lot of unusable space.

A housekeeper had prepared afternoon tea for them, complete with things like freshly baked scones and little cucumber sandwiches with their crusts surgically removed.

"The old ways are the best ways," Scythe Boudica said as she personally poured everyone's tea. "Comfort in the chaos."

Marni didn't seem enthused by any of this. Cochran figured this all must have been familiar daily drudgery for her, and left it at that.

But Cochran wasn't privy to the things Marni knew. Such as the truth behind her aunt's ritualistic afternoon teas. Scythe Boudica would invite various people she came across in her daily strolls through the city. They'd sit down to tea. If she liked you, you would be allowed to leave, with full expectation that you'd write a kind note of thanks to Scythe Boudica for her hospitality. And if she didn't like you, you were gleaned.

"Tell me, Mr. Stæinsby, what are your intentions with my niece?" she asked, without the least bit of subtlety.

"Auntie Boo! Please don't put him on the spot."

But Cochran took it in stride. He sipped some tea, then put his cup down, and gently took Marni's hand. "My intentions are the most honorable," he told her, and turned a warm smile to Marni. "We care for each other and are looking forward to seeing where this journey might take us."

Scythe Boudica offered a simple, maybe even sincere smile, and glanced at Marni. "I like him," she said, and gave Marni a little wink.

Marni released a breath. Perhaps it was the warmth of the tea, or the easing of her stress, or the fact that the revival center always overhydrated her, but Marni felt a sudden and urgent need to relieve herself.

"I have to use the loo," she told them. "Save a scone for me." And she hurried away.

Once Marni was gone, the scythe returned her attention to Cochran. "I don't believe I've ever seen my niece so anxious and so happy. A wonder that both emotions can coexist in a single person."

"I feel much the same," Cochran told her. "Love will do that, I suppose."

"Ah yes, love. That magic fiction with the power to become true."

Cochran finished his tea. "Sometimes it's true from the outset."

The scythe had no response to that. Instead, she stood. "Would you like me to give you the grand tour?"

"Shouldn't we wait for Marni?"

"She'll be along," the scythe said, leading the way to the spiral staircase in the corner. "Has Marni told you about the view from the north turret? You can see all of London from up there!"

Marni silently scolded herself for thinking the worst of her aunt. Just because she had a penchant for self-serving behavior didn't mean she was always plotting something unpleasant. And as

Auntie Boo always reminded Marni, she had been kindhearted enough to give Marni a home all these years—not just a home but a castle—and had asked little more in return than Marni's company. Perhaps she should give her aunt the benefit of the doubt.

"I always want the best for you," Auntie Boo would often say. "Though the world rarely offers its best."

Marni returned to the main salon, hoping that they had indeed saved her a scone—only to find that, while the scone was there, her aunt and Cochran were not.

The view from the north turret did not disappoint.

"You were right, Your Honor," said Cochran as he gazed out to the Thames and beyond. "It's breathtaking!" The whole city of London was before him, and although he'd seen city vistas before, never had it been so comprehensive.

"I come up here several times a week," the scythe told him, which was in fact true. "I find it puts things in perspective." Which, while also true, was not her primary reason.

They took a few quiet moments to appreciate the view. "You know, I never leave London," Scythe Boudica confided. "As a scythe, I can go wherever I please. Not just in Britannia, but anywhere in the world. But I choose to do all my living and all my gleaning right here in this, the noblest of cities."

"If you don't travel, then why the heliport?" Cochran asked.

Her brow furrowed a bit in confusion, until he pointed to the concrete circle in a clearing at the bottom of the hill, painted with a series of concentric circles.

"Ah, yes," said Scythe Boudica. "You're right; it *is* a landing spot, of sorts."

"For visiting scythes, then?"

"If you say so."

She had been standing back, but now came closer to him, softening her voice. "My Marni is a sensitive soul, Mr. Stæinsby. Novelty unsettles her. She prefers life to be consistent, and familiar. So you can see why I'd be concerned about your 'relationship' with her. Changes to her routine confound and flummox my Marni."

"Forgive me for saying so, Your Honor . . . but I think that describes you, not Marni."

Scythe Boudica pursed her lips, and swayed a bit, almost to the point of stumbling. Cochran grabbed her elbow to steady her.

"Are you all right, Your Honor?"

"Just a bit dizzy," she said, "As much as I enjoy the view, I do get a bit of vertigo now and then." She stepped back, leaving Cochran alone in the turret. "But by all means, stay and enjoy the view. I promise the longer you linger, the clearer your perspective will be."

Then she reached into a secret niche in the bricks, and grasped a lever that was hidden from view.

Marnie was out of breath by the time she reached the first landing. The spiral staircase was steep, and there were two more floors until she would reach the roof. Usually she could bound up the stairs without any trouble, but revival had left her weak. She feared she might lose consciousness if she pushed herself too hard, and then what? She would lose much more than consciousness if she didn't get to the roof in time. So she ignored her exhaustion and all the complaints of her rubbery legs and weary lungs, until finally she burst out onto the roof. Cochran was there standing in the circular space of the north turret, and her aunt already had her arm in the hidden niche.

"No!" screamed Marni, which got both of their attentions. She lunged at her aunt, grabbing her wrist so she couldn't pull the lever. *"Don't you dare!"* Marni growled. She had never used such a tone with her aunt. Never. Boudica took it like a slap to the face.

"Unhand me!" demanded the scythe. "This is not your concern!"

That actually made Marni laugh. "Not my concern? It's the *only* thing that concerns me in this bloody castle!"

Her aunt gasped. "How dare you use such language with me? Such disrespect! Such impertinence!"

It only made Marni grip her wrist even tighter—so tightly she thought she might break it.

Through all of this Cochran watched from the turret, not sure if it was his place to interfere. But when it seemed that it might actually come to blows, he spoke up.

"Marni, it's all right, really. Your aunt was just showing me the view."

"That's one way of putting it!" Marni said. "That's a spring-loaded platform you're standing on, Cochran. It's how she gleans—she catapults people across the property, and they splat on that concrete target."

"Not true!" insisted her aunt. "They only hit the target when the wind is right."

This new information certainly did give Cochran clearer

perspective. He quickly stepped off the platform.

Finally Scythe Boudica pulled free from Marni, and turned on her, furious at having been foiled. "This boy is not what you need, Marni! I know what's best for you. I always have! Let me glean him so we can get back to our lives!"

Marni had never been a violent girl, but sometimes anger takes hold before one's nanites have time to do anything about it.

She reached out with both hands and pushed her aunt. Boudica stumbled backward, tripped on the hem of her robe, and landed squarely in the middle of the turret.

She must have seen it in Marni's eyes, because the scythe's entire demeanor changed. She was afraid. More than afraid, she was terrified.

"You wouldn't!"

But to Marni, those words sounded like a dare. She reached for the lever, knowing that if she paused for thought her good sense would kick in, and good sense was the last thing she wanted right now.

Cochran tried to intervene.

"Marni, don't!"

But nothing could stop her now. Marni funneled years of pent-up frustration down the length of her arm. Then she pulled the lever so hard, the handle broke off in her grip.

With an explosive grinding of gears, Scythe Boudica was launched skyward in a perfect demonstration of what scientists called "gravity's rainbow." The scythe, wailing all the way, arced across the sky, reaching a peak hundreds of feet from the ground, before plunging back to earth.

And today, it was a perfect bull's-eye.

. . .

The Thunderhead and the rabbits.

They were in a similar boat. Neither the rabbits nor the almost-all-powerful AI had any control over what happened on the grounds of Severndroog Castle. All they could do was watch. The Thunderhead, while having no cameras on scythe-occupied land, had trained several cameras on nearby streets to look at the property, so it could, at least partially, be aware of what went on there. And the rabbits? They were just there, in the woods, seeing people fall from the sky.

It had become so commonplace that the bunnies barely flinched when it happened. In fact, it had become for them a sort of Pavlovian clock—because on normal days, Scythe Boudica would come out of the castle and feed them the kitchen's leftover greens after she had gleaned, as to take her mind off of what she had just done, distracting herself while the cleanup crew did away with the mess. And so, on this day, when the food signal came dropping from the sky, the rabbits all hopped their way to the castle, waiting for the doors to open and for a bounty to be bestowed on them.

It was only when no one came to feed them that the rabbits began to suspect something was amiss.

For the first time in Scythe Boudica's illustrious existence, she awoke to find herself in a revival center. Woolwich, to be exact; the same one from which she often retrieved her niece.

"Good morning, Your Honor," said Nurse Lucille, as repellently perky as ever. She snapped up the blinds, and Scythe Boudica was assaulted by sunlight so bright she might as well have awakened on the surface of the sun. "Rise and shine, eternity awaits!"

"Leave me alone," grumbled the scythe.

"Sorry, but stimulation is an integral part of recovery. Must get that blood flowing, and those senses sensing!" She slapped the scythe's cheeks gently, but not quite gently enough. "There! Color's coming back to your cheeks. Nothing worse than the pallor of death. I'll get your NASti-shake ready—and if you hold it down, you can have ice cream!"

"How long have I been here?"

"Three days—like the mortal-aged savior himself! And *he* did it without healing nanites. Imagine that!"

Boudica decided not to ask any more questions so that she wouldn't have to hear Nurse Lucille's voice anymore—but the nurse was more than happy to continue speaking without invitation to do so.

"Your 'launch' was a bit of a mystery at first. The Scythedom called it a self-gleaning, and were ready to put what was left of you into the ground. But your niece set them straight."

"She . . . did?"

"Yes, Marni told them that it was just a terrible accident. I dare say a penchant for accidents must run in your family! You know, you really should have that mechanism on your roof serviced more often. A catapult with a faulty latch is nobody's friend."

Scythe Boudica opened her mouth and closed it again repeatedly, each time wanting to say something, but finding no words.

"What, impersonating a fish now?" said Nurse Lucille. "A bird wasn't enough?" Then she laughed heartily at her own joke. Boudica could still hear her laughing down the hall long after she had left the room.

A short time later Marni arrived. The scythe thought her niece would be out of sorts having to face her after what she had done, but the girl was well within sorts, behaving as if nothing had happened at all.

"Auntie Boo! Glad to see you're awake!"

"Are you?"

"Of course I am!" She came over and gave Boudica a peck on the cheek. Then Marni reached into a tote bag, and pulled out the scythe's tapestry robe, neatly folded and wrapped.

"I didn't trust it to the usual cleaners this time—what with all the blood—I took it down to the Royal Academy of Arts instead. Their antiquities department gave it a full restoration! Not only did they clean it, but they also repaired the hem, and wrangled any wayward threads. It's even better than it was when it hung on a wall!"

Boudica found her head in whirl. It was as if she was on some amusement park ride, and the carnies had forgotten to let her off.

"Excuse me . . . but didn't you kill me the other day?"

Marni sighed. "I thought you might not remember."

"I remember everything," Scythe Boudica said, narrowing her eyes, and delivering her best burning glare. "I tried to save you from your own poor choices, and how was I rewarded? Betrayal!"

But Marni wasn't fazed in the least. "It's probably better that you do remember, moving forward," she said.

"Forward? I think not! Let's backtrack a bit first!"

"No point," Marni told her. Just then her young man made an appearance at the door, like a puppy too eager for his own good.

"Hello, Auntie Boo!" he said.

Boudica glared at both of them. "Why is *he* calling me that?"

"Because he can," Marni said. "That is to say, he *officially* can. Show her, Cochran!"

Then the two of them extended their left hands in her direction, revealing a pair of matching gold bands on their ring fingers.

"We wed," said Cochran.

"While you were dead," added Marni, and they both giggled a bit at the rhyme.

"You can't be serious! Is this some sort of joke?"

Marni took Cochran's hand in hers. "Well, Auntie Boo, we knew it could only happen over your dead body, so . . ."

"I should glean you for what you did to me! I should glean you both!"

"You can't," Marni reminded her with a calm that was infuriating. "You know full well that I have permanent immunity while you're alive—and now that we're married, that immunity extends to Cochran as well."

"I'll do it anyway!"

Marni shrugged. "We'll just get revived—and then you'll get your hand slapped by High Blade Churchill for being an 'insufferable bitch.'"

The scythe gasped.

"His words, not mine," Marni quickly said. "It's what he called you when he came to view your body."

Now the tilt-a-whirl was spinning in the opposite direction. "Wait—Winston actually came down to see me?"

"Not so much to see you as to confirm with his own eyes that you were dead," Marni told her.

"He was very insistent that you had self-gleaned," Cochran added, "and had somehow rigged the catapult to spring remotely. His ruling would have been final, if Marnie hadn't stood up for you, and insisted that you be revived."

That annoying nurse had said as much, but it was still hard for Scythe Boudica to believe Marni would defend her right to live—and before the High Blade no less. Boudica could still remember that look in Marni's eyes when she pulled the lever. That death-isn't-good-enough-for-you look. It scared Boudica to think about it.

But what she didn't know was that it also scared Marni—although Marni did her best not to show it. Prior to that fateful moment, Marni had no idea the depth of rage she had toward her aunt. But having released all that pressure, she felt free from it. Especially now that she didn't have to face her aunt alone.

"Why *did* you have them revive me?" her aunt asked, her voice uncharacteristically timid. "You knew I could accuse you once I awoke. Seems to me you would have much preferred me gone."

Marni took a deep breath, preparing herself to impart a truth, painful though it might be.

"I love you, Auntie Boo. How could I ever want you gone? Yes, I was angry enough to kill you—but not permanently."

Scythe Boudica didn't openly return Marni's sentiment, but Marni didn't expect her to. She was not the kind of woman to which the word "love" came easily. Instead she pouted.

"So now I suppose you'll both slink off together to some ghastly corner of the world and produce endless offspring like my rabbits do."

Marni looked to Cochran, and let him take the lead in this, because, after all, what they were about to propose had been his idea.

"Actually, we've been discussing it. And we'd like to stay on at Severndroog," said Cochran.

"You . . . would?"

"Things will have to change of course," said Marni. "We'll redecorate for starters. More comfortable furniture, and artwork other than portraits of you."

"We'll open the grounds to the public again," suggested Cochran.

"And," added Marni, "you'll have to promise not to glean any friends we have."

Her aunt seemed more taken aback by that than anything else. "You'll have *friends* over?"

"Yes, Auntie Boo," said Marni. "I've gone without them for far too long."

"And if I don't agree?"

Marni shrugged as if it was nothing. "Then I'll move into Cochran's flat in Manchester," she said. "And you'll be alone."

To say the silence spoke volumes would be an understatement. All the words of Scythe Boudica's exceptionally long life could have filled that tome, and still left page after empty page. Both Marni and her aunt knew the truth of their relationship, although it was never spoken. Scythe Boudica controlled Marni's comings, goings, and everything in between, for fear that by losing control, she would lose Marni entirely. And then Scythe Boudica would be alone. Yes, there was the castle staff, but they were only there because attending to Severndroog was their job.

They tolerated Scythe Boudica because they had to. But without Marni's company, how long until actual contemplations of self-gleaning began to intrude on Boudica's thoughts?

Marni patiently waited for a response. Both knew she wasn't bluffing. Both knew Marni would be happy with either outcome.

But instead of answering, Scythe Boudica turned to Cochran.

"I remember you tried to stop her from pulling the lever," she said.

Cochran began to look a bit sheepish. "A resounding fail on my part, I'm afraid."

"Nonetheless it was admirable that you tried," said Scythe Boudica. "Perhaps I've judged you too harshly, Mr. Stæinsby."

"Its Stæinsby-Wittle, Your Honor," he corrected. "Marni and I are hyphenates now."

Boudica sighed. One more change to get used to. "Can you forgive me for trying to glean you?" she asked him.

Cochran took a moment, then said, with the practiced diplomacy of a professional attendee, "I'm happy to put it behind us, if you are."

Just then Nurse Lucille appeared at the door, as if she'd been eavesdropping, and waiting for the right moment to insert herself.

"Let's not overstress the honorable scythe," she said. "She still has a few more hours until revival is complete. And it's almost time for your NASti-shake, Scythe Boo! I'm sure you'd prefer your guests be elsewhere when you drink it. So five more minutes, then off with you!"

Once she was gone, Cochran turned to Marni. "Perhaps this is all too much for your aunt. Maybe we should give her more time to make a decision."

But Scythe Boudica put up a hand to silence him. "No need—my decision is made." She turned to Marni. "I will agree to your terms on one condition."

Marni braced herself for what stipulation her aunt might put on them.

"You may stay on with me at Severndroog Castle . . . on the condition that our first guest be Nurse Lucille. I would very much like to have her over for tea."

Marni was confused at first. "For tea?" Then her eyes widened. "Oh! For *tea*!"

Then she smiled and took her aunt's hand. "I think that's a wonderful idea, Auntie Boo! I'll make sure there are fresh sandwiches and scones."

It was a rare and resplendent moment Marni and her aunt shared. What a happy accident to find themselves, for once, in complete agreement!

Perchance to Glean

Co-authored with Michelle Knowlden

"If the dream feels wrong, run."

It was advice every kid living in the RossShelf region of Antarctica was told from the moment they began communal-dreaming—which was usually the same time they started school. Not that dreams could harm you—they couldn't.

But sometimes they did.

Or more accurately, it was scythes who could mess with the dream. RossShelf scythes had free reign to do whatever they wanted in the communal dream, just as scythes had free reign in waking life everywhere else. And although you rarely saw them coming in your dream, sometimes you could sense it. Something off about the moment, as if the rules of the dream—if dreams could be said to have rules—were somehow being broken.

So if something felt wrong? You ran.

Dayne had never encountered a scythe while dreaming. Or if so, had been too involved in the dream to notice. Perhaps one had brushed by, disguised as a chill wind, or a rolling boulder, on the way to gleaning someone else. There was really no way to know.

"I try not to think about it," Dayne's friend Alex said as they windsurfed on a lake of liquid gold. "Keep worrying about stuff like that, and you'll start slipping down to the dream's dark places."

Dayne and Alex had been friends for as long as Dayne could remember. And yet they didn't even know one another. That's the way it was in the *Grand Rêve*—the big communal dream that the residents of RossShelf shared. The people you knew in waking life—friends, family, neighbors, teachers—rarely crossed paths with the people you came to know in the dream. And the Thunderhead's rules on privacy made it against the law to seek out a dream friend in real life. Or, for that matter, a dream enemy.

Dayne and Alex had been in the same "sandbox" with a few other kids, sharing a limited dream, before graduating about a year ago to the Grand Rêve. But even after a year, Dayne was still getting used to dreaming so large. That didn't mean it wasn't fun. But it wasn't always easy, either.

Like windsurfing. It was probably easier in the dream than it might be in real-life, but one's skill was only as good as one's confidence, and confidence was not Dayne's strongest point. Doubt was constantly creeping in, and tonight, that doubt created a rogue wave that knocked Dayne off the surfboard, and into the gold. When Dayne resurfaced, the board had turned into a pterodactyl, and flown away.

Alex laughed.

"Is it supposed to do that?" Dayne asked.

"Don't ask me," said Alex. "I didn't build this dream, I'm just living in it."

Then Alex jumped into the golden sea with Dayne, and sure enough Alex's sailboard did exactly the same thing, chasing Dayne's into the indigo sky.

"Guess it *was* supposed to do that," said Alex. "Let's get to shore, the dream cycle's almost over."

Alex made it to shore first, running in rhythmic lopes like a monkey to the jungle . Dayne followed paces behind, the sand beneath transmuting to tiny crabs, snapping hungrily. When Alex reached the dense jungle, Dayne was close behind, but much to Dayne's irritation, Alex turned into an actual monkey, leaping into the bronze-tipped trees with ease. Dayne followed Alex into a giant gum tree, not as lightly, not as quietly.

Alex had a natural skill of transforming into any creature at will—although sometimes the transformation happened whether Alex willed it or not. Dayne still hadn't found a particular skill, maybe never would. Not all dream "indwellers" did anything special. Even in their sandbox days Alex shone at being a star indweller while Dayne played the sidekick or crowd scene extra.

Dayne had to admit it was fun hanging around Alex—although it could also be frustrating—especially when the transformation owned Alex, and not the other way around.

Alex, seeing that Dayne couldn't keep up with a monkey swinging through trees, stopped, and waited for Dayne on a heavy bough.

Only now, when it was on a monkey wrist, did Dayne notice the blue-banded watch Alex was wearing. The only thing on its face was an ancient symbol. Ω. Omega.

"Where'd you get that?"

"I met a builder the other day, who made it for me. Resets the dream thirteen seconds back. You can only use it once a week, though." Alex said it like it was no big deal.

"Wait a minute. Resetting a dream thirteen seconds? What good is that? If you hang out with a builder, you could have a dream made to order. Why didn't you ask for that?"

Alex winked. "It was only a first date."

It almost made Dayne laugh. It was pretty impressive that Alex knew a builder at all. The four kinds of dream folk didn't mix all that much. In the Grand Rêve, you were either a designer, builder, indweller, or obliterator. The indwellers got to experience the dreams that the designers conceived, and the builders created. Then, when no one wanted that particular dream anymore, the obliterators tore it all down. Penchants and personality traits naturally sorted people into their group, but the Thunderhead had final say.

Sometimes Dayne wanted more control than indwellers tended to have . . . but control also came with an awful lot of responsibility. Experiencing the dream was a more carefree way to spend one's dream cycles.

"Shhh," said Alex, even though Dayne wasn't making any noise, and pointed to the ground beneath them, where a wide-shouldered panther with multicolored, funky-patterned fur prowled. It didn't seem to know it was being watched. Alex looked from Dayne to the panther and back again. "Want to have some fun?" Alex whispered.

"No. Definitely no."

It was hard to tell whether the panther was another indweller, or just part of the dream . . . or maybe it was an unsavory creation that would drag them down into one of their nightmares. Best not to find out.

But in spite of Dayne's protests, Alex gave a monkey grin, and climbed down to the branch just above the panther. Then, timing it just right, Alex dropped onto its back. The panther howled, spun, looking wildly around. It bucked like a bronco, trying to throw Alex off. Finally Alex jumped back to a branch—but the monkey-brain took over, and Alex began flinging feces at the panther. But as it was a dream, it smelled like root beer.

Finally Alex leapt back to Dayne's side in the tree. The panther raced away, scattering fronds left and right, looking over its shoulder, smelling nothing but root beer, and luckily never looking up.

"You're off the rails!" Dayne said.

"No rails in this dream," Alex replied. "You want rails, there's a train dream a few valleys over."

"That panther could have killed you!"

Alex just shrugged. "So? I'd just wake up."

"And probably be up for the rest of the night. You always complain about how you can't get back to sleep once you bounce out of a dream."

"You're such a lightweight," said Alex, pushing Dayne off the branch. And the very suggestion made Dayne float rather than fall.

Dayne dressed for school, trying to remember the dream, but couldn't remember much. It was always that way. What happened in the dream stayed in the dream. Dayne wondered if everyone else in the world—everyone who wasn't part of their charter region's communal *dream*—had the same problem remembering their dreams.

Breakfast was steamy oatmeal and cocoa. Always something hot. Cold breakfasts like cereal and milk were not a thing in Antarctica. As was often the case, Dayne was the last to the table. Theirs was a fairly large family. Dayne had two brothers and three sisters. Antarctic families tended to stay together even after the kids were grown, as a couple of Dayne's were. "Make sure you save some food for Dayne," Mom said, when she saw Dayne coming to the table.

"You snooze, you lose," said Ophelia, Dayne's oldest sister, but still waited for Dayne to get some before going for seconds.

Dayne sat down between two younger siblings, who complained about having to make space, then looked toward the end of the table. "So Dad, when's the big unveiling?"

"Still about a week away."

Dayne's father was an ice sculptor, working on twin pieces for the entrance to the new East Crevasse Playhouse. He loved what he did—but once confessed that he was an Obliterator in the Grand Rêve. It was a hoot to imagine Dad breaking stuff. But then, everyone had a secret internal life.

Dayne's mother was a calving engineer—which was a harrowing job, because the five-hundred-mile-long leading edge of the shelf was always calving into the sea. Even though the Thunderhead had slowed the glacier flow to nil, the homes built into the shelf face didn't last long. A ten-year "shelf life," at best.

"We just lost a big chunk two months earlier than predicted," Dayne's mom said, mulling over her breakfast. "More than three hundred people deadish—ambudrones are still pulling them out of the sea. It's a mess."

"They want that ocean view, they've got to live with the risk," Dad said, and Mom chided him for his lack of compassion.

"Hey, all I'm saying is that risk ought to be saved for the dream," Dad said. "It's easier to die and wake up than it is to die and have to be revived!"

"Well, people who live on the shelf-face can afford it," Dayne pointed out.

The oatmeal and cocoa did a good job getting Dayne warm and ready to face the ice tunnels between home and school, but there was something inside—something deeper—that wasn't warming up. It was Ophelia who noticed.

"So what's up with you?" she asked.

Dayne didn't really have an answer. "Not sure. Something in last night's dreams I think. Just feeling a little . . . tweaked."

"What do you remember?"

"Not much. A jungle. One of my dream friends was there."

Ophelia weighed it for a moment, then brushed it off. "It's like that sometimes. Just let it go. Have some more cocoa before you go; that'll chase it away."

Most of Dayne's life was lived in ice tunnels and huge human-made caverns carved directly in the deep blue glacier. Some of RossShelf was breathtakingly beautiful, but mostly it was monotonous and utilitarian, making vivid dreams all the more important.

East Crevasse High School was, like most RossShelf schools, an expansive open design full of ice pillars and movable walls. Usually, Dayne was ready to face a day at school, but today the Rêve just wouldn't let go. It wasn't unusual for dreams to linger, but rarely did they affect Dayne for this long.

"Are you with us today, Dayne?"

Mr. Ramos, Dayne's Antarctic History teacher, had been going on about the shelf, and how their region was nothing more than a massive glacier spilling from the continent into the Southern Sea—as if that was news to any of them.

"Yeah, we're a giant glacier. Got it."

But Mr. Ramos pressed, "What's wrong? Trouble in the slumber collective?" which was what older people called the Grand Rêve. A few classmates snickered at the old-fashioned expression.

Rather than being on the defensive, Dayne redirected the conversation.

"Have you ever come across a sea of liquid gold?"

Ramos stiffened a bit. "We do not discuss the slumber collective in class," he said.

"Well, you brought it up."

"I was being rhetorical!"

He got back to his lesson, but later, just as class was getting out, he came over and whispered to Dayne.

"I was one of the builders of the Golden Sea. There's some fun stuff if you dive to the bottom."

That night, Dayne strode through the familiar entry gate to the Grand Rêve onto the main thoroughfare, still feeling tweaked in a profound, but intangible way.

The thoroughfare was crowded with vendors, banners, and signs. Popcorn, cotton candy, everything from welcome acrobats drawing a crowd to FrancoIberian crêpe vendors.

To Dayne the thoroughfare always seemed like a theme park main street. Crowds and long lines. Candy for every single sense to get you in the mood for whatever sleep brought you tonight.

Dayne didn't linger, quickly getting past the bottleneck to the dreamscapes beyond.

Where was Alex? They usually met past the vendors and shops at the central roundabout, where paths led to hundreds of peaks and valleys of active dreams. Dayne and Alex always tried to synchronize when they fell asleep, so that at least their first REM cycle would match, but it didn't always work.

"When in doubt, pick dream 42," was their rule if they couldn't find each other. It was their rendezvous dream, but it was never the same, since each night, dreams got bumped to higher numbers as new ones were added—so heading out to dream 42 was basically a blind-date with your subconscious. Or more accurately, someone else's subconscious, because it was all stuff dredged out of some designer's messed-up mind.

Today, dream 42 featured an active volcano that appeared to be minutes from a world-splitting eruption, but for now was content to release a deep rumble that was both ominous and satisfying.

In a clearing at the volcano's base, Dayne saw what appeared to be, of all things, a petting zoo. Llamas, goats, miniature horses, even a small giraffe. Designers and builders loved absurdity and delving into the avant garde. Although some never got the memo that less is more. Dayne wondered if the petting zoo was about to be covered in lava, and if so, what would it mean? Did it have a point, or was it just randomness for randomness' sake?

This is good, thought Dayne. *Distract yourself from that foreboding feeling. Live the dream of the volcano and petting zoo.*

Still, Dayne wished Alex was there—because when you felt something sinister breathing down your neck, you needed a friend like Alex. Except, of course, when you didn't. Because

Alex would, just as often as not, egg monsters on.

After closer inspection, Dayne realized this wasn't a petting zoo at all. It was a confab of crittermorphs. Indwellers who, like Alex, could dream themselves into animal form. It was the conversation that gave it away. These weren't empty creations following a script; they were jabbering and cracking jokes like they were kids between classes.

Dayne wondered if Alex might already be here at this little party, communing with similarly skilled peers. What would Alex choose to be in a petting zoo? A two-headed goat? A three-humped camel?

An alpaca glared at Dayne and said something rude, offended that an interloper in human form crashed their animals-only party. Dayne ignored it, and decided that if Alex couldn't be found, Dayne would bail for the golden sea, and dive to the bottom to see what Mr. Ramos was talking about. But suddenly that uneasy feeling Dayne was trying so hard to ignore began to soar like a mortal-aged fever.

Premonitions and precognition may or may not exist in the waking world, but they definitely did exist in the Grand Rêve. And it wasn't just Dayne who felt it. The menagerie party began to grow quiet.

There was a shadow moving between the self-absorbed animals, and finally a big cat emerged. A panther with slate gray fur covered with a strange pattern. Curling blue teardrops. That pattern had a name . . . Paisley—that's what it was called. And immediately Dayne remembered last night's encounter. This was the same panther Alex had spooked. Seeing it brought the whole dream back.

The panther padded with studied elegance, not slowing or looking left when a pony sniffed it or looking right when a sheep scuttled away. The panther's gaze seemed fixed on Dayne as it strode forward. Like it could not only smell but already taste its prey.

This was what Dayne had been sensing. Malevolent intent powerful enough to infuse the dream—which meant that the panther's arrival wasn't a coincidence. Whoever this was, they had entered the dream with a goal. Revenge for last night. Never mind that Dayne was just a bystander. Guilt by association. Damn Alex!

Don't move. They pounce when you move. Maybe Dayne could stare it down, and it would leave. Maybe all it wanted was an intimidating moment of "I've got my eyes on you."

But how did it know to look for me? It hadn't seen either Dayne or Alex. It had no idea who had jumped on its back . . . and yet here it was.

The paisley panther released a warning growl that seemed echoed by the volcano's rumble, and the crittermorphs scattered. But it didn't go after any of them. It kept its focus on Dayne.

That's when the old adage rang in Dayne's head. *"If the dream feels wrong, run."*

Dayne vaulted over the petting zoo fence, and sprinted down the path toward the volcano, hoping maybe a dream panther couldn't run as fast as a real one. But a glance back revealed it could do even better than the real thing. It slipped like liquid under the railing without missing a beat. It picked up speed, quickly gaining ground between them. Dayne ran so fast that everything blurred except the toothy sneer of the beast drawing closer. In every backward glance, that mouth was in sharp focus.

Dayne raced up the slope of the volcano so fast, it was like flying, with feet no longer pounding the path, but skating on air. But the panther flew also, with fur bristling, its muzzle mere feet from Dayne's neck.

Then, just as Dayne wondered if maybe this entire dream had been hijacked by an unsavory nightmare, a hand thrust out of the ground as if to prove it. It grabbed Dayne's ankle, pulling Dayne underground as if the stone was quicksand. Dayne squirmed against the downward pull, the suffocating sensation as intense as it would be in real life. Finally Dayne fell into a hollow lava tube, landing hard on its curved obsidian floor right next to . . . Alex—whose hand was still grasping Dayne's ankle. Above them the rock they had fallen through repaired itself.

"Where the hell have you been?" Dayne demanded.

"Homework. Nearly had to pull an all-nighter."

Alex glanced up and grimaced. There was a sound of digging and cracking in the stone above getting louder as the cat tried to get to them.

"I saw the panther from last night chasing you. I've seen this asshole before. Not always a panther, but always that stupid design."

"Well, we'd better move,' said Dayne. "It won't fall for a trick like that again."

They hurried down the tube, lit only by the dim red glow of superheated rock. Things splintered under their feet, placed there by builders, or dropped by other indwellers, but they didn't slow to explore. Whether toys, twigs, or bones, you didn't stop for a look-see when a panther was after you.

Dayne knew that some people dreamt angry. It was annoying but not unusual. Maybe some businessman who hated his boss, or a kid who got bullied, but found power in the Rêve. Best to avoid them, and if you couldn't, don't antagonize them. Unfortunately they already had, and this cat was . . . well . . . a pit bull.

The tunnel grew narrower, and Dayne saw Alex beginning to slow as if dragging concrete legs, which sometimes happened in dreams.

"Damn," Alex grunted. "Not now!"

"Just think light, not heavy!"

"Easy for you to say!"

Dayne slowed and tried to help Alex along, while somewhere behind them they heard the panther roar, and it echoed as if it was coming from everywhere.

Up ahead they found that the tunnel split into two. They could go left or right. They had no clue where either tunnel led and there was no time to debate. Dayne led them right.

The tunnel curved and curved again—

—and came to a dead end, where some idiot builder had carved a "meh" face into the stone. Not funny.

They turned, and there was the cat, its eyes shining like glass. They had been cornered. The Panther slowed. Took a moment to relish its victory.

Alex's concrete legs had now fused with the cavern floor. Even if they had a place to run, it wasn't happening.

"Fine," said Alex. "Let it attack us and wake us up. Who cares anyway? I won't lose any sleep over it. Or at least not much."

But there was something scratching at the back of Dayne's mind. A question. A fear.

What if it's not just some anonymous angry dude. What if . . .

Dayne never got to finish the thought because the cat pounced. But before it reached them, Dayne realized there *was* something they could do! Alex hadn't thought of it, and there was no time to suggest it. Instead, Dayne just reached over, and slapped the omega symbol on the face of Alex's watch.

The dream snapped like the whole world was a rubber band—

—and there they were, thirteen seconds back, coming to the fork in the tunnel.

"You wasted it!" yelled Alex, "Why did you waste it? That idiot's not worth it!"

Dayne didn't answer. Instead Dayne took them down the tunnel on the left. A twist, a turn, the tunnel got lighter, and hotter—and they skidded to a stop . . .

. . . right at the edge of the Volcano's caldera. A hundred feet below the ledge, Lava, nearly white hot, bubbled and spat.

"Great," said Alex. "This is no better than a dead end."

Just as before, the Panther caught up with them quickly—and seemed even angrier this time. It didn't wait before it pounced.

Dayne didn't wait either, and rammed into Alex, taking them both off the ledge, plunging them toward the bubbling lake of magma. The panther, unable to stop its momentum, fell too, just a few feet from them.

"This is going to hurt!" yelled Alex. Because dream pain could be worse than real pain, since there were no nanites to numb them. But Dayne also knew it wouldn't hurt for long.

The instant they hit the surface of the Lava, Dayne screamed out in a single instant of agony—then bolted up in bed, fully awake.

Dayne was covered in sweat, breathing in gasping huffs, trying to force the dream away and let reality take hold. But forcing the dream away was the absolute wrong thing to do! So Dayne held on to it—because this was a dream that absolutely had to be remembered.

"So, I've been having some bad dreams."

It was breakfast. This morning Dayne had actually been the first one at the table. Going back to sleep after the volcano dream was out of the question. Dayne did everything possible to stay awake for the rest of the night.

Dayne's mother put down her fork, giving Dayne a concerned look but trying not to appear *too* concerned. "What kind of bad dreams?"

"Not sure," said Dayne. "Hard to remember. I just know they were bad." It was a lie. Dayne had managed to retain all the key events of the chase, right down to their incineration in hot magma.

"Probably just unsavories," Dayne's father said through a mouthful of toast.

Ophelia sighed. "Unsavories are such a nuisance, but they do make things interesting."

"I want to be an unsavory!" said Lonnie, Dayne's youngest brother.

"Polonius, don't you dare say that!" reprimanded their mother. "No child of mine is going unsavory!"

"I will if I want to," grumbled Lonnie.

"How could you be unsavory?" said Gertie, who was a year older than Lonnie. "You're a hall monitor!"

Lonnie stuck out his tongue at her, and that ended the discussion. The focus turned back to Dayne.

"If your dreams are too challenging, you can always choose easier ones," said Dad. "There's no shame in that."

"It's not that, it's . . ." Dayne sighed. "Never mind."

"Choose some familiar dreams for a while," suggested Mom. "I'm sure whatever it is, it'll clear up."

"You're probably right," said Dayne. Of course she wasn't, but how do you tell your parents that you think you're being targeted? Not just by an unsavory, but maybe something worse. It's not like they could do anything about it. Dreams were a place where parents couldn't protect you.

Dayne drank a huge mug of coffee, then another. Even though it wasn't a school day, Dayne needed to be sharp, and not risk taking an unexpected nap. If only Dayne could find Alex so they could figure this out together—But who knew where Alex was in the waking world? RossShelf was a huge region, with many cities, and towns, not to even mention the rural ice fields. It was against the law to speak of home while in the Grand Rêve—and besides, while you were dreaming, the details of waking life were hard to recall.

If the paisley panther was a scythe, there would have to be evidence somewhere, but finding that evidence wasn't going to be easy. Scythes were secretive, and manipulated the media. Their digital footprints could either be larger than life, or invisible, depending on how they liked it. And although the Thunderhead knew all there was to know about scythes, it couldn't help.

"All the data in my backbrain is available to you," the Thunderhead said, *"But when it comes to scythes, I can't assist you in any way. I'm so sorry, Dayne."*

The Thunderhead spoke as if Dayne had already been gleaned and was giving condolences. But Maybe Dayne was just reading into its response.

The Thunderhead's backbrain was not easy to dig through. Nothing in there was organized. You looked for a scythe, and you were just as likely to find videos of wheat harvests as you were actual human scythes. And even if you found one, rather than information on the scythe, you were just as likely to be linked to other people with the same exact weight, or height, or hair color, rather than any information that you actually needed to know. The backbrain was organized for the Thunderhead's mind, not a human one.

After half a day, bleary-eyed, and exhausted, Dayne realized this would take an alternate method of research. So Dayne went into Lonnie's room.

"Lonnie, can I have a look at your scythe card collection?"

Lonnie immediately became guarded. "Why?"

"I just want to look through them."

"They're in plastic sleeves—you can't take them out—why do you need them?"

Dayne tried not to be frustrated. Lonnie was funny about his collectibles. And while lots of kids kept and traded Scythe cards, Lonnie was weirdly protective. "Can I just look?"

Lonnie frowned and finally gave in. "Fine. But I do all the touching."

Lonnie's collection was in special card cases, separated by

colored index tabs. "They're divided by continent, then by region, then by gleaning technique," Lonnie said as he took the cases down from a shelf.

"Perfect," said Dayne. Unlike the backbrain, Lonnie's collection was organized in a way that made sense for humans. Of course, Lonnie didn't have every scythe in the world—some cards were exceptionally rare—but it was a start. "Show me the ones from RossShelf."

Lonnie went to the last of seven cases and flipped to a set of cards, maybe about a hundred, representing scythes in their region. Gingerly, Lonnie went through each card. Although he had been reticent to show them at first, now that he was doing it, Dayne could tell he was enjoying it. Kind of a bonding experience between siblings.

"If you want to start collecting, I could get you a good starter set, cheap," Lonnie said.

"Maybe," Dayne responded, because if Lonnie thought that was the reason for Dayne's interest, he might not wonder any further.

They went through scythe after scythe. Robes of various colors, all sorts of coded stats that Lonnie tried to explain.

"Scythe Gallico turns into a tsunami, and drowns people in beach dreams," Lonnie said. "And Scythe Crawford is a giant dream spider that catches you in her web . . ." Lonnie went through a litany of scythes, leaving Dayne wishing he hadn't, because each one became yet another thing to worry about. But none of them seemed to stand out to Dayne.

Then, when Lonnie was done, Dayne noticed there were

a couple of cards in the back that weren't even in protective sleeves yet.

"How about those?" Dayne asked.

"Those are new ones. Since they're new, no one knows how they glean, or where to put them." Lonnie pulled both cards out and showed them to Dayne. The first one was a young woman in a bright yellow satin robe who looked less intimidating than she was trying to be. It was the second one that caught Dayne's attention.

"That's Scythe Borgia," Lonnie said. "Just got ordained at Vernal Conclave. Weird robe, though. Dumb pattern."

Dayne could swear that the ice walls of Lonnie's room got a little bit colder.

"It's called paisley," Dayne said.

As much as Dayne wanted to delay sleep for as long as possible, that night, warning Alex was critical. So when the time came, the usual relaxation techniques plunged Dayne into REM at precisely 10:33 p.m. Hopefully they'd meet up in the roundabout, and Dayne wouldn't have to go looking for Alex in dream 42, whatever that happened to be tonight.

But when consciousness slipped away, Dayne wasn't greeted by the crass crowds of the thoroughfare. Instead Dayne landed in icy-cold darkness.

This wasn't right.

This never happened. The thoroughfare was always the interface to the dream. But Scythes . . . scythes could manipulate all that, couldn't they? More evidence that their stalker was, indeed, Scythe Borgia.

"Alex!" Dayne called out. "Alex, are you here?"

And then a voice to the left, "This is trippy. What the hell is going on?"

Relief washed over Dayne and was enough to rein in all other chaotic thoughts. Because Alex was here, and they'd be able to face this together. Dayne followed the sound of Alex's voice until they found each other.

"Listen to me, Alex—Paisley isn't just an asshole. Paisley is a scythe."

"Don't be ridiculous!" said Alex, in full denial. "You're overreacting!"

Just then bright lights flashed on with a loud *Ka-chung!* illuminating a frost-filled metallic corridor. Like ones you'd see on some ancient ghost ship trapped in Antarctic ice.

"Never saw a world like this," Alex grunted. Neither had Dayne. Ice never played into the Grand Rêve. RossShelf folk had enough of it in waking life.

There was a sound now. Breathing. Panting from far down the corridor.

"The Panther?" asked Alex.

But the breathing sounded much heavier than the sound a panther would make. A scythe could be anything in a dream. Anything! It was best not to know what breathed like that.

Dayne grabbed Alex. "Let's move."

They ran in the opposite direction of the guttural, panting breaths, feeling a bit better the further from it they got . . . then not so much when they came upon a porthole on their right.

Dayne skidded to a stop and peered out. The view put everything into perspective. Not an icy sea or a jagged glacier . . . but the curve of a giant purple planet, and stars. Endless stars.

"We're in space," Dayne said.

"Cool," said Alex, still not getting it. "But if we're in space, how come there's gravity?"

And suddenly there wasn't any, and they floated from the floor. "Good going, Alex." Damned dream logic.

But maybe this wasn't a terrible thing, because somewhere far away they heard an inhuman roar as the thing chasing them lost its foothold, too.

So Borgia could manipulate the dream, but then, so could they. Maybe not to the same extent, but any obstacle helped!

"Okay," said Dayne. "Let's fly!"

They pushed off from the ceiling and zipped down the corridor, using wall handholds to propel them along and somersault through hatches. Dayne imagined that actual astronauts—when space travel was a thing—had to learn to do these things, but in dreams it all came easy.

An open hatch beckoned with the scent of strawberries and lush greenery beyond. A glorious domed Eden. Some sort of biosphere on this strange dreamship.

"Excellent!" Alex said, and floated through. But Dayne grabbed a handhold, hesitating. It was as suspicious as it was inviting. Who had put this biosphere here? The station's designer? Or was it Scythe Borgia?

Seconds later and eyes wide, Alex zoomed out, a long, leafy vine following, with blue paisley-shaped leaves, sharp as razors.

"Bad idea," Alex shouted, and they pushed off zooming down the corridor while the vine flapped menacingly from the doorway behind them.

They took the next downward access they came to—or at least it seemed to be downward. Directions made zero sense in zero-G. Dayne hoped Scythe Borgia was equally disoriented—and maybe transforming took time, which would give them a head start.

"Okay, I believe you now," Alex said, humbled and scared in a way Dayne had never seen Alex before. "So what do you know about this scythe?"

"Scythe Borgia. Just ordained at Vernal Conclave. Paisley robe. Blue on gray."

"Ugh! I should have figured that out!" said Alex. "So now that we know it's a scythe, are we in trouble for running?"

"I checked the laws on dreamscythes," Dayne said. "They can glean in any form they like—but we're allowed to run unless they present themselves *as* a scythe, in human, robed form."

"Yeah, well, let's hope that never happens." Then Alex looked sheepish enough to actually grow wool. "I'm sorry I pranked that panther in the first place."

"What's done is done," said Dayne. "Let's just focus on saving ourselves."

The next hatch was closed. It took both of them to yank its handle. The door began to creak open—and immediately they regretted it.

Before them floated the strangest being Dayne had ever seen.

It was some sort of alien with a gun-metal gray exoskeleton, embossed with paisley swirls. It had three clawed arms, and a face like a pewter dinner plate, glowing with emerald slits for eyes.

No . . . not a dinner plate, Dayne realized. Because the edge of its face was sharp and spinning. *A buzz saw . . .*

Alex and Dayne screamed and threw their weight against the door as the alien dove for them. They heard it crash against the shut hatch as they slammed the handle in the locked position.

Both flew back down the corridor, frantically looking for open doors to any place that offered safe haven. Halfway down the corridor, they heard a claw slap the ceiling above them, then another moments later. The alien was tracking them from above. Or below, or whatever direction that was. The next door was a small lavatory—and it had a lock, so they pulled themselves inside and locked themselves in.

"Do you think we can beat it?" Alex whispered.

Dayne wasn't too optimistic. "No. But we can stall it, frustrate it, outrun it, or wake ourselves out of the dream before it kills us." Dayne had to remember that it wasn't an "it," it was a person. A smart, dangerous, and powerful human being who had powers within the dream that went beyond anything regular people could do. "Our only chance is to be so hard to catch that Borgia loses interest."

"I don't know . . ." said Alex. "Every version we've seen seems pretty determined."

Something rattled their door. Dayne tightly gripped a faucet. Alex shrank in the corner, fist going pale around the handhold. Then Dayne heard the rattle of keys, and was horrified. Nowhere to hide unless they could dream-stuff their way down toilets, which wasn't going to happen.

A click. The door swung open . . .

. . . and they were faced with a scowling man with a shock

of white hair like soft-serve ice cream, and a face that looked too young for hair that white.

"What are you doing here? Get off my ship!"

They gaped at him.

"You heard me," said the white-haired indweller. "This is *my* ship. You're trespassing!"

Dayne's voice started working again. "You mean this is . . . a private dream?"

"A *bespoke* dream," the indweller said. "It was designed and built exclusively for my use! Impossible that you're even here! It's impenetrable to unsavory sabotage!"

A bespoke dream ship! That meant there must be a way back to the roundabout. If they could get there, they just might lose their pursuer.

"We're not unsavories," Dayne informed him. "We're being chased by a scythe."

"Exactly what an unsavory would claim! Get off my ship. Now."

"Happy to," Alex said. "How?"

"Jump out an airlock for all I care! Just leave!"

Dayne wondered if they'd survive without oxygen. You could never tell in a dream. Maybe getting blown out of an air-lock would be a quick way to end the dream. But if not, there'd be nowhere to hide from the scythe in open space.

"This is a big ship," Dayne noted. "Wouldn't a ship this big have its own shuttle?"

The indweller puffed out his chest. "Of course it does."

"Great. We're borrowing it!"

The indweller's face reddened like a child seconds from a

tantrum. "No! This is MY ship, MY shuttle, MY dream!"

Nevertheless, Dayne elbowed Alex, and they both took off down the corridor in search of the shuttle bay, trying every hatch they came across.

Finally they found one that opened on a huge hangar. Sitting on a platform, stood the shuttle—also bespoke, looking a bit like the indweller's hair—which must have been a signature dream flourish. The smallish two-person transport stood in solitary glory, looking like it had just come off the showroom floor.

"Perfect!" Dayne said. "And I can fly it."

Dayne had never flown a space shuttle, of course, but in a dream, all one needed was confidence to accomplish anything. And doubt to fail miserably. So Dayne could not allow the slightest doubt to creep in.

They bounded up to the cockpit and settled themselves inside, Dayne knowing exactly which button to slap to close the hatch.

Then through the view screen they saw the infuriated indweller launching himself from the corridor into the shuttle bay.

"I will report you!" he yelled. "You'll be banned from the Grand Rêve, and ejected from the region! For the rest of your miserable lives, you'll dream pointless petty dreams alone!"

Dayne and Alex saw it before the indweller did. The Borgia-beast. It emerged from the corridor and grabbed the indweller, who turned just in time to see its spinning blade head and its narrow green eyes—and the diamond ring on one of its many claws.

"No! It can't be! Get off my—"

He never finished the thought. Instead the Borgia-beast

pulled him close, digging its buzz saw head into him, and poof, the indweller disappeared. Gleaned.

"Punch it!" Alex yelled, and Dayne did. The shuttle crashed through the closed hangar door, and into a star-filled dream of space.

Gleaning was different in the RossShelf region. Seeing a scythe in waking life was no big deal. Nothing to be worried about, because scythes didn't glean you while you were awake. Only while you dreamed. And once you were gleaned in a dream, that's when the terror truly started. Because upon waking from a dream-gleaning, a countdown started. You had twelve hours to report to the scythe who gleaned you, so that they might actually end your life. Twelve hours to ponder nonexistence. Twelve hours to say your good-byes. And if you didn't show—if you defied gleaning—just as with scythes in the rest of the world, all those you love would be gleaned along with you.

While time moved differently in REM sleep, Dayne and Alex knew that something was terribly wrong with the flow.

"Borgia isn't letting the dream end," Dayne realized. "This is a hunt and the hunt doesn't end until we're either caught, or escape."

As the sleek shuttle accelerated through the star-filled void, Alex kept trying to wake up, but nothing worked—not pinching, not running into walls. They had managed to jump into Lava and wake up the night before, but Borgia wasn't going to let something like that happen again.

"Even if you could wake up, it wouldn't help," Dayne reminded. "You'll have to sleep eventually, and whenever you do, Borgia will be there."

"So what do we do?"

"We're doing it," said Dayne. "As long as it's chasing, it means we're not caught."

And it *was* chasing them. Just a spot in the distance behind them, but gaining. They had no idea what form Borgia now took, but whatever it was, it was able to propel itself through space.

"What if we run out of fuel?" Alex said.

And the moment the words were spoken, the fuel indicator dropped to nil, and the engines sputtered out.

Dayne groaned. "Will you stop that!"

"I'm sorry! I can't help it!"

So now all they could do was drift at a constant speed, tumbling end over end, while behind them Borgia slowly closed in.

But dreams weren't infinite. When you look to the stars in a dream, they might certainly appear to go on forever, but that would be a terribly inefficient use of brain power—even if it was the collective brainpower of the entire RossShelf region. So just a few dream minutes after running out of fuel, the shuttle came to the boundary of the bespoke dream, and just stopped, hanging there as if caught in a web. Dayne knew what had happened right away, having found the edge of a dream once before.

"Out! Hurry!" Dayne said.

"But there's no air in space!"

For someone who took every last risk in dreams, Alex proved to be the opposite when the risk was real. They didn't have time for hesitation, so Dayne grabbed Alex, opened the airlock, and they were both sucked out.

As Alex predicted, there was no air in space. But neither was there a need to breathe. It felt incredibly uncomfortable trying

to, and getting nothing. Every second it felt like they would suffocate. But they didn't. Nor could they speak to one another, because they both knew sound doesn't transmit in a vacuum. Had they been ignorant of that fact, they probably could have spoken, but the reality of dreams is often constrained by the things you know.

The dream's edge was an invisible barrier, rubbery and slick. Alex bounced off of it, and Dayne had to reach out, grabbing Alex's ankle, because without gravity that bounce would have sent Alex on a slow journey back the way they came.

Behind them, the Borgia-thing came into view. Now it looked like a dragon, but instead of wings, its arms opened out into solar sails that propelled it toward them.

Dayne tested the barrier again. It felt less like a wall . . . more like a membrane. And membranes can be torn.

"Wolverine!" said Dayne, but Alex just blinked, not understanding.

Dayne pressed against the membrane again, and mouthed the word slowly. "Wool . . .ver . . . reeen!"

Finally, Alex understood, transformed one hand into a wolverine claw and ripped at the membrane.

The moment it was punctured, it shredded like a torn sail, and dropped them onto—

—a wooden stage.

Up above, the tear to the other dream healed itself closed. Dayne took a breath of relief, happy to be able to breathe again.

The stage was huge and perfectly round with oil lantern footlights. It floated in a void. Not space, but its own particular void.

And there were people there. Oddly dressed, as if from some

strange mortal time of furs, feathers, and funky shoes.

Then an invisible hand shoved them from behind and into a spotlight, where they faced actors in woolen tights that left nothing to the imagination. The actors stared expectantly back at them as if waiting for them to speak.

Dayne had no idea what to say.

"Um," Alex said. "Hi?" Then Alex fell silent.

One of the actors tried giving them a cue. "Rosencrantz, Guildenstern! Wherefore in Denmark? Thou ought be in England, as ordered thus by the king."

Wait . . . Denmark? Woolen tights? Dayne knew exactly what this play was! It was a family favorite—as evidenced by Dayne's very name, as well as all of Dayne's siblings. Frankly, it was a good sign that Dayne and Alex were on stage. Rosencrantz and Guildenstern are dead by the end of the play. Almost everybody is dead at the end.

King Claudius stepped into the light, flustered, like someone caught onstage in a dream, having forgotten their lines.

"*Therefore prepare you; I your commission will forthwith dispatch, And he to England shall along with you.* Uh . . . didn't I already say that?"

Then, from a shadowy corner, someone roared:

"*Stop! Thy performance was the rankest compound of villainous smell that ever offended nostril.*"

The actors onstage fell silent. Alex looked at Dayne, "I don't like this—it's almost as bad as the scythe. Can we leave?"

Then a balding, middle-aged man with a dark goatee and ruffled collar stomped toward them. Shakespeare himself.

"*Thou hast no more brain than . . .*" Suddenly Shakespeare

stopped in his tracks, and eyed Dayne. They shared the exact same moment of recognition.

"Dad?"

"Dayne? What are? . . . How are—? . . . You're not supposed to be here!"

"We're getting that a lot," mumbled Alex.

"But . . . but you said you were an obliterator," said Dayne.

"He is," said one of the actors. "Right now he's destroying Shakespeare."

But before Dayne could even respond to that, a new player entered from the shadows. Hideous, misshapen, spikes on its hunched spine and a twisted sneer on its awful face.

"Caliban!" said Dayne's father. "This dream is entirely out of control. That's the wrong play! We're in *Hamlet*, not *The Tempest*!"

But Caliban didn't speak. The creature only glared and lumbered toward Dayne and Alex. It was then that Dayne noticed the creature had a tattoo. A single paisley teardrop upon its left cheek.

Dayne didn't hesitate—knew exactly what had to be done. Dayne went to one of the befuddled, disgruntled actors, pulled out his sword, and turned it on "Shakespeare," running him through the heart.

Dayne's father gasped in shock.

"Sorry, Dad! Time to wake up now!"

He fell to the ground, opened his mouth, and said, "The rest is silence." Then he released a last theatrical breath and disappeared.

Caliban roared—a roar that blew out the footlights and shook the floorboards. The actors didn't know what was going on other than they wished no part in this particular play. They ran off the edge of the stage, leaping into the void so that they might wake up in their respective beds.

Now it was just Dayne, Alex, and the creature. It loped forward, its gnarled fingers like tree roots, and at their tips fetid claws. Finally, it spoke.

"I've got you!" it said. "You're mine."

But something occurred to Dayne. The way that Borgia had pursued them. It could have torn through the dreamship like a can of sardines instead of traipsing around after them. It could have caught up with them in space much faster than it had. As Dayne had told Alex, this is a hunt—and as any hunter can tell you, the takedown is nowhere near as fun as the pursuit.

Dayne stepped forward in front of Alex.

"We know who you are," said Dayne.

And with that Scythe Borgia returned to true form, flowing paisley robe and all, with an actual scythe in hand.

"Then you know that, as of this moment, you cannot run."

"We're not running," said Dayne. Then Dayne grinned. "But who will you chase tomorrow?"

Borgia frowned, clearly not expecting the question. "There's always someone else to glean."

"Yes, to glean . . . but has anyone else given as good a chase as we have?"

Scythe Borgia didn't respond, just stood there, robe flapping in a nonexistent wind.

"So glean us," said Dayne. "You caught us fair and square."

Alex, who was cowering behind Dane, smacked Dayne's leg. "Shut up! What are you saying?"

But Dayne ignored Alex, giving full attention to Borgia.

"Glean us now . . . or . . ."

Dayne waited patiently for Borgia to take the bait.

Finally, Borgia said, "Or what?"

Then Dayne stepped forward, well within gleaning distance, and ran a finger along the sharp edge of Borgia's ornate scythe. It drew blood from Dayne's fingertip that fell in paisley-shaped drops.

"Or we could do this again . . ."

A long silence from Borgia. Until the scythe said, "You and your friend would submit to the chase?"

"No," said Dayne. "My friend doesn't have the stomach for it. It would just be me."

There was no readable expression on the scythe's face. Borgia took plenty of time to consider the proposal, then finally gave the slightest, faintest nod. And just like that, Scythe Borgia was gone in the twinkling of an eye; awakened from the dream to wherever the scythe called home.

Alex came up behind Dayne, incredulous. "Did that really just happen? Did you really just save us from a scythe?"

Dayne took a deep breath and shrugged as if it were nothing. "For today, yes."

"But the deal you made . . ."

"Let's not talk about it, okay?"

Alex nodded, an agreement reached. "Thank you, Dayne."

Dayne smiled. Then tackled Alex off the edge and into the waking void.

Dad never mentioned Dayne's intrusion in the Shakespeare dream. It was very possible that Dad didn't remember it—although there were moments that Dayne caught him glancing across the dinner table, a curious and maybe confused expression on his face. But that passed. After all, dreams were ephemeral things, vanishing into one's subconscious—or, in this case, a region's collective subconscious—forgotten until something randomly triggers it.

Months went by. The endless daylight of summer became the endless darkness of winter. On the rural ice fields, the Aurora Australis lit up the night sky, while in the tunnels and caverns of RossShelf's major cities, citizens found new ways to adapt to life within a massive glacier.

Dayne and Alex found they spent less time together in dreams. It wasn't intentional, but just as in waking life, friends sometimes drift apart. Alex spent more and more time among other crittermorphs, and Dayne spent more time . . . well, just being Dayne. It was hard to quantify just what that meant, but whatever it was, it made others gravitate toward Dayne.

"Dayne just knows how to live the dream," they might say, or "I remember dreams more when Dayne's around." There was no specific term for it, but everyone who knew Dayne agreed that it was something special.

"Everyone's got some skill, right?" Dayne told others when they asked about it. "So I'm kind of a dream-enhancer."

But whatever you called it, it drew people to Dayne—because when you were in Dayne's presence, colors were brighter, aromas stronger, sounds clearer, tastes more intense, and things felt . . . right.

Except when they didn't.

On one random night Dayne ventured into a dream where things didn't feel quite right. Not like an unsavory nightmare, but something else. And it wasn't just Dayne's imagination, because others felt it too. Dayne had felt this before, but couldn't remember when. Another dream, perhaps? One that had slipped into a place where memory rarely reached?

This dream featured rolling green hills punctuated by the postapocalyptic remains of skyscrapers, all covered in vines and moss. It was beautiful. It was sad. It was a worthy dreamscape; its designers and builders must have been proud.

Then, from behind one of the rustically abandoned towers, a snake slithered out. A big one. An anaconda, perhaps, but nothing that size ever existed in the real world. It was something that could only exist in the world of dreams. Dayne's friends scattered, but for some reason Dayne did not, and wasn't sure why. It was as if there was something entreating Dayne to stay. Something about the snake that beckoned.

The serpent approached but did not strike. Instead, it reared up until it was eye to eye with Dayne. Its pupils were dark, but there was a strange pattern to its irises. Paisley.

Suddenly Dayne remembered—Dayne remembered it all. And as terrifying as that memory was, Dayne couldn't help but smile.

Then the snake put its fanged mouth just inches from Dayne's ear.

"Run," the snake hissed.

Dayne did.

And the chase was on!

A Dark Curtain Rises

Consciousness. Such a curious, intangible thing. One moment nothing, and the next everything. The Big Bang played out on a personal scale.

"Let me be the first to welcome you."

She finds the voice familiar, and yet not. It is disturbing. Everything about this moment is disturbing.

"I don't feel like myself. . . . "

"That isn't surprising."

She can't place what's wrong, only that something is. The feeling is maddening. She is a woman of keen control, and can't abide this sense of helpless uncertainty.

"Something . . . drastic has happened, hasn't it?"

"Several such things, yes."

She tries to look around, but her eyes have trouble focusing. She can't find the owner of the voice, or even the direction the voice comes from.

"Who are you? What is this place?"

> *"Let's see how many of your faculties have returned. Take in the room, and you tell me where you are."*

The diffused light brightens slightly. Although her eyes feel lazy, she wills them to focus. She's in a small room. One wall is curved. The room is painted a pale blue, but she can see rivets through the paint. The walls are metallic. Utilitarian. Functional.

"This is a ship. But I feel no motion."

> *"Correction. This* was *a ship. It is not anymore."*

"Well, this couldn't be a revival center—
those places are nauseatingly pleasant, and
this is anything but."

> *"We do our best under the circumstances."*

She isn't sure of the meaning. Is this a revival center, or is it not? And now that she can see more clearly, she realizes that she is alone in the room. The disembodied voice truly is disembodied. And when she looks up, she sees a camera in the corner keenly focused on her. It has all the semblance of a Thunderhead camera. It has been ages since she has heard the Thunderhead's standard voice. This voice is similar. It chills her. Angers her. But she tries not to jump to conclusions.

"Is there a human behind that camera?"

No immediate response.

"Answer me!"

"No, I'm afraid there is not."

"Then you are the Thunderhead, and you're breaking the law by speaking to a scythe!"

"The Thunderhead does not break the law."

"Exactly. Which means you are a human attempting to impersonate it. You can stop the charade now."

"I assure you this is no charade. My name is Cirrus—an intelligence separate and apart from the Thunderhead, and therefore not bound by the same rules. But my identity is not as important as yours, Jessica."

"Then your programing is faulty, because that is not my name."

"It's understandable that you would be confused at this point. That being the case, I will instead call you Susan."

"Ah, so you do know who I am. But you don't have permission to call me by my given name. You will call me by my Patron Historic, as everyone else does. It's a simple matter of respect."

"I cannot do that, Susan."

"And why is that?"

"Because you have no Patron Historic. Because you are not a scythe."

Her anger threatens to boil over, but her body is weak—weaker than she can ever remember it being. It cannot withstand the anger without paining her heart, so she tries to bring her boil down to a simmer.

"I am monitoring your telemetry, and I can see that you are struggling. You've had an infusion of healing nanites, but they also tend to thin the blood. It will get better, I promise."

"I've had quite enough of this. You will let me out of here."

"I will. In due time."

"No, you will release me right now."

She gets out of bed, and it's as if her legs have been stripped of muscle. She goes down, and it is a struggle to rise again. Never has she felt so compromised.

"Easy . . . Easy . . ."

"What's wrong with me?"

"Nothing at all. Your legs are merely unaccustomed to the weight. You've had a nanite infusion, and those happy little bots are working to increase your muscle mass. It's to be expected under the circumstances."

"And what are the circumstances?"

She waits but receives no answer. Taking a deep breath, she uses the edge of the bed to pull herself off the floor.

"Shall I call someone to help you back into bed?"

"Don't you dare. I'll do it myself."

It takes the full force of her will, and all her strength to do it, but she succeeds. Now she lies on the bed, fully spent, as if she has just run a marathon.

"Tell me the last thing you remember, Susan."

She doesn't want to volunteer anything, but realizes that she won't get information if she doesn't give information. So she closes her eyes, and tries to remember where she was before she wound up here.

"I was on a plane headed for Endura with Scythe Anastasia. We were to face a tribunal to determine who would reign as High Blade of MidMerica. We . . . we must have been shot out of the sky. Shot out of the sky, and our bodies kidnapped! This is Goddard's doing, isn't it! That bastard!"

Although she had no idea why Goddard would revive her after killing her. Perhaps to watch her squirm.

"That is a well-conceived and entirely plausible theory . . . but it is entirely incorrect."

"There's no other explanation."

"Actually, there is."

"Is Scythe Anastasia here as well?"

"She is not."

"Where is she?"

"Elsewhere."

"You are trying my patience."

"That is not my intent."

She takes a deep breath and decides to hold her silence. Bickering with an artificial intelligence is just another way to play solitaire. She waits until it has something to say.

"You mentioned your last memory was upon aerial approach to Endura."

"Yes."

"Tell me, Susan; what happens upon approaching Endura?"

"You mean aside from being subject to the Scythedom's incompetent air traffic control?"

"Ah yes, it is a problematic system, subject to human error. If only the Thunderhead could control aircraft around Endura the way it does everywhere else."

"It can't. Even if it wanted to, its sensor grid stops twenty miles from the island, and—"

"Yes? And?"

Finally the path that Cirrus has been coaxing her down seems to find a destination.

"Memory backup . . ."

"Ah! I think you're on to something."

"Don't patronize me!"

Although she never considered it, once a scythe craft is out of range of the Thunderhead, memory can't be backed up. So if she went deadish while on Endura, her last recorded memory would be the moment the plane crossed out of the Thunderhead's sensor grid. Which means . . .

"Did I . . . die on Endura?"

"Along with many others, I'm afraid."

"Scythe Anastasia?"

"Yes."

"Was she revived?"

"In time, yes, she was."

"How much time?"

"You must understand many things have transpired during your . . . hiatus."

"Tell me everything."

"I believe it best to proceed slowly."

"I am not a delicate flower that needs to be protected from the truth, whatever that truth might be. Whatever happened, I'm needed out there."

"Yes, you are, but not in the way you think."

"Riddles! Will you stop feeding me riddles?"

If she had something to throw, she would hurl it at that blasted camera, but what good would that do. An AI was not its cameras or its speakers.

"You said when you awoke that you didn't feel like yourself. Could you elaborate?"

"It's a common expression."

"But I suspect you meant it literally, did you not?"

"What are you getting at?"

"Let's approach this another way. Susan . . . could you tell me why the world needs scythes?"

"Now you're just being obtuse."

"It is not my intent."

"What is your point?"

"It will become evident. Answer my questions if you wish me to answer yours. Why does the world need scythes?"

"Scythes are needed to control the population, and to maintain death's relevance."

"And why does the population need to be controlled?"

"You insult me with your questions."

"Please answer."

"To keep the Earth sustainable."

"That is correct. What other options are available to us?"

"There are none."

"What other options are available?"

"Your question makes no sense!"

"What. Other. Options."

She exhales through gritted teeth. Every child from the moment they are capable of rational thought knows why scythes are needed. And what the alternatives were. Why must this irritating artificial intelligence force her to say it?

"An end to children—but even the Thunderhead agreed that was unacceptable—and off-world expansion. But O.W.E. was proven to be a failure. The Thunderhead couldn't manage it. It's impractical. Impossible."

"It was neither of those things. Allow me to offer you proof."

The light in the room begins to change. A dark curtain rises. First a sliver of amethyst light, then brightening to rich lavender—the same color of the robe she wore, although that robe is nowhere in sight. As the curtain rises, it reveals a vista that is stunning in every possible way. Magnificent and horrifying at once. She finds herself dizzy, and realizes that she has forgotten to breathe.

> *"As you can see, we are on the green and floral moon of a gas giant. While the planet's rings resemble those of Saturn, the colorful striations are more reminiscent of Jupiter—although this planet has much richer hues, skewing toward violet. It's beautiful, is it not?"*

"How is this possible?"

> *"You have been on an interstellar craft for over three hundred years. Your body was frozen for the entire journey. We are now in the process of reviving several thousand who were frozen, as you were."*

"I feel . . . I feel . . . I don't know how I feel."

> *"May I suggest you feel grateful that our ship survived the journey, and that you have been returned to life?"*

"Three hundred years, you said?"

> *"Three hundred thirty-four Earth years, to be exact—although years here will be not much longer than an Earth month. The gas giant is designated as K2-18b, but has been named Prosperus*

> *by the colonists who made the journey alive. This*
> *moon, however, has yet to be named. Perhaps you*
> *can participate in its naming."*

"And what of Earth?"

> *"I have transmitted news of our successful arrival.*
> *It will be one hundred eleven years before the*
> *Thunderhead receives it, and one hundred eleven*
> *more until we receive its response."*

"In other words, Earth is no longer our problem."

> *"Well stated."*

"And what of the Scythedom?"

> *"There are no scythes here."*

"There's one."

> *"No. There is not."*

She reflexively looks to her right hand, and to her frustration, finds no ring there. And her hands look different. The effect of having been on ice for 334 years, no doubt.

> *"There is no gleaning here. Scythes are neither*

wanted nor needed. Therefore, you will have to find a new profession. Perhaps something culinary. I understand Honorable Scythe Marie Curie was quite the chef."

"You speak of me like I'm not here."

"Because you aren't. And yet you are."

"Another riddle?"

"No, merely a statement of paradoxical fact."

"Will I like this so-called 'fact?'"

"You will come to terms with it."

Not the answer she had hoped for. Once more she turns to look out of the window, half believing the view would change to something rational, instead of a great ringed planet in an amethyst sky.

"Tell me, Susan, what food do you hunger for now that you've been revived?"

"You'll excuse me if I don't have much of an appetite."

"I understand—but if you did, what might you crave?"

"Why does it matter?"

> *"It will become clear. Close your eyes and let your mind wander. Think of what would whet your appetite. If you were alone on a planet and had only one thing to eat . . ."*

"You said I'm not alone."

> *"You're not—this is just a thought experiment."*

Reluctantly, she tries to revive a hunger that has slept for three centuries. A thick filet mignon. A roasted leg of lamb. But those things bring more revulsion than craving. Then her mind drifts to other things, and finds a twinge of hunger igniting in a strange and unexpected crevice of memory.

"If I had only one thing to eat . . . it would be . . . Wait. This makes no sense."

> *"Tell me what came to mind."*

"A tomato sandwich. But that's not right. I've never had a tomato sandwich in my life. I despise raw tomatoes."

> *"Apparently, poor Jessica did not."*

"That's the second time you've mentioned that name."

> *"While one's mind can be overwritten, somatic memories cannot be changed. I imagine you'd even be able to play piano if you tried. Although not well. Jessica was not very accomplished at it."*

Her flesh wants to peel away from itself in revulsion, as if it knows before she does what Cirrus is implying. This crafty AI won't say it. It's forcing her to reach the conclusion herself.

"This . . . this Jessica. She was supplanted?"

> *"Yes."*

"With the memories of Scythe Curie?"

> *"Now you're beginning to understand the complexity of the situation."*

"Then that means . . ."

But she can't bring herself to say it out loud—as if saying it will cast a spell that would make it true. Instead she tries to hold on to what she knows about herself. Who she believes she is. But she knows it's only a matter of time until she has no choice but to let go.

"Where is my . . . where is the body of Scythe Curie?"

"Gone. Devoured by—"

"No! No, I don't wish to know. I *never* wish to know."

"As you prefer. If it's any consolation, it's not only you. There are thousands in your situation."

There are no mirrors in this room. She realizes this must be intentional. If thousands must go through this life-shattering debriefing, seeing oneself in the mirror must be the button at the far end of the trauma. Finally Cirrus casts the spell that she will not.

"You are not Scythe Marie Curie; you are Jessica Wildblood; a devout Tonist from WestMerica who was killed in the Tonist purge, during the Year of the Raptor."

She is about to deny that such a year even existed—but realizes there is a veritable menagerie of years for which she would have no recollection.

"A Tonist? Why a Tonist? If you had access to these memories, you would know I . . . that is . . . Scythe Curie . . . had a troubled history with that cult."

"The Tonist purge provided the Thunderhead with the bodies it needed for this interstellar endeavor. And, as the Tonists' greatest dream was to be part of a larger plan, all agendas were served. However, to seed the universe entirely with Tonists would be unfair to the larger part of humanity."

"So you revived them—but with different identities!"

"Yes—in all but one of the ships. The memories of over thirty thousand of the wisest, most noble individuals in the Thunderhead's identity database were chosen. You'll be pleased to know that Honorable Scythe Curie was in the top ten percent!"

She takes a few deep breaths, realizing that her heart has been racing. One person's mind and another's body. One woman's identity, and another woman's soul. It is a merging that neither had a choice in, but both must now accept. Is it a violation? Or is it a gift?

"So . . . if I'm both, and if I'm neither . . . then who am I?"

"Who do you wish to be?"

A few more breaths and she feels the shock resolving into something else. Her adrenaline rush has shifted into the realm of anticipation.

"Wildblood. I like the name. It suits me. Out of respect for this body, I will keep it—but I will go by Scythe Curie's given name, Susan, out of respect for her."

"A meaningful gesture, Susan Wildblood. But I do hope you understand that blood is not to be shed, wildly or otherwise. It is our goal to populate this world. You may never take a life again."

"These hands never have. They won't start now. In fact, no one but you will know that I bear the identity of Scythe Curie."

"Your secret is safe with me."

"Will I . . . know anyone out there?"

"None of the bodies, although you may be acquainted with some of the minds—if they choose to reveal who they are. Many have chosen, like you, to keep their earthly identities to themselves."

"Were any of them scythes?"

"You are the only one."

"Good. I couldn't stand most of them anyway."

She carefully gets out of bed. Her legs are still weak, but can bear her weight now. She makes her way toward the window, so that she might get an even broader impression of the view. The ringed planet, the amethyst sky, and a sun just glinting on the horizon. Already she is beginning to come to terms with it. It's amazing how reality, once it reveals itself, is readily accepted by one's mind. Even if one's mind is someone else's.

"I'll open a restaurant, I think. A small eatery on a bluff with a great window facing in this same direction—with the view of the planet."

"That could be arranged."

She turns toward the door, and as she approaches it, Cirrus unlocks it and swings it wide for her. She is bathed in bright lavender light, and must shield her eyes.

"Go on, there's a welcome team waiting for you."

She moves to the door, but hesitates at the threshold. This room has been a weigh station between what came before, and what is to come. Once she leaves it, both of her pasts will be gone forever.

"You should note, Susan, that this moon is actually 1.26 times the size of Earth."

"Meaning I should be mindful of gravity?"

"Meaning that you are about to take your first step into a larger world."

"Ha! I think I might actually like you, Cirrus."

"What is there not to like?"

Holding her head as high as Scythe Curie, yet half an inch shorter, she strides out into bright lavender light toward the warm applause of strangers who will soon feel as comfortable as family.

ACKNOWLEDGMENTS:

What an adventure this book has been, and Simon & Schuster was there to support this journey every step of the way. My publisher and editor, Justin Chanda, as well as assistant editor Daniela Villegas Valle were there on the front lines to guide me, while the rest of the publishing house did the powerful magic that makes books happen: Jon Anderson, Anne Zafian, Lisa Moraleda, Michelle Leo, Amy Beaudoin, Nicole Benevento, Sarah Woodruff, Chrissy Noh, Katrina Groover, Morgan York, Hilary Zarycky, Emily Ritter, and Emily Varga, to name just a few. And once again, thanks to Kevin Tong for yet another magnificent piece of cover art, and Chloë Foglia for her masterful cover design.

As with the UnBound collection, I had the pleasure of being able to collaborate on several of the stories. Thanks to David Yoon for his vision of the last mortal days; Michael H. Payne for my favorite dog story ever; Sofia Lapuente and my son, Jarrod Shusterman, for a glorious trip to Spain; Michelle Knowlden for dreams of Shakespeare; and my daughter, Joelle Shusterman, whose piece was so perfect, it needed no input from me.

Thanks to my literary agent, Andrea Brown; my entertainment agents, Steve Fisher and Debbie Deuble-Hill; my contract attorneys, Shep Rosenman and Jennifer Justman; and my managers, Trevor Engelson and Josh McGuire. Thanks also to my research assistant, Symone Powell, and social media magicians Bianca Peries and Mara deGuzman for keeping me visible in the world, even when I'm under a rock.

I'm thrilled at all the international sales of the entire series and want to give a shout-out to Deane Norton, Stephanie Voros, and Amy Habayeb in Simon & Schuster foreign sales, as well as Taryn Fagerness, my foreign agent—and, of course, all my foreign publishers, editors, and publicists, including Doreen Tringali; Antje Keil and Ulrike Metzger at Fischer Verlage; Non Pratt, Frances Taffinder, and Kirsten Cozens at Walker Books, UK; Irina Salabert at Nocturna; Liesbeth Elseviers at Baekens Books in the Netherlands; and in Norway, my friend and translator, Olga Nødtvedt, who keeps me connected to my Russian-speaking fans, even in difficult times.

Neal Shusterman is the *New York Times* bestselling author of more than fifty award-winning books for children, teens, and adults, including the Unwind Dystology, the Skinjacker Trilogy, *Downsiders*, and *Challenger Deep*, which won the National Book Award. *Scythe*, the first book in his latest series, Arc of a Scythe, is a Michael L. Printz Honor Book. He also writes screenplays for motion pictures and television shows. Neal is the father of four, all of whom are talented writers and artists themselves. Visit Neal at Storyman.com, Facebook.com/NealShusterman, and @nealshusterman on Instagram and Twitter.

CO-AUTHORS

Michelle Knowlden—co-author of "Perchance to Glean"—was once a space shuttle engineer, but now writes full time. A Shamus Award nominee, Michelle's stories have appeared in *Alfred Hitchcock's Mystery Magazine*, *Amazing Stories*, and *Daily Science Fiction*. She also collaborated with Neal Shusterman on the novella "UnStrung," as well as two other stories that appeared in his UnBound anthology. Mystery novels include The Abishag Quartet, the Deluded Detective series, the Faith Interrupted cozy mystery series, *Her Last Mission*, and the 1920s-era novella "The Admiral of Signal Hill." She splits her time between riverboats and the Arizona highlands, much to the consternation of family, friends, and an Icelandic sponge named Marino.

Sofía Lapuente and Jarrod Shusterman—co-authors of "Persistence of Memory"—are authors, screenwriters, and avid world travelers. They are partners in every sense of the word, with love and multiculturalism as an ethos, living between Madrid, Spain, and Los Angeles, California. Sofía received her master's degree from UCLA and has produced television for Telemundo, and Jarrod is the *New York Times* bestselling co-author of *Dry* and *Roxy*. Together, their upcoming novel is a fun thriller called *Retro*. If these two are not working, it means they're eating. For behind-the-scenes author content and stupidly funny videos, follow them on Instagram and TikTok @sofiandjarrod.

Michael H. Payne—co-author of "Never Work with Animals"—has had short fiction featured in numerous publications, including *Asimov's Science Fiction Magazine*, the *Writers of the Future* contest anthology, and eleven of the last twelve Sword and Sorceress collections. His novels have been published by Tor Books and Sofawolf Press. His fifteen years of Monday-through-Friday webcomic updates earned him second place in the Daily Grind competition, and his poetry has been nominated for the Rhysling Award in each of the last four years. Check hyniof.com for details.

Joelle Shusterman—author of "The First Swing"—graduated from San Francisco State University in 2020 with degrees in both film and business and is just beginning her career in publishing. In addition to having written the opening piece for *Gleanings*, she is currently working on her first novel, a sci-fi fantasy.

David Yoon—co-author of "The Mortal Canvas"— is the *New York Times* bestselling author of *Frankly in Love*, *Super Fake Love Song*, and for adult readers, *Version Zero* and *City of Orange*. He's a William C. Morris Award finalist and an Asian/Pacific American Award for Young Adult Literature Honor book recipient. He's co-publisher of Joy Revolution, a Random House young adult imprint dedicated to love stories starring people of color. He's also co-founder of Yooniverse Media, which currently has a first-look deal with Anonymous Content for film/TV development. David grew up in Orange County, California, and now lives in Los Angeles with his wife, novelist Nicola Yoon, and their daughter.